# Poultry-Geist

## By C.S. Ramahon

The pseudonym, **C.S. Ramahon**, is an amalgam of both the first initials and last names of the co-authors.

**Email Authors:** shannindoe@yahoo.com

# CHAPTER 1: Crying Fowl

Long ago, I heard the saying: "The art of living is more like wrestling than dancing." How true. My name is, Dabney ... Dabney Doodledoo. Sure, go on and laugh. Most everyone else does. I know it's a wacky moniker, but one which has continually caused me to perpetually deflect teasing and taunting. However, it's my heritage and one that has been fixed upon me since my birth throughout these past thirty-seven years.

And yes, if I had a dollar for every time somebody (mostly a guy named, Alvin Snorkelpuss) kicked me in the shin and yelled, "A little dab in the knee will doddle-doo you," well, I'd have a bunch of dollars for sure.

When I was sixteen, it was no wonder I got teased and bullied by that rabbit-brained moron. He was eighteen, a senior in high school, and 6'3" tall. Muscular and almost two-hundred-forty pounds, he liked throwing his weight around and in general being a real jerk. Back then, I tipped the scales at a meager one-hundred-two pounds and was barely 5'4".

Except for my facial hair, I was a late bloomer. I began shaving when I was fourteen and had more hair on my arms, legs, and chest than most of the other guys in school. With my dark auburn-colored hair, I always had what looked like beard stubble, no matter how close I shaved. Snorkelpuss sneered and often remarked that I looked like I'd eaten a muskrat.

Three years later, I grew almost five inches that summer and gained enough weight to be like an uncut version of a young Tom Cruise ... errr ... make that, Tom Cruz, the Hispanic guy that lived two doors down from where I grew up. Yeah, but he too was a nice-looking dude.

In those years, I developed a sort of eager, almost appealing amiability and became instinctive, and spontaneous, plus exhibited the magic of youth and the joy of life.

Yet, here I was in the last days of this year, whereby I collapsed into a dreary and hysterical depression. I was deep in thought with my mouth wide open ... and before I managed to close it, I lost a bit of drool down my shirtfront. Yet, when I shut it and clenched my teeth, I presented a facial expression that suggested the look of a man on the brink of insanity. I moaned as if attempting to answer an imponderable question. I knew what I had to do. I must rid myself of this abnormality and free my family of these infernal pests I called ... <u>Poultry-Geists.</u>

Except for eating and cooking it, the only thing I knew about poultry before all this happened was that the chicken probably came before the egg because it was hard for me to imagine God sitting on an egg. At any rate, on my way out the door of the lavish Lancaster Hotel where my family and I were holed up for the past four days, I strolled out of the lobby and stepped outside from under the lodge canopy.

Looking upward, I craned my neck and scanned the skies, noting that the frosty, thick clouds above me looked like white cotton balls. The freshly falling flakes of snow that all night tumbled silently toward Earth were like a ruptured featherbed and the size of American silver dollars. The lighted electronic sign outside the bank building across the street stated the time as 9:38 A.M. and registered the temperature as being eight degrees Fahrenheit. With the stiff breeze, I imagine the wind chill must be far below zero.

My eyes watered and cold tears rolled down my rosy cheeks. As I breathed, my exhaled fog froze and formed ice upon the curly hairs of my manly mustache. In the biting cold, I pulled my woolen storm collar tightly around my neck and lower face. My toboggan cap drooped just above my eyes. A few seconds in this extreme cold and already I couldn't feel my nose. I had on a heavy, downy-filled, duck-feather-stuffed coat with a hood. {The very thought of ducks made me cringe} Despite these cold blockers, I experienced profuse perspiring inside all that wrapping. Even with my insulated pants and lined leather gloves, I still shivered and the cold penetrated me as if a worm was crawling through my brain.

From the open doorway of the hotel came a familiar voice, "Dabney! Where are you going this early?" cried a concerned, Daisy Doodledoo.

"I have to go downtown," I sincerely replied to my dear wife.

I hoped she'd accept that simple declaration without further quibbling, but it was not to be.

"Downtown? For what? Why?"

"I have to go see a ... oh, never mind. I just have to go, that's all."

"In this weather? Are you crazy?"

"Ouch!" I declared in a shrill, small voice like that of an expiring mouse. Maybe she was right and I was crazy at that. I replied, "Believe me, I have my reasons. You and the kids just stay inside and keep warm."

I figured lunatics in an asylum had it more together than I did right now.

"Come on, darling. Don't be foolish. We've all seen your ... odd enhancement. We love you and know how upset you are ... but ...please, come back inside," she pleaded.

I shook my head, which indicated—no. Even from the doorway and despite the extreme cold, I still caught a whiff of the marvelous, fragrant perfume Daisy was wearing. It was a scent that I presented to her on our fourteenth wedding anniversary last month. I loved her with all my heart and hated to be so evasive, but the throbbing bells of absurdity rang through my vaporous skull, having been placed there by a madcap, unexplainable, ominous enchantment that we'd all been experiencing.

I could wait no longer. I needed to seek help before my mind drifted away ... before I became some storm-tossed wreck cast aground and an indefinable resemblance of our unwelcomed visitors. I must quell this impenetrable cloud of lunacy that had bound itself to me and my family.

Stepping onto the walk, I babbled to myself, as my rubber goulashes sank into a foot of new-fallen snow. I had to carefully slosh and goose-step {ooh, another fowl reference I should have avoided} as I made my way towards my four-wheeled drive Jeep parked ten feet away. It awaited me next to the valet driver that pulled it out front for me. A blast of icy wind whizzed by me and sent a chill to my bones that momentarily drifted the snowflakes sideways through the air. In my muddled mind, I knew going out in this type of weather was risky, but after what we'd been through, it was a small wonder that I had the slightest bit of reason left in me.

This was something that could no longer wait, and there was no way I could rationally illustrate or explain to any non-professional my condition and what had been happening to us over the past few weeks. Although the hotel parking lot cover prevented a pile-up of snow on my vehicle, before I could enter the Jeep, snow already began to accumulate on the windshield and hood. Using my leather gloves, I wiped away what I was able to and got inside the car. I slid into the driver's seat and momentarily removed my gloves. I rifled through my pants pocket for the car keys and glanced at the passenger window. There in the frost was a handprint from long ago left there by my young daughter, Cah Cah. As I gazed at the handprint, the image began to crust with iciness and slowly altered. It began to resemble the shadowed silhouette of a thumb and hand with fingerprints forming the shape of a turkey. I cringed again.

Silly me. I then realized the motor was already running and the valet had put the key in the ignition and turned on the engine when he drove and parked it here for me. Sitting there, I let the motor idle a bit and the opportunity to warm up ... it and me. The valet stood next to my car with a wet towel slung over his shoulder that he'd used to wipe away the frost inside my car's windshield. He smiled broadly and held out his hand, palm upward. I rolled down the driver's window and handed him the ten-dollar tip I knew he expected. He thanked me and backed away under the hotel canopy, tracking snow from his overshoes like dust trailing off a ranch hand's boots. I rolled up the window and turned on the car's heater and window defroster. My teeth were chattering from the miserable, inescapable cold.

Sitting there, the inside glass had already begun to fog up from my body heat and breathing. With my gloves back on, I wiped away the frost building on my driver's side window. It was then that I heard and spotted the neighbor from our adjoining hotel room, a mister Milton Moosejaw. He was behind my car attempting to drive his 1970 Volkswagen Beetle out onto the slick streets in front of the hotel. He told me he had the notion that his air-cooled engine required no need for anti-freeze and was the perfect vehicle for Pennsylvania winters. I knew that it was too lightweight and that this ignorant migrant from the south had no true idea of what driving was like here in January.

With a foot of snow falling the night before, his efforts to drive were futile. His lead foot on the gas pedal had little effect on the spinning wheels, and there was hardly any traction for the common road tires he had on his small car. From experiencing many winters here in the northern U.S., I knew vehicles needed chains or spiked snow tires that would fare much better in this climate. This was poor Milton's first foray into the near north of southeast Pennsylvania, so he was ignorant of that fact.

Daisy, the kids, and I moved into our dream home in Paradise, Pennsylvania, about ten miles outside of where we were now at this Lancaster hotel. We'd moved there about a month before. That now seemed light-years away from our apartment and condo in sunny Miami. I'd accepted a partnership position within the poultry processing plant a few miles away. I loved the area, except for the long, harsh winter that had recently begun with a vengeance.

At first, I contributed my sudden wacky visions and sounds to delusions perhaps brought on by the result of some unforeseen reaction to a chemical produced within the plant. However, the sphere and possibility of my exposure to any sort of hazardous substance that would create such havoc upon my mind and body were minuscule and very unlikely. I even wondered if perhaps I hadn't contracted Mad Cow Disease, but dismissed that idea because Daisy and the kids also experienced their trauma. No, whatever deviled-ham fowl play was haunting us came not from the existence of toxic material. Rather, the madness was thrust upon us from a tepid landscape garnished by the oddball, feathered entities that disturbed our reverie, and then invaded our home life and intruded like thieves in the night to steal away the common sense of reality. Thinking about it all now, made me pinch the bridge of my nose to subdue an instant headache. Haunted with a chill and unearthly foreboding, I shivered in the cold.

As I have tried to expel the nonsensical gathering of the absurdity of what I call, Poultry-Geists, my emotions ranged from a display of comical disbelief, livid rage, a sense of dread, gloom, the doldrums of depression, stomach-twisting astonishment, pangs of heart-pounding surprise, excruciating embarrassment, and then ultimately into a bout with a physical abomination. All that said and done, now I was off to town and nothing ... snow, sleet, ice, or a break out of lions from the Lancaster Zoo was going to stop me from going into town to see a medical doctor. Even the old Indian oracle we'd used couldn't explain or help rid me of that which has tortured my soul and what transpired to leave me as I am.

Once underway, I drove ten miles into Lancaster on slick streets void of traffic for an appointment to see a doctor. It would be my first visit to a physician since coming to Paradise. I didn't know this doctor, but in calling around his was the only office I could find open on this wintery Saturday morning. I called him in private, so as not to disturb or alarm Daisy.

After finding the street where his office was located, I pulled onto the paved road and began to look for addresses on the buildings I passed. As I drove, I had to use my wipers to clear the snow accumulating on the car's windshield. With the snowdrifts by the roadsides, I had to be careful, even though the snow plows cleared and treated the slick, icy streets earlier that morning.

Despite the defroster, the windshield began to frost up inside and I had to lean over the steering wheel to wipe away the foggy glass. The flurries got heavier as I drove and the winds picked up, which made the drive even more stressful and annoying.

About ten blocks from my destination, I turned on the car radio in hopes to find some soothing music to help calm my nerves.

A weather bulletin came on first, "Heavy snowfall will continue throughout the day. In the Lancaster area, we can expect around eight to ten more inches of fresh flurries before dark."

I grumbled and switched through the stations till I found one with pleasant, easy-listening classical music. As the street veered off and around a bend, like a bolt out of the blue ... or a snowball rolling downhill I should say ... to my complete amazement I was suddenly confronted with a dozen two-foot-tall cartoon hens {as in chickens} dancing arm-in-arm {wing-to-wing that is} right there in front of my car on the street. I blew my car horn and swerved to try and miss them. As I did, the music on the radio instantly changed and began blaring out the beating instrumental sounds from the "Can-Can." While stricken in silence, I watched as these high-stepping floozies {Toon hens} pranced, danced, smiled, and wiggled their feathered fannies wildly in the snowy street. In the seconds when my car began to spin out of control, I stared in disbelief, as I saw them blink their long eyelashes, raise and ruffle their plump feathers, and invoke their skinny dancing legs and three-toed feet that were crammed into and sheathed in crimson red high-heels in synch to the music on my car radio. All of the sudden, hearing the music I was overcome with an inexplicable urge that I could not resist. My hands left the steering wheel and I grabbed my head and the soft, floppy object underneath my woolen toboggan. My rear itched and I began to uncontrollably sway my hips to the music of the "Can-Can." I raised and kicked my legs around the steering wheel and upon the dashboard. Then, without reason, I unexpectedly began to crow like a rooster. Madness ... total madness possessed me. My thoughts were a clamoring of confusion.

In an attempt to regain control of myself and the Jeep, I lowered my legs and slammed on the brakes, which was not the thing to do. Before I knew it, I was doing a corkscrew tailspin directly into the path of those dancing hens ... scattering poultry, feathers, and them like bowling pins being tossed around all over the place.

My car spun a full revolution, two, three, and then four times ... and somehow slid directly and miraculously into an open parallel park next to the street-side curb. The stunned hens were flung on top of parked cars, wedged into snow banks, hung from traffic lights, lampposts, and a few were thrust upon flashing store signs ... where their plump feathered rear ends displayed their bright red petticoats.

The engine on the Jeep fouled, sputtered, and then turned off. I tried to restart it, but it would only grind and seemed like it wasn't getting fuel. The gas gauge showed full, but I supposed either the cold had frozen up the fuel intake, or the tailspin and the crash with the hens somehow temporarily drained the fuel from the engine. Whatever the case, I sat there in shock. Breathing heavy, I watched as the formidable cold began to quickly affect the car windows, for they were fogging up so much I could barely see out.

I sighed deeply and relaxed my iron grip on the steering wheel. I dropped my hands to my lap and a few seconds later tried to wipe away the icy window next to me to peek outside. I knew I was close to the doctor's office, so I checked for addresses across the street. While I did that, I saw no sign of the hens I'd hit. As had been the case many times before, these types of visions just seemed to vanish into thin air ... as they had this time as well. As a defense mechanism, I heard myself exude a deep-bellied laugh at the lunacy.

Then, to make things worse, from the passenger side seat of my car, I heard a flapping of wings, and then there was a stern, all too familiar male voice, which sounded a good deal like the formerly famous actor, John Wayne's character in the movie, "True Grit."

"Whoa there, Pilgrim," he said. "You realize that you just took out half my harem of breeding hens?"

My eyes narrowed and I frowned. My demeanor quickly evidenced my displeasure by forming a contemptuous sneer and a grim scowl. The bewildered, bemused expression on my face changed quickly, for this voice was one I'd heard way too often of late and it provoked me to anger. I reached and flung the toboggan cap off my head, which revealed my smooth-skinned bald head, now mysteriously donned on top by a crimson red, attached by the root, rooster's comb that flopped to one side of my slick noggin.

"You again!" I screamed angrily.

Wanting nothing more than to release my fury, my hands formed an intense strangling pose. At the moment, I wished I'd had one of Daisy's old cast-iron skillets to bash against the thick noggin of this antagonist. This was the last straw and I seemed to be spiraling out of control. Livid, I confronted my unwelcomed passenger. For a brief moment, it seemed as if I might cry, but then I was too bitter for tears. No, this barnyard intruder that plagued me now brought out in me a raging fury.

Meanwhile, on the icy sidewalk, a brave young woman challenging the elements and carrying a plastic bag filled with her shopping goods was herself bundled up in a scarf and heavy coat with a hood. She trudged her way through the blinding snowfall, to be suddenly drawn toward my rocking vehicle and the loud commotion that was taking place inside it. With the fogged windows, she couldn't tell what was happening. Her startled eyes reflected her astonishment at what she heard, for it sounded all the world like … two roosters were fighting.

She stopped, leaned over, and peered closely into the window on the passenger's side. However, the windows were just too hazy for her to see into the car. Suddenly, two eight-inch-long chicken feet were thrust onto the passenger window. Completely startled, she screamed, turned, dropped her bag, and in her fleece-lined boots quickly toddled down the street in a panic. She almost slipped twice on the icy walkway.

Inside the car, brown and white feathers drifted in the air and began to settle onto the dashboard and seats. In one hand, I held up a small, black piece of cloth with an elastic band binding it on each end. In my other hand, I held a pair of snake-skin cowboy boots. My breath came in gulps, and my coat was torn and tattered in several places. Scattered downy feathers floated across the car seats. My sunglasses used for driving in the blinding snow were twisted and one lens was missing. I snarled at my unwelcomed passenger, who also seemed winded and rattled.

His gruff voice spoke again, "All I said was that's a good look for you, Pilgrim. Now be a good sport and hand me back my boots and eye patch, before I have to plug you with my Colt Dragoon."

I replied, "You bird-brained, bone-headed sidewinder, this has all been your fault. And if you aim to frighten me with that hardboiled egg shooter of yours, forget it."

I sneered and reached for my toboggan cap up on the dash. I angrily slammed it down over my slick scalp, which covered the rooster's comb and my now grotesque-looking skinhead. I growled at the voice, tossed the boots at him, opened my car door, and exited into the snow, wind, and freezing weather. I looked back inside the car and pointed a trembling finger.

"Wherever they went, gather your flock of floozy hens, and don't be here when I get back."

"Wait, Pilgrim! My eyepatch. I need it," he grumbled.

I snarled, "No you don't. You're neither blind nor deaf, but you definitely are dumb."

Slamming the car door and gripped in the blistering winter snow, I ambled towards the sidewalk and passed by a parking meter. There, I stopped and hung the eyepatch over it. Inside the car, I heard a loud rooster crow coming from the throat of that vile, unbalanced, surly, conceited fowl that caused my family and me such distress these past few weeks.

Because of the commotion, my nerves began to affect me physically. The undigested scrambled eggs I'd had for breakfast came up and spewed onto the snow. When I finally stopped puking, I gasped deeply and then inhaled the cold air like a man coming up out of the deep of a swimming pool. I stepped over the pile of steaming egg puke and looked around. I felt a qualm of apprehension but focused on my task at hand ... to get to the doctor's office.

Out of sight from where I stood, under my parked car was one of the dancing hens. She pecked the pavement and a tear ran down her beak.

She whispered sadly, "Oh my, I hope that wasn't junior that man just churned out all over the pavement."

Somewhat relieved, I waddled off towards a commercial building I saw down the street. At the end of that block, I'd made it to my destination, the doctor's office where I'd made my appointment.

Despite all the clamor and distractions, I'd somehow made it in time. I fought with the stiff winds to open the glass door and stammered inside.

The name on the front door was, "Doctor, Yu Muzzkauff, General Practitioner of Medicine, Surgery, Cosmetician, Dermatologist, Obstetrician, Dietician ... Etc., Etc., Etc."

Although a bit wary and somewhat uncomfortable with the thought of seeing a doctor I'd never met, I knew I had no choice but to have an exam and get checked out by a physician. So, I came and was determined to overcome my anatomical infirmity. Now fully matured, I was built thick through the shoulders, with stout legs and thin angular bones that were physical traits passed down to me through many generations of Doodledoos. I'd not allow any more fowl culprits to steal away that legacy of my ancestors.

Inside I removed my coat, scarf, and gloves, then signed in at the reception desk. I kept on the toboggan cap. After taking my insurance info, a few minutes later a tall, young nurse wearing a white uniform and nurse's cap stepped inside the waiting area and called my name.

"Mister Doodledroop?"

Accustomed to people mispronouncing my name, I stood up and corrected her.

"It's Doodledoo. My name is, Dabney Doodledoo," I said quietly.

Others in the waiting room snickered and some repressed laughter. As I mentioned, I was accustomed to experiencing such a thing when I gave my name. At any rate, the attractive nurse that I guessed was in her mid-twenties ushered me back into a dimly lit examining room. My first impressions of this doctor's facilities were that it looked a bit ramshackle and unsanitary for a medical office. My first clue to the competency of this doctor should have registered when I noticed that most of his office plants had died.

"I'm nurse, Nova Caine. Have a seat Mr. Doodles; I need to take your blood pressure and temperature."

As she wrapped the blood pressure cup around my left arm, she then urged a glass thermometer into my mouth and stuck it under my tongue.

She pumped on the tube that inflated the cup, while the pressure on my arm increased. She gradually let out the air to read my blood pressure.

She asked, "Are you in any pain?"

With the glass thermometer in my mouth, all I managed to mumble was, "Only mentally."

She smiled and had not comprehended what I'd said.

"That's good," she commented. "Well, your blood pressure's a bit high, but not critical."

She then pulled out the thermometer and remarked, "And you don't have any fever."

After that, I was guided to a well-worn scale where she weighed me and inquired, "So what brings you out in this storm to see the doctor?"

I replied sheepishly, "I'll wait and explain that to him."

She crossed her arms defensively and shrugged, "Very well then."

She handed me a thin white hospital-type gown ... the type that is tied in the back and is open exposing one's rear end.

"Remove your clothing and get dressed in this gown. Have a seat here on this examining table and Dr. Muzzkauff will be in to see you soon."

I reluctantly took the gown and questioned, "Why must I get undressed?"

She ruffled, crossed her arms again, and stated firmly, "Do you want the doctor to examine you or not?"

"Of course, I do. That's why I'm here," I replied.

She waved the gown at me, "Then do as I asked. Get undressed and into this gown."

She pointed to a clothes rack where I could hang the remainder of my things, smirked, and then left the room.

I grumbled under my breath but granted her request. I slipped off my pants, shirt, and everything except for my underpants and toboggan. I wasn't ready just yet to expose the cursed appendage atop my head.

As the minutes dragged by, almost a half-hour later the door to the examining room opened and I got my first glimpse of Dr. Musskauff. Walking with both hands behind his back, underneath his wild-looking thick mustache, between his teeth he gripped a burning cigar. He raised his bushy eyebrows. They fluttered up and down, as he grinned at me. For a moment I thought he was a kooky clone of the deceased comedian, Groucho Marx. I stood, for my barren backside was cold from having sat on the stainless-steel table. As he pranced about, I was a bit jumpy and anxious. None more, however, it seemed than this spastic, elderly, gray-haired doctor dressed in his white physician's coat that was garnished by what looked to be crimson stains. In looking closer, I knew they were not caused by blood, but rather I gathered perhaps from dripping tomato sauce ... possibly from having eaten something like a sloppy pizza, or a bowl of spaghetti.

Immediately, my muddled mind queried, "Who eats pizza or spaghetti this early in the morning?"

Then I wondered if maybe the stains on the coat were from when he'd eaten supper the night before. At any rate, this disheveled-looking man had a stethoscope slung over his wrinkled neck and wore gaudy eyeglasses with coke-bottle thick lenses. He entered with a stupid-looking smile and a restless expression of confusion on his face. His hands trembled as if he'd just dipped them into the frozen snow outside. He had on a headband with a thin, three-inch round, silver metal device attached to it. There was a tiny hole for him to peep through in the middle of the device.

He seemed blissfully happy, faced me, and had a squint in his eyes. He then flashed a reassuring grin that seemed to be aimed at the wall rather than at me. He seemed not unlike a cat ready to pounce on some unsuspecting mouse. Laden with the strong scent of tobacco, he puffed his cigar and laid it down in a steel bedpan nearby.

Slamming down on a small, silver stool that rotated, he then reached out and clumsily gripped me by the waist. With a lighted otoscope, he had me bend down as he checked my ear cavities. He robustly pulled me towards him and used his stethoscope, which he pressed not to my chest, but rather to my neck and jugular vein.

He then declared, "I'm Dr. Muzzkauff. Your lungs sound a bit congested. Tell me the secret word, Miss Doodlebug, and win a hundred bucks or a free tonsillectomy. Now, when did you learn you were pregnant?"

I straightened up and gripped the gown I had on, using my left hand to close it around my rear end.

Feeling as if the last bolt holding my brain together had come loose, I exclaimed, "I'm not a woman, nor am I pregnant ... and what do you mean a secret word?"

Nurse Nova Caine, or whatever her stupid name was looked panicky. She snatched the chart out of the doctor's hand and replaced it with another. She shot me a silly, embarrassed grin.

"Sorry, doctor," she told him. "That was the wrong chart."

Dr. Muzzkauff widened his eyes as if to see better, but then he grabbed a large magnifying glass off a nearby table. He grabbed his cigar from the empty bedpan, took a long drag, and then puffed smoke in my face. He then studied the new chart she gave him. He reached into a drawer and removed a pair of latex gloves that he slipped onto his hands. It was then that I noticed he had no index finger on his right hand and no pinky on his left. The nurse took his cigar and stamped it out in the metal bedpan.

The doctor snarled, "I beg your pardon, Mr. Doodlebaum. Stand please, turn around, drop your underpants, and cough."

He lowered the metal eyepiece, turned on a built-in light attached to it, stared through the small hole, and then at me ... his ever-increasing annoyed patient standing in front of him.

I shrugged and stated, "It's Doodledoo ... Dabney Doodledoo. I then asked, "So, why the gloves and why must I turn around?"

"Come, come, Mr. Doodlebrain. I can't check your prostate unless you turn around."

With that, Nurse Caine jauntily cocked her head to one side and winked at me. I threw up my hands in frustration, slapped them to my face, and gritted my teeth.

"There's nothing wrong with my prostate. I'm not here for that type of exam," I snarled.

I squirmed and began to scratch at my head through the toboggan cap.

The doctor flipped down the metal eyepiece. As he did so, his ballpoint pen fell to the floor. Out of breath, he bent and his fumbling, fat hands began to blindly pat across the cold tile, as he searched for the pen. Wearing his latex gloves, he rustled under the toe-kick of a cabinet. When he rose back up he was holding a plastic hypodermic, sans the needle. Stuck to his latex gloves were chewed gum, a bobby pin, a paper clip, and a crumpled tissue. He picked away the strange grouping of items and scribbled at the chart with the plastic syringe. The sticky items again fell to the floor, where his nurse kicked them back out of sight under the cabinet. He then looked angrily at his nurse.

13

"Make a note, Miss Candycane. Order some new pens ... ones that will write." He seemed annoyed and then asked, "Alright, Mr. Doodlesoup, just why are you here then?"

Restless and agitated, but also tense and uneasy, I knew I had to address the real reason for my visit. I quickly searched my mind and imagination for the endless vista of plausible possibilities, but none developed.

I then stated meekly, "To see about removing some ... growths."

The doctor, in a lapse of absurdity momentarily swayed and turned mechanically on the stool that caused him to be facing the wall rather than me.

Speaking towards the sheetrock, he stated, "I see." Which of course he could not.

"What type of growths?" he asked the wall. "Warts, skin tags, moles?"

Nurse Nova Caine twirled the doctor's stool around till he again faced me. Between fighting with that flimsy gown, Miss Sunshine's annoying attempts at embarrassing me, plus the good doctor's assured senility, I began to feel like an alien from the planet Uranus.

With my eyes pointed downward and my hands on my hips, with misgivings I said, "No, they're a bit more uncommon than those. I'm embarrassed to say."

The doctor fiddled with his thick eyeglass lenses and narrowed his eyes.

"Come now, Mr. Doodlenose. There's no need to be apprehensive. There isn't much I haven't seen."

The irony of this half-blind doctor's absurd statement made me gag and I did my best to mask my agitation

"Well, I'll wager you've never dealt with growths like I have," I stated bluntly.

"No?" he queried. "Well, you've piqued my interest, Mr. Doodlespot. Show me what you have."

Before I'd remove my toboggan, I carefully raised my arms revealing to the doctor and nurse my armpits. A shocking gasp escaped the nurse's throat, and she quickly backed away. The doctor adjusted his eyeglasses and then used the magnifying glass to confirm what his weary, dim eyesight revealed. He almost fell off his stool at the sight he saw there under my arms, for instead of hair, my armpits now sported a full tuft of downy-soft chicken feathers. I quickly dropped my arms and slumped back onto the cold, steel table.

"See what I mean, doctor?" I proclaimed.

His face twisted and he glared cock-eyed at me. With his eyes wide and open, he urged my arms to rise again. He stared through the magnifying glass and then tugged at the feathers. I winced in pain, as the doctor lowered the glass. His mouth dropped open in surprise.

"My goodness, man. These look like—"

"Feathers. Yeah, I know."

He tilted his head back and squinted his eyes.

"I don't understand. Such a thing isn't possible."

It had taken a lot of gumption and a build-up of my courage to come here, and now that I was here, I knew I must confront head-on this strange dilemma. I had to find a solution to ridding myself of this foolishness.

The doctor tossed his nurse a look of sheer puzzlement.

He asked her, "It isn't possible, is it?"

"Not unless you're a bird or some form of poultry," she replied.

Her eyes suspiciously narrowed and I saw her eyeing me with frosty calm.

As the doctor closely examined my pits again, he ran his hands across the feathers. The nurse also carefully leaned forward to get a closer view. I reacted to the doctor's touch by giggling, for his fingers on the feathers tickled me. At my surprising reaction, he yanked his hands away like he'd touched a live electric wire. I suddenly felt like a half-opened bag of flour, as he gawked at me through those coke-bottle lenses of his. He then cocked his head sideways, hobbled backward on his rolling stool, and looked around the room.

Like a windless bellow, I sat holding my breath and awaited his words and a genuine reaction to my reveal.

He smiled and said, "Oh, I get it. This is some sort of prank, isn't it? Where's the hidden video camera?"

The nurse laughed, rose, and began to gaze into a wall mirror to touch up the hair beneath her cap. She unruffled her white uniform and she too glanced around the dimly lit room, as if she was also searching for a hidden camera.

"Prank?" I asked, as my mental agitation grew.

The doctor grinned and said, "Come now, Mr. Doodlehickey. What'd you do, shave under your arms, tear up your pillow, and super glue feathers to your pits?"

I again scratched at my head. The doctor reached, grinned, and looked suspicious about what I showed him. He grabbed the unlit cigar from the bedpan and when he couldn't suck in any smoke, he rolled it between his lips and sneered.

"Your head cold, Mr. Doddlebug? Take off your cap. You've got a microphone hidden under there, don't you?"

The doctor then reached over and grabbed my toboggan cap. He jerked it upwards ... and off my skin-head. Despite his poor vision, the doctor's smile quickly changed to a look of horrified disbelief. He cried out, as this revelation sent him rolling back again towards his office wall. Squinting and staring at my head, he then scampered away and rolled into a corner of the room. Nurse Caine screamed and ran off through the open doorway like someone with a swarm of hornets chasing after her. She slammed the door shut behind her. My bald head revealed my fully formed rooster's comb. It flopped lazily to one side of my head as if it were a rare steak tar-tar plastered to my noggin.

The commentary quickly spiraled out of control, as did the doctor's emotions.

"Uhh, Mr. Doodlesnoop, I'm afraid I can't help you. I'll refer you to a specialist more suited for your ... problem; say a nice barnyard veterinarian."

With his body, the doctor then accidentally backed into and flipped off the light switch on the wall. The windowless room went completely dark. A moment later, I groped in the dark which was all of a sudden slightly illuminated by the built-in light on the doctor's flip-down, metal eye device. The light shined directly onto my face and into my wide-open eyes and pupils. My face formed a blank expression and I was overwhelmed by a strange sensation demanding I perform my daybreak duty. Quick as a blink, my body quivered and reacted. I jerked upward, and then involuntarily leaped feet-first upon the stainless-steel table.

As in the car, I threw up my head, crouched, flapped my arms up and down, and then began to <u>crow</u>. The door to the examining room flew open, as the terrorized doctor stood and bolted down the lighted hallway like a frightened hare, with his entangled stethoscope dragging at his feet.

Like the doctor's unlit cigar, my goal of solving this dilemma was immediately and suddenly snuffed out in the middle of my ambitious attempt to rid myself of this brooding curse that befell me. I quickly restored my garments and hastily left in a gloomy reverie.

# CHAPTER 2: Duck Sauce

Of course, you're curious and I know what you must be thinking. What was all that about in that kooky old doctor's office? Now, despite the furor and confusion I caused, I survived that rather awkward and embarrassing trip to Dr. Muzzkauff. I think it's best that before I go any further with this story ... let me back up and explain how I got this way.

No, I was not the casualty of some idiopathic disease, nor was I smitten by some environmental contamination that irradiated the cells of my body causing me these physical abnormalities. No, I wasn't imagining all that, and yes ... those two-foot-tall dancing hens and that crazy rooster passenger of mine were indeed real. At least that's the way I perceived it. Whatever reality might be these days, is it any wonder why I feel like I'm going crazy? So would you if such things happened. So, what did occur and how'd I get those puzzling pullet anomalies that I displayed before the good doctor and his hysterical nurse?

Well, I could say it was caused because of some quantum mechanics theory going haywire or resulted from a queer phase of the moon that re-arranged the molecules in my body and through another dimension pell-mell turned me and my family into crazed lunatics. That might explain this perfect storm of screwball incidents, but alas it mostly started just because of my stupidity, two grilled chickens, two wild ducks, and two shotguns. The difference between genius and stupidity is that genius has its limits. I know you do too, so let me not further digress and move forward with my explanation.

\* \* \*

A year or so before, in the driveway at our thirty-acre farm in Johnstown, Ohio ... steam rose off my head and my shoes were soaked and soggy. I shivered under the wool blankets wrapped tightly around my aching, cold, naked body and sat on the back edge of an ambulance. My trembling hands were swathed around a Styrofoam cup containing hot coffee. Yep, that was me again ... very cold and in a pickle ... rather make that stewing in a slow marinate.

I lifted the cup and drank down the warm brew. Daisy wore a thick overcoat, walked up, patted me on the knee, and hugged me through the blanket. She then leaned and kissed me on the cheek. Her sad eyes reflected her concern and she also looked remorseful. I dearly love that woman, but sometimes marriage is not a word, but a run-on sentence. Such was the case that day.

Yes, I do love her, but it's because of her nagging, sentimentality, and brainless action that got me into that current mess. A paramedic with a stethoscope around his neck stood in front of me. He placed the scope end to my hairy chest and my body quivered from the coldness of it. I sneezed and Daisy handed me a tissue.

The male paramedic queried, "If I might ask sir, just exactly what were you doing in the middle of that frozen pond?"

I sneezed a couple more times and wiped my runny nose with a fourth tissue that Daisy handed me. She looked away and back at our warm farmhouse forty yards away. My two sons, Dooby and Dippy Doodledoo, plus my little daughter, Cah Cah Doodledoo, stared outside through the den window at me and the flashing lights of the emergency vehicles. The comical scene of bedlam that was going on in their driveway had to be amusing to them.

So, let me explain what occurred here and tell you about the first of the two ducks and the shotgun.

You see, about forty minutes ago, I was dressed in thermal underwear and wore, a thick, lined, canvas coat with a pullover hood, thermal leather boots, and fleece-lined, leather gloves. Yep, I was similarly attired to what I wore that day to Dr. Muzzkauff's office.

At any rate, there I was ... laying fully prostrate over the frozen solid, three-acre pond behind our farmhouse. Around my waist was tied a one-hundred-fifty-foot nylon rope, anchored securely to the solid post on our pond's fishing dock near the shoreline.

Fully committed and almost sixty feet out from shore, I struggled to shimmy my way forward towards the center of the pond and my intended target and destination. With a steady ice-cold north wind blowing, snow falling, and outside temperatures nearing twenty degrees Fahrenheit, I knew I had strolled up fool's hill with this errand. With my ever-increasing red cheeks and nose, my exhaled breath formed a wave of white fog before my watering eyes.

I slapped one hand in front of the other; bent and flexed my knees, and used whatever leverage I could get to creep slowly ahead. I didn't exactly have all-wheel drive and the ice beneath me began to creak and weaken under my body weight, made even heavier by the thick layer of clothing I wore. Annoyed and cold, I felt dumber by the second.

I mumbled to myself, "Don't know what that woman's thinking, or me either."

I was pushing the envelope and was crazy for letting her talk me into this; out here in this freezing weather ... all because of a <u>stupid duck</u> that didn't know he was supposed to fly south for winter.

Warmly tucked away inside our farmhouse, Daisy witnessed me ... her idiot husband and every precarious move I made. She grimaced and sipped hot coffee from her cup. She intently watched me from the kitchen window about a hundred yards away.

Sitting quietly in a chair pulled up to the breakfast table was my daughter, three-year-old, <u>Cah Cah</u>. Oblivious to anything going on outside, she grasped her spoon and dished her way through a bowl of milk and frosted cornflakes. About as much cereal spilled out onto the tablecloth as what was taken into her bird-like mouth.

Daisy's attention was momentarily diverted, as our youngest son, nine-year-old, <u>Dippy</u>, screamed and came running through the kitchen. He was being chased by his older thirteen-year-old brother, <u>Dooby</u>. Their dog, Goldie, a year-old Golden Retriever raced along next to them and barked its approval of the chase.

Dippy yelled, "Mom! Dooby says he's going to make me into a popsicle."

Laughing, the older brother caught Dippy and pulled him into a headlock. He rubbed his fist into his brother's curly, blond hair. Their ruckus almost caused the two boys to knock over the dining table where little Cah Cah was eating.

Dooby repeated his veiled threat, "Yes, I will! I'll pour water over you, toss you outside, watch you freeze stiff, and then hammer you into the ground like a tent spike. You won't thaw out till summer."

Goldie continued to bark and yelp, as she tried to get the boys' attention. She wanted to have them chase her.

Setting her cup down on the window sill, Daisy quickly turned and loudly clapped her hands.

In a stern voice, she said, "Stop that barking, Goldie. And you two boys break it up! Dooby, let go of your brother."

Dippy whined and complained, "Momma, I don't want to be no popsicle."

"You won't be. Your brother is just teasing you."

She picked up her coffee and took another sip. She turned back to see me perched precariously outside near the middle of our icy pond.

"I'm not certain about the fate of your daddy though," she whined.

She watched me crawl and slowly scuttle across the ice, while the intensity of the falling snow increased. Noting their mother's outdoor distraction from their indoor play, the two boys stopped their roughhousing and strolled over to the den window. They looked out, and both boys saw me, their smart father, on my belly, inching my way forward over the ice-covered pond.

Confused, Dippy asked, "Momma, why's Pop crawling around in the middle of our frozen pond?"

Not quick to answer, Daisy took yet another slow sip of her coffee. She winced and stared out the window.

She sighed deeply and then explained, "I've been up since daylight and saw that poor duck out there. I've watched it flying around here since the start of winter. I saw it land there this morning and it hasn't moved since. I convinced your father that the unfortunate thing is stuck to the ice and that he should go out there to free it."

Dooby laughed and replied, "You mean Pop was dumb enough ... I mean ... so he's trying to un-stick a duck?"

She seemed annoyed at the logic of our son's questions about the absurdity of the situation.

She ruffled and said, "Never mind. You two just sit down and eat some cereal. Your dad will be fine, I hope ... and he'll free that duck. I'm sure of it ... well maybe."

Dippy and Dooby sat down at the table, where each grabbed a clean bowl. They glanced at each other and began laughing.

Dooby whispered to Dippy, "Pop's the one that's gonna become a popsicle!"

While the ice continued to creak and act as if it might crack open at any moment, I inched my way ever closer to the center of the pond and that web-footed foul fowl, feathered creature and the reason that brought me out into this blizzard.

From her vantage point in the kitchen, Daisy grabbed a paper towel. She wiped away the frost forming inside the kitchen window. Her face registered an expression of concern and she chewed on a fingernail.

Meanwhile, the male Mallard duck in question lay quietly. Its butt was turned towards me and its duck bill and the contour feathers that regulate its body temperature were facing south in the icy breeze. Its eyes were closed, and except for a few feathers that waved about in the wind it appeared almost to be in a cryogenic state of suspended animation. I winced at the thought, for at the moment, my mind felt as though it too were in a cryogenic state.

About five feet from the duck, my expression was one of relief, for my struggle to reach this stupid duck was almost complete.

I stopped squirming and took a deep breath, as I again grumbled to myself, "Well, fool, you're almost there. Jerk that wayward duck up by the roots and get back to your wife and kids in your warm farmhouse."

With a couple of quick heaves, I found myself within two feet of the duck. At that point, the dim-witted fowl's eyes suddenly opened. He waggled and stretched his wings, flapped them three times, and then stood up. It was then that I noticed something unique about that duck. It was a drake Mallard with three white-feathered-neck-rings instead of the normal two. That was odd, but not as odd as my being out there. What happened next said it all about this foolishness and how dumb I'd been to attempt this folly.

As I watched in complete idiocy, the duck lifted to its feet and turned around. When it saw me so near, it flapped its wings harder, leaped into the air, and then did the 'alley-oop' ... as it steadily and easily flew up and away.

I was stricken with stunned silence and rolled over onto my back ... my disbelieving eyes laser locked upon the surreal scene that unfolded as if it happened in slow motion.

From outside the kitchen window, I spotted Daisy, as she clutched both hands to her cheeks and mouth. Her eyes depicted to me her total shock and surprise that the duck she was so worried about ... just up and flew away.

I imagined that from a view a hundred feet above, one could see the single tear drop that formed, and then quickly froze on my cheek.

In a detached manner from reality, I watched as the duck soared away, flying only about two hundred yards, and then landing on my neighbor, Joe Thompson's, frozen pond; where it settled comfortably down, just as it had done on ours.

Not surprisingly, the ice around me began to crack and displayed severe fissures, which formed all around my body. As I attempted to move, the ice cracked more. It appeared at any moment to possibly shatter into a thousand pieces that would send me plunging into the icy waters below.

My self-deprecation continued and I whispered, "I feel like a man with an unfinished attic. Now what do you do, genius?"

Lying there, I realized that this was all she wrote and I had no hold of that dabbling duck, but rather only a can of worms. Yep, my dumb-downed, doe-si-doe, cha-cha-cha across the ice here to save that goony bird was about to result in my being deposited into a freeze-dried glory hole in the middle of my icy pond.

No sooner had I realized that inevitable brain cloud than I began to experience it. Like glass breaking and some Ali Baba character yelling, "Open Sesame," the ice shredded beneath me, and sis boom bah ... I quickly plunged and was deposited into my ice bath. My thick coat, heavy boots, and insulated pants weren't exactly buoyancy aids, so I was dragged under by the weight. For a moment, I was certain that I'd soon be playing my golden harp and sporting my wings, as my spirit floated toward heaven ... or at least I hoped that I was going up and not down.

As I squirmed and panicked, I thrashed my legs and arms and tried to stay afloat. However, the instant cold made every pore of my body scream from the shock. Inside the house, Daisy screamed and the kids all went crazy, while they watched me go under the ice. She immediately grabbed the phone and dialed 911.

As I was about to give in and give up, I felt my boots settle solidly into the muddy bottom soil below. I was amazed that when I pushed against the bottom, I was able to situate myself ... and all of a sudden recognized that the freezing water was only about five feet deep and that I was tall enough to stand up.

Although I chattered and was as cold as I've ever been, I inhaled deeply, relieved that I wasn't drowning. The corporal punishment I deserved from having been so foolish wasn't going to claim me after all. Still, there I stood like a prairie dog poking its head out of its hole.

I whispered a quick prayer and cried, "Thanks, Lord!" I then mumbled, "Okay, Cro-Magnon man. You're still alive, but not out of the cracker barrel just yet."

* * *

As the snow let up a bit, a fire truck and an ambulance were parked in the long driveway of our Doodledoo homestead. Daisy stood nearby in a hooded coat and warm boots. She shuddered in the cold and shook hands with three volunteer firemen and two paramedics. She thanked them for coming so quickly to help pull me out of the icy pond.

I was then led to the back of an opened-up ambulance where my body shook from the cold. I removed my boots and clothing, while the paramedics wrapped my wobbly feet in fuzzy, dry slippers and the rest of me in two lined and dry wool blankets.

"Duck your head and have a seat here, Mr. Doodledumb. I have to take your vitals," declared a paramedic.

I winced and uttered, "Ooooh! Don't say duck, and my name's, Doodledoo. Please, hurry. I feel like I've got one wheel down and my axle's dragging."

I winced and plopped down near the opened, rear ambulance doors, while the paramedic checked my pulse and temperature.

My hands shook, as one of the firemen handed me a hot cup of coffee.

"Here you are, Mr. Doodlemaflich. Drink this; it'll help warm you up."

I took the coffee, and despite its bitter taste eagerly sipped it from the cup.

"Thanks!" I said, "And thanks to all you guys for saving me."

Daisy walked up. "How is he?"

"His pulse rate is high and his body temp is low, but that's to be expected. No worries though, he avoided hypothermia. If he doesn't thaw out soon, we'll stick him in the microwave for a few minutes," stated the paramedic humorously.

Humiliated, I again mumbled under my breath and sipped more of the coffee. Although it tasted like battery acid, it warmed my innards. I flashed my wife a weak smile, as my teeth chattered from the cold. Inside, I was fit to be tied, but I kept my temper in check and ate my humble pie. Although I'd given in to Daisy's request, it was ultimately my doing that got me into this mess.

Fifteen minutes later, Daisy and I were left alone. The fire truck and ambulance departed, and I stubbornly refused any more help from them. Holding onto my arm, Daisy gently guided me toward the house. As I shuffled my way across the paved drive, I stopped and stared across the way towards the neighbor's pond. There on that frozen pool of ice sat the accursed duck. My jaw tightened and I glared at it with reproachful eyes. I frowned at Daisy, who stifled a laugh, but sheepishly did not desire to annoy me further and chew the fat with me over what I'd tried to do. Sure, I had a bone of contention with her about the incident, but there was nothing to be gained from my chewing at the carpet or losing all my emotional control.

I commented calmly, "Apparently, it wasn't stuck to the ice ... dear."

Daisy patted my wrist and listened to me whimper, as she edged my wobbly steps towards the back door of our farmhouse.

"I know, sweetheart. I'm so sorry I asked you to do that."

"Not as sorry as I am for having tried it."

"Poor thing must've liked it out there. I can't imagine why," she stated.

As we got to the door and Daisy reached for the doorknob, all of a sudden, we heard a sharp, loud and booming noise ... that of a shotgun being fired.

Both of us turned towards our neighbor's house and saw Joe Johnson standing outside on his back porch. His shotgun breech was open, smoking, and slung over his arm. Joe's black Labrador retriever rushed out onto the frozen pond, where it slipped a bit, but then handily retrieved the dead duck. It then raced back to Joe with its bounty between its teeth. Joe took the duck from his dog and glanced over at Daisy and me ... who stood like statues with our mouths wide open.

Joe triumphantly held up his quarry and yelled over at us, "Hey Doodles! Guess what's for dinner?"

Joe laughed and headed inside his house with the duck and his dog. I had a blank, stupid expression on my face. I sighed and glanced at the window where the kids and our golden retriever sat and watched us. I looked at Goldie's sad eyes and felt like I was trapped in his bone orchard of ignorance.

"Now, why didn't I think of that?" I whimpered.

"Well, forever more. After all, you did and that poor duck still got shot." cried Daisy.

I looked at her, and although I snickered, a few other tears fell slowly from my eyes. I opened the door and quietly ambled inside, as I glanced over at my three kids.

"Are you okay, Pop?" asked Dooby.

"Sure, but if you'd put my brain in that duck it would've flown backward," I moaned.

Little Dippy perhaps said it best, "Yeah, Pop. I can't believe you let Mom talk you into trying that."

Daisy shot me a look of disdain and quickly poured me a fresh cup of her coffee. I winced and saw the annoyance on her face at her son's logic.

"Careful," I cautioned. "Don't rile the mother alligator until after you've crossed the river."

Daisy suppressed a laugh and her lips curled into a smirking grin.

After my first sip of her coffee, I sighed and told her, "That paramedic's rot gut brew would make a sword-swallower gag, so yours is a welcome gift to my gullet. Thanks, dear."

I stumbled to my recliner, plopped down, and wrapped the blankets around me. Daisy walked by and again kissed my cheek.

"Relax hon. Now that you've got your ducks in a row, I'll bring your slippers and get you some dry, warm clothes to wear."

I swallowed hard and shot her a look of defiance for her annoying tease referencing '*ducks.*'

In a thawing tone, I replied, "That sounds nice, for I'm in dry dock and starting to experience combat fatigue."

"I'm very sorry, dear, but that the poor duck is a gone goose—"

I winced and interrupted her, "Oooh! Don't say goose either, or anything about feathered fowl or that brainless duck winging it."

"No, dear, Joe didn't wing it, he shot it dead."

"I know, Daisy. And its swan song almost became my own. I'm so tired, if I'm dead when you get back; just toss me outside in the snow onto the compost pile."

Dooby and Dippy turned on the T.V. and began watching a Loony Tunes cartoon. After it was over, they started a pretend argument. Their faces got close together, as they smiled and giggled.

Dooby exclaimed, "It's wabbit season!"

Dippy grinned and stated, "No, it's duck season!"

"Wabbit season."

Dippy then repeated, "Wabbit season."

No, it's duck season ... and I demand you shoot me!" cried a laughing Dooby.

Dippy pointed his finger as if it were a gun at Dooby. "Bang!"

I grimaced and pulled the warm blankets around me. I closed my eyes, but forced a grin and whispered through gritted teeth ... as in synch with the two boys I growled, "You're despicable!"

# CHAPTER 3: The Sky Is Falling

Two weeks later, I came through the front door and slammed it shut behind me. Daisy entered the foyer from the kitchen and saw that I was upset. She walked over to me and we hugged.

She asked, "Hard day, hon?".

I broke away from our embrace, took a piece of paper from my pocket, and gave it to her.

"What's this?"

"Read it and weep," I said.

As we walked together into our kitchen and sat in a chair at the table, she began to read:

"It is with a sad heart that we regretfully announce that as of April third, Booker Industries will be closing. We appreciate every employee's contribution over the past thirty-two years, and we regret that because of low profits and rising costs, the time has come to retire our facility and close the plant."

Daisy's hand dropped the paper to the floor and she walked dejectedly into the den. I followed her and hugged her, as she fell back into an armchair. She hid her face in her hands. I sat down beside her and tried to comfort her from the shock.

"We've enough to live on for a while and I'll get severance pay," I told her.

She looked up at me and said, "I'll get a job. We can find one together. Besides, for years you've wanted out of that old factory."

"Yeah, but not this way. Look, we've been doing the same old six and seven routines, day in and day out for a long time now. What say we break out of our stale existence? I trained as a chef for years before getting on at the plant. Maybe it's time I tried out my culinary skills. It could be fun."

I leaned and gave her a smile and a kiss. I then surprised her, "How do you feel about going south to someplace warm ... say like, Miami?" I asked.

"Miami? That's a long way from here, but the kids would like it. Sure, why not? We'll both get jobs in a nice restaurant there," she answered.

"Yeah, we'll turn sour grapes into sweet wine. I'll call the realtor and you go online and look for us an apartment or some other place to rent down there."

She then paused and grimaced, "I will, but we'll have to sell your farm implements, our cows, and if we rent an apartment, we can't take Goldie."

I sighed and said, "Okay, but the Jacksons have wanted a dog. I'm sure they'll give him a good home."

\* \* \*

Six months later in Miami, Florida, on an eighth-floor, open, outdoor balcony patio, Charlie Cole stood over his fired-up grill. He sniffed the delicious smell of what was cooking and a smile formed on his face.

With his grilling fork, he lifted the lid of his stainless-steel grill and poked at the two whole chickens slow grilling to a golden brown. He lifted and turned the two simmering yard birds. They sizzled and sent smoke and dizzying, appetizing aromas that raised into the air above his plush condo balcony that overlooked Miami's downtown and south beach area.

He used a sharp carving knife to slice off a small piece of white meat. He tasted it, savored the flavor, and then licked his fingers.

His terrier dog, Buster, sat up on its hind legs with its tongue hanging out and begged for a morsel. It pedaled in the air with its front paws. Charlie grinned and tossed a small, sliced portion of chicken to his dog, which gobbled it down in one quick bite.

He quipped, "Good stuff, huh, Buster?"

Moments later, in the alleyway below Charlie's luxury patio and condo, walked Daisy and me. We quickly strolled down the alley towards the back entrance a half-block away towards a restaurant where we each now worked as assistant chefs.

As I briskly strolled ahead, Daisy's right shoe came untied and slipped off her foot. She stopped to replace the shoe and retie the laces.

I declared, "Hurry! If we're late again old man Applegate will fire us for sure."

"That pointy-headed old skin flint. How long are you going to let that miserable Frenchman abuse you?" she asked.

"Till we can find better employment elsewhere," I stated. "So, please hurry, dear."

"Applegate's a reprobate. To him, we're just pod people, kitchen slaves lacking personality or originality."

She finished tying her laces and stood. She then shook a fist at me, "You have more culinary talent in your little finger than he does in his entire scrawny body."

"Alright, dear, but let's not argue the point right now and just report to work."

High above, Charlie heard the doorbell ring. He watched through the glass sliding door as a lovely woman in a bright yellow and orange party dress answered their front door. Gloria Cole, Charlie's beautiful wife, welcomed their dinner guests, Barbara and Jim Evans, plus Faith and Bill Smith.

Gloria exchanged hugs with them all and showed the two couples into their home.

"Hi everyone. Please, come inside, Charlie's on the patio."

"Thanks for inviting us, Gloria," said Jim.

Bill glanced towards the balcony and sniffed the air.

He commented, "Something smells delicious."

Barbara carried a large straw purse slung over her forearm. As she went to set it down on a chair, out hopped a small, orange and white striped cat. Before she or anyone could react, the cat darted towards the open glass door that led to the balcony patio.

She screamed, "Oh dear! Snuffles crawled out of my purse. Come back here, Snook-ems."

Jim snarled and grumbled, "Stupid cat."

Charlie poked at the two grilling chickens with long-handled grilling forks. He proudly speared them and lifted them off the grill. He stood holding the two cooked morsels with his arms straight up over his head as if he were a gladiator standing over a fallen opponent.

He yelled, "Hey gang, right on time. These two beauties are grilled to perfection."

No sooner did he get the words out, than Snuffles the cat raced out onto the balcony.

Seeing the feline, Buster reacted vigorously and instinctively took in after it.

Barbara pleaded, "Snuffles, come here this instant."

The cat ignored her owner's wishes, hissed, and then began to scurry across the patio. It quickly fled and tried to avoid the snarling, barking little dog that chased after it.

As this was happening, Charlie's arms extended outward and back, with each chicken still impaled on a grilling fork. When the cat ran under his legs, Buster followed. Charlie wobbled backward, lost his balance, and then stumbled towards the balcony's half-wall railing.

Gloria hollered, "Look out, Charlie!"

Charlie's arms flung back and as he hit the half-wall the grilled chickens flung off the forks like two large lumps of clay ... and plummeted off into mid-air. A stunned Charlie turned quickly, only to catch a fleeting glimpse of the savory, cooked poultry, as it tumbled down towards the alley below.

He babbled like a child that just broke a favorite toy and this event seemed to him as fatal as being bitten by the fangs of a venomous snake.

A painful, low moan exuded from Charlie's watering mouth.

"Oooh, no!"

As I raced toward Daisy to assist her, the tumbling fowl dropped like a bolt from out of the blue.

She stood tall and informed me, "Alright, I retied my laces. Let's go."

No sooner had she said this, than came the loud, dull thud of two fleshy objects hitting the pavement directly beside us. I quickly recognized that the two whole chickens were fully cooked and descended from the condo building next to us. We each raised our eyes upward and then back down at the two grilled yard birds before us. A long slit of remaining daylight seeped through and between the downtown buildings like pointing fingers that shone brightly upon the two grilled hens. For just a moment I had an epiphany and these two morsels seemed like orchids in a cornfield.

Daisy scratched her head and commented, "Now, where do you suppose those came from?"

"Who cares? I'm just glad that they missed hitting us," I replied

Filled with intense tension like that of a drawn bow, instead of leaving them be, I rushed to pick up the two hens and placed one under each armpit.

I then said, "Let's go, I'll dispose of them when we get to work."

High above on his balcony, Charlie removed his cooking apron, sat down his grilling forks, smiled at the others, and said, "How do you all feel about tuna fish sandwiches?"

With a cooked bird under each of my arms, Daisy and I raced down the alley and through the back door of the <u>Chez Appétit Restaurant</u>.

Daisy found and punched each of our time cards and we hurried to our assignment areas in the kitchen. The middle-aged owner, a Frenchman named, Morris Applegate, wore a dark suit with a bow tie. A tall, lean man, he sported a long, dark handlebar mustache and thick eyebrows. He busily shouted orders to his other kitchen and wait staff.

"Sacré bleu! What's the hold-up? Get that order out to table fourteen immediately," he demanded.

He continued his rant to a chef next to me, "You there, finish up the order for the Chef's Salad at table eighteen."

Adding more orders, he reminded the waiter, "Be sure to recommend the Sauvignon Blanc wine with their meal."

Glancing at the order tickets, he yelled, "Who's got the chicken order ready for table nine?"

He then turned his head towards me to see Daisy and me quickly busying ourselves with other orders. He passed by the two chickens that I casually set upon the steel counter.

Rudely, as was his style, he shouted his orders, "You there, Doodleman, slice these birds and ready them to serve table nine."

My face formed a sneer and I started to comment to Applegate, but the ornery, green-eyed monster didn't give me a chance to do so.

"Did you hear me, man? Get the four orders of chicken out to table nine ... now."

Since no one in his kitchen experienced laissez-faire or was allowed to do their own will, I glanced at Daisy, who shrugged her shoulders and winked at me.

I sighed and mumbled, "What the heck."

As Applegate walked away, I brushed and picked away a few specks of dirt and small bits of debris from the two grilled chickens. I didn't even know if they were fully cooked, but I had my marching orders, and since he was the one calling the shots, I complied with them. I flicked away a small pebble, grinned, and began to slice into the two chickens. As I did, my nose got a whiff of their delicious aroma. I sniffed a few more pieces and then gave a slice of the chicken to Daisy to sample.

I told her, "Taste this and tell me what you think."

When she did, her eyes lit up like a bright ray of sunshine. She savored the juicy morsel of white meat, licking her lips as if she'd just tasted the piéce de résistance.

"Mmmmm, my goodness. That's incredible and I'm not even that fond of grilled chicken."

I quickly prepped the four chicken entree orders and garnished the plate with a creative swirl of parsley, food coloring, and the side dish complement of veggies. Seeing the order was ready, Applegate grabbed a passing waiter with a tray. He took and slapped the four plates down onto the tray and pointed to the dining room.

"Table nine, now," he ordered.

I glanced at the sliced chicken before me. Again, I sneaked a slice and tasted both the dark and white breast meat. As I savored the scrumptiously flavored chicken and licked my fingers, that mealy-mouthed Simon Legere Frenchman slapped the back of my hand. An uneaten morsel fell and landed back on the dish below me.

"Do not bring your voracious appetite into my kitchen, Doodleface. My food is for the paying customers, not you or your lady."

I lowered my head like a sad sack and cowered away to work on another order. As I left, Applegate sniffed the two chickens. He then took a piece of the meat to sample it.

His bushy eyebrows rose and his thin, drawn face twisted and formed a huge grin. He glanced about his kitchen and then used a sharp knife to slice away more pieces of the chicken, quickly devouring them.

Surveying his group of chefs in the kitchen he asked, "Which of you grilled these two hens?"

When his other staff shook their heads in denial, as the father of coquetry reviewed his royal harem of hired cooks, I reluctantly turned and faced my slave master.

"I cooked them, Sir. That is to say, Daisy and I did together."

He shook his head, "No! You? You cooked these?"

I nodded my head, but my conscience bothered me and I felt compelled and poised to tell him the truth. However, Daisy stepped forward and continued our sleight-of-hand shell game.

"Yes, we cooked them, Mr. Applegate," she said. "Delicious, are they not?"

Before he could reply, a waiter burst into the kitchen. "Sir, table nine wishes to speak to the owner."

I recognized that as being the table where the chicken had been sent. I cringed, wondering if perhaps I'd missed some pebble or stone and that some patron had gagged or choked on it. Applegate removed his apron, straightened his bow tie, and glared at me.

He then emphatically stated, "Very well, Doodlebum, henceforth. I'll expect you to produce this palatable grilled chicken every night."

With that, he exited the kitchen. As he approached his patrons at table nine, the two couples greeted him with a smile. Applegate noticed the two male customers were happily devouring their orders. Their knives and forks were in hand and they were chewing vigorously. The two women ceased eating, patted their dainty mouths with napkins, and smiled at him.

"Good evening, sirs and Madams. I trust the food is to your liking."

The first woman said, "We just wanted to tell you, this chicken is divine."

The second woman added, "Our compliments to you and your chef. This is the best grilled chicken I've ever tasted."

The two men formed silly grins and nodded in agreement. Like ravenous wolves, they each continued to consume the flavorful fowl.

"Excellent, we aim to please," remarked a please Applegate. "I have directed our chef to make this exquisite cuisine a regular item on our menu. Thank you for coming and for the compliment. I'll have the waiter send you some complimentary hors d'oeuveres."

# POULTRY-GEIST

* * *

A few minutes after quitting time at 10:00 P.M., Daisy and I stood alone in the dimly lit alleyway. We gazed upward at the exterior of the glass and steel condo building. I took notice that each of the eight floors had an array of outdoor balconies.

"From which of those balconies do you reckon our two chickens fell?" I asked.

Daisy replied, "Who knows? Maybe they tumbled from heaven. They sure impressed old man Applegate."

"Yeah, but you and I know I didn't cook them. I'm a good chef, but how do I repeat that juicy, aromatic, and tasteful success?"

She said, "It's getting late, so I'll call and see if Judy will stay another hour with the kids. That way, we can stop on the way home at the all-night supermarket to buy six or eight grilling hens and try to duplicate the taste on our grill."

I pulled a rolled-up wad of tin foil from my coat pocket. I peeled back the foil and there inside were several left-over grilled pieces of the two chickens we picked up here on the street.

I looked at Daisy and eagerly replied, "Okay, Let's do it. I'll test the ingredients from these saved pieces to see what was used as a marinade or basting."

At home, when Judy left and the kids were asleep in their beds, Daisy and I worked most of the night cooking hens. We tried spices, herbs, sauces, and grilling at various temperatures in an attempt to duplicate the aromatic taste of the two chickens we served at the restaurant. With each try, they wound up failing to match the same savory flavors and tenderness of those two chickens.

Later, I nibbled on a slice of the chicken I'd just cooked. Disappointed, I shook my head in disgust. It tasted okay but was not near as tasty as that of the two grilled chickens in the alley.

"I just don't get it. The bastings used were nothing but butter, a store-bought hickory sauce, and a little Tabasco for flavoring. What are we not doing that made the other two chickens taste so good?" I sleepily asked.

Daisy pulled up a bar stool. Exhausted, she plopped down onto it. Her arm rested on the counter, and she yawned. Also drowsy, she placed a hand under her chin and weakly tapped her other fingers on the counter for a few seconds. As if a light went off in her brain, she then bolted upright and was suddenly alert and anxious.

"Wait! I think I know what's missing," she stated anxiously.

I yawned too and commented, "Then for heaven's sake, tell me so we can get some sleep."

"Maybe it's gravity," she said.

Barely able to keep my eyes open I quizzed her, "Gravity?"

"Look, those two pullets fell, or were tossed off that balcony on that building, falling who knows how far to the ground."

"Yeah, so?" I mumbled.

"What if from that height, when they hit the ground the force from the fall tenderized and injected them with a marinate in some way? Perhaps the flavor just splattered throughout the meat."

I smirked and started to dismiss the idea, but then I had second thoughts, and my expression plus my interest was piqued. I cleared my mind and thought about what she'd said.

"You know, that sounds crazy, but maybe you're onto something."

"Sure! We'll need to discover from how high they dropped, and then we may be able to duplicate the taste," she exclaimed.

I yawned and issued a drowsy murmur, "Let's get some sleep. We'll refrigerate the chickens we cooked tonight, reheat them tomorrow, and take them down there before work."

"But how do we test from which floor they fell?" she queried me.

At the moment, my brain was fuzzy like an out-of-order elevator.

"I remarked, "Let me sleep on it. I'll think of something."

# CHAPTER 4: Kockle-Doodledoo

Beneath a sky as fair as summer flowers, Daisy and I arrived in the alleyway with our cooked chickens before noon the next day. I looked up at the glaring sun as it reflected off the glass building. A light wind drifted between the building and I wondered if that would have any effect when the chickens fell. I then noticed near the top of the building and bright as a diamond in the sun an aluminum platform about ten feet long attached to cables from the roof. Situated on the sturdy platform were two male window washers.

Seeing them suddenly gave me an idea. I smiled, waved my arms, and eventually got their attention. Creeping downward like a snail, the platform slowly descended from halfway up the building towards us on the ground level.

I told Daisy, "I think we may have our way of testing from what height the chickens fell."

She nodded and soon the men and platform gradually lowered and neared the ground. It was then that I noticed the odd contraption attached to the right side of it. Of the two young men dressed in white overalls, the one on the right side was strapped into his harness and the other wasn't. The one on the right had in front of him a large pane of glass about five feet tall in a metal frame that covered half of the platform. The way he was strapped in, it seemed as though he was only capable of cleaning the large pane, but not any of the windows on the building. That made me curious as to why he was even part of their window-washing assignment.

It was when they neared the ground floor of their descent that I noticed the man on the right had on dark, tinted glasses. Though he was calm as night, to me it seemed apparent that he may have poor eyesight. The platform came to a stop a couple of feet off the ground.

The well-built young man on the left grinned and hopped out, while the other man had the look of a bewildered, blind moth. With eyes as blue as a clear forest pool, the man on the left greeted us. The other man looked to be his twin and except for the way they were dressed had the same build, dark complexion, and handsome features. For certain, I could tell Daisy noticed their attractiveness.

"Hi, my name's Wayne Kockle, and this is my twin brother, Dwayne. I saw you waving, is something wrong?"

The other man held out his hand to the air in front of him, I suppose in a gesture to shake hands.

He smiled and commented, "Yes, we're twins, but I'm the good-looking one."

Wayne held what appeared to be a device of some sort. As he departed the platform, he flipped a switch on it.

The platform jerked and caused Dwayne to hold onto a rail. It then started to ascend and slowly lifted three floors, where Dwayne began again to eagerly clean his large glass pane.

Wayne extended his hand to me and I shook it.

"No, nothing's wrong," I said. "Thanks for coming down. I'm Dabney Doodledoo, and this is my wife, Daisy."

I paused and looked up. I saw a contented Dwayne, as he used soap and water to wash the glass pane. He then took a rubber squeegee and began to wipe it dry. I started to say something to Wayne, but stopped and chuckled.

Wayne then yelled to his brother, "Good job, Dwayne. Relax a while as I talk to these nice folks."

Dwayne smiled and waved down in the direction of Wayne's voice. He stumbled a bit on the platform.

Wayne then quietly explained, "Dwayne was temporarily blinded while playing golf."

"Oh my, how'd that happen? Was he hit in the head with a golf club?" I asked.

"No, he was struck by lightning. The doctors say it damaged his optical nerve and it will take several months before it heals back and he can see again. He's stubborn and refuses to accept he has a handicap, so I had that big glass pane rigged up. He believes he's helping me clean the windows. He has very keen hearing, so I sent him back up to wipe while we talk."

Daisy and I smiled and nodded our heads.

She asked, "Aren't you afraid he'll fall?"

Wayne grinned, "Oh, he falls out all the time, which is why I use two harnesses on him and a safety net that deploys under the platform when he does."

Daisy and I both suppressed a hearty laugh but did giggle under our breath.

He then asked, "What can we do for you folks?"

"Wayne, we need your help and I'll pay you a hundred dollars for your time."

"That much?" he said. "What is it you have in mind, Mr. Doodledoo?"

He noticed the grouping we brought of cooked chickens in the basket.

"Having a cookout, are you?" he questioned.

"Thanks for getting my last name right and you can call me, Dabney. No, we'd like you to take these cooked chickens and say ... start on the second floor of the building. Then, when I tell you, toss one off."

"Toss one off? Just one? What do we do with the others?"

I handed him a radio. "Take this two-way radio. As you get to each floor, I'll call and ask you to toss off another chicken. Do that on each floor till I say stop."

That sounds simple enough. I won't ask why you want this, as I imagine you have your reasons."

"Yes, we do. Can you tell which floor your platform is at ... when you toss over a chicken?"

"Yes, the floors are marked by a sensor that the platform reads as it passes by it."

Daisy handed Wayne the chickens and basket.

"Okay then, I'll bring Dwayne down and we'll get started."

He pushed a button on the control device and the platform moved downward. When it reached the ground level, he turned with one hand on the remote control, and the other holding the basket of chickens. He grinned and hopped up to join Dwayne on the cable-drawn stand.

* * *

When ready, Wayne raised the platform to the second floor. Holding the small portable two-way hand-held radio, I keyed the microphone. Daisy stood nervously nearby.

"Okay, Wayne, stand by to drop the first one," I said into the microphone.

Wayne stood next to the stack of cooked chickens he took from Daisy. Holding his portable handheld radio, He keyed his microphone.

"Ready when you are, Dabney."

Almost low enough to be heard without the radio, I spoke into the microphone, "Roger that."

Dwayne laughed and let out a mock rooster crow.

He then commented, "Now let's see if I've got this straight. He wants us to toss over a grilled chicken from different heights of the building. That's weird but entertaining. And you thought it'd be just another boring day."

He then sat down on the platform, leaned back against the back rail, placed his hands behind his head, and smiled. I used a broom and swept the alley pavement below as clean as I could get it. Wayne then heard his radio being keyed.

I said, "Okay Wayne, we're ready down here. Toss over the first one."

"Ten-four," called Wayne.

He released the mic and issued instructions to his working partner.

"All right, Bro. Fire one."

Dwayne rose and his hands fumbled inside the basket. He picked up a chicken, leaned over the front edge of the platform, and as if a bombardier released it.

"Bombs away!" he yelled. "Make that cluck-cluck-and-away."

Both men laughed, as the pullet dashed rapidly towards the ground.

Wayne chuckled and said, "I'd say we're in the catbird seat, but I suppose it's more accurate to call it the yard bird seat."

"This is the easiest and most fun hundred bucks we've ever made." declared Dwayne.

Backing away to a safe distance, Daisy and I waited and watched, as a moment later the first chicken slammed into the pavement.

Like scientists careful not to destroy a test tube sample, we rushed in, but carefully gathered the poultry carcass, dusted it off, placed it on a folding tray, and then sliced away a parcel of meat. Each one of us tasted the sampling and then looked at the other for a response.

She looked at me and remarked, "It is better, but the meat's too ragged and stringy."

I nodded my head, took the microphone, and keyed it again.

"Wayne, please take it up a couple of floors and try again."

"Sure thing, Boss."

Daisy and I again backed away and looked upwards. Seconds later, another cooked bird smashed against the ground. We rushed in and repeated the taste test. Afterward, we looked at each other and had a similar reaction as before.

"It's getting better, but it's still not right," I stated sadly.

I then repeated a request to Wayne, "Take it up a couple of floors at a time now, and then toss over another bird."

Meanwhile, at the end of the alleyway, a couple of homeless, displaced hobos hid behind their makeshift, cardboard shelters and watched the goings-on with interest. One turned to the other and blinked his eyes. He seemed completely baffled by what he just saw and heard.

The other hobo hoisted a bottle of his liquid lunch and swigged down swallows of some cheap adult beverage. He wiped his mouth with the back of a grimy, stained, fingerless glove.

The first hobo stirred a can of mulligan stew that warmed over a half-used can of lit Sterno.

He remarked, "They're at it again. As best I can make out, the man below is on the radio trying to talk them fellers into not tossing them chickens off that aluminum ledge up there."

The second hobo alleged, "A fat lot of good that does. Those chickens are trapped up there by those two guys like serpents trying to escape a vulture. As soon as the yard birds land, that man and woman rush over to stab and slash at 'em with a knife."

"Yeah, but that doesn't matter anywho. Them namby-pamby fellers we've watched go up and down the outside of that building on that mobile ledge up there already nipped them bird's heads off and plucked the chicken's feathers even a-fore they got tossed off."

Dwayne faced his brother and shrugged.

"This ruins all my illusions about us ever being overachievers."

After the drop from the sixth floor, Daisy and I bent over our tray and tasted the chicken that just fell to earth. I winced and was frustrated. I keyed the microphone one last time.

"All right, Wayne. We may be wasting our time, but take it up to the eighth floor and let a couple more fall. If they don't turn out right, then this has been all for naught."

At the pinnacle edge near the top of the building, Dwayne reached in and removed two cooked chickens. He crawled over to the edge of the platform and tossed them over the side.

He sighed and asked Wayne, "Can we get back to washing windows now?"

When the final two cooked fowls splattered to Earth, Daisy seemed less confident and enthusiastic. She rolled her eyes and slowly walked over to the two pullets. Despondency and doubt clung to me like a cast-off cloak. My throat was dry, and I felt a flush of anxiety that rushed over me. She and I both knew this was the moment of truth.

Nervous, but eager, Daisy approached the two carcasses with the headlong zest of a big game hunter. Emotions flashed across her face like the sweep of sunlit clouds over a quiet landscape. Silently, she approached the chickens and swiftly sliced away a piece of meat from each bird. Slowly and deliberately, she closed her eyes and tasted the slices. I cringed as her lovely face formed a blank expression.

As my breath caught in my throat, I noticed her eyes flash open and become luminous and bright.

A broad smile suddenly appeared, and her cheeks became rosy. She suddenly seemed as joyful as a wave that dances on the sea.

Unable to contain my curiosity any longer, I then took a knife and sliced myself a sampling from the two chickens. As I chewed, I stood silent for a moment and then dropped to my knees like a broken branch. I squatted like a maniac on his throne and became giddy with delight.

Daisy's face glowed and I grinned, but then to be certain of our test, I keyed the microphone once more and in a soft voice I said, "Wayne, just to be sure, please toss off another chicken."

Against a sky as clear as sapphire I watched the yard bird tumble, fall, and then smash into the ground. The two hobos stared about like calves in a pen.

However, for me, it was like something divine clung around us as if it were a holy vapor.

Cautiously and with some bit of trepidation, we gathered this final grilled chicken and whacked off a larger piece for each of us to taste. As we licked our fingers in triumph, the beating of my heart sounded like a drum in my ears. I grabbed Daisy's hand and gleefully jumped for joy. We held hands and began dancing in circles. Our laughter depicted our mirth and we were happy as bees in clover.

From atop the building, high above on their perch, Wayne glanced below at the two giddy adults frolicking in the alley.

He held his handset and keyed the microphone. "Uh, Major Tom to ground control. From up here, it looks as if you're splashdown was a success. Whatever that means."

I screamed into the microphone. "Yes, it was. Thank you so much. You can come down now and join us. There's something I want you to try."

The two hobos watched all this with the complacency of a stray cat. They took in all the drops and tasted as if it was a pungent, displeasing odor. As Daisy and I danced around the pile of grilled chickens, they winced and shook their heads. One gathered their cardboard home, folded it under one arm, and then picked up a grimy old blanket and ragged, canvas backpack.

He snarled and grunted, "Come on, Reginald. This is too nerve-racking. We ain't living in a neighborhood where witches are dancing around dead chickens."

The other hobo remarked, "You know, Gerald, I think they're affiliated with some enchanted, nomadic tribe. Either that ... or perhaps they are practicing butchers."

The hobos slinked away like they were escaping from dragons. Daisy and I ceased our dance and above us, we saw Wayne and Dwayne depart their platform and disappear onto the rooftop.

While the twins made it off the roof and into an elevator headed back to ground level, I found myself experiencing a jumble of anxious thoughts. As I stared at my gleaming wife and those savory chickens before me, every nerve in my body seemed like a strained harp-string ready to snap at the slightest thing.

My mind envisioned us in a restaurant of ours serving up this delicious grilled chicken to customers. The promise and prospect of that scenario would mean no longer having to crawl like a snake before the slanderous, villainous venom of old man Applegate, or endure his oppressive orders and criticism. Cheerful emotions raced through me like a tempest. Inside, I leaped with the delight of a fawn at play.

"Eureka!" I shouted.

Wayne soon came forth from the overhead door of the plush condo. Behind him, Dwayne held onto his brother's elbow and was led into the alleyway. Questions quickly came forth from both brothers as they approached us.

"So, if you would, please explain to us what that was all about," stated Wayne.

"My, that is an intoxicating perfume you're wearing Miss Daisy. What is it?"

Wayne queried, "Yes, it is nice, but please ... you've piqued our curiosity. Why were you so seemingly disappointed until we tossed those last yard birds down?"

Dwayne asked, "Satin Dreams, that's your perfume, isn't it? And yes, why did we play bombardier with your grilled pullets?"

Daisy smiled and said, "No, Dwayne, the perfume is called, Night Mist, and it's one that Dabney gave me on our anniversary. As for what we were doing, I'll let him explain. However, before he does, I'd like you each to try a piece of the chicken that fell ... from the sixth floor."

She winked at me, quickly sliced off two pieces from those chickens, and handed them to each brother.

She asked, "Well, what'd you think?"

Wayne chewed on his piece and remarked, "It's not bad, but kind of dry though."

Dwayne added, "I agree. It's okay but what's the point here?"

She told them, "That piece came from the one you dropped off the sixth floor."

She then sliced off two other pieces from different chickens.

"Now, taste this, which comes from the ones you tossed from the eighth floor."

Dwayne and Wayne tossed away the previous pieces. They took the ones offered them now by Daisy. They bit into the chicken and rolled the meat around on their tongues. Dwayne's face formed a queer expression of surprise. He gobbled down the piece of chicken, as did Wayne.

They each appeared as if the sweetness of what they just ate tickled every pleasurable sense inside their palettes and brains.

Wayne smiled broadly, "Wow! That's the tastiest piece of chicken I've ever wrapped my lips around."

Dwayne followed, "Me too. What'd you do to it?"

I stepped up and told them, "We cooked all the chickens the same. It was the drop from the proper height that made the difference."

"Huh? You mean the drop off the eighth floor did this?"

"Apparently so. That's why we had you drop from different floors until we could discover if a fall is what made the grilled chickens we found here last night so tasty."

"Wait, you found cooked chickens here ... just lying in the alley?"

Daisy laughed and explained, "No, we were walking down the alley on our way to work when two grilled chickens fell from off someone's patio above."

"Yes, and I picked them up and carried them with us to the kitchen of the restaurant we work at down the street."

Wayne looked up towards the eighth floor of the building and nodded his head.

"The eighth floor ... yes that would be Charlie Cole's place. He does grill out a lot. That's amazing! Can I get another piece?" Wayne asked as he licked his lips.

I cut other pieces and gave some to him and Dwayne. They each gulped them down with eager anticipation.

Wayne turned and then whispered into his brother's ear. Dwayne smiled and nodded his head. Wayne sighed deeply and then reached to pat me gently on the shoulder.

"You must market this great discovery."

"Yes, but I'm thinking we keep it a secret and maybe go see a banker about opening our own restaurant," I said.

Daisy seemed surprised but pleased by my bold statement.

"Yeah, I believe that's what we'll do," I proclaimed.

"No need," declared Wayne. "Dwayne and I will fund the money for your venture."

"We sure will. With chicken this good, serving it in a restaurant's bound to succeed."

My mind swirled with dizzying possibilities. "That's a nice gesture, fellows," I said. "But it would take a couple hundred grand or more to open a restaurant."

"Is that all? Then let's open four, one east, west, north, and another here in South Beach," replied Dwayne.

I was befuddled by his statement. Daisy and I both look confused by their boldness.

"No disrespect guys, but you two are window washers to whom I owe a hundred bucks. Where'd you get that kind of money?"

Dwayne snickered a bit and Wayne's face formed a suspicious grin. Before anything else could be said, a man came rushing out of the back door of the building. He saw Wayne and Dwayne and headed towards them. I worried that he might be their boss and had come to chew them out for not having finished washing all the windows.

Instead, the excited man reported to them, "Thank goodness I found you. Pardon my interruption, Sirs. Your architect called and said the city approved your plans for adding six more stories and a penthouse here to your building. He wants you to meet him at his downtown office at 3:00 P.M. to go over the plans and discuss the details."

What the man said pealed through my brain like a muffled bell. Daisy and I both were surprised and confused by the man's statements. It was as if a door had been opened to expose the shaft of a gold mine.

"That's good news, Joe. Call him back though and tell him we'll make an appointment for tomorrow. We have other matters to attend to today," directed Wayne ... to his associate.

When I was able to speak, my words stumbled out, "Hold on. Are you telling me you two own this building?"

"This one and three more like it. Our deceased father was a wealthy inventor. He bought this building ten years ago. We come down here for a few weeks each year to escape from the cold Pennsylvania winters." stated Dwayne.

"Of course, we've sold all the condo units here, but still own the land, facilities, and common areas," added Wayne.

Daisy swallowed hard and asked, "Then, you aren't quacks selling banana oil and spouting hogwash. You two are rich?"

Dwayne waved an arm in the air and this scenario seemed like manna from heaven to us.

He then stated, "On second thought, let's open a dozen restaurants around the area. That'll mean more revenue across the board, plus more coverage in the market."

"Of course, we'll have to come up with a more sanitary way to prepare and drop the chickens, but the cost-benefit of production will make for higher margins," said Wayne.

"You mentioned Pennsylvania. Why there?" I asked.

"We own a hatchery and poultry processing plant back in Paradise, Pennsylvania. We can furnish any chickens, turkeys, or any sort of poultry you'll need for your restaurants," declared Dwayne. "With this grilled recipe, you can offer whole or half chicken orders, shish-ka-bobs, a buffet, tenders, finger foods, or whatever pleases you."

"What do you say, Dabney and Miss Daisy? Do we have a deal?" asked Wayne.

He extended his hand toward them. So too did Dwayne, except he was facing the wrong direction. Wayne quickly twirled him around to face us.

"Shake on it, partners," said Dwayne.

Daisy and I look puzzled, paused a moment, and then I eagerly took Dwayne and Wayne's handshake. Daisy hugged them both and happy tears formed in her eyes.

"Okay! I shouted. "You are our investors."

"Now, let us go get out of these outfits and we'll go somewhere to celebrate and discuss what and how we'll get things started," said Wayne.

All of us broke out in laughter. However, Daisy glanced at her watch and became panicky.

"Oh no. It's almost 2:00. We have to be at work at 3:00—"

Before she finished, she realized the absurdity of what she was saying. We didn't need that job anymore. Slaving at Applegate's restaurant was like wearing a too-tight girdle around her waist.

"Her voice trembled, "Wait a minute. If you're so rich, what's with the window washing? Is all this talk of wealth just a ruse?"

"All we've said is true. Washing windows is just something to do, plus we enjoy the sunshine and fresh air."

# CHAPTER 5: A Plan and Plumping Out

Late October and three months later, Daisy and I greeted customers at one of our highly successful Miami grilled chicken restaurants. The sign over the entrance read: <u>Kockle-Doodledoo's Ate-Plate Café</u>. By spelling "Eight" as "Ate" about our method of tenderizing and marinating, we were able to disguise the process and avoid others from knowing our trade secret ... somewhat like Colonel Sanders and his finger-licking-good KFC motto.

The casual restaurant was full of hungry diners that stood in the cafeteria-style line with trays waiting to sample one of our Florida famous grilled chicken dinners. A man with a clipboard stood nearby and marveled at how busy it was. He and I stepped aside and into the kitchen, where we began going over the comments and data on his printed forms.

"As always, everything looks spic and span, Dabney," stated the man beside me.

"Thanks, Bob. That's what we require of every café," I said.

"Three more new restaurants this month. You, Daisy, and the Kockle twins are quite a success, Dabney."

"If you prepare a tasty menu and product, people will come," I replied

The Inspector tore off the bottom portion of the form and handed it to me.

"Except for that curious asphalt-covered pebble I found in your chicken last month, you run a very clean operation."

Filled with a bashful tinge of remorse, I grinned and said, "Yes, I am sorry about that, Bob. Is your tooth better now that we got you a new crown placed over it?"

Bob ran his tongue across the incisor tooth that got cracked when he bit into a small pavement stone while eating one of our meals. I of course could not reveal from where it may have come, but realized after that we must be more careful when harvesting our grilled hens.

He shook my hand, "Congratulations, Dabney, and well done."

We then walked back into the dining room. The Health Inspector tossed his clipboard on a nearby counter, took a food tray, and then took his place in the serving line behind the other customers.

"My mouth's watering, and my stomach's growling. I can't wait to dig into some of your incredible grilled chicken," he said.

Daisy handed him a wrapped napkin with silverware inside.

"It's our pleasure to serve you, Bob. Enjoy your lunch."

* * *

Near midnight on a Tuesday, when we were sure none of the other tenants were on their patios, from a condo six doors down from Charlie Cole's, Wayne and Dwayne rolled out onto the balcony of their eighth-floor penthouse, four large stainless-steel carts loaded down with grilled chickens. They glanced over the balcony to the alleyway below. Once again, Wayne used a headset radio, and microphone to relay his message.

"Sky-Bird One to Ground-Hog. We're ready to fly at your command."

Eight floors below in the alley, I listened to his words through my radio headset.

"Roger, Sky-Bird. Commence 'Operation Sky-Dive' on my order."

I then backed a black panel van with no markings into position. Behind my truck, on the pavement was an X –mark in infrared paint. Daisy stood nearby wearing glasses capable of recognizing infrared markings. She waved and cued me when I backed the van into position over the X.

With a smug delight, I pushed a button and the van's rear door opened. A second or so later, a large four-foot by six-foot stainless-steel platform pan emerged and flipped open onto the ground directly over the infrared X. I straightened myself with a sense of dignity and felt a numbed comfort and elation from our having discovered this unique, but strange way of infusing our poultry with its amazing flavor.

Daisy checked the deserted alley and with nobody around, she gave me the thumbs up. As a precaution, we set up a wooden sign rail that stated, "Men Working. Alley Closed."

I spoke into my headset, "Sky-bird, the table is set. Commence Dive."

Seconds later, the alley began to resound with thud after thud, as each of the numerous cooked chickens pummeled from the eighth floor onto the sanitary stainless-steel pan below. The whole operation took about ten minutes. As Daisy raced to gather and fold up the wooden rail that blocked the alley, I pushed another button on the van's dash. The pan, now full of cooked chickens lifted and retracted inside the back of the vehicle.

Again, in a dark corner at the end of the alley and unknown to us, two different hobos than before were draped in shredded clothing and watched with confused bewilderment at what we were doing. One scratched at his gray, shaggy beard and stuck his head out from behind their shoddy, makeshift shelter. Sleepy-eyed and somewhat inebriated, he yawned, as his bunkmate on the straw mattress rolled over and went back to sleep.

The awake man muttered to himself, "No wonder we got this spot so cheap from Reginald and Gerald. Who can sleep with that chicken-plopping racket going on here every night?"

Daisy opened the van's side door and tossed in the Men Working sign rail. She then jumped inside as the van whisked away down the alley and onto the dark street.

* * *

A week later, Daisy and I met with Wayne and Dwayne to discuss our progress and how to improve our methods of marinating and tenderizing. We all agreed that it was becoming risky to keep doing it the way we had been. Dwayne said he had an idea. With him being somewhat of an inventor like his dad, he claimed to have come up with another more convenient method than the stealthy sky drops we'd been doing these past few months.

Although his eyesight hadn't fully returned, he was able now to discern a bit of light from the darkness. We agreed to let Dwayne work on improving our repeatable technique and he told us he should have an improved way by the start of December. After the meeting, he and Wayne caught a plane back to Paradise, Pennsylvania. They wanted to check on their poultry processing plant and give Dwayne time to develop his idea.

* * *

On a crisp, chilly Thanksgiving Day inside a comfortable, luxurious, suburban home five miles out of Paradise, Pennsylvania amid Lancaster county and Amish country, there a cheerful family sat around a dining room table.

From the corner of the room, they heard a squawk, as their pet parrot shuffled around on her T-bar perch. This green-feathered, curved-beak pet was called, P. Patti Parrot. The P. stood for Peanut, which was Patti's favorite snack. Known by the Plump family to be rather candid, Patti often repeated words that ruffled the feathers of her owners.

At the table of the Plump family unit, Paul Plump, the leader of the household weighed in at three-hundred-fifty pounds. His gray eyes shined and narrowed as he sat proudly at the head of the table. Dressed in slippers, a pullover, a plus-sized sweatshirt, and corduroy pants, he was the epitome of casual, homey attire.

Seeing him, Patti Parrot squawked, "Pappy Person."

His wife, Polly, with her svelte two-hundred-eighty-pound frame, leaned over the table and then busily touched up and finished with the table settings. Her rosy cheeks glowed, and her short, disheveled blond hair curled about her head. Her deep blue eyes shined, and happy laughter bubbled from her high-pitched voice. She wore a plus-sized apricot-colored dress with three-quarter sleeves. On her fat, but tiny feet were Nike leather walking shoes with Velcro straps to secure them.

Patti Parrot saw her and squawked, "Pappy's partner."

When done, Polly turned; left for the kitchen, and then a moment later returned and brought out a huge serving plate with her featured dish: A large, golden-brown, twenty-three-pound roasted turkey complimented with her family's favorite cornbread dressing.

Patti Parrot became agitated and eager as a racehorse at the starting gate. "Pleasing platter ... Pleasing platter," she squawked.

Paul licked his lips, as drool ran down the corners of his mouth and double chin. In his pudgy hand, he held a fully charged, cordless electric carving knife. As if it were a bandsaw, he readied himself to forge into the bird-like it was a wooden hobby project ... only this one he could eat.

No doubt, he aimed to use the sharp cutlery on the turkey, once the pre-meal festivities were complete. Seated around the table were their two children. Twelve-year-old, Petunia, attired in her flared bottom velour pants and tank top was already over one-hundred-fifty pounds. Perky five-year-old, Pansy, in a pink, frilly dress her mom made grinned from ear to ear. She had her hair in pigtails and was a comparatively skinny seventy-five-pounder.

To the kids, Patti Parrot screeched, "Precious Pansy ... Pretty Petunia."

Both kids were already poised near the deviled eggs, jellied cranberry sauce, sweet potatoes, and pumpkin pie. With their forks in hand, they were ready to dig into the large meal. Tucked down their dresses were white-laced bibs so that they wouldn't stain their clothes.

Patrick Plump, Paul's father and the elder of the clan was an easy-going study of relaxation. Reeking with the untantalizing smell of his cheap aftershave, he was dressed like an unmade bed. Weighing in at an even four hundred pounds, he presented quite a captivating presence. He happily presided over the opposite end of the long table from Paul. He too was bibbed and gathered with fork and knife in hand.

Patti Parrot saw Patrick, raised her beak in the air, and turned her back to him. She then squealed, "Paternal patriarch ... Pathetic pudgy pachyderm."

Papa Plump growled and tossed a roll at Patti, causing her to <u>duck</u>. (<u>Ouch! There's that word again</u>)

Once everyone was seated in their chairs, Paul tapped his spoon lightly against an empty tea glass. He pushed himself to a standing position and called for his family's attention. Everyone bowed their head and except for a few giggles from Pansy, the room became silent.

Paul then delivered his prayerful Thanksgiving liturgy, "Please, let us properly profess our profound pleadings of purpose, as I preside and present a pertinent prayer. Permit Lord our praise, as we partake and participate in these perfectly prepared premium parcels and poultry."

He paused and slapped the back of Pansy's hand, as she opened her squinted eyes and reached for a warm roll.

He continued his prayer, "Please purge and prohibit our pitiful sins, plus pardon our pathetic problems, as we progress with proper passion. Amen."

Paul and the others raised their eyes and heads. Each one began salivating over the feast before them. Paul smiled, as he flipped the 'ON' button of the cordless knife. He listened to its distinctive whir and hum. The knife proved ready to carve and slice into the big bird before them. However, as a tease,

Paul surprisingly sat down, as the plates began to clang and side dishes began to fill each Plump's plate.

Patti Parrot protested when she was not given any roasted peanuts. Polly then reached under the table and came back holding a bag of Patti's much-beloved snack. She leaned over and poured out a proper portion of the nuts into Patti's feed dish.

Patti Parrot proceeded to crack open the peanut shells and quickly became a contented bird.

"Peanut Patti is pacified pet parrot," she squawked.

Paul pretended to ignore his family's intense hunger for the delectable poultry I before them, as he instead curiously requested his father.

"Papa Plump, please pass the peas."

He winked at his confused wife and asked perky Petunia. "Please pass the piping hot potatoes and a portion of that premium produced pudding platter my pretty partner, Polly, has so promptly and properly prepared."

Little Pansy snarled and her face took on a serious smirk of disappointment. Papa Plump intervened.

He growled, "Pardon, but passing is performed. Don't perpetuate or prolong practical pranks, as patience is passed, and hunger pangs provoke possible protests from your patriarch and other puffed up plucky playful Plumps."

Paul let out a huge laugh, as his robust stomach rippled up and down like an ocean wave. His eyes then focused on the bronzed, large-breasted roast turkey before him. He again pressed the button on the electric knife that raced the tiny slicing device as fast as it would go. As the gluttonous group of family members drooled and dropped what they were doing, each set of eyes focused on what was about to take place ... the ceremonial carving and serving of the Thanksgiving turkey. What happened then ... nobody expected it. Suddenly, the plates began to rattle and bounce up and down about an inch off the dining table. The elaborate dining room crystal chandelier began to clatter, shake, and then twirled as if it were one of those mirrored balls on a disco ceiling.

Paul gasped, but continued to grasp the whirring, humming knife. Polly's mouth flew open, as she and the others then witnessed the large turkey ... as it slowly rose off the platter. Defiantly, it somehow re-animated and stood up on its short, stumpy legs. Because of this riveting, heart-pounding action, Polly and the two girls screamed and drew back from the table.

Unbelievably, out of the turkey's neck popped a tiny head that wore a white hockey mask with two fierce-looking red eyes glowing out the eye holes. To Paul's astonishment, quick as a martial arts expert, the turkey wobbled over towards him and grabbed the knife away with a hand-like protrusion from the end of its featherless wing.

The turkey then let out a weird, evil, fanatical squeal and gobble laugh. It wielded the cordless knife into the air and raced its slicing motor, much like the menacing psycho from the movie, "The Texas Chain Saw Massacre." It took a swipe with the knife at Polly, whose hair stood on end when she heard the resurrected fowl's frightening squeal. The knife sliced away hair and left Polly with a Grace Slick type flat top, as she departed golden-colored locks twirled silently down upon the table.

Patti Parrot wailed, "Preposterous predicament." She flapped her wings and flew off into another room.

Quickly backing away from the table, the plump family dropped their utensils. Then they watched in stunned horror, as the deviled eggs suddenly leaped up out of their plate, sprouted tiny little forked tails, spindly-hoofed legs, and small demonstrative arms that held shields and a tiny pitchfork. The creamy half-egg fillings moved to the center of the table and began to form an eerie snarling face that stared out at the family of potential diners. The eggs then quickly gathered, squatted together in a huddled mass ... and looked forever more like a horde of zealous Spartan warriors about to attack.

Paul spoke in a choked, panicky voice, "Possible precarious predicament."

Papa Plump added, "Probable perilous problem."

The turkey used the knife to slice away into the cranberry sauce, splashing purple jellied sauce all over the nearby Plumps. It then glared at them out of the shadows of the eye holes in its mask. It plunged the knife into the pie, all the while squealing like a stuck pig.

"Oh my, not the pumpkin pie," sighed a disappointed Polly Plump.

The obsessive re-animated turkey waddled towards the edge of the table and in the direction of Papa Plump and the kids.

Papa yelled, "People, I propose we pursue a path pronto to the pantry to preserve our persons."

Petunia rose and began to run. She screamed, "Panic! It's in pursuit. Proceed promptly, or perhaps perish."

Papa Plump lifted his fat belly and lumbered off, followed closely by Petunia, Polly, and Paul. The very plump Plumps ambled a few yards away, crammed themselves inside the kitchen's large walk-in-panty, and then slammed the door shut behind them. No sooner were they inside than they saw the knife blade, still whirring and humming, as it ominously slid under the bottom of the closed door.

It eerily rattled back and forth, slicing at the air between it and the floor an inch away. The sound of the creepy turkey gobble and its apparent laughter and squeal resounded through the door.

A single sixty-watt bulb lit up the crowded pantry, filled now with four frightened fatties. As they ran for the pantry, Polly instinctively grabbed her purse. Inside it, she found and removed her cell phone.

Paul directed her, "Please place a plea to police to provide protection and put asunder this possessed and perverted poultry that places us in peril."

When she made a connection, Polly appealed to the 911 operator, "Police! Please proceed promptly to 70 Pleasant Place in Paradise, Pennsylvania."

With the speaker function on the phone, Petunia yelled, "Particularly come pound this packing house pullet into portions and pieces!"

As the others panicked, desperately hungry Papa Plump spotted some promising food in the pantry. His face took on a serene look of contentment and he grabbed three packages off the shelves, opened them, and began to nibble while offering some of his bounties to the others.

"Perhaps panicked prodigy will partake of packaged pecans, peanuts, or popcorn," he said calmly.

"Please, Papa, pick a more proper time to partake," declared Paul.

After being assured that help was its way, an annoyed Polly then realized something was amiss. It suddenly went dark in the room, as the sixty-watt light bulb above them flickered out, burst, and sent shards of glass to the floor.

Outside the door, they heard the distinctive sounds of the family cat, as it let out a shrill meow. There was then a loud squeal that came forth from the turkey, followed by a stark feline shriek, and then silently, orange fur came floating in under the pantry door.

Petunia sighed sadly and said, "Pity the poor pussy."

In a voice tinged with panic, Polly resonated, "Oh poop! Perplexed am I for one particular Plump isn't present. Please don't let that putrid, prowling pitter-pattering poultry pest, paw, or paddle my precious, pampered little Pansy."

She stood and, in the dark, grappled for the doorknob, she intends to race out and save little Pansy. As she reached for the knob, the knife again sliced under the door. She screamed and sat back down.

Paul then spoke, "Puzzled I am by the proximity of that peculiar, plucky parasite. Wish I do for a periscope to peek."

Polly yelled out, "Pansy! My precious, pretty, pee wee pumpkin. Please pardon me as persecuted am I that you're not present."

She heard no response; only the continued sounds of the turkey's gobble laughter, plus the incessant thrusts of the cordless blade slicing through under the door.

Lighting a penlight attached to her key ring, Polly and the others watched as the pantry doorknob slowly began to turn. Mustering all her motherly courage, Polly grabbed the knob, turned it, and flung open the pantry door. As the light streamed in, the others huddled at the back of the pantry in the shadows. To Polly's surprise and delight the menacing turkey was nowhere to be seen.

Screaming sirens approached, as Polly shuffled her way back into the dining room. There, on the table were the scattered, smashed remnants of what had been the deviled eggs. Laid out with her head down on the table cloth and her tongue sloshing out the side of her mouth was little Pansy. Polly gasped, as she witnessed that the nice, purple and pink cotton dress she'd made Pansy was cut into shreds. Parts of it hung from her child's back as if it were now ribbons. She grabbed hold of Pansy and pulled the young girl away from the table. As the others slowly and carefully sauntered out from the pantry, a panicked Polly checked the physical status of her youngest daughter.

Relieved, she saw no broken skin, bruises, or cuts on Pansy.

"My pampered, prissy, half-pint, Pansy ... in your pretty, purple, and pink shredded dress. How are you, precious?"

Little Pansy's head fell back, and she grinned up at her mother.

Unharmed, between her two missing front teeth she yapped, "Pooped my panties, but didn't pout. Pounded and paddled I did to that pile of pesky peppered egg people."

Polly remarked, "I'm perplexed how you escaped painful punches by that puffy, prowling Poultry-Geist."

Little Pansy giggled and looked at her carved-up dress. She rose in her chair and without a single knick grinned and answered her mother, "Pansy played possum."

Seeing his little girl safe, Paul smiled and commented, "Proud am I Pansy of my little progeny."

He glanced around the room but did not see the crazed turkey carcass.

"Presume do I," he said. "That plundering pest is passed from this place."

Papa Plump came bounding through the kitchen while he snacked on something green and crunchy. He carried it in an opened jar and withdrew what he was eating to offer some of it to them.

Smiling he said, "Paternal papa offering pickles."

No sooner had he said that than the police burst through the front door. They entered with pistols and shotguns drawn and at the ready.

Paul expressed, "Punctual protectors, please patrol premises and purge property of that pathetic pullet predator that pounced upon my people."

After that perfect directive, from the corner of the room out jumped the psycho turkey, its slicing blade held at full height. Its silly scream echoed through the halls of the house.

In unison, the five police officers let loose with their shotguns and pistols, pummeling the angrily energetic turkey carcass and splattering it to pieces. It exploded into shards of roasted flesh and bone.

As the room became quiet and the gun smoke cleared, Papa Plump had a pickle dangling loosely from his lips like a limp cigar. Patti Parrot, who'd been hiding, flew out the front door when the cops arrived and Pansy removed her hands from over her ears.

A nervous Petunia began to rifle through her mother's purse.

# POULTRY-GEIST

Curious, Polly first stated and then inquired, "Peace to the proper pieces. I may purely puke. Petunia, for what in my purse do you peruse?"

An exasperated Petunia replied, "Prozac."

\* \* \*

The following day, Paul Plump was outside standing next to a local realtor. In Petunia's arms was an orange-haired cat with its three-inch tail wrapped at the end by adhesive tape and a gauze bandage. In the front yard, the realtor shook hands with Paul, and then placed a *"For Sale"* sign up in the yard.

# CHAPTER 6: Ducks and Moving Targets

Now, let me relate to you the second of my duck and shotgun stories. Our two wealthy twin brothers from Pennsylvania were on the verge of asking Daisy and me to come to Paradise for a surprise reveal and an offer they wanted to make us.

Before that though and before the harsh Pennsylvania winter weather set in, Wayne and Dwayne chose a chilly, but dry November day to go on a duck hunt. Or at least, that was Dwayne's perception of the outing. The brothers were each dressed in warm, camouflaged outfits and adrift on a pond in an aluminum flat-bottom boat. Wayne watched his twin who sat cross-legged in the front of the boat. It was a cloudy and misty morning with fog that began to roll in across the pond.

Dwayne was going duck hunting with Wayne ... or so he thought. At any rate, Dwayne sat anxiously with his twenty-gauge shotgun cradled in his lap. Still not healed, his damaged eyes could not discern much except being able to tell day from night. On this day, he wore dark-tinted sunglasses, even though it was dreary and overcast.

A while ago when playing golf, Dwayne was stuck blind when lightning hit a tree close by him. The doctors remain confident that his blindness is not permanent, but he's disappointed that after six months he still can't see.

That rather rotund purebred, one-hundred-seventy-five-pound Tibetan Mastiff sitting next to him is Sweet-roll, his loyal service companion and a seeing-eye dog.

As they mentioned to me and Daisy, the twins' father was a wealthy entrepreneur and inventor, a talent he passed on to Dwayne. Besides numerous other investments in real estate and buying golf courses, the brothers owned and operated the poultry hatchery and processing plant there in Paradise, Pennsylvania.

With Dwayne getting anxious, Wayne waved an arm in the air. The silence was then suddenly broken by the sounds of quaking duck calls. Waving his shotgun precariously, Dwayne stood clumsily in the boat and caused the small craft to rock back and forth. However, the aim of his shotgun was away from the frontal direction of the quacking sounds and rather was positioned instead toward the port side of the boat.

Before Wayne could stop him, Dwayne pulled the trigger on the shotgun and a loud blast echoed through the misty fog. At the rear of the boat, Wayne had to steady and catch his brother before Dwayne fell backward into the water.

From sixty feet away near the shore, the garbled, mournful sound of a gasping gobble was heard. Accordingly, after the shot, a large turkey with white feathers slammed down against the dirt and fell dead as a doornail upon the ground.

Wayne looked in the direction of Dwayne's wayward blast and his face formed a scowl. He took off his hunting cap, wiped the sweat from his forehead, and gave Dwayne a curious, exasperated look. He sighed and watched as the smoke from the shotgun barrel rose into the overcast skies.

His brotherly hunting companion sat eagerly rubbing his hands together. His still unsighted and unfocused eyes stared excitedly into the dim, clouded light of his existence.

He excitedly asked, "Did I get him, Wayne?"

On the shoreline, the soft, mostly inaudible sound of human footsteps quickly approached through a sea of cackling turkeys. A strong male hand reached down and picked up the large, dead turkey. As he did so, hundreds of the same such birds gobbled and waddled nervously away from him. He held up the spent bird and glared out at the small boat bobbing about on the pond. He shrugged his shoulders at Wayne who sat in the rear of the boat.

Onshore and above the man's head was a sign proclaiming: Kockle's Hatchery and Processing Plant.

Wayne held up his hands to the man on the shore, shrugged, and then turned toward Dwayne.

"Uh ... No, Bro, you missed. Yet, I'm sure there'll be others along shortly."

Dwayne remarked, "I thought I heard the duck call and then a gobble. What sort of ducks were those?" (*Ducks, ducks, ducks* ... why must it always be ducks?)

Wayne looked over at the man and the nearby shoreline of the poultry plant. He waved and gestured at him to take the dead turkey away. He then motioned towards a grove of waist-high cattail plants about a hundred feet off the starboard side of the boat.

"Yeah," he said. "I think those were a rare breed of Tur-duckies."

"You may be right, for I think I heard a whole flock of them quack-gobbling across the pond."

Dwayne smiled and by his good nature nodded, giving no outward indication that he was wise to the trick his brother was playing on him. He then pulled two more shotgun shells out of his hunting vest pocket and reloaded. He swiveled in his seat and the shotgun barrel now pointed towards Wayne's head.

Wayne gulped, dodged the gun, and ducked down in the seat. (Again with that word, whoever's writing this stop saying DUCK). {I'm not saying it, stupid … I'm writing it stupid … so shut up … I'm the author of this story … no I am … are not… sigh!}

Sweetroll whined, jumped down off his seat, turned his butt into the air, and tucked his tail. He hid his head and eyes with his paws.

Wayne yelled, "Yipes! Uh, turn around, Bro. I think see a few mallards coming in from the other way."

Near the cattails were two men that wore armored, Kevlar full-body suits, complete with bullet-proof headgear and reinforced clear face masks. They waved at Wayne and gave him a half-hearted thumbs-up signal.

Wayne waved back and the men began to chortle on their *duck* calls. The sound mimicked that of flying ducks. {I'm not even going to comment anymore … neither am I … shut up, you}

Dwayne's keen ears homed in on the quacking noise. He fired off two shotgun rounds in the direction of the calls. The shotgun pellets hit the two men, knocking one back into the pond.

"Aha! I heard a big one hit the water that time. I must've winged him," claimed Dwayne.

The downed man scrambled to his feet in the muddy mire and brushed away a shredded Lilly pad plant from his chest. He then made his way as quietly as possible through the cattails towards the shore. There, he grabbed onto a rope attached to the front of Wayne's boat a hundred feet away. He slowly took up the slack in the line.

"Yeah, Bro. You smacked that one right out of the sky. I'll crank up the outboard, and Sweetroll will bring it in for you," declared Wayne, as he waved at the man with the rope.

Wayne reached behind him towards a portable Mp3 player and pushed the <u>PLAY</u> button. The loud hum of a small outboard motor blared over the boat's rear speakers.

He nodded at the man on shore, who began to pull on the rope. The boat slowly began to travel forward towards the shoreline.

About five feet from shore, the second of the two men waved at Wayne, reached into an ice chest, and held up an unplucked dead duck.

"Okay, we're close enough now for Sweetroll."

Dwayne laid down his shotgun and pointed ... in the wrong direction of course.

"Go fetch him, boy," he told Sweetroll.

The large, overweight dog bounded out of the boat. He groaned as he hit the cold water. Barking for effect, he lurched, stumbled, and swam all five feet to shore. Out of the water, he took a moment to shake and gave the man holding the duck a quick pond water shower. Sweetroll then took the duck into his mouth and trotted proudly back to the boat, which had now been pulled up onto the bank.

Wayne assisted Dwayne out of the boat and onto shore, just as Sweetroll came toddling up with the ... the supposedly fallen fowl. {<u>There, are you happy now? I didn't write duck ... Oops, I suppose I just did ... Oh well, get over it</u>}

Dwayne bent down on one knee, patted his faithful service dog, and took the prized quarry from Sweetroll's jaws.

He smiled and triumphantly held it out at arm's length.

Wayne acted excited and said, "That's a nice one for your trophy case, Bro."

"Yeah, but it must've flown in from northern Canada, for its ice-cold," groaned Dwayne.

With a free hand, Dwayne reached into a canvas pouch around his waist and removed two cinnamon rolls.

He patted his canine companion, "Good, boy, Sweetroll. Here's your reward."

He held the buns out and Sweetroll immediately latched onto both, slobbering and eagerly the dog chomped them down. With the fowl in one hand, Dwayne grabbed onto the raised harness handle on Sweetroll's back with his other, as he, the dog, and Wayne happily headed for Wayne's truck, and then home.

The man hiding in the bushes and the one that pulled the rope waited till the twins were gone. The two men then sloshed off towards the opposite side of the shallow pond. There, they began to remove their heavily clothed armored suits. Sweat poured from their brows and cheeks and they seemed exhausted. They plopped down on the muddy bank.

The first man stated, "Man, Wayne was right. Instead of using the blank shells we put in his ammunition box, crazy Dwayne replaced them and used live rounds from his hunting vest."

"Thank goodness we wore this armor," replied the second man.

"One thing for sure, plucking chicken feathers is a lot easier work. ... and I want a raise."

# CHAPTER 7: Parade to Paradise

Although we were doing a fantastic business in Miami and growing our wealth, for Daisy and me, overseeing seven restaurants was very stressful and demanding. That meant we didn't get to spend as much quality time with our kids as we'd liked.

Before Wayne and Dwayne left for Pennsylvania, they arranged to have us move out of our leased Miami apartment and into their plush condo penthouse. It was very nice, but the kids didn't have any outdoor places to play. The indoor pool on the ground floor helped release some of their youthful energy and provided them with watery fun, but it wasn't like the open land we had before on our small farm in northern Ohio.

Our move had a two-fold purpose, as we then became the ones to cart up the grilled chickens and toss them over twice a week to two of our most trusted employees below in the van. Our kids often wanted to help, so we sometimes let them, but worried about being up so high and having one of them slip or fall over the half-walls edge. We were delighted when we discovered our process worked equally as well on all poultry as it did with the chickens. Turkeys, quail, geese, pheasant, dove, squab, and yes ... it even worked on ... you know that other fowl whose name also begins with a "D."

On Thanksgiving, we closed all our restaurants, took a few days off, and then took the kids to a nice hotel in Fort Lauderdale for a couple of days. The weather was warm, even in November. The ocean was calm and the slight breezes from Caribbean trade winds presented us with two marvelous days of beach fun and relaxation.

Instead of our usual vast Thanksgiving spread of turkey and all the trimmings, we chose instead to pack lunches and picnic on the beach, which we did. We played games, took turns burying each other in the sand, made sandcastles, laid out in the warm sun, and the kids and I splashed and played in the ankle-slapping waves that gently rolled into shore. Daisy joined in most of the fun, but because of her morbid fear of the ocean, she refused to even wade into it. Nor was she crazy about the idea of the rest of us doing so. She'd had a traumatic experience as a child when she excitedly raced into the ocean waves as a kid and stepped on a manta ray. That incident frightened her and now she was paranoid and would not go in the saltwater.

* * *

When we returned from our days of frolicking, we got a Skype call on my computer from Wayne about their progress on improving our tenderizing and marinating procedure.

"We've developed and quickly built a new facility here in our Paradise plant that will vastly increase the speed and efficiency of producing our flavorful marinating process," explained Wayne.

"That's great!" I told him. "But if the procedure is up there in Pennsylvania, how will you get us the product down here?" I asked.

"We worked that out too. Dwayne developed a freeze-dried process that will preserve the texture and flavor but allow for shipping the birds out to various states without compromising the taste when the birds are thawed in the restaurant kitchens."

Daisy commented, "So, you're going to handle all the tenderizing process from up there and ship us the chickens?"

"Yes, chicken or any other poultry needs you have," remarked Dwayne. "And there's one other thing."

"What's that?" I asked.

"You and Daisy have been working too hard and burning the midnight oil long enough. We want you to come up here and join us in sort of a semi-retirement. Here, you can relax and assist us with the operations, plus Daisy can quit working and become a stay-at-home mom again."

I glanced at Daisy, whose eyes lit up and watered at the thought of being able to do that again.

"That's a generous offer, guys. We like the warmer weather here, but what you propose is tempting. Who'd oversee things down here?" I questioned.

"Not to worry, we've been in contact with some other successful Miami restaurateurs, and one has agreed to join our team and run things for you down there," replied Wayne.

"Yeah, what's his name?" I asked. "Maybe we know him."

"A Frenchman named, Morris Applegate," said Dwayne.

Daisy about fell out of her chair and I moaned as I felt the blood drain from my face.

"Applegate?" I yelled. "Yeah, we know that tyrant. He was the slave driver we worked for before we discovered our grilling process. I hope you didn't reveal anything of how we do it to him."

Wayne's expression, even over a computer monitor reflected his surprise and disappointment.

"Uh, oh ... we didn't realize that, Dabney. Not to worry though, we didn't tell him anything about the process. Since the idea of using him seems upsetting to you, we'll look into finding someone else."

I paused a moment and then calmed down. After I thought about it a while, the idea of him having to deal with Daisy and me made me rethink that possibility.

"No, wait for a second," I said, as Daisy pinched my arm. "Maybe him working with us might work out anyway. Would we be his boss and he'd have to report to us on every major decision?"

"Of course," replied Wayne. "You'd direct him and he'd report to you about all operations down there. We'd also have him sign a confidentiality non-competition agreement that would bind him to secrecy should our process ever become known to him."

I glanced at Daisy, whose eyes widened, and she shrugged.

"Well, at least it might relieve some of his employees from having to deal with him daily," she declared.

I glared into the monitor. "Okay, guys. We'll think about Applegate, but we'd require him to alter his intimidating and rude methods of managing. We'd hold him to a strict code of conduct. I'd even require regular polling of employees to make certain he follows our rules and doesn't become the tyrannical taskmaster he was when we worked for him."

Wayne forced a smile and then added, "Alright, Dabney. Now for the other news. We've hired a firm that specializes in franchising and marketing. We're going to have them work the southern region of the U.S. first, and then when that's up and going with many new franchise cafés underway, we'll branch out to the east coast, the mid-west, and then the western states."

An excited Dwayne remarked, "We'll go national to Alaska and Hawaii. Maybe even international. By then, you two will be so rich you'll be able to afford to just sit back and count your money."

My brain became dizzy thinking about the possibilities. "Wow!" I spoke. "Are you sure we can keep up with demand like that?"

"That's what we want to show you. Now that you're okay with Applegate, we'll fly down next week to meet him. You and Daisy can read him his rights and after that deal's set up, we'll move the two of you up here and fly back to Paradise to show you the new setup. How's that sound?" Wayne queried.

We both sighed and nodded our heads. I had a tinge of anxiety, but the prospects of this new venture did excite me.

"We look forward to seeing you guys again. How's your eyesight coming, Dwayne? Are you any better?" I asked.

"I saw the doctor last week and I am healing, but so far all I can make out are unfocused blurs, and can't identify anything I see."

* * *

Two weeks later and into the second week of December, after signing up Applegate, Daisy and I made our way into the first-class section of a jet airplane. We were shown to our seats across the aisle from where Wayne and Dwayne would be seated. Our kids were left at home under the care of our long-time daycare worker and friend, Judy. The kids wanted to come, but this was to be a trip up to go over the details of franchising and for us to view the new process Dwayne had so confidently and rapidly developed.

Dwayne's service and seeing eye-dog, Sweetroll, was permitted to come on board with him. Wayne guided his brother into a seat, while Dwayne used his steering cane to feel his way along. An out-of-breath and exhausted Sweetroll plopped down underneath Dwayne's seat. After he was seated across from us, Dwayne reached into his carry-on bag and removed a bottle of water.

He then reached back inside his bag, removed a small, plastic bowl, and set it on the plane's floor next to Sweetroll. He unscrewed the bottle's cap and bent to pour the water into the bowl.

Unfortunately, the water missed the bowl entirely and the water ran forward across the floor of the plane. Sweetroll lapped at it as best he could before it drained away toward the fashionably dressed young female passenger sitting in front of Dwayne.

He leaned and patted Sweetroll's behind instead of the dog's head.

"There you go boy; you must be thirsty too."

As water puddled under her feet, it took a few seconds for the woman to realize what had been done. She moaned, released her seat belt, and stood up in the aisle. Annoyed, she kicked off her expensive high heels shoes and shot Dwayne a cold stare ... of which he could not see. She limped off toward the plane's restroom carrying her wet shoes.

An excited Daisy commented, "This is neat. We've never flown first class before."

From his seat next to Dwayne, Wayne looked over at her and smiled.

"From now on, only the best for you two."

"That's right, and you're going to love living in Paradise," added Dwayne.

"How far from Philly is Paradise?" I asked.

Wayne said, "It's close to Lancaster and about an hour's drive northeast of Philly."

Before Wayne assisted Dwayne to strap on the seat belt, I leaned over and placed a kiss on Daisy's cheek.

She smiled and said, "I hope the kids don't give Judy too much trouble."

"They'll be fine. I just hope we're doing the right thing. Miami is searing hot and humid at times, but the winter months there are so mild," I said.

"Yeah, but they also have hurricanes, with which we won't have to contend. Besides, it'll be nice to have snow again," she replied. "And you're to be Wayne and Dwayne's new plant director."

"I know, but I do have trepidations about leaving that smug Frenchman in charge of what we created. So help me, if he doesn't follow the rules we've set up and doesn't treat the employees fair, I'll fly back down there and toss him off that condo balcony."

Daisy giggled, "Imagine his reaction when a dozen chefs he hired couldn't duplicate the flavors of our chicken. Thinking of the frustration that must have caused me helped me get a good night's sleep last night."

Daisy then leaned back in her seat and glanced out the window. The young woman with wet shoes soon returned to her seat. In a few minutes, the plane taxied out to the runway, and we all prepared for take-off.

Before that, an attractive young flight attendant came down the aisle, stopped at the row where Wayne and Dwayne sat, and then reached and pulled down the overhead bin door. She withdrew what appeared to be a canvas backpack-like bag with a harness in front of it.

Dwayne seemed to know exactly what was taking place and he stood up and took the canvas bag from her.

"Thank you, Celia. You're a lifesaver," he said to the attendant.

She smiled and commented, "Actually, I'm not Celia. My name's Betty. Celia's off today, but she told me what to give you before take-off."

"Well, thank you, Betty," he told her. He then asked Wayne, "Here' Bro, help me get into this."

Daisy and I watched with inquiring minds, as Dwayne stepped into the straps and Wayne helped fit the bag around and onto Dwayne's backside ... to then fasten the thing's straps together in the front.

We weren't sure what it was until Wayne pointed to a metal ring fastened to the strap.

"Now this is your ripcord. If or when you jump and clear the plane and engines, pull this and your chute will open," he said.

"Got it," said Dwayne. "How long do I have if I wait? Thirty seconds or so before I pull the ripcord?"

"The rest of your life, Bro. No, don't do that. Count to no longer than ten and then pull it." said Wayne with a smile on his face.

He glanced over at me and saw the puzzled look I gave him. There sat Wayne in a modern jet airliner that travels 35,000 feet into the stratosphere ... and he was wearing a parachute. Daisy and I giggled, and Wayne just shrugged and leaned over the aisle.

He spoke softly to us, "Dwayne listened to an oration about catastrophic engine failure on passenger jets and some folks having to jump out of a plane during emergencies. Since then, he won't fly anywhere without wearing a parachute."

"Got it," I said, mimicking Dwayne.

Even though we knew it was just paranoid Dwayne being himself, others sitting in first class began to question the flight attendant, asking her if this plane was safe, or if everyone else should have a parachute.

Wearing the bulky parachute, once Dwayne was able to cram back into his seat, Betty came forth with a seatbelt extension and fastened Dwayne into his seat. He then reached above him with the supposed intent to point the cool air vent onto him. Instead, he hit the buttons to page the flight attendant and the one that turned on the overhead light. Sweetroll barked and as the plane began take-off and lifted off into the air; the dog's bark became a piercing, agonizing howl. Dwayne reached out to pet Sweetroll, but only managed to annoy the women in front of him more ... when instead he patted her on the head.

In a soothing voice, he mildly scolded, "Calm down and quit acting like a frightened sheep."

\* \* \*

About halfway into the flight, Wayne opened up his briefcase, removed a book, and began to read. He sat the open briefcase on the console between him and Dwayne, who had the window seat. A few minutes later, Wayne glanced up from his reading when he saw Dwayne rummaging through a vest pocket removing a folded paper packet of white powder.

He whispered, "What's that? I hope it's legal, Bro."

Dwayne chuckled and opened the packet of powder. "Relax; I've had trouble sleeping of late, so my doctor gave me strong sedative pills to knock me out."

"And since you don't like taking pills, you crushed and ground them into that powder."

"Right, and I'll mix them with my water and take some swigs before bedtime tonight."

Another half-hour into the flight, Wayne put down his book, unclasped his seat beat, and stepped into the aisle. It had already been a long day for Daisy and me, so with the smooth air we had on the trip, I used the time to nap and renew my energy. Daisy did as well.

Before we boarded, Daisy sprayed herself and the aroma of her intoxicating perfume wafted throughout the plane's cabin. Wayne told me Dwayne noticed it, complimented her for it, and seemed to take pleasure in the scent.

Wayne remarked, "I've got to make a pit stop, Bro. Can I get you anything while I'm up?"

Dwayne pulled his tray table down and was drinking from another bottle of water.

"Maybe see if they have any fruit or snacks."

After Wayne left, Dwayne rummaged through his bag and removed a small plastic funnel. He then reached for the water bottle he'd sat on the tray table, but as he did his hand accidentally knocked the bottle off onto the floor. He leaned over for it, but it rolled under the seat in front of him.

As Betty, the flight attendant passed by, Dwayne motioned to her. Thinking he was pointing to his bottle on the floor, instead, she thought he was pointing at Wayne's open briefcase in the seat next to him.

"Pardon me, Sir. Would you mind putting that bottle here on my tray?"

"Sure thing, Dwayne. And it's me, Betty."

Dwayne blushed and apologized, "Oh, I'm sorry. I thought you were the male attendant."

Betty smiled and removed a bottle of grape juice from Wayne's briefcase. She then placed it in front of Dwayne on the tray table.

Dwayne felt the bottle and said, "Thank you, ma'am. She started to walk away but saw the water bottle on the floor and bent to pick it up. She started to ask him if it was his, but then just shrugged, placed it on his tray table, and then went about performing her other duties.

Dwayne unscrewed the grape juice bottle cap, placed the funnel inside the bottle, and began to empty the sedative powder into it. After he'd emptied about a third of it, he scratched his head and decided to just empty all the very potent sedative powder into the bottle. He then replaced the bottle cap, just as Wayne exited the restroom facilities and began making his way back to his seat. He sat the bottle on his tray table.

When he got to his seat, he saw both the water bottle and the one with the grape juice there on Dwayne's tray table.

"What's this? I'm glad you didn't drink this yet," stated Wayne.

Thinking Wayne meant the bottle of water, Dwayne grinned and told him, "No, I'm not ready for that yet, but would you mind putting the water back into my bag there?"

Wayne looked at the two bottles and replied, "Will do, Bro."

Wayne picked up his briefcase, took the bottle of grape juice, and placed it back into his briefcase, and then he grasped the bottle of water and stuffed it down into Dwayne's bag. He then sat down and buckled his seat belt, unaware that he'd just put into motion a situational mix-up that would later lead to an unimaginable paradox.

As he completed the task, he touched Dwayne's hand and presented him with a bag of fruit-flavored Gummy Bears.

"Here, these are all they had," said Wayne.

Dwayne took the bag, opened it, and began to chew on the rubbery snacks.

"Thanks, Bro. These are good."

"Are you feeling any better?" asked Wayne.

"Somewhat. I'll be better after I take my sedatives and get a good night's rest."

Wayne reached and took the earphones from the seatback in front of him and began listening to the soft music he chose to play."

The flight attendants soon came through the cabin to serve a luncheon meal. Dwayne did not eat and instead sat his plate on the floor, where Sweetroll downed the boneless rib-eye steak and potatoes.

I woke Daisy and we each scraped down the surprisingly tasty food. Neither of us had ever had such fine dining before on a plane ride. Afterward, Dwayne fed Sweetroll two of the cinnamon buns he had brought on and stored in a plastic zip-locked bag.

\* \* \*

Soon after eating, the plane landed safely at the Philadelphia International Airport. As everyone stood and began de-boarding, Wayne assisted his brother, who struggled out of the parachute and then gathered his belongings and a walking cane. Sweetroll seemed eager to exit, and his tongue lapped over his nose, as he stretched and yawned. Finding Sweetroll's harness handle, Dwayne grabbed hold of it and stepped into the aisle.

After we got to the gate and the plane stopped, the flight attendants opened the plane's front door. A handsome young pilot exited the cockpit. He immediately saw Dwayne and Wayne. Smiling, he walked toward them and extended his hand.

"Good to have you two with us again. I hope you enjoyed the flight," he told them.

As the men shook hands, Sweetroll bounced around and seemed eager to get off the plane. When he saw the pilot, he greeted the jet's conductor by hopping up with his rear legs and placing two huge paws on the pilot's chest.

The pilot laughed and petted Sweetroll's ears. "Well, hello there, Sweetroll. Yes, it's nice to see you again as well."

Daisy stood in the aisle, as Wayne picked up his briefcase, turned, and introduced us.

"Captain John, these are our friends and new business partners, Dabney and Daisy."

We shook hands with the pilot and he said, "A pleasure to meet you, folks."

Sweetroll's nose nudged the pilot's hand, seeking more patting and attention.

"Okay, boy. I'll shake your hand too ... make that your paw."

We then all started toward the exit door. John offered Dwayne an arm, as Dwayne shuffled along, with the others following.

Sweetroll, with his guide harness attached, bounded away from Dwayne and out the open doorway. He trotted a few steps, and then looked back at the plane for Dwayne.

He began to bark and pace about on the catwalk leading to the terminal.

Wayne commented, "I think Sweetroll's trying to tell us he has a bladder issue."

John nodded, "I think you're right. I need to stretch my legs before taking off for New York. I can walk him to the pet relief area, and then meet you all at the baggage claim."

Dwayne replied, "That's very nice of you, John. Thanks."

Wayne handed his briefcase to Dwayne and took hold of his brother's elbow. In that way, he became Dwayne's guide.

It was a bright sunny day in Philadelphia and an unseasonably warm sixty-seven degrees for a December day in Pennsylvania. Captain John put on his sunglasses, took hold of Sweetroll's guide harness, and began walking out of the breezeway into the building's airport terminal. The cheerful duo of man and beast nonchalantly strolled past the airline ticket counter, where a woman, her husband, and three children were readying to purchase tickets on John's plane for the continuation flight to New York City.

They witness the tall, charming young man in aviator sunglasses being led by the seeing-eye dog. The woman sneered and then turned to the lady behind the ticket counter.

"Pardon me, Miss. Do you know that man walking there?"

The woman glanced up to see Captain John strolling happily along with Sweetroll.

"Why, yes. That's Captain John Jenkins. He'll be your pilot on the flight to New York."

The woman's expression went blank. She glared at her husband, reached over the counter, snatched their credit card from the service lady, and turned to leave.

Her husband hadn't seen John or Sweetroll and was confused by her actions.

She angrily told the lady, "Cancel that request. Come on kids, we're not going on that flight."

Her husband questioned her, "Why? Aren't we going to New York?"

She sneered at him, "Yes, but with a different pilot, on another plane and airline."

* * *

With his hand grasping Wayne's elbow, Dwayne followed his brother through the airport. After a few hundred feet, Dwayne tugged Wayne's arm.

"Like Sweetroll, I too need a restroom stop," stated Dwayne.

Wayne saw a restroom coming up soon and turned to look back at Daisy and me that followed close behind.

"You two go on to the baggage area, we'll be along after taking this break."

Although I could use a break myself, Daisy nodded and tugged at my arm. We continued through the terminal towards the baggage claim area.

Minutes later when they exited the restroom, Dwayne held the briefcase in one hand and with the other took Wayne's elbow. Then they proceeded toward the area where they'd meet back with Daisy and me.

In a nearby coffee shop, a very attractive young woman wearing high heels and dressed in a femininely chic outfit sat next to an elderly man with a thick bandage tied around his head and eyes. He tugged at the mask-like gauze, but she carefully spanked his hand.

"Now, Dad! Quit messing with the bandages. The doctor said to keep the bandages on until tomorrow."

He removed his hands from the gauze and smiled at her.

"Okay, okay. What time is it? He said for me to use the first round of eye drops around 2:00 P.M."

"Yes, Dad, and we'll do that. It's 1:15 P.M. If you hadn't insisted on having cataract surgery on both eyes on the same day ... and in Baltimore no less, we could have been home hours ago."

"I know, but as I told you, doc Goodman was my optometrist for over forty years and I wasn't about to trust my eyesight to anyone else. Now, let's get our bags and head home. We've been gone two days and I miss my recliner."

She rose, slung her purse over her left arm, and guided him onto his feet. He took her elbow with his left hand and followed her out of the coffee shop. As the two began walking, the terminal became very crowded. It was impossible to forge through the crowd without bumping into other people trying to get to their boarding gates.

At the same time about ten feet to the left of them, Wayne was attempting to guide Dwayne through the throng. They headed for a baggage claim in the opposite direction. By sheer chance, the young lady and Wayne are funneled together in the crowd. Soon the two meet up and bump headlong into one another.

# POULTRY-GEIST

In an instant, Wayne's eyes take in the loveliness of this woman, which somehow reacts in his brain and momentarily disengages his oratorical abilities. In other words, he was momentarily stunned into silence by the picturesque beauty before him. She too was immediately enamored by this handsome stranger, for neither of them seemed to notice that the other was leading someone else by an elbow.

Exhilarated after a dramatic pause among the frenzied multitude, jovial Wayne regained the power of speech that eluded him. He smiled and started to speak, but before he could do so, someone pushed him from behind. His body lurched forward and in an unintended forceful manner knocked the purse off her shoulder. The bag fell and tumbled to the floor. As Wayne bent and dropped to one knee to retrieve it, so too did the young woman.

Neither was aware of what else was happening, as Dwayne and her doting father were compelled to release and let go of their guides. When they did, someone rushed into them and spun each other around in a circle. This confused and provoked them to lose their bearings, which caused them to inadvertently exchange places. Dwayne almost lost hold of Wayne's briefcase, but managed to hold onto it.

Bent down, Wayne grinned sheepishly at the lovely woman, picked up her purse, and handed it to her. As their fingers touched, it was as if they were suddenly alone among the crowd, as their eyes locked on one another, and they slowly stood.

The young woman withdrew her hand quickly and gave him a curt nod of appreciation.

From somewhere behind her she heard her dad's voice, "I lost you there for a minute, Let's go and get out of here before the herd stampedes."

Barely aware of his words, she nodded her head and managed a tremulous smile.

Hearing Dwayne murmur a similar statement, Wayne also paid little heed to comply with his twin's annoyance and request.

In a courteous voice, he said to her, "I'm very sorry. It's packed together in here. My name is, Wayne."

They shook hands and she replaced the purse over her shoulder.

In a cordial voice, she stated, "Yes, it's busy as a beehive in here. I'm Karen."

Wayne was no doubt captivated by her underlying sensuality. She paused a moment, clumsily exhaled, and then signified with a pointing finger her intent.

"Well, we'd better get going. Nice to meet you, Wayne."

Without looking, each took the hand of the man they were to lead and placed it around their elbow. Like bashful a sheep, Wayne smiled, and then the pairs meekly went their opposite ways.

A few minutes later, as Wayne reached the baggage claim, he spotted Daisy and me. Captain John left Sweetroll there with us, who wagged his tail when Wayne approached. With his elbow-led passenger in tow, Wayne strolled over to us.

Bags were being dumped out onto the conveyor. He saw two familiar bags and pointed with his left hand.

"Here come our bags, Dwayne."

Daisy scrunched her face, and she and I were puzzled by whom he had at his elbow. Suddenly, Wayne heard an unfamiliar voice behind him.

"Karen? Who is Dwayne and have they sent out our bags yet?"

I asked, "Who's your friend, Wayne ... and where is, Dwayne?"

Wayne turned his head, and for the first time since he'd left Karen noticed that it was not Dwayne, but instead, it was Karen's dad that he'd lead here. Not recognizing the man, he looked around for Dwayne.

Momentarily alarmed he demanded, "Who are you, and where's my brother?"

"Me? Who are you and where's my daughter?" Emphatically inquired the dad.

Daisy and I grabbed the twins' bags and stood looking quizzically at a nervous and worried Wayne. As he began to panic, he then heard a feminine voice behind him.

"Dad, I know we may not always see eye to eye, but in this case, we should walk hand in hand ... make that hand on an elbow."

Dwayne wheeled and turned to see Karen standing a few feet away. Dwayne held onto her elbow. She had a broad smile on her face and a hand to her mouth to suppress laughter. Seeing the relief in Wayne's eyes, Karen nodded cordially and led Dwayne toward his brother. Sweetroll barked and broke away from Daisy. He rushed to Dwayne's side, who then bent over and patted him. Karen also petted Sweetroll.

"Well, aren't you just the cutest thing? What's your name?" she asked in her lyrical voice.

Dwayne blissfully replied, "Thanks! I told you I'm Dwayne. The dog's name is Sweetroll."

Karen giggled, and then purposely glared at an embarrassed Wayne.

"Sweetroll! That seems ... appropriate. He's a big fellow, what breed is he?"

"He's a Tibetan Mastiff. He was trained as a service dog and is my eyes until I can see again," replied Dwayne.

With a smug delight, she winked, and then told Wayne, "I believe we need to exchange passengers."

She guided Dwayne and Sweetroll over to Wayne, and then took her dad's hand.

He demanded, "Karen? What's going on here?"

"I'm ... I'm so sorry for the mix-up. My apologies, Karen," stated Wayne.

Karen answered her dad, "Just a slight side-track, Dad. It's okay now."

Dwayne gloried in the shared moment and added to Wayne's humiliation.

He grumbled, "Thanks for losing me, Bro. This one is fun and smells much better than you. The way she distracted you, I'll wager she's also much prettier too."

"Being as how you're my identical twin that doesn't speak well for either of us," commented Wayne.

Karen's dad was still confused. He curiously patted his daughter's hand and then tugged again at his eye bandages.

"Will someone please tell me what's happening? Have our bags come out yet, Karen?"

She scolded him, "No, not yet, Dad, and I asked you to quit messing with your bandages."

Looking teasingly at Wayne, she scrunched her nose.

With lips like two budded roses, she said, "We got diverted a bit, and wound up at the wrong baggage area. Keep a tight grip on my elbow and we'll go to ours now."

Still puzzled, Daisy and I looked on in confusion, as Karen and her dad turned to leave. Before doing so, Karen batted her long, black, curly lashes, and then laughed.

"Bye Dwayne, I had a great time. Call me."

She kissed Dwayne on the cheek, as Wayne stared stupidly at his brother ... who smirked and raised his thumb to her.

Before she and her dad sauntered out of sight, Wayne saw her whisper in Dwayne's ear. She then gave him a small piece of paper. He grinned and quickly stuffed it into his pants pocket. Wayne's face became green with envy, and her melodramatic, riveting act proved without a doubt to be the cause of an instantly symptomatic case of jealousy between Wayne and his twin.

He sadly watched her and her dad disappear into the mass of humanity. He angrily snatched his briefcase out of Dwayne's hand, turned away, and then jerked his bag off the conveyor. Before he reached Dwayne's bag, one of their employees, Clancy O'Riley entered the baggage claim and lifted Dwayne's bag. He too watched Karen and her dad leave, and then he approached his twin employers. He patted Dwayne on the back and shook Wayne's hand.

In his thick Irish brogue, he asked, "Welcome home, lads. Have a nice trip, did ya?"

Dwayne grinned and quipped, "I don't know about the others, but for me, it couldn't have been better."

After introducing Clancy to Daisy and me, the five of us made our way out of the terminal.

\* \* \*

Clancy guided us all outside to a late model black sedan parked in the handicapped spot directly near the exit. He approached Wayne, who excused himself from the others, and talked to Clancy alone.

I said to Daisy, "My, what a wonderful day we picked to come. It feels like a warm spring day here. I'd expected it to be cold here this time of year."

"It usually is. This weather is the exemption rather than the rule," stated Wayne.

Away from us on the other side of the car, Clancy told Wayne, "The sedan's gassed and ready, she is. I'll take Sam's car and meet you back at the Paradise plant tomorrow."

"Thanks, Clancy. Did you get the modifications made to the car according to Dwayne's specifications?"

"Aye! That we did and tested everything on the trip down here."

"Great! How'd it perform?" Wayne asked.

"Amazingly well. Your brother's a regular genius, he is. Much like the old mister."

Wayne ruffled, "Yes, I know, but right now I prefer not to be reminded of that."

Clancy shrugged and walked to the rear of the car. He opened the trunk with the key remote and loaded all the bags inside.

Before saying any more, Wayne confronted his brother. "What's on that piece of paper Karen gave you that you stuck in your pocket?"

Dwayne stood next to the car door and held Sweetroll's harness. "How should I know? I'm blind, remember? Anyway, it's nothing for you."

"It's her phone number, isn't it?"

"Maybe, but I saw her first."

Angry, Wayne stated, "No you didn't. You can't see anything. Let me have it."

"No chance. She didn't give it to you."

"Come on, Dwayne. You can't read it. Give me the paper."

Daisy and I stood silently by and watched the two bickering like obstinate, pre-pubescent adolescent teens.

Dwayne declared, "I can too! She wrote it in Braille."

Wayne countered, "What? You're nuts."

"You're trying to extinguish my fire with her because you were unable to start one of your own."

Wayne snarled in anger and tossed his briefcase into the front seat of the car. Clancy shook his head, smiled, and then opened the passenger door to help Sweetroll inside the sedan. The dog immediately hopped into the back seat, and Clancy then assisted Dwayne, settling him into the front seat. He bent to buckle Dwayne's seat belt, as Sweetroll climbed up on the seatback and gave Clancy a slobbering, wet lick on the face.

"Whoa, big fella! Nice to see you again too."

Dwayne took hold of Clancy's hand on the seat belt catch.

"Did you see her, Clancy?" whispered Dwayne.

"Aye, that I did, Lad."

"And was she beautiful?"

"As radiant as the rose and lovely as a bonnie spring morning, she was."

Wayne plopped down in the driver's seat. He grimaced because he overheard their quiet conversation.

He added, "True, but for you, dear brother, she's as unapproachable as a star, or a faded cloud on the horizon."

Wayne grabbed at Dwayne's pocket. "Come on! Give me the paper."

Dwayne slapped his brother's hand and snarled. Clancy opened the back car door for Daisy and me. She glided in next to Sweetroll. I went around and got in from the street side and scooted up close to between them.

Clancy stood on the curb outside the open passenger's door.

"Good folks, welcome you are to the city of brotherly love ... such as it is. Now, it's on to Paradise with you, and good luck."

Wayne sneered at Dwayne and Clancy closed the car door.

* * *

Clancy drove his other car, while Wayne started up the sedan and they all left the airport. Wayne soon pulled onto the Interstate highway leading towards Paradise. Not much conversation ensued and Daisy and I were curious if the two brothers were still going to quibble, or if they'd cooled off now that we were on our way to that fair gem they spoke about called Paradise.

There was medium traffic on the roadway today, and when he had ample space between him and the traffic in front of him he took his right hand off the wheel and glanced back at Daisy and me.

"You two all right back there?"

Daisy was nestled like a dove into the seat. I kept Sweetroll at bay, as she gazed out the window at the passing countryside.

I answered for us, "Yes, we're good and excited about seeing Paradise and Lancaster County."

"Shall I tell them now?" asked Dwayne.

Wayne nodded his head and grinned.

"Sure, go ahead."

"Tell us what?" Daisy questioned.

"We've got a surprise for you. We bought you a house. It's just outside of town in a nice subdivision."

"This exciting news quickly got Daisy's attention.

"You bought us a house?"

"As we said, only the best for our partners. It has five bedrooms, four baths, a chef's kitchen with a large pantry, a media room, a game room, an efficient office, and a big backyard with a pool for the kids," replied Wayne.

"You and your kids are going to love the area and the schools, plus the fact that the house sits at the end of a cul-de-sac."

The beating of Daisy's heart was suddenly like a drum.

"But ... that's such an expensive gift."

"We got it at half its value," stated Wayne.

Dwayne explained, "Kind of odd how that happened. Paul Plump and his family lived there. He worked for us as an accountant, but after Thanksgiving he just up and quit. He moved out of the house immediately and priced the house so cheap we had to buy it."

"Yeah, that was weird. Not to worry though, the house is quite nice," commented Wayne.

Silence then brooded like a gentle spirit within the car, as the pulse in Daisy's and my veins raced through our bodies. Then, Daisy leaned over, hugged me, and then sat forward and put her arms around both Wayne and Dwayne's neck. She kissed each one on the cheek. Laughter then rang out inside the car and Sweetroll howled.

Since we'd met these two generous and wonderful young men, our troubles had melted away like snow in the bright spring sunshine. Our future now seemed just as bright and loomed before us as alluring and varied as the road ahead. How were we so blessed? I knew we owed it all to the good Lord and blind luck. I'd considered the odds of us discovering our gravitational method of preparing poultry and decided that the chances had to be about the same as finding a snowflake in the ocean. Yet it happened and here we were just a few months later.

"You guys have been so good to us. How can we ever repay your kindness and generosity?" I said sincerely.

"It's we who are fortunate to have met you. If not, we wouldn't have the promising distribution channels we do now for our poultry, nor the potential for growth that your discovery brought us." declared Wayne.

A few minutes later, Wayne pulled the sedan into a roadside rest stop.

He shut off the sedan and opened the briefcase he'd carried on the plane. He withdrew the bottle of grape juice he'd saved for the occasion ... the very same bottle that Dwayne had accidentally filled with his strong sedatives earlier on the flight.

Wayne instructed us, "Flip that tray table down on the back of the seat. Inside is a shelf and four small glasses."

Daisy did as he asked and handed him the glasses. He opened the two-quart bottle and filled each glass with a large shot of the grape juice. Daisy and I took our two glasses and paused as Wayne continued.

"We don't drink strong spirits, especially while driving. This is only grape juice, but it'll serve our purpose,"

He handed Dwayne a full glass too. We all smiled and raised our glasses in a happy toast to our association and friendship.

"Here's to successful new ventures and great friendships," he said eloquently.

We all laughed and clinked our glasses together.

"Saluté!" I replied.

My mind raced with thoughts of our good fortune. It seemed like we'd uncovered a great hidden treasure from a great depth buried beneath a block of granite.

Wayne and all of us guzzled the fruity juice and savored the moment, as well as the taste. I thought it did have an unusual twang to it though. That 'twang' was about to make itself known.

Soon, we finished off the bottle and Daisy gathered the glasses, replaced them on their seatback shelf, and then closed and fastened the trays to the seatback. Wayne then started the sedan and pulled back onto the freeway. What happened after that was incredibly amazing, ingenious, innovative ... and downright wacky.

# CHAPTER 8: The Attraction Reaction

A few minutes later, Wayne gunned the car's engine, sped ahead, and edged the sedan to within thirty yards of a big rig eighteen-wheeler truck. I was curious as to what he was up to and our eyes met in the reflection of the rearview mirror. We stared silently at each other for the beat of a few seconds. As I broke eye contact with him and as the interstate passed beneath us, I became mesmerized by the thrum of the tires on the asphalt. For some reason, I began to feel a little nauseous. I glanced at Daisy, who began to sweat and blink her eyes as if she was losing focus.

Wayne broke the silence by commenting, "At times Dwayne's real a twit."

He snarled at his twin, who returned the barb with one of his own, "As are you, my brother."

"But Dwayne's also a gifted inventor like our dad. We were able to construct an ingenious way to perform the chicken gravity drop from inside our plant. We'll show you tomorrow," said Wayne.

As he paused and began to fiddle with some knobs on the dash, I could feel the blood drain from my brain and Wayne's words seemed to tumble from his lips in slow motion.

"Watch now, as I demonstrate another of Dwayne's brilliant ideas."

As he commented, my mind tried to decipher what he was saying. He reached and twisted another knob until a lit number five appeared in an L.E.D. window near the car radio on the dash.

I looked again at Daisy whose head bobbled back and forth and drool began to dribble down her chin. I then recall hearing a warning from Dwayne.

"Careful not to turn the dial past five, or the electronics may overload."

Wayne assured him, "I know. I've only got it on five."

The door to my consciousness began to close ever so gently and slowly. One of the last things I recalled before my mind began to flutter was that Wayne reached over and turned off the ignition to the car. The sedan's motor stopped, however, the car continued to speed along at the same pace.

I looked over at Daisy, who was now resting her head on Sweetroll's back. My words slurred and fell from my lips like mush.

I heard myself mumble to Wayne, "How ish it we're still moo-ving at the same shpeed? Ish this a bat-ree lectric car too? "

Wayne's reactions seemed also to be slowing down a bit.

He said, 'No, but then ... sort of." He yawned and continued, "We're emitting an electromagnetic signal that's locked onto the metal in the truck in front of us."

Dwayne seemed okay, but he too began to smack his lips as if they were getting numb.

"It'll pull us at the same rate of speed the truck travels, and the system monitor will maintain a safe ninety theet ... I mean thirty yards distance from its bumper," stated Dwayne as he too began to slur his words.

"Yeah, and we amuse gero zas ... that is ... use zero gas," explained Wayne, as his head bobbed forward and then back up in a reflex action.

I slurred, "Talk about your alter-nut fool source ... use some bobby's else's dee-shell."

I sat there with my knees pushed up against the seatback. I closed my eyes and listened to my breath enter through my nose. I felt it swell in my chest and then release. As I struggled to open my eyes again, I saw telephone poles zipping past one after another. Their wires fell and then rose again in a never-ending series of waves. I couldn't move my hands and it felt like they were duct-taped behind me. My thigh was now somehow under Daisy's head.

Everyone in the car went silent once more as Wayne released his grip go on the steering wheel. He reclined his seat back, closed his eyes, and relaxed.

The final thing I heard Dwayne say before I passed out was, "See the USA...in your Chevrolet."

To that, an ever-sleepy Wayne replied, "I wish you could ... see ... it, Bro."

When no one commented back to him, Wayne's remaining conscious words were to himself, "We're not just humans being. We're humans ... doing."

About five more miles down the road, with all of us passengers in the sedan having drunk from the bottle of grape juice that Dwayne earlier spiked with powerful sedatives, we succumbed to the powerful drug and were now fast asleep. Our heads bobbed and weaved as the sedan obedient to its programmed command continued to follow speedily down the highway closely along behind the big truck ... just as predicted ... well almost.

# POULTRY-GEIST

* * *

Twenty-five miles out of Philadelphia, a large Hummer vehicle raced into the narrow space between the big rig truck and our group's sedan. The car automatically fell back to a safe distance from the Hummer, and then locked onto it instead. Slumbering inside the sedan our foursome had no idea of what was happening, or what was about to occur.

My face was plastered against the rear window and slobber ran down the glass from my open mouth. Daisy was leaning back with her head resting on the rear package tray. Wayne slumped over the steering wheel and Dwayne's arms were crossed under him. His head rested on the dashboard. Sweetroll was asleep too, between Daisy and me in the back seat.

A few more miles down the road, the Hummer made a quick move and turned off at an exit. It headed northeast and away from Paradise. Our sedan then followed close behind the Hummer where a few miles later, the large vehicle turned again onto a two-lane dirt road. Dust kicked up as the trailing sedan followed along behind. There was a definite shift in the landscape going by, as many of the simple farm residences passed were older two-story clapboards with wood-frame windows, run-down barns, and walls scabbed with peeling paint and large front porches.

A few more miles down the road, the male driver of the Hummer glanced into his rearview mirror. He was a stocky man with short-cropped hair and a bulbous nose. Dressed in a faded long-sleeve, red fleece shirt and ragged jeans that were two sizes too large for his squatty body, he looked like he'd been fitted by clothes from a garage sale. He snarled and noticed the black sedan that still tagged along behind them.

In the passenger seat, sitting next to the driver was a middle-aged muscular man who wore dark sunglasses and a blue tank top under a tattered denim jacket. Both men's shoes were worn and scuffed. The muscular man with a large bald head had a lit cigar that hung from his big, full lips. He exhaled a stream of smoke and turned to look back through the rear window at the car following them.

"For sure, they're following us, Draco. What should I do?" asked the driver.

Draco, the passenger, growled, turned around, and looked forward down the road.

"Lose them, Rowdy. There's a crossroads up ahead. Speed up. When we get there, I'll tell you what to do," declared Draco.

Rowdy began to panic and acted nervously. "What if they're the Feds? They'll get us and send us back to the pen. If they run our plates they'll find out this is a stolen car."

An angry Draco reached over and slapped Rowdy on the face with the back of his hand.

"I ain't going back in the slammer, see!" He screamed. "Get hold of yourself and do what I tell ya."

Draco reached inside his denim coat and withdrew a semi-automatic pistol. He waved it in front of Rowdy's eyes as if to make a point.

"If they are lawmen, and don't quit tailing us ... they're gonna become un-Feds."

Through the windshield of his car, Draco saw something coming over the hill. It was also approaching a crossroads. Ambling steadily down the dirt road was a large, green International Harvester tractor with a full implement plow attached behind it.

As the Hummer sped up, so too did the sedan. Nearing the crossroads, the muscular man made his decision.

"Quick! Make a left at the crossroads. That'll shake 'em off our tail long enough for us to make it back to our hideout," he shouted.

At the last second, when at the crossroads, Rowdy spun the steering wheel sharply to the left.

The Hummer skid, fishtailed, and almost skidded off into the bar ditch. Instead, it wavered and took the sharp turn left onto the other dirt road.

Our sedan spun too but did not make the turn. Instead, it twirled around and faced the opposite direction. It sat still, as the electromagnetic pull on the Hummer was lost. As the Hummer plowed along down the crossroad, only a dust trail in the sky became visible.

However, the tractor continued to saunter along and soon approached the sedan. When it came within ten yards of the car, the young, male teenage tractor driver that wore earphones was jamming out to some tune on his I-pod. He barely noticed the car on the opposite side of the road. Pretty much oblivious to anything around him, he never so much as glanced inside our stalled sedan, but instead passed it by and turned onto the crossroad in the opposite direction from what the Hummer had taken.

The sedan shook, as the electromagnetic force then locked onto the tractor's plow and began to trail along behind the farm boy's large tractor.

Inside the sedan, though still asleep, Daisy and I were entwined like limp spaghetti, with our arms and legs tangled together.

Wayne's arms were wrapped around the steering wheel and Dwayne's now slumped over near the passenger door. Sweetroll barked and licked his master's face, as he tried in vain to wake Dwayne.

The farm boy drove the tractor and had not a clue that the sedan was tagging along close behind and thirty yards back. Minutes later and a few more miles from the crossroads, the tractor headed down a steep incline in the dirt road. With its raised axle and large tires, it had no problems crossing through a three-foot deep creek and about fifty feet wide that overflowed from recent rains to the area.

As you might have guessed, our sedan soon followed into the creek. The muddy water surrounded the car up to the windows, and then the forceful water began to flow inside the cab.

The water seeped in and soon all of us were knocked out passengers and soaked to our waist or better. The car's interior, plus our clothing was saturated. Sweetroll howled and his fur looked like a wet mop. He whined and shook the creek water from his body.

The electromagnetic gauge on the dash began to shoot off sparks. The L.E.D. readout jumped up from five ... to ten. The sedan closed to within twenty yards of the tractor. Another five or six miles down the road and the tractor puttered slowly along still followed closely by our sedan. The landscape changed again as the tractor entered the main street of a small Pennsylvania farm town. Many of the houses were prefabs with vinyl siding and patchy lawns. Being it was a Friday, near the weekend and the weather was so nice for this time of year, many town folks were out and about on this fine day.

The sedan passed a man using a lawnmower with a bagger to catch leaves and was rolling the bagger across his yard. The running lawnmower suddenly jerked from his hand, rolled quickly down the street, and magnetically attached itself to the back of the sedan. The man that had been using the mower raced after our car and for a block or so was able to keep up with it before he started to give out.

"Hey, come back here with my mower," he yelled.

He saw all of us reclined in the car and pounded on the windows, but when he got no response he dropped back, leaped, and grabbed onto his mower attached to the sedan. He was dragged about twenty feet before he got tossed off and laid prostrate and frustrated in the middle of the main street.

Moments later, in front of an outdoor farm implement store, all manner of hoes, rakes, small plows, scythes, shovels, nails, hammers, saws, barbed wire rolls, and other metal objects went flying through the air. They too magnetically slammed into and melded onto our sedan.

A couple of old men were playing horseshoes in their front yard. Suddenly, the iron u-shaped shoes diverted into mid-air and were quickly drawn toward and onto the sedan. The two men shrugged, fussed, and with eyes that glowed with a blind rage waved their arms when the sedan passed by them.

"Tarnation! That's a humdinger of a whodunnit," cried out one old man.

Seeing what happened, a young boy full of eager vigor hopped on a bicycle and took to chasing after our sedan. Soon he realized he was not peddling, yet the bike was catching up with the car. As he came within a few feet of it, he panicked and leaped off into a ditch, while the bike joined the parade of other metal objects that attached to the automobile via Dwayne's electromagnetic invention gone haywire.

Further down the road, two women sat chatting on a park bench on that fine day. One lady had on a charm bracelet and the other wore eyeglasses. A man that sat across from them on another bench was feeding sesame seeds to some pigeons. The tractor passed them and moments later, like a skilled pickpocket, the one woman's bracelet was snatched from her wrist, while at the same moment the other woman's metal-framed eyeglasses ripped from her face and dashed away. That action stunned the man on the other bench, but not as much as when his pants ripped open and his pocket watch along with the other two items were whisked away like they were shot out of a canon. Rapidly they were added to the growing potpourri of magnetically influenced metal articles that were attached to the sedan. All three people were stunned.

The man growled, "For heaven's sake, that was my granddaddy's watch."

A few minutes later, the car and its piled-on objects passed by a residence wherein the backyard a hungry man taking advantage of the fine day wore an apron and chef's hat. He was cooking six T-bone steaks on his charcoal kettle grill. He paused a moment to sniff the lingering aroma and then stabbed one of the tender and juicy steaks with a grilling fork.

As the tractor and sedan passed down the street, as quick as the movement of some wild animal, the grill violently started to shake. What seemed to him without a reason, it jerked into motion and quickly plowed through his wooden fence, the front lawn, and into the street. Taken completely by surprise, he was pale as a ghost when he observed the grill wobbling and chasing down the street toward the sedan like an arrow shot from a bow. It soon plastered itself firmly upside down against the top of the sedan.

Three of the steaks were still under it and sparks flew as hot charcoal bounced off the car and onto the pavement. Defiantly, he too ran after the car.

He yelled and waved the grilling fork, "Hey, come back here with my steaks and grill."

It was to no avail. His one remaining steak was still speared to the fork. He stopped and the final insult occurred when the grilling fork along with the steak was also snatched out of his hand. As the tractor and sedan rounded a bend in the street, the man stopped, sat down in the middle of the road, placed his face in his hands, and began to sob.

On the way out of town, the sedan passed by an automotive junkyard where there were pegged plywood displays with hundreds of old hubcaps hanging from them. Like flying Frisbees through the skies, the hubcaps flung one after the other at our sedan. They smothered its hood, trunk, and top completely with the metal wheel covers. None of us were the least bit aware that all this was going on and that the sedan now looked like a deranged tank.

Across the street from the junkyard, a man was pushing his three-year-old son in one of those old-time metal pedal cars that kids in the '50's played with back then. Without warning, the car began to speed up. His son giggled, but the dad knew something was amiss. He dove and grabbed onto it ... as it too rolled quickly into the street and began racing toward the sedan.

"What the heck? Hold on, Buddy. I'll get you out," hollered the dad to his son.

With all his might, he reached with one hand and grabbed his kid. He managed to get his son out and the two of them spun and rolled along on the pavement.

Unharmed, the little boy laughed and said, "That was fun, Daddy. Let's do it again."

A few miles out of town, the tractor, followed by the sedan, pulled onto a well-traveled two-lane paved highway. Soon, passing by a billboard, the two vehicles approached a stop sign. Hidden behind the billboard was a motorcycle patrolman. He was stationed there and watched for those who might run the stop sign.

The patrolman paid little heed to the tractor. Instead, he continued to eat his sandwich and drink from his bottled water. A second or two later though, our clattering tank sedan passed by him. His mouth flew open, he dropped his sandwich into the lunch pail on the ground, tossed away his bottle of water, flipped on his cycle's wig-wag lights, and started up his powerful two-wheeled machine. He secured his helmet and sunglasses and then sped out to chase down our sedan. About a hundred yards away, the tractor heeded the sign and came to a stop ... as did our accumulated, metallic sedan, now fifteen yards behind.

The farm boy, still unmindful of his surroundings, did not see or hear the patrolman or motorcycle behind him. With the sedan stopped, the patrolman pulled to within twenty feet of it and shut off the cycle's motor. He flipped up the dark visor of his helmet and stared in awe at the mass of unusual, collected metal. His nose began to wiggle, as he got an unexpected whiff of the steaks still grilling somewhere on top of the sedan.

In dark blue, bloused pants, he slung one leg and his knee-high boots over the seat of the cycle, and then with his foot engaged his ride's kickstand. No doubt curious and confused by this sight before him, he began to slowly approach the sedan from the rear driver's side.

# POULTRY-GEIST

As he walked towards the car, the farm boy accelerated his tractor through the stop sign. As he did that ... the sedan followed and unfortunately, so too did the patrolman's parked motorcycle. The law officer watched in disbelief, as the kickstand disengaged and the cycle raced past him, locking itself next to the bicycle onto the rear trunk and bumper of the sedan.

Astounded by this action, seeing his motorcycle pulling away from him both surprised and angered him. Furious, he quickly withdrew his sidearm and began chasing after the rolling, mangled collection of oddball objects now covering the sedan.

"Stop!" he yelled. "Come back with my cycle. Pullover or I'll shoot!"

No sooner had he issued that warning than his 9 mm pistol got sucked out of his hand. It too flew through the air and attached itself to the car. The frustrated law officer could do nothing but watch, as his cycle and pistol slowly pulled away in the distance.

A man no longer in prime physical condition, he could only sustain his chase for about fifty yards. Exhausted, mad, and confused, he stopped, bent over, and placed his hands on his knees. He gasped for air and tried to catch his breath. With his hands on his hips, he rose and stood straight, looked around at the vacant farmland about him, removed his helmet and sunglasses, and then angrily tossed them to the ground. The last sound he heard before the conglomerate of queer objects disappeared down the road was that of a dog's bark that came from within that strange assemblage of metal.

Moments later left alone there among the peaceful, silent, plowed fields of God's tabernacle, all that was heard were the chatter of crickets, a few birds chirping, and the whimpering moans of a quaking, quivering, and thoroughly perturbed lawman.

He mumbled, "I think it's time I retired. I know the chief is never gonna believe me when I tell him about this."

Meanwhile, the tractor rolled down the road and soon approached a set of railroad tracks. The farm boy stopped, looked down the line, and then crossed his tractor over the rails. The first set of rails was rather smooth, but then the tractor climbed about fifteen feet away across an elevated incline and the second set of tracks. Although the sedan crossed easily over the first set, before the next inclined set of tracks, sparks again began to fly from the

Electromagnetic L.E.D. readout dial, which then leaped ahead to fifteen. The word 'Danger' then appeared on the dial.

The tractor bounced across the elevated second set of tracks, but as it did the sedan lost its magnetic lock on the tractor. Instead, the sedan hit the tracks, bounded upward, and then rolled back down the incline about five feet off and away from the tracks.

Fifteen minutes passed, and then in the distance, the blaring horn from a railroad engine could be heard. A few moments later, the speeding train raced towards the crossing like a roaring lion. As it dashed by at better than fifty mph, the sedan lurched forward. Now on full power, the magnetic pull latched onto the last train car passing by it. The sedan was jerked like a slingshot suddenly onto the tracks where it got dragged behind the train.

Inside the sedan, Wayne and Dwayne were tossed into the back seat. They were spread eagle on top of Daisy and me, who were each still deep in slumber and under the influence of Dwayne's sedative. Sweetroll whined and was plastered against the rear window with his tongue hanging out and his eyes bulging to reflect his fright. The car's tires soon blew out and the rims were giving off sparks, as the sedan and all its additional metal parasites rolled along behind the train car.

About thirty minutes later, the train slowed and began to pull into a station. Sparks began to fly again on the L.E.D. screen. Finally, smoke poured forth from under the car's hood, and the L.E.D. quickly reflected a fall to zero on the dial. Instantly, the metal objects that had been attached to the sedan begin to fall away.

An older couple parked at a nearby rail crossing, watched all this as the motorcycle, with its wigwag lights still blaring, rolled toward the wooden arm-like barrier now let down to keep cars from crossing the tracks. The cycle stopped and it leaned against the wooden barrier arm.

"Hmmm," mumbled the old gentleman. "I guess the policeman that rode that is writing out tickets in the promised land now."

As the myriad of old hubcaps began to drop off and roll around, the man's wife remarked, "Look, Sam. I think I see a hubcap that will match that missing one on our front wheel."

"Yeah, and look at that new charcoal grill. You get the hubcap. I'll remove the stupid cop's cycle and put the grill in our trunk. That's a good-looking hoe and rake too," he remarked. "Too bad we don't need another lawnmower."

The sedan, now released from the train, rolled on its rims down the tracks to a stop in front of the small rail station. The sign over the wood building stated: 'Welcome to Paradise.'

As the train soon left the station and pulled away, the sedan with us in it sat idle on the tracks.

The surprised station manager raced outside and scratched his head when he saw the car on the tracks, plus the vast array of metal items scattered around it. As restless as a blue-tailed fly on a hot summer's day, he waved a wary finger at us, four unconscious people, inside the sedan. He tried, but couldn't open the locked car doors, and instead pounded his fist on the windows attempting to get the attention of we passed out passengers.

In a state of great agitation, he shouted, "How'd this car get here? You must remove it immediately. There'll be another train along here in about twenty minutes."

Wandering around like a panicked June bug, he seemed in complete and confused wonder. He became even more curious as he watched the elder couple picking up items scattered around the tracks.

He withdrew a cell phone and placed a frantic call, "This is station master Smith in Paradise. Get hold of Red Line 1200 Express and tell them to locate a siding to pull onto and delay coming into the station here until we can clear the tracks."

He paused a moment and then replied to the person on the other end of the phone. "What? Sure, I'm authorized," he said as his blood pressure rose. "Look, you want to know what the chain of command is? It's what I'm going to beat you with if you don't stop that train and do what I told you."

With all the pounding and yelling going on, Daisy yawned and instinctively tried to stretch her arms.

She yawned and moaned, "Be quiet kids. How can a body sleep with all this racket going on?"

It was then that she realized she couldn't sit up, for Dwayne was draped over on top of her.

She shook Dwayne. He stirred a bit, as did Wayne and I. Sweetroll's paw was on my chest. His mouth was next to Wayne's face, which he slobbered all over with his tongue. As we passengers began to slowly wake from our groggy stupor, Sweetroll barked loudly, no doubt urging us all to rise.

Wayne had the uppermost seat position, so he was somehow able to sleepily reach the driver's side rear door handle. The station manager stood by with a hammer and was about to crash in the driver's window when Wayne weakly pulled at the door handle and it quickly flew open. Gallons of creek water spilled out and soaked passengers plummeted onto the ground.

The station manager's face twisted into a grimace.

"Great, that explains it. Drunks on the track having a joy ride. I can't wait to hear how you all explain this to the sheriff."

We four adult humans tumbled onto each other in the wet dirt next to the train tracks. Sweetroll bounded out and jumped right on top of Dwayne. Wayne sat up, his wet clothes grinding into the dirt. Daisy crawled out from under me, her matted hair and soaked clothes made her appear like a Raggedy Ann doll.

Wayne and I tried to make sense of all this, but with still fuzzy eyesight and dazed brains, we had a hard enough time trying to figure out whose legs belonged to who. We struggled to untangle and all four of us attempted to stand. Only Daisy made it temporarily to her feet. She forced her half-shut eyes as open as she could get them, squinted in the sun, and gazed about her as she deeply yawned. Through blurry eyes, she saw and read the sign over the train station, as did Wayne, who crawled onto his knees.

"Oh good, we're here." He sighed, and then fell onto his backside.

Daisy put one foot ahead of another and tried to take a step. Uncoordinated, she too dropped to her knees. I fought to clear the cobwebs in my head, but I was completely confused and disoriented.

The station master disconnected his phone conversation with the sheriff and waved an accusing finger at Daisy.

"Lady, I don't who you people are or how you managed in your intoxicated state to drive a car onto the tracks, but I'm going to tow it and have it impounded after I have you all arrested."

Daisy had a confused look on her face and tugged at her clothing. The condescending angry station manager was annoying her.

She yawned and asked, "What happened, and why are we all soaked?"

"Look lady, I'm not sure what you've been drinking, smoking, or snorting, but I'm sure it isn't legal."

Daisy rubbed her temples, sneered, and then replied harshly, "Mister, my head hurts, and I feel like a wet noodle. I'm going to need you to turn down your babbling for just a bit."

The station master shot her an icy glare, threw up his arms, and stomped away.

Dwayne got his feet under him, but then fell back against the fender of the car. He sniffed, reached, and his hands grasped to peel away a grilled steak from off the hood of the car. He sat holding the steak with a blank look on his face. He took a bite of the tender, well-done beef and grinned. Sweetroll then tumbled him over trying to get at the savory prize. He gave up fighting off his dog and Sweetroll made quick work of devouring the steak and gnawing on the T-bone.

"My one bite was delicious. Wish I'd had some A-1 sauce."

# CHAPTER 9: Palatial Paradox

An hour later and nearing dusk, our group was all sitting in the back of a stretch limo. A doctor had drawn blood samples from each of us to test for substances that might be illegal. We were arrested and then released ten minutes later when the sheriff found out that he'd detained the Kockle brothers, the largest employers in town, plus two of their business partners.

Though each of us had almost dried out and regained some of our composure and ability to function, we were all still dirty and disheveled. Dwayne had a torn shirt, and one shoe was missing. We could never quite figure out where it went. My pants were split in the rear, and thanks to the overly apologetic station master's safety pins, I remained decent. Daisy had several missing buttons on her blouse, and it took a while to locate her purse, which was wadded up under the front seat of the sedan. My wallet was soaked, as were the four hundred dollar bills I had inside it.

Sitting in the limo, Wayne turned to our familiar driver and said, "Thanks for coming to bail us out so soon, Clancy."

"Ah, tis my pleasure and duty, Lads. I still think a thousand dollars donated to the sheriff's re-election campaign and not allowing you to drive for a month was too steep a fine," he said.

"Maybe, but if the sheriff's son didn't work for us, it'd have been more. Besides, you're the one that drives us most of the time anyway," replied Wayne.

"Glad to help, I am. If I may ask, Sir, why was the car parked on the railroad tracks?"

"I'm not sure. Neither do I know why it wouldn't start, nor how it got all those dents and scratches."

Dwayne asked a fatigued Daisy and me, "You're certain you two want to see the house before going to clean up at the hotel?"

I yawned and stated, "Yes, please. We want to see it before it gets too dark."

Ten minutes later, Wayne looked out the window, as the limo entered a lavish suburban neighborhood.

"This is your street. The house is at the end of the block," he said.

Daisy read the street sign, "Pleasant Place. What a perfectly prim, proper, and peaceful primrose path." She said, and I wondered silently why she'd used all those 'P's.

Her hair was a mess, and her clothing was wrinkled. She slid closer to the window and gazed out, as the limo approached our new home. She reached over and nervously squeezed my hand.

When the limo neared the end of the cul-de-sac, in front of them in the street, according to Clancy, dozens of chickens suddenly appeared out of nowhere. Clancy did a double-take and his foot slammed on the car's brake. He quickly turned the steering wheel and tried to avoid hitting them. This unexpected, irrational event caused all of us to be tossed about inside the limo.

He saw several hens splatter against the windshield and when he turned the wheel to miss others, the limo rammed into the brick mailbox at the front of the property ... knocking it to pieces.

Wayne yelled, "Clancy! What on earth made you do that?"

"Sean and Begorrah! Chickens, there were. You saw them. Dozens of them ... all over the road, they were. I couldn't avoid them," he excitedly stated.

The bewildered driver looked at Wayne, opened the door, and leaped out. He no doubt expected a bevy of fractured chicken parts to be scattered about, but instead, Clancy saw nothing. No dead chickens whatsoever. Not even a stray feather. He stood gawking about in the street, as Wayne exited the car and looked around and then at Clancy.

"Clancy, are you off the wagon again?"

"Nay, Lad, I swear to you. Not a nip of the holy nectar have I consumed. There were chickens I tell you ... dozens of them."

"You need some time off. Back away from this mess and pull up to the house," instructed Wayne.

Clancy removed his chauffeur's cap, scratched his head, and frustratingly reentered the limo.

He mumbled, "Chickens there was, I swear by the Blarney and my mother's old bones. It's a load of nonsense; codswallop it is."

Hearing Clancy's comment, Dwayne inquired, "Chickens? Where? Are we at the home or the processing plant?"

Wayne answered, "We're at the home." He then commented to Daisy and me, "Nice covered porch, don't you think?"

Clancy backed off from the destroyed remnants of the brick mailbox and slowly pulled into the driveway of our spacious and luxurious new home.

Moments later, the four of us exited the vehicle and left Clancy in the limo while he tried to make sense of what just happened to him. As we walked toward the front door of the house, Wayne smiled at Daisy, and then glanced back at the ruined mailbox. Clancy opened the driver's door and stepped out onto the driveway. He glared back at the street, removed his chauffeur's cap and the breeze blew his red hair about his pale face and rosy cheeks.

Wayne led Dwayne by the arm and remarked, "Before you all move in, I'll get a bricklayer by here to repair the mailbox."

Dwayne also held onto Sweetroll's harness, as we approached the three steps to the front porch of this spacious, custom-built Victorian-style home on a lovely professionally landscaped three-acre lot with woods in the backyard. It was in a quiet and highly desirable estate neighborhood.

Still weakened, I tried to lift my leg to step up but seemed unable to do so. I pawed at the air with my foot and with great effort finally made it up to the next step.

I smiled and said, "Sorry. I'm still weak in the knees. Whatever it was that knocked us out lingers yet within me." As I tread on the first porch step, I swear I heard the sound of a duck's quack. {Yes, I said duck ... again}

Surprised, I asked Daisy, "Did you hear that?"

"What?" she questioned.

Thinking it was just my imagination, I replied, "I'm still dizzy. I guess it was nothing."

That was before reaching the next step, which issued a loud quack and a boisterous, geese honk. This time I glared at Daisy, plus both the twins.

"Don't tell me you all didn't hear that."

"Hear what?" queried Dwayne.

By now, I was becoming annoyed. "There was a loud honking goose, plus a duck quacking."

Daisy looked at me like I was going crazy. "I think you're just tired and 'quacking up,' dear."

I then withdrew and let the twins and her go forward onto the next step, which when I stood upon it there were three calls: that of a turkey gobble, the honking goose, and then the duck quack. I shook my head and had to wonder if indeed I wasn't quacking up. Daisy too had to have Wayne assist her up the steps.

"Thanks, Wayne."

We approached the elaborate twin doors with the ornate lead glass patterned inserts. Wayne punched in a passcode on the keyless entry, opened the door, and stood aside to allow Daisy and me inside.

Daisy shuffled inside and I followed. The two of us quickly became wide-eyed, and a huge smile formed on Daisy's lips, as we beheld one of the nicest homes we'd ever seen. She gazed about at the high ceilings, the finely crafted moldings, the fabulous entryway, and rich, hard scraped oak flooring that flowed into the formal dining room. The posh, sunken family room had plush carpet, a rock-faced gas fireplace, and two sets of French doors that led to the outside.

Daisy gasped and said, "Oh, guys! This place is just lovely. Everything is superb."

We began to explore our new house. Daisy screamed with delight when she entered the bright and cheery gourmet custom kitchen with granite countertops, beautiful oak cabinetry, and high-end stainless-steel appliances.

She opened the door to the walk-in pantry.

"My goodness, what a nice pantry. You could fit a whole family in here."

One feature that we liked was that between the den and kitchen wall, there was a hundred-gallon saltwater aquarium, complete with colorful, growing coral. It was stocked with numerous brightly-hued tropical fish.

After touring the first-floor master suite with a large walk-in closet by herself, Daisy stepped into the elaborate master bath area. She didn't notice the eight-foot-long vanity cabinet with the many drawers and space for her to sit on a stool to do her make-up. Nor did she take note of the large, jetted tub, or the huge shower with granite walls, three overhead sprinkler heads, and two granite shower seats. No, all she could focus on was the toilet, which had a seven-foot-tall ostrich bent over with its head in the John.

She screamed and we all entered the bathroom, thinking hers was a scream of delight at what she'd seen there. Instead, the look on her face was one of fright and surprise. Her finger nervously shook and pointed at the toilet.

I hugged her and turned to look at where she pointed. "Yes, it's a very nice toilet, dear. Almost all houses have them now." I said sarcastically, but with no malice intended.

"Did you see it?" she asked me.

"Yes, hon. As I said, it's a potty. A very pretty potty in a properly, pleasing place."

I walked her back into the bedroom where she broke away from me and ran back to the bathroom opening. When she peeked in, there was nothing there except the toilet and other accommodating items appropriate and needed in a bathroom.

Still a bit nervous, we then saw the other upstairs bedrooms, the daylight basement with a full game room, a kitchenette, and an amazing bar with a wine closet. I thought that this fantastic house was set up for entertaining large gatherings or when we had out-of-town guests.

Wayne asked, "Do you like it?"

"Like it? Replied Daisy. "We love it! So will our kids, especially Cah Cah, who loves fish and aquariums."

I added, "Yes, we can't thank you enough, guys. This is a quantum leap ahead from our simple old farmhouse in Ohio or even your penthouse condo in Miami."

Dwayne grinned and remarked, "Take them out back to see the yard."

When Wayne opened those French doors and we stepped out into the lavish landscape there, the first thing we saw was a shady two-tiered deck with awning and pool deck leading to a gorgeous swimming pool that now was swathed over with a winter safety cover.

Seeing the pool, Daisy couldn't suppress her joy. "Oh, wow! We've never had a pool. I can't wait till summer to try that out."

We were blown away by this elaborate place. There was an oversized driveway that led to a detached three-car garage and a breezeway with a full, easily accessible staircase to a garage attic and more storage.

When we returned inside, Wayne handed Daisy the keys and passcode to the home.

# POULTRY-GEIST

Dwayne told us, "We had the deed put in your names and the taxes, plus the insurance are paid for the next three years. All you've got to do is arrange for your furniture and things to be shipped up here and move right in when you're ready. In the meantime, we're putting you up in the best hotel in Lancaster."

I paused to catch my breath and struggled for words to say, "My Lord! This is beyond generous, guys. How can we ever thank you or pay you back for such a glorious gift?"

Wayne grinned and patted me on the back, "No need to do that. We just want you to enjoy living here. If there's anything else you need or something you'd like us to change, let us know."

Like me, Daisy was overwhelmed by their generosity. She paused a moment, looked at the den, and then at the plum-colored wallpaper in the dining room.

Then she politely remarked, "Perfectly pleasing pink and pastel palette patterns in the parlor. Perhaps probably to permit paisley pinstriped purple paint to perish in their partaking place."

We all looked at her strangely.

She shrugged and remarked, "Whoa! Where'd all those words come from?"

I awkwardly cleared my throat.

Seemingly without control of my vocabulary, I stated, "Pretty, posh, palatial palace provides plentiful pleasure and presents a perfectly plush place."

Then I grabbed at my throat and said, "Yikes, me too. This passel of 'P's is peculiar and poses a possible perplexing problem." Then I cried out, "Stop it!"

Daisy flinched at the tone of my voice. The amusement and excitement died from her tired eyes and she regarded me with a searching solemnity. My congested mind became cluttered with questions.

I asked the twins, "Who did you say lived here before?"

Dwayne's words too seemed to spasm, as he stated, "Paul and Polly Plump, plus their Papa and pampered prodigy." He sneered and also appeared puzzled by his choice of words.

Daisy then questioned, "Why'd they leave here and where'd you say they went?"

Without thinking, Wayne replied, "The puzzling, portly Plumps promptly proceeded to pursue other prospective possibilities." He seemed stunned by saying it that way.

"Doing what?" I asked.

Evidently Dwayne was without any mental effort or control to stop it.

"He became proprietor of Pepper's Pasta and Pizza Place in Pittsburg."

Little did Daisy, I, nor either of the twins know why we said those 'P' words, or that we were all about to go from eggs over easy ... to scrambled. We'd have all been better off if we'd high-tailed it out of that house while we still had our perky pride and before our plucky prominent potential perished. {Who's writing all that? I am ... who are you? ... I am you, stupid}

# CHAPTER 10: Processing Plant Pullets

The next morning it was cooler and there was frost on the ground. After a continental breakfast and being delivered some dry clothing, Daisy and I joined Wayne and Dwayne for a limo ride through the countryside to take in all the amazing Amish farms and culture that surrounded Lancaster County. Clancy drove us and we stopped by an Amish farm where Daisy and I got to milk a cow and tour through an Amish Museum, plus a store where Daisy purchased some apple butter, apricot preserves, and other Amish-made items to take back to the kids. One unusual item Daisy bought was a girl rag doll for Cah Cah. It was odd because the handmade doll had no face, eyes, mouth, or nose.

When Daisy asked why Wayne explained, "Their handmade rag dolls, dressed in Amish attire, and typically don't have faces. The Amish believe a faceless doll indicates that all children are the same in God's eyes."

Dwayne added, "All together, there are over five thousand Amish farms here in Lancaster County alone. All of them raise chickens and other poultry, so in a way, we compete with them, but not really since we market to larger corporate stores and the restaurant business."

Wayne then remarked, "Yes, but we do furnish chicks for many Amish farms, and we've learned from them to provide poultry with no growth hormones or preservatives. Until the turkeys or chickens are harvested, they live in spacious buildings where they get fresh air and drink purified well water. They are not force-fed and grow at their own pace."

By noon, Wayne and Dwayne had Clancy stop at one of their favorite family cafés that served home-style cooking. Although Wayne invited him to come with us, Clancy broke out the lunch he'd brought.

He told Wayne, "Tis mighty nice of you to ask, Lad, but I'll be dining on me own rations."

"Aye," said Dwayne, "And a nip or two of your sherry I presume."

"Perhaps so, Lad, but only for medicinal purposes ... you understand."

"Yeah, well make certain if we're stopped by John Law on the way home you have your prescription handy."

Daisy and I laughed, and then followed the twins and Sweetroll into the plain-looking diner. Some of the younger kids in the diner were somewhat nervous and overwhelmed by the size of Sweetroll, but Dwayne assured them he was harmless and even let them pet him. That is, they petted the dog ... not Dwayne.

When we were seated at a booth the waitress brought us menus, and then took our drink order. Daisy and I ordered orange juice; the twins preferred iced tea. The waitress then turned to get our drinks. Daisy and I wore comfortable walking shoes and casual clothing that the twins supplied us and looked forward to the plant tour to come after lunch.

When the waitress brought our drinks, she took her pencil and readied to take our food order.

An uncertain expression formed on my face, and I asked, "May we possibly proceed to place proper picks for partaking on plates to please our palettes."

Daisy and the twins looked at me like I was an alien from Mars. A sudden unforeseen gloom seemed to drift over us like a cloud.

Wayne wet his lips with his tongue and glanced up at the confounded waitress.

He cleared his throat, and then asked her, "What do you recommend?"

Without hesitation, she then went into a 'P' rant of her own.

"Perfectly prepared pulled pork and potatoes; peppered Panama perch; pleasing portions of pleasant pheasant; pretzel packed pasta; pulverized Peruvian Pufferfish; and a choice of prickly pear pudding, or a piece of peach and pineapple pie," spouted the waitress wearing the pleasingly plump pair of puffy pants.

She shook her head and thumped her noggin as if to clear out the cobwebs.

"I'll have a cheeseburger, fries, a coke, and nothing else than begins with the letter P," I said.

The twins and Daisy nodded their heads and agreed with my choice.

While we were waiting for our food, Daisy used her cell phone to call back home to see how the kids were doing. With only two weeks till Christmas, they were out for the holidays, and I was sure they were anxious to learn if we were moving up here.

Judy answered. Daisy placed her phone on the tabletop, and we all listened in as she activated the speaker function on her phone.

"Hi Judy, we're here in Paradise and stopped for lunch. How are the kids?" Daisy asked.

"They're fine." Replied Judy. "Hold on they want to speak with you and Dabney."

Our excited kids all tried to talk at the same time and most of what we heard was a lot of giggling and chatter we didn't understand.

"Hi kids. I'm right here with your mom,"

Daisy told them, "Wayne and Dwayne have been taking us around the area up here to see all the beautiful farms. Your dad and I even got to milk a cow."

"That's neat," declared Dippy. "Judy took us to the zoo yesterday and we saw all sorts of animals."

"That was nice of her. What animals did you see?"

There was an unexpected, strange pause and an excruciating, lingering moment of silence that worried me. Under the circumstances, it wasn't like our kids to ever remain quiet during a phone call, even for a few seconds.

Then in a droning voice almost in unison they calmly spoke into the phone, "Pandas, porcupines, peacocks, pigs, panthers, penguins, and pelicans."

Then after a brief moment to catch their breath finished up with, "Ponies, porpoises, prairie dogs, primates, and puppies."

Daisy, plus the twins, and I were speechless and completely stunned. My square jaw tensed, and I twirled at my mustache nervously. Daisy had a tear in her eye. Wayne leaned back on his elbows and seemed dumbfounded. Dwayne gathered a wrapped cinnamon bun from his vest, and then obviously thinking it was Sweetroll, patted the arm of the leather chair in which he sat.

"Sweetroll, who cut your fur so short? He questioned. "Here's your dessert and your lunch will be here soon ... I hope."

After a few minutes of small talk, Daisy told the excited kids about the new home we'd have here and that we'd be back in a day or two to start packing for Paradise. I ate only part of my cheeseburger, as I was too confused and worried about the odd effect something was having on all of us ... even on our kids.

After she nervously consumed her cheeseburger and fries, Daisy slid back her chair and stood.

"Pardon, please, as I proceed to powder place to properly perform pampering and perhaps perfume."

She bit her lips in dismay and a look of puzzlement passed over her face.

I sighed and said, "Pathetically peculiar problem."

\* \* \*

That afternoon, the twins gave us a tour of their poultry and hatchery plant. We watched in wonder, as the twins escorted us around and showed us the facilities. They stopped us in front of a room with what appeared to be thousands of eggs on large carts.

Wayne explained, "These carts contain crates of fertilized eggs. An automated incubation system turns the eggs forty degrees every hour, much as does a mother hen."

The next thing we saw was the hatching area. There, young chicks with downy, yellow feathers began to break through their shells.

Wayne continued, "At around nineteen days, the chicks hatch. They then tumble down a conveyor that separates them from their shells."

Daisy and I observed the process, as hundreds of tiny chicks tumbled aimlessly down a conveyor onto a steel roller. The chicks are bigger than the shells, so the shells fell in between the rollers onto another conveyor below.

Daisy sighed, clasped her hands together, and stared at the chicks.

She remarked, "Seems like a rude way to be welcomed into the world, but I suppose it's necessary."

We watched as the chicks entered a round room, where dozens of female workers sat next to the conveyor line. When the chicks passed by, each woman grabbed one, examined it, and then tossed it into one of two openings on the conveyor.

Wayne said, "The openings there allow the chicks to fall down a chute, and onto separated conveyors below."

I asked Wayne, "What are the women doing?"

"They are separating the male chicks from the female ones."

Daisy seemed to search for a plausible explanation. "How on earth do they determine which is which?"

"By their feathers," stated Dwayne. "If the wingtips are uneven, it's a female. If they are all the same length, then it's male."

Daisy and I were impressed, but a bit uncomfortable by the dispassionate method and assembly of these small tufts of poultry. A warning signal seemed to go off in my head.

Dwayne then said, "As the chicks tumble down into crates of a hundred each, they pass under an antibiotic spray."

Wayne added, "The hens go one way and the fryers another."

Daisy seemed to become increasingly uneasy with the rough treatment the chicks received before being even a few minutes out of their shells. Before they knew what was happening, they were separated, packaged, sprayed, and sent out for shipment to other parts of the plant.

I heard her mumble, "Poor little things."

Wayne heard her remark and stated, "They don't remain little for long. In around forty-five days, chances are you'll find them pampered, fed, plump, and soon in a supermarket's meat counter section, or as one of those delicious grilled hens, we supply to your restaurants. Some may become egg-laying hens too."

I nodded and accepted the fact that mankind is the only animal that remains on friendly terms with those he intends to eat ... right up until it comes time to eat them.

Our group turned to go, but as we did, Daisy and I took note that one of the small chicks hopped out of its box and onto a nearby table. To me, it seemed that the chick was staring right at us.

I said to Daisy, "I could swear that little chick had an angry expression on its face."

"Yeah!" she remarked. "I'd say he's hopping mad ... and who could blame him?"

* * *

After we toured the hatchery, rather than taking us inside the processing plant where the mature hens experience a rather unpleasant treatment ... resulting in them being prepared for consumption, Wayne and Dwayne escorted Daisy and me to the rear area outside the plant. About twenty yards away, we saw a tall, corrugated steel silo building. It had two adjoining one-story metal buildings attached to it on each side. The four of us approached the silo and I was curious as to what was inside.

"I remarked to Wayne, "I saw this driving up. What's in the silo? Is that where you store corn or other grain to feed the chickens?"

Sweetroll led Dwayne, who smiled and said, "No, not grain. It's my surprise for you."

"Well, it'll have to go some to beat the drive here from Philly, or you're giving us a house."

Wayne clicked a remote. The door to the silo opened and we all walked inside.

Once in, Daisy and I gawked at what Wayne and Dwayne had constructed. Rising exactly eight stories into the air was a steel tower-like frame about five feet square. On top of the tower were a chain and sprocket-driven device that had stainless steel, spoon-shaped paddles every eighteen inches on the chain.

Wayne flipped a switch on a nearby wall. A conveyor near the bottom of the tower began to roll out cooked grill chickens that flowed down the conveyor towards the tower.

"Watch this," said Wayne. "As the chickens get to the tower, each one slides onto a spoon-like paddle."

We observed in wonder as the process did exactly as Wayne described.

"When at the top, they glide five feet down and across to the other side onto the edge ... that then drops them eight stories onto a sterile steel pan platform at ground level."

We watched, as this began to happen. The first chickens spilled over the top and dropped to the pan just as Wayne said they would. As they hit, a steel-powered arm pushed and slid them onto another conveyor that took them to a packaging system where they were freeze-dried, wrapped, and then placed in a truck to be shipped.

"Cool, huh!" said Wayne.

"Way cool," I replied. "It sure beats our nighttime drops off your Miami condo."

"Sure does," declared Daisy. "But what about long-distance hauls? How do we keep the chickens fresh and ready to serve?"

Dwayne commented, "This way, we manage the amounts needed, and after they're cooked, no humans are required to control the process. It's automated. For the birds we need to ship long distances, as I told you in Miami, we developed a rapid freeze system that will preserve the cooked texture of the chickens, which can be defrosted, heated, and served without losing any of the flavor or tenderness."

"Besides us, you two and two confidentially sworn employees, plus the contractor that built this facility knows about it ... so, our secret is intact," added Wayne.

Dwayne then stated, "This plant will supply enough freshly cooked chickens for all our southern franchisees. When we expand our franchises to the east and other areas, we'll purchase land and build a regional tower set-up like this one to serve those areas."

"It's amazing, Dwayne. You truly are a genius," remarked Daisy.

# CHAPTER 11: Moving In ... Moaning On

The next afternoon, Daisy and I were reunited with our kids and back in Miami. On the flight there, neither Daisy nor I spoke of the strange, unaccountable, and uncontrollable manner in which we and our kids spoke all those 'P' words. Nor did we mention what we thought we saw and heard at the house the twins bought us. I think we each tried to believe that our odd speech pattern {Oooh, another 'P' word} and what happened at the house were due to hallucinations derived from whatever source knocked us out that day on the way to Paradise.

We got some information from the toxicology results of having our blood drawn that day. The labs identified the primary substance in our blood to be a strong sedative ... though none of us knew how that got into our systems. What bothered Daisy and me the most, however, was that they wanted me to get another blood test, claiming that I had very peculiar DNA matter in my cells. {Yet another pitiful 'P' word}

"The technician told me on the phone, "When you get moved here, we'll re-test you, as somehow your sample must have gotten contaminated."

"What do you mean by that?" I then asked.

The man on the phone laughed and said, "Well, although an impossibility, your blood sample revealed that a third of your cells resembles that of a fowl ... namely ... a chicken."

I joined him in laughing so hard that spittle came out my nose. I began to then "cackle" and before I could control myself ... I heard a loud rooster's crow exit from my throat.

The man on the other end of the phone laughed even harder, but I gasped and almost fainted when I heard myself doing that. I faked going along with his interpretation of my action, for I knew by his cynical laughter that he'd thought I was pretending by crowing.

"That's a good one, mister Doodlegood. We'll see you when you get back."

My voice tinged with apprehension, "Okay, and thanks for calling."

# POULTRY-GEIST

$* * *$

By the end of the week, the movers the twins hired came and packed everything, including our Jeep, loaded it all into vans, and then headed out for Pennsylvania. We spent our last Miami night going out to celebrate with our kids at one of our restaurants. The kids wanted pizza, {Yep, <u>another 'P'</u> <u>word</u>} but Daisy and I insisted that was not an option.

A week before Christmas, we were all met by Clancy at the Philly airport and driven by limo to our new home in Paradise. This time, none of us lost consciousness.

"So, my darlings, I think your parents and you will like it here. Tis a nice, quiet town where a body can rest and enjoy life," alleged Clancy.

He grinned at Cah Cah, who sat next to him in the front seat. She looked up at him and returned a smile of her own.

He told her, "And you, my little angel, are a precious jewel indeed."

"Yes, I'm sure we'll all love it and be happy living here," remarked Daisy.

$* * *$

Once in Paradise and driving toward their new home, near the front curb a bricklayer was almost finished rebuilding the brick mailbox that Clancy ran over a week before. On the opposite side of the property, Dwayne was putting the finishing touches on the mailbox that he had nearly constructed.

He slapped the last brick into place and then turned towards Wayne, who walked up just as Dwayne finished raking off the mortar.

Clancy pulled into the driveway and our wide-eyed, excited kids raced up the walk and rushed inside through the front door. I started to yell at them to wait, but I knew that wasn't going to work, so I let them go. I nodded at the bricklayer and smiled my approval of his work. Daisy and I saw Wayne, who motioned at us to come to the other side of the yard.

Dwayne heard us coming and when we got close, Sweetroll greeted us with his usual flair and almost knocked me down. Dwayne Points toward the house and away from his bricklaying catastrophe.

He stated, "There you go, folks. I rebuilt your mailbox. How does it look?"

Daisy giggled and Wayne put his finger to his lips to shush us. My eyebrows rose, and I looked at the convoluted mess that Dwayne made. Sweetroll growled, lifted his leg, and peed on the twisted stack of kiln-dried clay brick. The metal mailbox itself was upside down and with the pivoting red flag pointed downward. Besides leaning to both the right, and then to the left, some of the mortared brick was laid with the holes facing outward. Others were turned crooked.

Grinning from ear to ear, Daisy said, "Yes, well thank you, Dwayne. We appreciate your efforts."

Dwayne smiled, as Sweetroll pulled him towards the house.

"You're welcome, Daisy. I'll go clean up now."

After Dwayne began to walk away, Wayne, Daisy, and I stood back and looked queerly at Dwayne's awkward work.

"More of that same window washer treatment I see," I declared.

"Yes," said Wayne. "I'll have the brick mason tear it down tomorrow."

I nodded and patted Wayne on the back. The two of us burst into laughter.

"You're right. He is independent and stubborn, but he has a good heart and intentions."

\* \* \*

With the furniture arrived, it is being set up inside by workers that Wayne hired, we got to spend our first night in our new, elaborate home. The kids fought over which of the bedrooms each got, and when they saw the swimming pool outside, they loved it so much they almost went speechless … almost. When they realized they were going to have a place to swim when it got warm, I believe I counted about twenty Yippees and a dozen or so Wahoos. Of course, Cah Cah wanted to go get in the pool right then, but it was only 51 degrees outside.

"Sorry, Sweet Cheeks, you'll just have to wait till it gets warmer and we can remove the pool cover," I told her.

# POULTRY-GEIST

The furniture was put in place in all the rooms and later after the kids were settled into their beds, I was in our downstairs bedroom. Daisy strolled in from the bathroom. Her hair was damp, and her face was covered in cold cream. She sat on the edge of our bed and began wiping the cream from her face with some Kleenex. Before she could finish, I leaned over, grabbed her, and gave her a big kiss. When I retracted, my face too was covered in cold cream.

"Nice cucumber flavor ... yuck," I said as I tasted the cold cream on my lips.

She laughed and handed me a Kleenex. I wiped away the slippery substance from my face.

I told her, "Well, we made it, Daisy. Welcome to Paradise."

She smiled at me, and then I stood and walked into our master bathroom. I ambled to the long vanity and my sink. I opened a drawer, removed my toothpaste and toothbrush, and began brushing my teeth.

As I bent over to spit the paste into the sink, I heard a sound behind me. I spit and then listened to the low, cooing, and cackling sounds of what I interpreted as that from hens. As I rose from the sink and saw my startled reflection in the vanity mirror, I witnessed six large hens perched on the large glass shower stall door behind me. Unlike me, they seemed to be calm and asleep.

I wheeled about rapidly. When I did, I was just as startled because there was nothing there upon the shower stall door. There were neither chickens nor any sign they were ever there. That nerve-racking incident caused my heart to skip a beat and my legs gave way as I slumped down onto the toilet seat. I silently wondered if perhaps we hadn't moved into a house that was a Petri dish filled with inconsolable fowl spirits determined to taunt and haunt us. As it turned out, that hunch was pretty much on target.

When I returned to our bedroom, I had a worried and puzzled expression on my face. Daisy held up the alarm clock from off the nightstand by our king-sized bed.

She asked, "Something wrong, dear?".

I slowly sat on the edge of our bed and glanced back into the bathroom.

"Dabney, what is it? You look as if you've seen a ghost."

I winced and told her, "Huh? Oh, it's nothing. I think I'm just tired."

Daisy fiddled with the alarm clock dial.

"Me too. It's been a long day. What time shall I set the alarm?"

"I want to be at the plant by 8:30 A.M. tomorrow. It's the last day the plant's open before closing for the Christmas holidays and Wayne and Dwayne are introducing me to the franchise salespeople."

"I'll set it for 7:00 A.M.," she said.

She flipped off the lamp and she and I snuggled up together. In the dark, and on our first night in our new home, my eyes were drawn back towards the bathroom.

* * *

Around 5:30 A.M., from out of somewhere strange, a large rooster hopped up onto the end of our bed. He cackled a few times and then spread his wings. Then, like the blast from an air horn, he let out an extremely loud daylight cock-a-doodle-doo. I about jumped out of my skin and wished he had cock-a-doodle-didn't.

I kicked off the covers and bolted upwards in the bed. A much calmer Daisy slowly stirred and sat up next to me. We each cleared the sleep from our eyes and stared into the newly dawning light streaming in through our bedroom windows.

She inquired of me "Huh? What?"

The rooster flapped its wings again and again, and then let out another bellowing crow.

This time, I stumbled out of bed and fell onto the carpeted floor. Daisy looked over at the alarm clock.

"It's only 5:30 A.M. Why are you getting up so early?"

Angry, sleepy, and yet panicked, I lunged out of the bed and began searching the room for the rooster, which now was nowhere to be found.

I exclaimed, "It was a darn rooster. His crowing woke me up. Surely you heard it."

Daisy looked at me, as if I were crazy, "Rooster? What rooster?"

"The one that just crowed twice. Where'd that ornery critter go? I'll wring its darn neck."

"You're dreaming! Come back to bed. You can sleep another hour and a half before getting started."

"No! I ain't sleeping till I find that pest and have him for dinner."

I got into my robe and slippers, left the bedroom, and began to search through the big house, but my search was in vain for I found no rooster. It made no sense. The doors and windows were all closed, so how'd it get inside? Was there some secret poultry door hidden here someplace, or was I truly dreaming and had a hypnopompic hallucination? Yeah, I know that's a big psycho-babble word that I'll explain later. But then I digress, for a story is never improved by telling it all to somebody before it is finished. Suffice it to say, I silently wondered if indeed I had a screw loose.

It was a cloudy day, and I wore a sweater to ward off the chill in the air. I got to work on time. Later, at 10:00 A.M. that morning, Wayne, Dwayne, and I were seated in the plant's conference room. Still somewhat sleepy-eyed, I was introduced by Wayne to the gathering of men there.

He told them, "You sales reps will love working with him. Please welcome our new partner and operations manager, Dabney Doodledoo.".

One of the men gathered at the table leaned over and grinned.

"Did you say, Doodledorf?"

Wayne cast a scolding eye toward that franchise salesman. I shuffled to the head of the conference table and stared out at the men. They gave me a quick round of meager applause. My eyes were red and I appeared weak.

"Thanks," I said. "I'm happy to be here."

I paused and tried not to anger. I yawned but tried not to even blink. I siphoned words to my numb brain as if I needed a hoist to get them to the surface. What with all that hubbub and zany circumstance that occurred at home, my pot had been stirred a bit too much for my liking.

I quickly sobered and added, "My last name is Doodledoo. I inherited it, along with my grandpa's sharp kitchen clever that he used to chop off anyone's tail feathers that made fun of my family's name."

As I said that, I thought of Alvin Snorkelpuss and wished I'd shown more backbone long ago in dealing with him, as I surprisingly had just done here. The salesman held up his hands in surrender and smiled at me.

"Sounds like a nice Polish name to me," he mentioned politely and facetiously.

The room broke out in laughter.

"That's an egg-cellent guess, but egg-zactly not where we were from," I replied.

More laughter came forth.

I took a sip from the cup of coffee near me on the table.

"At any rate, it's a pleasure to be here, and I look forward to meeting all of you and working with you. With your help, we'll spread the Kockle-Doodledoo's grilled chicken brand to every corner of this nation."

As I spoke, I became more alert. However, after several moments, my eyes were suddenly drawn to the opposite end of the long conference table. There, my disbelieving eyes observed something that startled me into silent submission. It was as if my brain was suffering from a seizure from the depression era and a dust storm was blowing through it.

Sitting back in a chair with its feet up on the table was what appeared to be an animated cartoon character.

I stopped speaking in mid-sentence, rubbed my eyes, and stared at a large cartoon rooster. The others noticed my odd reaction, and they turned to and look towards the end of the table, but they saw no one there.

The rooster had on a felt cowboy hat, opened at the top so that its rooster comb could hang out. There was a black eye patch over its right eye, and around its wide waistline was a leather gun and ammo belt. He wore cowboy boots and spurs over his stumpy legs.

However, instead of bullets being in the leather loops of the belt, there were hen eggs, six of them, three on each side. In the holster, instead of a pistol, there was a large pearl-handled slingshot. Along with his boots and spurs, he wore a bright red and blue bandanna tied around his thick neck.

Then, clear as a bell I heard him say, "Howdy, Pilgrim. I'm Marshall, Rooster Galldern. That's a mighty fine speech. I know you must take a lot of pride in your cultured heritage, but turn off your fandango, because my hens and I ain't going anywhere. So, friend, you better get another line of work; this one doesn't fit your pistol."

I swallowed hard and wondered if my tortured stomach was going to re-send my morning pottage back up the pipe.

In a voice that was unmistakably similar to the sound and pattern of John Wayne, Rooster leaped to his feet, hopped up on the table, and began to mosey down it towards me. His spurs jingled as he strutted. He had a slight limp and came within a foot of my nose. He angrily stared me down with his one uncovered left eye.

"Step down off your high horse, Pilgrim. Cross the idea of franchising, whatever that means, off your list. And who pray tell are all these other jaybirds?"

He pointed at the man that remarked on my last name.

"That mongrel looks like the sidewinder that ran with Lucky Red Pepper when he pulled that bank job down in Parnell County. He probably has papers out on him from someplace."

Amazingly agile for a plump pullet, Rooster jumped down onto the floor. {Oooh! Two references in a row to roosters, plus there were another two 'P' words} He quickly withdrew his slingshot from the holster and twirled it several spins. He snarled and then waltzed out the door. I heard him remark before leaving.

"Be seeing you, Pilgrim. This apple ain't cooked yet, so grab your hat and hold on fella."

The world is never without surprises. I again rubbed my eyes and the men in the room stared at me, for it was as if I were suddenly cast into a trance.

Completely unhinged, I yelled, "Wait! Come back here Marshall, you lunatic, one-eyed pullet!"

Dwayne grinned and replied, "Marshall? I don't think there's anyone here by that name, Dabney. Oh no, the Fire Marshall's not here again is he?"

"Huh? You mean ya'll didn't see him? He was right here. He spoke to me. He's a big ugly rooster." I stated matter of factly.

My voice trailed off and I seemed near collapse. Wayne stepped up, took me by the arm, and led me back to my seat.

I heard another salesman whisper to the man next to him, "Great! We're going to be led by a low-hanging eggplant that must've been born during a lunar eclipse."

That salesman replied, "Yeah, and today he's battling and working out on his crazy mood swing set."

I don't drink strong spirits either, but now I'd rather have had a free bottle in front of me than feel as if I'd had a pre-frontal lobotomy. I remained speechless and stared out the door from which that crazy cock-a-doodle who called himself, Rooster Galldern, just left. I began to wonder if maybe I played too much playground football as a kid without wearing a helmet.

The men in the room stared suspiciously at me. I didn't blame them. I placed my hands on the table and folded them together in a tight grasp. Despite the cool temperature inside the room, my shirt collar began to sweat. It had not been a flattering light in which I had painted myself and my first impression must have left them with the idea that there were lunatics locked up in asylums who had it more together than I did.

"Well, thank you for those ... inspiring words, Dabney." Said a stoic Wayne. "The brain is a marvelous organ; it starts working as soon as we get up in the morning and does not stop ... unless sometimes it does when we get to work. Here, sit down awhile, Dabney. You seem a bit tired and bewildered."

"Huh? Yes, I'm not feeling too good," I replied, scarcely aware of his words.

There were several snickers from those in the room. The twins were reaching for the stars and instead today I'd handed them mud. Galldern that Marshall Galldern.

* * *

Later that day, the phone in my new office began to ring. I answered it. Daisy was on the line.

I spoke, "Hi, hon. No, I'm better now. A doctor gave me a shot to pep me up. I think I was just tired and delirious from having that darn rooster wake me up so early this morning. I suppose it'll take me a while to get used to these new surroundings."

"Wayne said something about you seeing another rooster. What's with that?"

"Just my mind playing tricks on me, I imagine."

"Come home early, and please pick up something for dinner. I don't feel like cooking."

"I hear tell they make a great grilled chicken here. I'll bring home a bucket."

"Terrific! See you in a while. Are we still going shopping with the boys for a Christmas tree tonight?"

"Oh, yes. I forgot about that. Sure, I should feel better by then."

When I got off, as I was driving home, I got hungry and reached into the bucket of chicken beside me. I took out a drumstick and began gnawing on it. It was delicious. Soon, I turned onto our cul-de-sac street and slowly approached our house. As I reached and readied to turn into the driveway, I suddenly saw dozens of chickens run into the street directly in front of my car. This was why the later incident with the dancing hens was such a déjà vu occurrence.

At any rate, I jammed on the brakes, but the chickens bounded off my grill and windshield. Feathers flew everywhere. My reaction was to swerve, and when I did ... the car ran into and knocked down the recently rebuilt brick mailbox. I quickly exited my car.

Like Clancy before me, I rushed to the front of my auto, no doubt expecting to see dead chickens lying everywhere. None were there; not a single feather or any sign of them.

I looked about, turned, and then looked up into the cloudy sky. I raised my arms and tilted back my head.

I mumbled, "Cut down on the caffeine, Dabney. Tomorrow, go see an optometrist ... and then a shrink."

I stared disgustedly at the mailbox, got back into my car, and pulled into the driveway. I parked and got out. As I did, I noticed the bumper and front right quarter panel of my car was dented, and the mailbox was ruined ... yet again.

I reached back inside the car to remove the bucket of grilled chicken I'd brought home for dinner. I forgot and left the drumstick piece I'd eaten laying on the console. As I strolled up the sidewalk, I heard the gleeful sounds of laughter that came from the backyard. I glanced over the waist-high stone wall into the yard and saw my two boys having fun and playing on their new slide, swing set, and play fort that Wayne and Dwayne bought for them. Little Cah Cah that was dressed warmly in her coat and gloves saw me and ran toward me at the wall. Also wearing a pink toboggan cap, she peeked over the short wall and grinned up at me.

"Yippee! Dah Dah's home."

I leaned over and patted her on the head. She ran towards the back door, I smiled and waved to the boys. With the bucket of chicken in hand, I headed back towards the front door.

When I made my way up the three front steps, I opened the door and attempted to walk inside. However, some inexplicable invisible force stopped me. Rather, I should say my body was inside, but I couldn't seem to bring the bucket of chicken into the house.

"What the heck?" I cried. "What's going on?"

I angered and pulled as hard as I was able, but the bucket remained outside the door. Frustrated, I yanked harder and the paper bucket holding the chicken tore in two. The pieces tumbled to the ground and spilled all across the concrete floor of the covered front porch.

I heard Daisy calling me. I tossed down the torn bucket and walked back out to pick up the scattered chicken. Before I could do so, each piece seemed to come to life. The two wings flapped and made their way over to where the two breasts were lying. Then the two thighs and the one uneaten leg all joined like wires retracting and pulling themselves together back into their original shape.

Before my disbelieving eyes, the carcass of separated grilled chicken parts reassembled itself and hobbled off the front porch, falling down the steps and onto the lawn. I could only stare silently in complete puzzlement, as then the other leg I had partially eaten rolled out of the front car seat and fell onto the concrete driveway. It then lifted vertically, as the reassembling chicken waved a beckoning wing to indicate it should roll over and join onto the other 'parts is parts' restored carcass. The bony leg spun several revolutions under the car, onto the lawn, and finally reunited and reattached itself to the self-reconstructed chicken carcass.

The grilled yard bird wobbled away, looking like a naked peg-legged sailor with no head.

It stumbled across the lawn and ran smack into an oak tree. It fell, backed off, wobbled out to the curb, and then into the street.

About that same time, little Cah Cah came racing through the house. She zipped through the open front door and leaped into my arms.

"Dah Dah, welcome home."

Unable to take my focus off the staggering chicken corpse, I hugged her and glanced over her shoulder at that re-animated, creeping, unknown species of meat that was attempting to escape to God knows where.

Suddenly, a large red-tailed hawk appeared in the sky, swooped down at the reassembled pullet, grabbed it in its claws ... and although struggling a bit, managed to fly away with it into a nearby, tall tree.

Daisy soon joined Cah Cah and me on the porch. I hugged and kissed my daughter, and then handed her off to Daisy. I was dumbfounded, and frustrated, and kept glancing up into the tree about a block away.

Daisy noticed my distraction and asked, "What are you looking at, dear?"

In a statue-like repose, I stood there gawking. I feared my sanity was evaporating like a ghost. My finger shook and I pointed it in the direction of the tree where that ... that thing got snatched up and taken by the hawk.

"It ... it got up and wobbled away," I said in a tormented voice.

"What wobbled away? What are you talking about?"

I shook my head, forced a smile, and clapped my hands to my face. Daisy shook her head, and then I saw that she noticed the dent in the car's fender and bent bumper. She pointed and I shook my head in sinking despair.

"Don't ask," I stated with a bowed head. Then I sternly told her, "We're going out for dinner."

"Why? Didn't you bring home the grilled chicken?" she asked. "I see the torn bucket here, but where's the chicken?"

Her face was quiet, and a curious look was in her eyes.

I exuded a sarcastic laugh. "Where's the chicken?" I paused and pointed my finger again, but soon retracted it. My frail soul was besieged with an image I'd never be able to forget.

"Where's the chicken, you ask? Uh ... well, I shall not one minute longer discuss that. Get your coat, and then you two get in the car. I'll go get the boys."

Once my family was all inside the car, I backed out of the driveway. As the kids played and cut up in the back seat, Daisy glanced out her passenger window. As the car pulled out of the drive, she noticed the fallen remnants of the destroyed mailbox lying in the yard and street. She pointed at the rubble.

"My gosh! What happened to the—"

"Don't ask about that either," I stated and changed the subject. "After diner, are you kids up to going to help pick out our Christmas tree?"

In unison, the three of them all yelled out, "Yes!" Cah Cah added, "Can we go see Santa too?"

"I'm not sure he's here yet, but you'll see him soon," I told her.

Daisy and I had a surprise in store for the kids that we were certain would take them over the moon, but we didn't want to tell them yet. Instead, we'd take them there and show them. It was something we discovered that was the likes of which we found amazing. We were confident the kids would too.

Up till then though, what a day it had been. It began with that stupid rooster crowing so early this morning, then that cartoonish Marshall Galldern, us inexplicably speaking in 'P' words, and now the reassembled carcass and incredible escape of our chicken dinner. One had to wonder what was to come next.

Although I acted calm and cool among the kids, in truth I was like an iceberg. That part of me that was visible above the water and sanity line appeared tranquil and composed. However, those other three-quarters of me below the surface were consumed by jerky agitation and a gnawing, creeping stupor that chiseled away at my brain. I needed clarity and instead, my mind was shuttered and could make no sense of it all.

* * *

We drove into Lancaster and ate at an exclusive Inn that combined old-world charm with innovative American cuisine. They served steaks, chops, prime rib, fresh seafood, and the chef's daily specials. As well as a full menu, we were also offered a children's menu. Daisy and I ate prime rib, while the kids ordered off the kid's menu. I seriously considered ordering just a salad and contemplated becoming a vegetarian. Although it was on the menu, now I had no desire to attempt dining on grilled chicken.

Anyway, it was an enjoyable outing and helped revive my spirits somewhat. My kids were always a good remedy when I felt depressed or in need of being cheered up. Daisy knew I was holding something back, but she didn't press the issue. Instead, she was the wonderful, supporting spouse and mate she'd always been.

After dinner, she grabbed my hand under the table, looked me in the eye, and then attempted to pull me out of my sinkhole doldrums.

"We love you, dear. I hope you're feeling better now."

I smiled at her and squeezed her hand.

"I love you all too and thanks. It was a long day and I'm just tired."

I was like a car driving in the dark with its engine running, but with the headlights off.

Twenty minutes later, we were strolling through a Christmas tree lot attempting to choose just the right tree to place in the large den of our new home. Dippy and Dooby had their favorites, but in the end, the final decision came down to Cah Cah's preference. The tree the boys liked would not fit on top of my car, but the one Cah Cah wanted was like the bed Goldilocks picked out upstairs in the house of the Three Bears. It was 'just right.'

Later back at home, we got the tree stabilized and in front of the den's big picture window that looked out onto the front yard and street. Dooby and I sauntered upstairs and into the sky parlor attic, where we began bringing down the lights, ornaments, and other items needed to decorate the tree and house. It was a happy, family occasion that brightened my outlook and took away the cloud of gloom I'd had earlier. Seeing the excitement on my kids' faces and after the boys set up our ceramic manger scene, it hit home to me that there was hope. I needed to be strong and overcome whatever it was that plagued me these past few days.

# CHAPTER 12: Dr. Peekup Andropoff

At daybreak the next morning, I was roused from sleep again by that phantom crowing rooster that only I could see or hear. I bounded out of bed, took a shower, and got ready ... but not to go into the plant. It was a Friday and Wayne, and Dwayne was going duck hunting again. I decided I needed professional help to discuss the things that had been happening since we got here. I'd gotten online before going to bed last night and searched for a qualified psychologist in our area. There were several, but I chose one and after breakfast, I was on my way to his office to see about arranging a session with him.

An hour later, after his 11:00 A.M. appointment got canceled, the psychologist agreed to see me. His female assistant took me into a quiet room with ornate, warm wood-paneled walls and thick, plush carpeting. There were no outside windows and the only light came from a dimly lit lamp next to a leather armchair. Across from the chair was a leather couch and on a nearby table there burned a scented candle whose flame gave off the soothing fragrance of blooming roses.

The assistant told me to lie down and relax on the backless couch that slanted upward to support one's head and upper body. I did as she suggested and then folded my hands across my chest. I noticed several framed certificates on the wall that touted the doctor's degrees, pedigrees, and the many certificates of achievement and certified affirmations of his professional accomplishments and abilities.

She left the room and a few minutes later, the oak door from the doctor's private office opened, and in he strolled. He was tall, thin, had thick, dark hair tapering to his collar, and a hawk nose characterized by its small bend in the middle and pointed sharp edge. The golden light of the candle reflected off his high cheekbones and below his long nose was a thin mouth lifted in mute invitation. He smoked a long, curved pipe, and what appeared to me clothing that resembled that of a man born a century ago. He puffed his pipe and then exhaled a circle of smoke that curled about his head. He looked at me, smiled, and glided into the comfortable-looking armchair next to the couch. Crossing his longs legs, his sharp and assessing eyes trailed over my form on the couch.

He had a pen and pad lying on the small table next to him, picked it up, and studied what was written on it a moment before speaking. I'd explained to the assistant that I wanted to see him and discuss some rather odd things that have been occurring to my family and me.

He grunted, turned in his chair to face me, and spoke in an odd, yet gentle tone, "Good morning, Mr. Doodledoom. I am Dr. Peekup Andropoff. I understand that you're here to discuss some issues of concern to you and your family."

"Yes, Sir, I am," I told him. "And my last name's, Doodledoo. You can call me, Dabney."

"Very well, Dabney. And you may call me, Dr. Andropoff."

Hearing that, I wondered if I was consulting with a doctor or a Ukrainian Uber driver.

"Now, suppose we start by you explaining to me ... what is it that brings you to see a renowned psychologist like myself," he bragged candidly.

I paused and immediately realized that this man with a thick Russian accent was really into himself.

"Well, doctor, I was brought here by my late-model Jeep Wrangler."

He lifted his chin, waggled the pipe in his teeth, and then I met his brown-eyed icy stare head-on with one of my own. I did not await further comment but presented him with a sneer.

"Your room has charming, rich paneling, an entire wall assembly of your impressive, renowned credentials, but I'm sorry that you can't afford better lighting in here," I said sarcastically. "I know that you're likely far better educated than me and probably much brighter than your lights here, but if you will just tone down your ego a bit and concentrate on the care of my id with your odd, I'd be grateful," I boldly commented.

I wasn't sure why I'd been so rude to the man, but I was frustrated and needed to take out my irritation on someone I suppose ... especially since it was costing me two hundred dollar bills an hour.

He came back with a response that I knew would be clever.

"You know, Dabney, people who think they know everything are very irritating to those of us who do."

At that, I broke out into laughter, and then we each chuckled together. Obviously, the ice between us had been broken and thawed somewhat, so now I could relax more and we could get on with the session.

He glanced down and began writing on his notepad.

"Where are you from, Doc, and is that Russian accent of yours real?" I asked.

"I am here from the next room. Did you not see me enter?"

I grinned and said, "Touché! I suppose I deserved that. Sorry about gigging you over the lights and paneling ... and you do have impressive credentials."

He smirked again and glanced at the items on his walls. "Yes, they are impressive. I think the man that framed and printed them did excellent work." He stated in his silky, sarcastic voice. His tone indicated to me that his intent was teasing and not malicious.

I saw his eyebrows raise and the mystery in his eyes beckoned me to open up and say something about why I was there. I smiled and didn't disappoint him.

"Well, you see, Doc, it all started a few days ago when we moved to Paradise from Miami. My wife and I are partners with the Kockle twins there that own a hatchery and poultry processing plant. We went into business with them in a lucrative restaurant venture. They bought us ... rather I should say, and they gave us a large luxurious home. Nevertheless, ever since then, wacky things have been happening. Whatever's causing it has also somewhat affected my family and even my twin boys and young daughter."

The doctor shuffles in his chair and sits up straight. I saw a gleam of interest spark in his eyes, or were those dollar signs?

"Now let me get this straight, Dabney. You're saying that you're partners with the Kockle twins ... two of the wealthiest people within Pennsylvania ... and that you're involved in a lucrative venture that will no doubt bring you a handsome return on investment? In other words, you are rich?"

I nodded my head, and he pushed a buzzer on the table next to him. He laid his pipe in an ashtray with a pipe rest. A moment later, the assistant opened the door to the front office and stepped inside.

"Ms. Williams, make a note. Mr. Doodledome here will require ... oh, let's say a dozen sessions or more. He will be an A-rated patient, so please schedule him a future two-hour session for next Monday."

I noticed that as he was speaking to her, the Russian accent he'd used dropped away and he now sounded like a guy from Brooklyn. The assistant acknowledged his commands and left the room. I would learn later that being an A-rated patient meant she was to raise my hourly rate from two-hundred dollars an hour to five-hundred dollars. While I thought of my problems as adversity, he saw them as an opportunity.

"Now, where were we, Dabney?" he said, returning to his fake Russian accent. "Please go on and be as thorough as you'd like. There's no rush. So what sorts of things have been happening that cause you grief?"

I looked at him with amused wonder. He was quite a piece of work, this one. We exchanged polite simultaneous smiles and I continued.

"I don't know how to accurately explain it, but I've been hearing and seeing things that are just absurdly weird and couldn't possibly be real."

"Weird how? Describe what you've been experiencing."

I laid back and stared at the ceiling and the shadows cast there by the flickering candle.

"Well, for one thing, I started hearing ducks quaking, honking geese, and turkey gobbles. I've been woken up at daybreak by a crowing rooster that only I can see or hear. If that weren't bad enough, at a conference meeting at the plant yesterday, I saw and heard a cartoon-looking rooster wearing cowboy attire that spoke to me and issued me some sort of caution ... or maybe it was a warning."

The doctor asked, "I see, and did anyone else in the meeting see or hear that rooster?".

"No, but I can tell you that to me it seemed very real and disturbing."

"So in other words, your problem is you're hallucinating; seeing and hearing things that no one else does. Is that correct?"

"Yes, and for some strange reason, my wife, me, the Kockle twins, and even my kids have at times had moments when we were plagued by predicaments and proceeded to pronounce in procession peculiar 'P' words like we were puppets." I cringed when I heard my own words.

In spite of himself, he chuckled, paused a moment, his dark eyes lowered, and he continued to write down something on his pad.

"Words that begin with a 'P' you say? And all of you were affected by such an anomaly?"

"Yes, all of us, and as I stated ... even my three kids," I told him.

"Might you have possibly just imagined that?" His eyes clung to me analyzing my reaction.

"I don't believe so. It was like we were all victims of some odd mental contagion that invaded our thoughts and made us talk like that."

"Hmmm, interesting. And what you're hearing and seeing has to do with chickens, roosters, and cartoon characters?"

"Yes!

"I see ... Go on!"

"And it's getting worse. Last night when I drove home, I saw a flock of chickens run in front of my car. I swerved to avoid them, but instead hit and knocked down our brick mailbox. Then, when I tried to carry in a box of grilled chicken I brought home for supper, some invisible force wouldn't allow me to bring it into the house. Instead, the pieces tore from the bucket, reassembled into a re-animated carcass there on my front lawn, and stumbled away ... only to get snapped up by a hawk."

"Wait, are you saying cooked pieces of grilled chicken just reassembled and gathered themselves back into a whole chicken?"

His face formed a bewildered look and he studied me like I was a lab rat in a cage.

"Except for the head and feathers...Yes. That's it exactly," I said. "And the one drumstick that I'd nibbled on didn't have much meat left on it ... when it tumbled out of my car seat and rolled onto the ground to connect up with the other pieces."

The doctor's eyes were shadowy and unfathomable. He muttered to himself, drew a deep breath, and then wrote a lot more onto his pad. I shuddered and felt humiliated, but sensed I had to tell him the truth.

"Am I going crazy, Doc?"

Before answering, he took a few moments; scribbled some more onto his pad, and then took another puff or two from his pipe. He uncrossed his legs, raised his head, and shot me a twisted smile.

"Uhhh, no more than the rest of us I suppose. From what you tell me, it may be that you're having hypnopompic delusions, perhaps the result of anxiety and stress ... due to the stressful move here from Miami."

I stared at him with intense astonishment and wondered how he was not stunned by what I'd told him.

Instead, he was cool and aloof.

"You told my assistant you lost your job of ten years in Ohio, moved your family thousands of miles away to Florida, and now you've started a new venture in the restaurant business. You've uprooted them again and moved here to Paradise, taken on greater responsibility, and you're in the poultry business. Therefore, perhaps because of the pent-up stress, you manifest visions and hear the voices of chickens and roosters when you wake. It's all quite simple really."

I was amazed by his composed appraisal and astonished by how confident he was of his presumption. Some of what he said made sense to me.

"You think so? I suppose it does seem plausible when you explain it like that, but –"

Before he could go on, his assistant opened the door again and stepped inside.

"I beg your pardon, doctor, but Bob Wiley is on the phone," she said.

"Bob? What about, Bob?"

"He claims to be on top of a bridge and says he's going to jump off unless he talks to you."

"Nonsense, he's only doing that to garnish my attention."

"Perhaps so, but he claims he has tickets to a Neil Diamond concert, and if you won't go with him, he's going to kill himself."

"Neil Diamond tickets? On what row and which night?"

The doctor slammed his pad down on the table, angrily stood, and turned to me.

"I'm very sorry, Mr. Doodledrip ... err, I mean, Dobney. I'd better take the call. I'll just be a moment. Relax here and I'll be back after I see where the seats are ... I mean when I settle this matter with my other patient."

The doctor and assistant exited the room and closed the door behind them. I was left alone in the somber, solitude of semi-darkness and surrounded by oak walls that seemed to be closing in on me. A few silent seconds passed, and then out of curiosity I sat up and saw that the doctor left the pad onto which he had been scribbling.

Unable to resist the temptation, I sat down in his armchair and picked up the pad. I read the words he'd written there and was disturbed by what I read:

"Mad as a March hare ... Irrational ... Rich, but his compass does not point north ... Perhaps he has mercury poisoning ... lives in a topsy-turvy fantasy world ... I'd need an industrial torque wrench to tighten all the loose nuts and bolts in his noggin ... on next visit, offer him a trail mix of nuts and fruits, for he's mentally ill ... has a brain as inflated as a soap bubble."

I was devastated and felt like I was a wedding cake left out in the rain. I wished I'd not been so nosey. The last words he wrote down before leaving to take the call were:

"Save Bob ... go to concert ... get Neil's autograph."

As I stewed in self-pity, I stood and returned to my place on the couch. I plopped back and put my hands over my eyes. Suddenly, I heard someone sit down in the doctor's chair. I thought he'd returned and caught me going over his notes. I shrugged, glanced over, and instead saw that cantankerous cartoon, Marshall Rooster Galldern, sitting there smirking. The doctor's lighted pipe hung from his beak and he exhaled a smoke ring with the image of a small chick inside it. When the smoke vanished in a whiff, so did the chick. As before, Rooster's dialect was in John Wayne's drawl.

"I don't favor talkin' to vermin, Pilgrim, but I'll listen to you just this once."

I was angered and raised my hand as if to say something. He scoffed at me and lifted his winged-tip hand.

I cried out, "No! You're not real. Like the doctor said; you're just some stupid figment of my imagination."

"Whoa! Take 'er easy, Pilgrim. I wouldn't make a habit of callin' me no figment."

Rooster pulled down his eye patch, glared at me with both eyes, and then snarled.

"Son, you're about as dim as a dyin' lightning bug. Out here, a man settles his problems and doesn't need to visit no, Bogeyman to look for answers. Courage is being scared to death but etting' up anyway."

I heard something scrambling across the floor. I rolled over on my side and saw a large cartoon rat scurrying across the room. Rooster whipped out his slingshot and loaded it up with an egg.

He aimed it at the rat and declared, "Mr. Rat, I have a writ, writ for a fat rat, which makes it a fat rat writ for a rat like that. You are hereby ordered to cease and desist."

The rat stopped, looked back at Rooster, and sneered. Rooster drew back his slingshot and let fire with an egg, which splattered on the rat. Soaked in the yoke, it moaned and stumbled slowly into a hole in the wall.

"See what I mean, Pilgrim? You can't bargain with a fat rat, you just have to shell it. Now get up, son, cause couches are only good for one thing ... and I don't mean a lyin' there and etting' that worthless varmint breeze through your noggin and trample his foreign-educated hoofs all over your whispering secrets."

Then the door opened, and the doctor walked back inside. He smiled and picked up his pad. As he sat down on his chair, Rooster's image quickly vanished, and he was gone.

"Now, where we, Dobney?"

I looked around and not seeing my fowl nemesis annoyed me.

"It's Dabney, and I think we're done here."

I was disconcerted, incoherent, and perplexed.

"Come now, tell me more about your delusions and the unpleasant anxiety you've been dealing with these past few days."

"Mad as a March hare, am I? Well, Mary had a little lamb ... its fleas were in the snow. I'm a squirrel with nuts and bolts ... and it's time for me to go."

I bolted off the couch, raced for the door, and bounded out of the office. The doctor calmly rose, walked to the door, and motioned to his assistant.

He waved at me as I left, "Okay, upsy-daisy you go, huh? Well, toodle-oo, Mr. Doodle-doo-doo. You tutti-frutti has gone twenty-three skidoo. See you on Monday."

He instructed her, "Send in the next patient, Ms. Décolletage, and bill Mr. Doodledork's poultry plant for an A-rated two-hour session."

He then paused and scratched his chin. "Second-row seats for Neil, eh? Not too bad, Bob."

# CHAPTER 13: Quacked Up Holidays

As I was leaving that "quack doctor's" office, Wayne and Dwayne were involved with their adventure ... another quacked-up duck hunt on the pond by the plant. As before, Dwayne was determined to shoot another fowl trophy for his den wall. The last duck he thought he shot here was one Wayne had brought from the freezer in their plant. It was forty-six degrees outside today and each of them was dressed in warm camouflaged clothing.

This time though, Wayne couldn't convince any of the plant employees to suit up in armor. Therefore, although he knew it would disappoint his twin, he planned to allow Wayne to miss targeting or shooting any ducks. Hidden speakers along by the cattails near the shoreline would blare out duck calls on Wayne's command.

After fifteen minutes of silence between them, as they waited, Dwayne remarked," I've been working on developing a computer program that will interpret a chicken's clucking into English so that we'll know what they're saying to us."

Wayne looked at his brother and gently rocked back and forth in his seat in the small boat.

"Yeah, and how's that coming along?" he asked, as he blew on his hands to keep them warm.

"So far, all I've been able to accomplish is that two clucks and a cackle mean they want food, and then a cackle, followed by three clucks, means they need to poop."

He mockingly asked, "You figured that out, did you?" Wayne laughed, and then said, "Pretend I'm a chicken. What am I telling you?"

Wayne puckered up his mouth and rattled, "Cluck, cluck, cackle, cackle, cluck, cackle."

Dwayne grinned and seemed disconcerted, as Wayne awaited Dwayne's anticipated response.

He teased, "I'm not sure I heard you right. Could you repeat that?"

Wayne sneered and said, "No! You heard it. What'd I say, Mr. Chicken?"

"Cluck, cackle, cluck cackle, cluck, cluck, cackle, cluck."

"That's no answer. What'd I say in chicken?" Wayne teased.

"I'm not sure, but I replied in chicken and said ... no, I'm not going to give you Karen's phone number, so quit asking."

"You rat fink. I told you, I saw her first, so when are you going to give up and let me have that?" Wayne demanded.

"Never! So, quit asking me, in English or in chicken," replied Dwayne.

"You know, you can't steal second base with one foot on first. What good is it with you having her number and not being able to read what it is?

"Clancy can read, and he did so for me," said Dwayne.

"You're lying. I told him not to do that."

"Yes, but he likes me better than he does you, so he told me anyway. I guess she does too, for it was to me that she gave her phone number," chortled Dwayne.

Wayne squirmed in his seat. He was incensed with his brother's stubborn resistance in providing the phone number of the attractive young woman he'd bumped into at the airport. He wasn't a hundred percent sure Dwayne had it, but he reasoned that it must be what was written on the piece of paper she gave him.

Wayne grumbled, "Don't tell me you've called her."

"Not yet, but I will any day now. It's the holidays and I expect she's busy with plans to be with her dad and family."

About then, to Wayne's utter surprise, a real flock of ducks began to fly overhead. Dwayne scrambled with his shotgun and stood up in the boat as the ducks began to circle and land a football field away. Wayne tried to steady his brother, but Dwayne stepped forward and as he did, he tripped over the aluminum seat in front of them. As he was falling forward, the shotgun pointed downward and his finger pulled the trigger.

With the shotgun blast, the ducks roused flew up in the air and were soon out of sight. Meanwhile, a hole the size of a softball was blown into the bottom of their boat. Pond water began to shoot up like a fountain through the hole. Wayne stuck his hands over the gusher, but it was to no avail. Their craft was beginning to fill with cold water.

Dwayne dropped his shotgun and grabbed the cell phone inside his jacket. He spoke in a voice command to his phone.

"Google, Dial 911."

As he did that, Wayne began to row towards shore. He'd not had anyone onshore this time with a rope to pull them in, and his efforts did nothing to delay the fact that the water was quickly rising in the boat. Where they were in the pond, it was about fifteen feet deep to the bottom.

A computerized female voice on Dwayne's phone answered and asked, "Did you say, dial 411?"

"No!" exclaimed Dwayne. "I said, dial 911."

The voice then stated, "Okay, I'll dial 191."

Dwayne got very annoyed and yelled, "No, Google. Dial the emergency numbers, 9-1-1."

"The voice came again, "I'm sorry but that function isn't available now."

Wayne grabbed the phone and dialed the numbers 9-1-1 for Dwayne. Then he handed the phone back to Dwayne and returned to rowing.

Soon, a composed male voice on the other end of the line asked, "What is your emergency?"

Dwayne said loudly, "Send help! Our boat is sinking."

The emergency operator then asked, "What is your position, Sir?"

Dwayne's face reflected his irritation and he retorted in cold sarcasm, "I'm Vice-President in charge of production at Stupid Questions, Inc."

As Wayne feverishly panted and rowed, the boat somehow remained afloat long enough to get them to within thirty feet of the shoreline.

The male voice of the emergency response operator stated, "Sir, I can't help you unless we know where you're located."

As the boat sank beneath them, each brother sloshed out into the cold pond, stood chest-deep in the muddy water, and wallowed onto the shore. Dripping wet, Wayne fell onto his back and lay onto the damp ground.

"Sir, are you still there?" He asks again, "Where are you located?"

Dwayne snarled and commented to the operator, "We're in a phone booth at the corner of Walk and Don't Walk. Disregard this call, as we've both drowned. This is a recording."

Wayne started laughing, as Dwayne disconnected the call and plopped down beside his twin.

"I'm glad we left Sweetroll at home this time. He'd be mad that his cinnamon buns got wet," said Dwayne.

Then the sound of something familiar startled them, as the noon alarm at the plant depicting it was lunch hour sounded. Its blaring buzzer made Dwayne smile.

He asked, "Is the ice cream truck here? And no, you can't have her number."

\* \* \*

When I got home from seeing Dr. Andropoff, I gathered my clan again and loaded them into our car for a foray into Amish country there in Lancaster County. It was a chilly day, but not cold enough to be much of a bother, plus from having lived in Ohio we were used to this kind of weather. As long as there was no rain or snow, we were ready to go. I figured the fresh air would do us all good. Besides, it was time for Daisy and me to show our kids something that would delight and amaze them.

It was only four days till Christmas, and snow was predicted for two days from then, so I wanted to let the kids experience some of what Daisy and I saw on our excursion with the Kockle twins.

One of the surprises I wanted to spring on the boys was that I'd heard the Amish were famous for their puppy farms, so perhaps on our visits today we could find a suitable dog for them. That would be a nice Christmas gift I thought. They had been real troopers in allowing Goldie to remain in Ohio with our friends. When in Miami, getting a dog was not an option, but now that we had a large home and huge backyard, a dog would be a welcomed addition to our family. I was certain Cah Cah would love one too.

So, I was determined not to allow the dissatisfaction of my visit to the psychologist to ruin the day. Instead, I focused my attention on the headlong zest of a big game hunter on enjoying this outing, the quiet landscapes of this beautiful land, and away from any of my delusional, shadowy world of Poultry-Geists.

On our drive through town, our first stop was at the place Daisy and I was anxious to visit and show the kids. Cah Cah was too young to read, but when she saw us pull up in front of the National Christmas Center Museum located right there in Paradise, her eyes widened and she became very alert. Dooby read the sign in front out loud, and when she heard the word Christmas, Cah Cah screamed with joy. The kids all bounded out of the car and headed inside, followed closely by Daisy and me.

While I bought the tickets, the white-bearded man that greeted us at the center called himself, "Santa Jr." He bore a striking resemblance to a certain jolly old elf. We learned that he was the owner and founder of the center and delighted in making people happy and giving them a place to forget about their problems. I for one found that idea very comforting and needing. He told us it gave folks time to think about the reason for the season, plus it was somewhere children could come and have the magic of Christmas their parents had when they were children.

He told us, "I wanted it to be a place that brings back the true spirit of Christmas that he felt had been lost in commercialism."

The first thing Dippy noticed and was drawn to was all the toy trains set up in the lobby. We each had our favorite displays, as we wandered the museum's fifteen main galleries. There was the "Tudor Towne's" animated storybook village, a "Journey to Bethlehem," and we were filled with glee over vintage decorations that Daisy and I remembered from our childhood. The center took us on a journey through Christmas history. There were Nativity sets gathered going back two hundred years; a "Street of Memories" and shopping; Christmas traditions around the world; toy trains; countless Santa figures, lighted trees; animated displays and decorations, plus much more. That day, there was even a live Santa there in the North Pole at the "Santa's Workshop" area. All the kids, even Dooby sat in his lap and whispered to the old gentleman what they wished for Christmas. We even learned that the first known written mention of a Christmas tree in America was found in the 1821 diary of Matthew Zahn, who lived near here in Lancaster, PA.

I enjoyed seeing the 1950s "Christmas Morning" display, for it made me think of my father and how he used to describe that decade when he was a child. We saw the old bubble lights he described, plus there was a rotating color projector under the tree, and also one under what looked like a silver tin foil tree that changed colors as the light shone upon it.

There was even a display for the old F.W. Woolworth five and dime store he used to describe to me. He said it almost always smelled like walking into a popcorn-scented lobby like that in a movie theater. There was even a life-sized Nativity scene with the baby Jesus. All in all, we had a marvelous time and the visit helped us all get in more joyful spirits. However, it did sadden us to learn the center had to close a week after New Year's due to the owner's advancing age and health, plus the fact that the center never turned a profit. The woman at the counter told us they were looking for a buyer to maybe keep it open, but no offers had come in as of yet. We all hoped it could somehow remain open and find a new owner.

Later that afternoon, we drove through Lancaster County and away from the hustle of city life to the quiet surroundings of Amish country. This was not our kids' first time witnessing how the Amish lived. In Ohio, we'd visited a few times the Berlin area of eastern Ohio where several Amish farms and families were located. However, here in Lancaster County, there was a much larger presence and Amish influence. Although it was a bit breezy, we took a ride in a horse-drawn carriage through the beautiful and unforgettable Pennsylvania Dutch country landscape, while we watched the everyday routines of the Amish through hilly back roads.

Later, Daisy browsed handmade arts, crafts, and other products and we all experienced the simpler life of the Amish people. We spent time on an Amish fifteen-acre farm. There was fun for the whole family, as we fed and petted farm animals, rode an Amish scooter, explored an Amish-built schoolhouse, walked across a covered bridge, sat in Amish buggies, and much more.

While on that farm, I learned about who I needed to contact about getting a dog for the kids. I took the info and would go back the next day to get a puppy. I decided I'd wait to give the kids that surprise on Christmas morning.

Nearing dark and back in Lancaster city, the joyous celebration continued as we viewed the vast array of festive, colorful lights that began to twinkle and shine right after dusk. We parked in town and got out to walk among the many venues, from delightful out-of-the-way shops selling unique wares made by local artisans, to outlet shops representing nationally known brands. It made it easy to find something for even that most difficult to buy for friends ... like the Kockle twins.

We strolled from shop to shop, taking in the decorations, the music, and the spirit of the season. As Daisy and the kids browsed one store, I discovered a unique shop that sold music boxes. I found one that I knew she would love to have. So, I bought it and had it wrapped for her to put under the tree at home. The music box had sapphire-colored Swarovski crystals and two beautiful, white doves sculptured on the lid. It played "On the Wings of Love."

Going home, we drove past residence after residence where we saw images from joyful holidays past, present, and future that appeared to us filled our eyes and made this one of the sweetest days I could recall in several years. For the first time to me, Paradise seemed like home.

# CHAPTER 14: Going Bonkers

That night, Daisy and I lay awake, each of us resting in bed on our backs. We had our eyes open and seemed to be in deep thought. I smiled as I remembered what we'd done that day and what we saw. Daisy stretched, yawned, and then broke the silence.

"So, what do you think about what the psychologist told you this morning?"

I rolled over and faced her, as my smile faded into a frown of surprise.

"Huh? What are you talking about?" I asked and feigning like I didn't know what she meant.

"Come on, dear, tell me what he said. His assistant called here to have me remind you of your follow-up session scheduled for Monday, at 1:00 P.M."

Knowing that the cat was out of the bag, I grumbled, "That sorry quack!"

She moved to hug me in a gesture of comfort and concern.

"It's okay, Dabney. I know you've been uptight lately, we both have, so if you felt you needed to talk to a psychologist I understand."

Her sweet voice caroled like a gold-caged nightingale. Shocked and embarrassed by her learning of my visit, I fawned before her and hid my face in her chest. I tried to remain calm, but words fell from my lips like I was a dumb, neglected lap dog.

"I ... think maybe he was right. Perhaps I am too stressed out, but the things I've heard and seen just can't be imaginary. At least not to me," I blubbered

My emotions got the better of me and I felt like my self-control was breaking up like some great frozen river's ice at the touch of spring.

"Am I going insane, Daisy?" I whimpered.

"Now, dear, who wouldn't be stressed? I mean with your new job and that stupid invisible rooster waking us up this morning, you have to be tired."

"Yeah, I guess so," I stated.

Suddenly realizing what she'd just said, I bounded up in bed and looked at her with a wide-eyed expression.

"Hey, wait a minute! You mean, you also heard the rooster crow?" I asked.

She looked at me and snarled her lips, "I did this morning. It made my skin crawl. Then, when I was making breakfast, I opened a cabinet door to get a pan. As I did so, I swear I thought I saw a hen race between my legs chasing after some scrambled eggs and ham."

"You saw a chicken? Are you sure it wasn't a rooster dressed like a cowboy?"

"No, it was a hen, and as I bent down and watched between my legs, it ran away ... and disappeared ... right into the wall." She paused and tears began to form in her eyes. "Am I going crazy too?"

I bit down on my bottom lip, leaped out of bed, and paced angrily about the room.

"No, I don't think so, for insanity isn't contagious. Something's going on here though that we don't understand, and that quack doctor I saw believes it's just some Hypno-something-or-other condition brought on by tension and lack of sleep."

"Then what is going on? Please, if you can explain this ... I may be able to get some sleep by tomorrow night."

The anxiety drifted among us like a dark, impenetrable cloud. Our new home and this isle of Paradise, although a gem, seemed like a brooding place with spirits drawing us into a landscape of unknown confusion and mental anguish.

Daisy put her hands on her face and wept into her pillow. I sat on the edge of the bed and tried to comfort her.

"I'm not sure what this is all about, but cheer up hon; at least you're not seeing cartoon roosters."

She sobbed again into her pillow, "No, not yet anyway."

With that, her pillow began to stretch and move under her head. I couldn't believe my eyes, as I saw it squirm, break free from her grasp, and then roll onto the bed covers ... where it then burst open and hundreds of goosedown feathers began to float through the air. We each bolted from the bed, ran from the room, and slammed the door behind us. Down the hall, we ran into the bedroom where our boys were asleep. Daisy raced into Cah Cah's room, grabbed her out of bed, and came in with the rest of us. We never explained our actions to the kids that night, but the next day I threw away all our down-filled pillows. Then, I planned on getting the, orneriest egg-sucking bird dog puppy I could find.

* * *

That next new morning our pesky, ghostly alarm clock rooster woke Daisy and me at the usual early hour. Despite our being in two double beds drawn together as one, we were wrapped around our kids. At least, they managed to get some sleep that night.

Dippy groaned and fell out of bed. He grumbled, "When did we get a rooster in the house?"

His words made me cringe, for I hated that our kids were now being drawn into this madness as well. We ate breakfast, but had milk and cereal instead and avoided my usual scrambled eggs, toast, and bacon.

It was bad enough that we were haunted by poultry; I sure didn't want to offend any hogs and maybe see pigs fly too. All went fairly normal, that is until we walked into the den and saw that the ornaments on the trees had all turned into chicken heads with glowing red, blinking eyes. Cah Cah screamed and ran upstairs to her room. Dooby strolled cautiously over, thumped one of the heads ... and it squawked at him.

Instead of a star crowning the top of our tree, there was now a rooster's head that began a loud crowing sound that made us all scramble behind furniture. When I peeked over the back of our sectional sofa at the tree, the heads were gone and the star and ornaments were all back to normal. Was I wrong and these mental visions truly were contagious?

All of us were on guard and ill at ease the rest of that morning but attempted to go about our lives and normal routines. I thought of the song, "If Today Was A Fish, I'd Throw It Back In."

Daisy went shopping for our Christmas dinner, and I stayed home with the kids. We began wrapping the presents we'd already bought for the Kockle twins and Daisy. There were even a few under the tree that I'd not noticed that had my name on them. I placed the package with her music box under the tree. She'd pestered me on the way home about it last night, being curious as to what I'd gotten her.

The house was a mess, as we didn't make any of our beds that morning, toys were scattered around the den, and Daisy left without cleaning up the kitchen.

She was going to straighten up, but I told her a Phyllis Diller quote:

"Cleaning your house while your kids are still growing is like shoveling the walk while it's still snowing."

Knowing we'd be pressed for time when we moved here, Daisy and I purchased the kids' toys and things they'd get from Santa before we left Miami. The items were in storage and the plan was that all of them would be delivered tomorrow on Christmas Eve. While Daisy took the kids to a movie, I'd have the gifts placed in the garage, and then lock it so only I could get in there.

Cah Cah's little battery-operated car, her dollhouse, an "American Girl" doll, a personalized chef's hat, a happy holidays teddy bear, a tooth-fairy box in which to place the baby teeth she loses, plus a Barbie backpack; all would be ready for her to find under the tree on Christmas morning.

Dippy was to receive a new bicycle, a walking toy robot, a Lego police station, Thor's magic hammer, a telescope, a pound of gummy army soldiers, and a Flash costume.

Although Dooby no longer believed in Santa, he wanted a motor scooter, but I told him he'd have to wait a few more years. Instead, I bought him a set of L.E.D. lights for his bike wheels, a pair of binoculars, a Wham-O Frisbee, a four-propeller drone with a video camera, and a new Play station game with three new, non-violent video games.

Being Santa was one of the best things I've ever experienced in my life and Daisy and I always cherished those Christmas memories we've shared with our children.

Daisy went supermarket shopping, while the kids settled into the den to watch some television. I went into the kitchen and cleaned the few dishes we dirtied at breakfast. It was almost noon, and I wanted to watch the local news and get the weather forecast. I'd hoped for snow, but doubted we'd get any for Christmas.

As I dried my hands on a kitchen towel, the news started. Dippy yelled at me from the den.

"Hurry, Pop! It's almost time for the weather, and you don't want to miss ... <u>Marshall Galldern</u>."

Had I heard him right? Had he said, Marshall Galldern?

Then Dooby added, "He's right, Pop. This crazy rooster is a riot. You've got to see him."

I thought, "See him? I can't get rid of him."

Were they suffering from delusions like mine? I wondered and hoped that wasn't the case. I was led into the den by Cah Cah who tugged my arm and guided me into my recliner. I looked at my watch and hoped Daisy would get back by 1:00 P.M. so that I could go find us a puppy. I tried to act coy with the kids and not let on that I'd already seen Marshall Galldern ... and wasn't impressed. I was very curious about their excitement to watch him on television. Why and how could that possibly happen ... for he wasn't real ... was he?

After a commercial, as the news came back on, I attempted to think of something to divert my attention from the television. Daisy had also reminded me that the one gift we had yet to find Cah Cah was a Clown Fish for the aquarium. Cah Cah had been to see the movie, "Finding Nemo." When she saw the new house with the large aquarium, she asked why there was no Nemo. I'd looked on the Internet and found a place in Lancaster that had one, so I'd called and reserved it. I was to pick it up today, and hopefully, get a nice dog for us too ... preferably a bird dog puppy that would dislike poultry.

I sat nervously as I watched the T.V. and listened. When it was time for the weather, the newscaster said something that almost made me fall out of my chair.

He announced, "And now folks, it's time for the weather, so let's throw it over to our new weather expert and prognosticator, Marshall, Rooster Galldern."

I drew back in my chair and leaned against the headrest. My head felt as if it was spinning around like I was that possessed girl in the movie, "The Exorcist."

The newscaster commented, "I like your horse, Rooster."

In his usual cowboy garb, Rooster nodded to the newscaster, placed one foot into the stirrup of a worn saddle attached to a wooden sawhorse, and then swung his leg over and plopped his fluffy, feathered behind into the leather seat. He reached over the saddle horn and grabbed some leather reins attached to the plastic horse head of the sawhorse. Its tail was a stringy mop head.

Rooster commented in his John Wayne drawl, "Yep, I 'saw' this horse and had to rope and ride it. It's not as game as old Bo, but I heard tell it's what was left of a three-rail fence."

He then withdrew his slingshot and held the end like it was a water-dowsing rod. He pointed it at the weather map next to him and said, "Days are like the weather... some you love and others you hate. For all you little deputies gathered out there, I can promise it won't be a rainy or white Christmas. Instead, you'll have a balmy fifty-eight-degree clear day to take Santa's toys outside and play."

He kicked at the stirrups as if to spur on his sawhorse and continued speaking at the camera.

"I'm glad because you know; it's hard for me to lead a cavalry charge during a blizzard on a horse with such short legs as these."

Then I swear he looked straight into the camera and said, "And as for you, Pilgrim—"

When I heard him say that, I felt the hairs stand up on the back of my neck.

"It's too cold to sweat, but I can see from here that you're mind's like a door with no lock or key, as mysterious as a dust storm, as shocking as a lightning bolt, and you're as curious as a rain cloud about what's happening."

It was as if he spoke directly through that television to me.

He concluded his diatribe with, "There are some things a man or rooster just can't run away from. So, Pilgrim, just slap some bacon on a biscuit and let's go. You're burnin' daylight ... and there'll be plenty of that till New Year's Day before an arctic front comes strolling into town."

Then he winked and the scene switched back to the normal newscast. The kids screamed in joy. I screamed in disgust, clicked off the set with the remote, and ran to the kitchen where I turned on the sink faucet and placed my head underneath the cold water. I had no idea what all those things he said meant, but I knew it wouldn't be the last time I had to contend with that fowl scoundrel.

What was he referring to about running from something? Why should I care or listen to that mocking John Wayne cowboy pullet anyway? He was crazier than I am. And how and why was he on television if he wasn't real? But ... how could he be?

As I stood hunched over the sink about ready to spew my morning's cereal back up, the rear door opened, and in walked Daisy with a couple of sacks of groceries.

Seeing me, she asked, "Can I get some help bringing in the rest of the bags?"

I raised my head from the sink and slung water across the tiled floor.

Daisy set the bags on the kitchen island counter and yelled at me, "What are you doing, Dabney? You're getting water all over the floor."

Brushing a hand across my face and brows, I shot her a look that got her pulse racing.

Her hands flew to her mouth and quickly she asked, "Oh my word, what's wrong now?"

Our conversation became a monologue, for though I tried to speak, no words could escape my mouth. I just stood there and dripped, as water began to flow over the top of the sink and onto the floor.

She sat the bags on the table and raced over, turned off the faucet, and slammed her hand into the sink to remove the stopper and drain the water out. She then grabbed me by the shoulders and shook me. My melancholy expression didn't change.

"For heaven's sake, snap out of it and tell me what's wrong," she urged.

She looked around and not seeing the kids she panicked, "Are the kids alright?"

I was able to nod an affirmative to that, and then I hugged her to me and she walked me slowly to a nearby chair at the breakfast table. I sat down and she did too beside me. She grabbed some paper towels off the counter and began to dry off my hair and head.

I managed to gather some semblance of composure and looked her in the eye. I could see she was worried. Finally, I somehow inhaled deeply and swallowed hard.

Speaking quietly, I told her, "The kids are fine, they went downstairs to play."

As I was speaking, in through the opened back door came the Plumps' missing parrot, Peanut Patti. It swooshed by me at breakneck speed and flew directly through the kitchen into the den. There, it landed on its familiar T-shaped perch.

Daisy and I quickly followed after it and when it saw us, the parrot squawked, "Pudgy Plump's parrot, Peanut Patti peacefully perched."

Hearing that, Daisy was quite amused and impressed by this talking bird. She asked it, "Your name is Peanut Patti and that is your perch?"

"Precisely!" squawked the parrot.

I scratched my wet head and stated, "A parrot's perch? So, that's what that thing is. I thought maybe it was some sort of exercise equipment."

Hearing their mom was home, the kids bounded up the stairs. Cah Cah was the first to see the parrot. She ran up to it and stared at it.

The parrot then squawked, "Prissy polliwog."

Dippy soon joined in the fascination of having a talking bird in the house.

He asked, "Wow! Did that bird just talk?"

"Perky playful person." squawked Patti parrot, as she looked at Dippy.

Cah Cah offered it a piece of cheese on which she'd been nibbling.

"Patti prefers peanuts," squawked the parrot.

Daisy laughed and tried to pet the parrot.

It leaned away from her hand and squawked, "Pretty, preening, perfumed partner please pass on petting."

It turned toward Dooby and called him, "Pimpled palace prince."

I snarled my lips and glared at the bird, trying to imagine what its scrawny body would look like dressed, cooked, and served at our dining room table.

It peered back at me with its beady eyes and squawked, "Paternal poppa partner."

Although I was opposed to having a parrot that was not caged in the house, the others all seemed to like it and were amazed at its odd manner of speech and amazing comprehension.

At least the bird had caused me to momentarily forget about Rooster. As I helped Daisy bring in the other groceries, the kids sat and talked to Patti. I opened up to Daisy about our having seen the rooster on the television weather forecast. That amazed and seemed to frighten her a bit, for like me she wondered if perhaps the kids were also having a bout with the taunting Poultry-Geists that plagued us. When I helped her to empty the sacks and put away the food items, I noticed a meat item that I did not recognize.

"What's this?" I asked holding up the two large cellophane-wrapped packages.

"I didn't think we were ready for a turkey for Christmas dinner, and I got the impression this morning that you didn't want ham, or a grilled chicken ... so, I found an Amish meat market that had rabbits dressed out and ready to cook. I haven't had Hasenpfeffer Stew in years, and under the circumstances figured two rabbits would provide a good meal for us and the twins"

"I've never eaten rabbit," I told her. "What's it taste like?"

"Like chicken, but without the feathers," she told me.

* * *

After resting until around 3:00 P.M., I left the house and drove to the pet store where I bought the Clown Fish for Cah Cah. The man sold it to me in a plastic container that had a battery-operated pump that fed air through a tube into the tank and supplied enough oxygen into the saltwater to sustain the fish until I could place it into the aquarium tomorrow night. I also bought some fish food for it.

I had the address and directions for the Amish farm that bred dogs. Following the map I was given the day before, I found the farm easily in twenty minutes. The Amish gentleman that greeted me wore simple clothing and had no mustache like I did, but instead wore a full beard under his chin and onto his neck. He had on a brimmed hat and he spoke with a German brogue that I'd come to know as Pennsylvania Dutch.

"Hello, mister, I'm Jonathon. You come to look at dogs, I reckon," he said.

I shook his hand and followed him into a large barn where there were cows, horses, sheep, pigs, and what seemed to be dozens of cages with both pups and grown dogs.

He asked me, "What breed of dog might you be interested in, mister?"

"I was thinking of something along the line of a bird dog," I stated.

He looked at me and his lips almost formed a smile.

"I see," he said. "Then you're a hunter. On my farm, folks from the city come to hunt pheasant, quail, and <u>ducks</u> on my land {<u>Not that 'D' word again ... after the day I've had</u>} ... for a nominal fee, you understand, brother."

I saw what he was getting at, but I had no interest in hunting ... although a certain cartoon cowboy rooster might be a prey I'd consider. I had other reasons for wanting a dog. I wanted one that would grow to become a loveable, loyal pet, but also perform like my Ohio neighbor's dog had done with that stupid duh ... err, I mean quacker from on our pond that I tried to save. Hopefully, a bird dog wouldn't wait for one of my winged antagonists to be shot before chasing it away from our home and family. The sooner the better.

After the farmer found I wasn't interested in hunting, he tried to sway me from purchasing a bird dog, but as we perused his stock, I found just the one I wanted. The pup had black fur with a white patch of fur over one eye. The tip of his tail was also white, as were his two front paws. I chose him because he was cute and I knew Cah Cah and the boys would love him.

The farmer and I dickered a bit on price but finally came to an accord. I paid him and took the pup with me to my car. That little rascal was feisty, even a bit hyper, and happy to be out of his cage. I held him in my lap as I drove away. In my rearview mirror, I swear I thought I again saw that accursed Rooster Galldern.

He waved at me, and then pulled his slingshot. Quickly loading up an egg, he drew back on the stout rubber tubing and flung the egg towards the back window of my Jeep. My anger provided me with enough conscious realization that what I thought just happened truly had. I screeched on my car's brakes, sat the pup down, and bolted out of my car door. I raced around to the back window and sure enough ... it was covered in egg-foo-goo.

I turned and watched Galldern gallop away on his sawhorse. He waved his hat in the air with one hand and with the sawhorse took head on a three-rail fence. Just as he got to it, instead of leaping over it, the sawhorse skidded to a stop and Galldern went tumbling into the wood rails. I raced towards him and was aware that this was reaching a new level of craziness. Feathers flew and I heard him squawk and moan, but he managed to low-crawl under the fence. He whistled at the sawhorse, which then climbed the fence and stumbled over onto the ground next to Galldern. He remounted the sawhorse and its unbalanced quirky 2" x 4" legs and then strode steadily as it galloped away and vanished over a hill before I could catch that pullet assassin.

Greatly annoyed and feeling as if he'd now thrown down the gauntlet, I felt a surge of adrenalin course through my veins. I was ready to get to the bottom of that meteorological run-amok rooster. I got back in my car and fended off a slobbering bunch of puppy kisses on my face. I then decided I'd pay a visit to that local Fox television affiliate and see if I can't get my hands around that miserable poultry terrorist. He'd become like a paper cut to my brain causing me to have a full-out sanity aneurism.

* * *

On the way home, I stopped at a gas station to fill up. While there, I used my cell phone to call Daisy. I didn't mention my incident with Galldern.

"Hey, hon. It's me. I located a shop in Lancaster that sells Clownfish. I purchased one for Cah Cah and it's in a plastic cube that pumps air into the water, so it should be fine till we get it in the tank tonight after Cah Cah's asleep.

"Oh, that's wonderful, dear. That's perfect for one of Cah Cah's Christmas gifts."

"The delivery guys are coming tomorrow at 1:00 P.M., so you'll need to do as we planned and take the kids to a movie around noon or so."

"That's great! The show starts a little after that, so you'll have plenty of time to hide their presents in the garage attic," she stated. "What did you find out about a puppy?"

"I'm looking at him through the window, while I fill up with gas. I may need my car interior detailed when I get home, for he's slobbered all over the windows. We'll also have to get his nails trimmed."

"Oh, goodness. All the kids are going to go nuts when they see they have a dog again. Cah Cah will be so happy, and she may leap into the aquarium with her Clownfish."

"Yes, with all that's happened I want the kids to have an extra special Christmas this year. Don't wait on supper for me. Rover and I will stop and pick up something on the way home."

When I got off the phone with her, I dialed the number of the brick mason and told him we needed another repair to our mailbox out front.

He laughed and said, "Si, Señor, I have enough brick left from a few days ago, so I'll ride out tomorrow and repair it. Do I bill the plant as I did before?"

"Yes, that's fine, but tomorrow's Christmas Eve. You should relax and be with your family."

"Señor, I have eight children, so a relaxing day for me is at work."

# CHAPTER 15: Roasting Rooster

Fifteen minutes later I pulled up, parked, and left the fish and dog in the car. I strolled irritably towards the front door of the television station. When I entered the reception area a nice middle-aged woman that wore a Christmas sweater and fuzzy, clip-on reindeer antlers greeted me. She had such a sweet smile and pleasant demeanor that I toned down my temper and returned her smile.

"I'd like to speak with your station manager," I told her.

"Merry Christmas, Sir. I'm very sorry, but he's already left for the Holidays," she said politely.

"Merry Christmas to you also, "I remarked with a sad face. "May I then see whoever is left in charge?"

"That would be our chief meteorologist, Marshall Goodbody. May I ask your name and the reason for your visit?"

"His name is Marshall? I should have expected as much. Anyways, I'm Dabney Doodledoo. I'm filing a complaint against your station and that wretched weather forecaster, Marshall, Rooster Galldern."

The woman looked at me and bit her lip as if to stifle a grin. Then she sat up and her left eyebrow raised a fraction.

"Well, Mr. Doodlehoop, have a seat just a moment while I page Mr. Goodbody."

She did that and the man on the intercom told her he'd be out in a moment to see me. When he did appear, he was a short, stocky man wearing a Santa suit, and Santa cap, plus had a banner that stated, "Merry Christmas."

"Mr. Goodbody, Mr. Doodleloop here has come with a complaint ... about Marshall Galldern."

I shook his hand and corrected the receptionist, "My name is pronounced, Dabney Doodledoo ... not Doodlehoop, Doodleloop, nor Noodlesoup," I exasperatingly declared.

He grinned at me and expressed regret, "Having a last name like Goodbody, I can certainly understand your frustration, Mr. Doodledoo."

The receptionist seemed embarrassed. He politely pointed towards a doorway.

"Please follow me to my office and you can tell me your concerns. Ms. Hodgepodge, see that we're not disturbed."

He led me inside to an office next to the newsroom. He walked behind his desk, and pointed to a chair across from it.

"Please, have a seat, Mr. Doodledoo."

"Call me, Dabney,"

"Certainly," Now, please tell me, Dabney, what issues you're having with our Marshall Galldern."

"To begin with, before I drove here, he egged my car using that silly slingshot of his. Besides that, he's been like a cloud on my horizon causing me to question my sanity. He appears and disappears at the most inconvenient of times and taunts me in that John Wayne drawl of his with backwoods cowboy logic that makes no sense to me. To make matters worse, I turned on my television to watch the weather forecast ... and there he was."

Remaining quiet and somewhat aloof, the meteorologist carefully studied my face, as if I were a cold front streaming down from Canada. That, or else he expected me to remove a mask and reveal a phantom underneath. He then reached down and lifted a large box. After that, he turned to his computer and logged onto his email account. Smiling at me with a sense of satisfaction, he turned the computer monitor around so I could see it. He pointed at the box first.

"Dabney, there are hundreds of letters inside that box from local station viewers of our weather reports. All of them are positive statements congratulating us on creating the comical animated character, Marshall Rooster Galldern. Furthermore, as you can see, my email inbox was overwhelmed with hundreds of more people contacting me to say how much they and their kids enjoyed watching the forecasts with Marshall Galldern. Of all these contacts, there's not a single negative response ... that is until today, for here you are in person."

"I don't care how many others like him; to me, he's been a dark well of sorrow that's drawn me into a spiraling shaft of despondency."

"A shaft of despondency ... you say?" he smiled and then asked, "This is a joke, right? You do realize that he's just an animated CGI character and not a real person."

"Of course, he's not," I stated firmly. "He's a dadgum, egg-slinging, mongrel rooster."

With that, Marshall looked at me like I was crazy. I could tell by him tightening his jaw muscles that he was losing his patience with me.

"Be reasonable, Dabney. You see, besides being a meteorologist, I studied computer graphics in college. To boost our ratings and inject some humor into my holiday forecasts, I developed the cartoon character, Rooster Galldern. Because my dad's favorite actor was John Wayne, I created a caricature of the role he played in the movie, "True Grit.""

"Don't patronize me," I grumbled. "He's as real as you and me. Tell me where I can find him. I'll fricassee him, pluck his feathers, and send him back to you in a stew pot."

Marshall then shook his head and shrugged. He stood walked around his desk and with an arm slowly pointed the way towards the back of the studio. I followed as he led me to a door.

"Alright, Dabney, if you insist. Marshall Galldern is right this way. I'm sure he'll be glad to listen to your grievance."

"Good," I said. "Thank you for your help."

With that, he opened a metal door and shoved me out into the back parking lot of the station. He then quickly locked the door from the inside.

"I heard his words exclaim through it, "Why do all the crazies come out on the holidays?"

I stood at the door, angry and upset. I was like that Mattie Ross girl in the movie, "True Grit," for I thought about her words to Rooster Cogburn when he led in prisoners he arrested, and then slammed the jailhouse door on her.

I uttered, "If he thinks I'll be put off by a closed door, he doesn't know me very well."

After standing there alone in my stupor for near fifteen minutes, I finally realized the foolishness of my situation. He wasn't coming back and I imagine by now the station's front door was locked too. Thus, I tromped around the building and headed back to my car.

When I rounded the corner and saw my Jeep in front, I became even more enraged. There, on top of it and completely covering its roof were dozens of cackling hens. In a charging fury, I ran screaming at them. As I did, they began to scatter, hopped down, and then they raced away. I heard the pup barking furiously inside the car and cringed at the mass of muddled chicken poop that was left behind from those accursed hens. Their excrement was on the roof, hood, side panels, windshield, and everywhere on the vehicle. It looked like a snowstorm of hen droppings.

I took out a handkerchief and carefully opened the door handle, scooted back the pup, and slid inside onto the driver's seat. I looked in back to make sure Cah Cah's Clownfish was doing okay. It was, so I enacted the windshield washing spray and wiper blades. After several squirts, the liquid and wipers removed enough of the droppings that I could see to drive.

Immediately, I drove to a full-service car wash in town to clean away the mess. The man that led me into the automatic car wash looked at my Jeep like it was a pale ball of bird poop. I guess it was at that.

Returning home, I forgot about my hunger and immediately carried the pup and the fish upstairs into the garage attic. I put out a bowl of water for the pup, some of the dog food I'd bought, and placed the fish and plastic cube onto a table. I fed the fish, and then locked the door behind me, as I went inside the house.

* * *

So, I'd again been assaulted by that Rooster Galldern and he wasn't even at the television station. In this mixed-up chicken-eat-chicken world that I was drawn into, it seemed like we were in Paradise Lost, not Pennsylvania. I supposed there was no cure for birth or death except that we had to exist and live in the interval. Right now, I felt like the land-line phone of my life had been left off the hook.

I told myself I was not crazy, but that the trouble with counting on reason and experience to guide me was that the final exam came first and then the lesson. I felt like a bad rendition of myself at a wax museum where I stood rigidly with a 'stupid' candle wick sticking out of my head.

To me, Rooster Galldern was like the fat old general that came down out of the hills after the battle was over to shoot all the survivors. Was he real, or was I indeed over the edge now and bonkers? Still, I knew that where there's smoke there's fire, so to me, he was real and tormented my soul like he was whipping it with a leather strap. I found no peace from him here in my home and sleep became to me like an eight-hour peep show into the absurd.

As I stammered to my recliner in the den, I heard Daisy and the kids upstairs laughing and enjoying their time together. At least they seemed happy. I glanced at the time and felt my stomach growl from lack of nourishment. Although the riches of the world were laid stretched before me like the open palm of my hand, I was depressed and miserable. As I closed, and then slowly opened my eyes, who sat across from me on the sofa? Why of course ... it was Rooster Galldern.

He smirked and shook his head.

"Pilgrim, you don't look too froggy and appear more like the galley slave on a doomed ship. Your fiddle's out of tune and if you don't take care of your body, where are you gonna live?"

I snarled at him and yelled, "Get out! You deranged hayseed, you're driving me nuts."

I stood and raced towards him. He quickly vanished and reappeared across the room from me. I turned and again headed at him with my hands out in a strangling position. Once more, he disappeared like a wisp of smoke and reassembled in the hall next to the stairs.

I declared, "Be still, you galloping gob of pot-bellied protoplasm. Let me get my hands around that plumed neck of yours and we'll be serving you on a platter tomorrow for lunch."

"Not gonna happen, Pilgrim. Quit squawkin' like a hen that laid a square egg. You may be more ornery and stubborn than a cross-eyed mule, but your noggin's as soft as a two-minute egg."

I stopped and stood silent, my breath coming in exasperated gasps. He was my nemesis, but there were all those other incidents with chickens and other fowl.

"Why do you and other poultry continue to torment me? What'd my family or I do to you or any of these other fowl?"

"You mean, other than using us as poached eggs on toast and as favorite entrees on your restaurant menus? You're cookin' on the front burner, son, and that puts a burr under the saddle for a bunch of us pullets."

There it was. We were undergoing this tribulation because we farmed, raised, processed, and served grilled chicken at our restaurants. In that case, what hope did we have? Even the promise of the oncoming New Year now only seemed to provide a midnight eve where we could watch our anticipation for a return of sanity descend into oblivion like that crystal ball on that New York City building.

"Listen, muttonhead," he grumbled. "You're short on ears and long on mouth. I know you're madder than a wet hen without a roost, but a rooster's gotta have a code, a creed to live by, and true grit. You gotta get it done, son."

I bemoaned, "You old snuff dipping side-winder; you've become like that rat you egged. You spring your traps in my mind and nibble at the crumbs before moving on to spring yet another trap on me."

"For sure, I'm no spring chicken, Pilgrim, but you're a few bricks shy of a full load yourself. So, get off my tail, you're walkin' too close. Besides, nobody ever saw a cowboy on a psychologist's couch," he stated angrily.

"Shut up, you sawed-off sawhorse. You've caused me all manner of grief. You're ruining my health and are the basis for all my muddled thoughts. For insurance purposes, an intern at the plant took my blood and urine sample the other day and later told me I somehow tested to have chicken DNA in me. She claimed it must be a mistake, for she also said that my pee was the consistency of a bouillon cube. So, Galldern-it, you back off," I ranted.

Hearing the commotion downstairs, Daisy came bounding down to see why I was so upset. As she appeared on the upstairs landing, Galldern melted away like a vapor.

Descending the stairs, Daisy asked, "What are you shouting about, hon? And who were you talking to?"

"Only a lingering flame that's burning a hole in my brain," I declared.

She looked around frantically but saw no one. "Was it that dreadful rooster that's been causing you so much dismay?"

"Yes, but he's gone now. I need to go eat something, take a bath, and go to bed."

She hugged me and we walked together into the kitchen. She led me to the table and like a magician soon had produced a plate of warm leftovers from the meal she and the kids ate earlier.

"Thank you, dear, "I said. "How are the kids?"

She grinned and told me, "Excited about Santa coming tomorrow night and Christmas morning. It's great that the weather is going to be nice and that they can play outside with their toys."

"Yes, I suppose so. I took the pup and fish up to the garage attic. They'll be alright till tomorrow. I did forget to get puppy pads, so when you're out tomorrow please pick some up."

"I will, but while we're gone don't you work yourself into a frenzy," she stated. "I think I'll go out and check on the pup and fish. I'll bet they're both cute," she remarked.

# CHAPTER 16: Manger Stranger

The next day, we all woke at nearly 7:00 A.M. I rolled over and looked at the alarm clock, obviously happy that we hadn't been awakened earlier by a rooster crowing. I got dressed and while the kids and Daisy were eating breakfast, I went to the garage attic and fed the fish and puppy. There were a few puppy surprises left for me there to clean up, but I did so and had to fight off the pup at the door to keep him inside the attic. He barked, but fortunately, it could not be heard from within the house.

I came inside, ate some cereal, and then went down the stairs to our below man-cave-like basement. There was a full-size pool table down there and two other game tables on which to play cards and shuffleboard. I wanted to check the fridge and cabinets there to be certain they had soft drinks and snacks for when the Kockle twins came over tomorrow. A large, big screen T.V. was also going to broadcast a pro football game, so the theater-like leather seats would provide us, men, a comfortable place from which to watch the action. I needed a place to relax after all that's happened and to take a break from the excitement of Santa's impending visit. Daisy too might find a respite down here from all her meal prep, serving, and cleaning.

Also joining me below was Peanut Patti, the parrot. She flew down and lit upon the back of a game chair. She bobbed her head up and down like a cork in a pond to get my attention.

I stopped walking, put my hands on my hips, and asked, "What is it you want Patti? I haven't any peanuts."

"Predict paternal partner to be pitifully pecked," squawked the parrot.

I ignored her, but as I began to decorate the handrails on the stairs with vinyl strands of pine and holly garland, I heard something shuffle about in the room. When I stopped to listen, I heard nothing. So, I placed lights and ornaments on a small artificial tree we'd brought down from the attic yesterday. As I hung a Merry Christmas banner on the wall, I again heard something rustle nearby.

The parrot squawked again, "Pappy partner is a peek-a-boo pawn."

I glanced around the room but still didn't see anything that would cause the dull shuffling sound. Then, a moment later I heard it again and began to worry. What I didn't see was yet another cartoon rooster ... walking upside down on the ceiling. When I took a step, so too did that rooster. This one had brown feathers, a full, crimson red comb atop its head, plus a round chubby body. Uneasy, I moved to the small walk-in bar area where I turned on the faucet and washed my hands with soap in the bar sink. Once again I heard the shuffling noise of footsteps and became increasingly annoyed and confused. I dried my hands and walked a few more steps. Then I had a hunch, stopped, and slowly turned my head upward toward the ceiling. When I did, I went nose to beak with the other rooster.

He sneered at me and remarked, "Hiya, Pard. Muh name's, Brighton Early. I must have overslept this morning, but I'll be back on duty by daybreak tomorrow ... not that you'll need it, for it'll be Christmas and your little pullets will be anticipating Santa's arrival and what he left them from his gift sack."

"So, you're the sorry crowing alarm clock that's been rousing us out of bed every morning at daylight?" I angrily asked.

"Yep. I'm proud to say that I am one and the same. Say, why are you upside down?"

"Me? I'm on the floor. You're the one that's on the ceiling," I told him.

With that, his clawed chicken feet let go of the ceiling and he fluttered down onto the pool table in front of me. He squawked when he saw me pick up a pool cue and pound it anxiously into my palm.

"Easy there, Pard. Reel in your wild crazies. I just do what I do," he declared.

"Which is what I'm about to do." I replied.

I lost all my composure and swung the pool cue as hard as I could at the rooster's body. The parrot squawked and flew out of the room.

"Preserve Patti, as I pass to the parlor."

Instead of hurting the rooster, the cue simply passed through him as if he were smoke. His image faded, much in the way Rooster Galldern's had. Then, he rematerialized behind me. Before I could turn around, he grabbed me by the head and pecked a few knots on it. He then went berserk. He teasingly kissed me with his beak, and then set off on a crowing binge. Bouncing off the walls, ceiling, and floor like a rubber super ball, he was in a blind rage of zaniness. Brown feathers drifted about the basement, but the overactive rooster showed no signs of fatigue from his hissy fit.

I put down the pool cue and in stunned silence slowly sat down in one of the leather chairs. I rubbed the knots rising on top of my head and snarled.

"You swung that at me faster than a chicken attacks a bug. As you can see though, I'm unharmed. Yep, Pard, you're green as a gourd and have been working without a full string of lights. Sorry if I flip your garter by waking you at the break of each new day, but that's what we roosters have been doing around here for longer than dirt."

I thought about what he said and shrugged, "Ouch! You roly-poly Poultry-Geist. My head hurts and I'm in a pucker over the pecks you landed on my noggin."

He smirked and said, "Yeah, I'm tougher than a stewed owl and don't take to being hit upon. Besides, it's not so bad to rise early and go to bed early. That's the Amish way around these parts, so maybe you'll get used to it."

Before I could say anything else, Brighton dissolved into the wall and disappeared. I leaned back in the chair and sighed. I noticed my hands had quit shaking, but I thought maybe I'd better keep that appointment with Dr. Andropoff on Monday after all. He was a bit of a quack too, but at least he listened to me.

* * *

At noon, Daisy and the kids set off for Lancaster to go see a movie. That allowed me to get the remainder of the toys in from the garage and to bring down the Clownfish and puppy. I placed Cah Cah's Nemo into the aquarium and it took only a few minutes for it to acclimate to its new environs and neighboring aquatic friends. I took the puppy into our master bedroom downstairs and locked it in our bathroom. I hoped not to find any more of its surprises before Daisy got home with the puppy pads.

We planned that when she got out of the movie around 3:00 P.M., she'd take them all to get some sweets at a local candy store. She'd then drive around until about 4:30 P.M. looking at decorations. A half-hour before dark, I told her to meet me at a pre-arranged restaurant where we could all eat dinner. In the meantime, I dragged in all the toys and gifts for the kids and sat them around and under the tree in our den.

When we got home from sightseeing, Daisy and I would make sure we led the kids upstairs before they could look into the den, so that Christmas morning would be a surprise for them. When the time came to meet them at the restaurant, I was tired, hungry, and eager to get this day completed.

As I pulled up and parked in front of the restaurant where we were to dine, I stepped, got out, and walked toward the entry. To my astonishment, Patti parrot flew up and landed on a sign over the entry door.

She squawked, "Probable preposterous paranormal predicament."

I'd about had it with that pesky loud-mouthed parrot. I ignored it and walked inside where Daisy and the kids were waiting for me. They all saw the twin knots on my forehead.

"What happened, dear? Did you fall and hit your head?' Daisy asked.

"Huh? Well, I ran into a door as I was getting dressed," I told them with not much conviction.

Everything went as we planned, for we enjoyed a nice meal with the kids, and after dark, we had a fun time watching all the frivolity going on in town. We stopped, parked, and got out to walk in the chilled night air to a place in a city park where others were gathered to watch and listen to Christmas carolers. We laughed and sang along with old standards like, "Silent Night," "Jingle Bells," "Rudolph the Red-Nosed Reindeer," and "White Christmas."

The kids, Daisy, and I were all in a pleasant, relaxing holiday mood. When the songs were over, we began to trek back toward where we parked my car.

When going to listen to the carolers, we'd passed by an inspiring, full-sized manger scene. However, as we returned via the same route we took to get there, when we came upon that scene again, each of us did a double-take on whom and what had replaced the livestock and three wise men in the scene.

There, towering over the babe in a manger was the same seven-foot-tall ostrich that Daisy had seen in the master bath that day when we first saw our house. Across from it was the rooster, Brighton Early, holding a staph. He wore a red beard that flowed from his beak and was dressed up like a . shepherd. Instead of three wise men ... three fancy-dressed, fat hens wore golden crowns kneeling beside the manger. One offered up a basket of eggs, one a basket of shucked corn, and the third a basket of popcorn.

On Joseph's shoulder, was the pug-nosed parrot, Peanut Patti.

Like some divine prognosticator, she squawked, "Pedigreed papoose is a perfect prodigy."

Atop the stable, there hung Rooster Galldern with a <u>halo</u> around his cowboy hat<u>, angel wings</u> attached to his back, and he hung by a rope tied to a tree above it that dangled him precariously over the manger. He grumbled and twisted, as the unstable rope twirled and turned him in circles, while the kids, me, and Daisy looked on in total wonderment. I glanced around to see if anyone else might be viewing this, but somehow, we were the only ones noticing this screwball scene. Cah Cah laughed and yelled, "Oooh goody! There's Marshall Galldern."

When the twisted rope circled and brought him back around to face us, Rooster began to sing in his out-of-tune, gruff John Wayne voice in the cadence of the song, "We Three Kings."

"<u>These three French hens ... from a roost that's afar ... are the same ones ... that pooped on your car</u>."

Cah Cah and the kids laughed, but I cringed and quickly gathered them and Daisy down the street. When I glanced back at the scene, it was again back to normal and the poultry that had "fowled it all up" had dispersed.

Nevertheless, the zany visions did not end with that incident. We passed by the bronze statue of a lion lying down with a stream of water coming from its mouth into a fountain pool. There, Cah stopped and asked for a coin to toss into the pool that would grant her a wish. I gave her a quarter, which she quickly tossed into the fountain.

As Cah Cah closed her eyes and made her wish, Daisy pointed to a nearby tree that suddenly sprouted ripe pears ... in late December. Up in the tree, on a small branch, she spotted a partridge. It flapped its wings and cooed at us. Yes, as you might have guessed ... it was a partridge in a pear tree. Oh, my!

Dooby then pointed out two white turtle doves that landed near the lion statue's feet. They were soon joined by the same three French hens we saw at the manger scene. They scurried around the fountain; then four calling birds lit in a tree nearby and began to sing out in their warbling voices. Fireworks suddenly lit up the sky and formed five golden, bright rings above us.

As we all stood immobile by that lion statue, onto the park lawn came six geese that flapped their wings and then lay down on the lawn. Just as suddenly, seven swans came zooming in on the wing, landed in the fountain's pool, and then began to swim around. A wide-eyed Dippy pointed at eight Amish women milking cows while being pulled by mules on a trailer down the street. I about fainted. Yet, there were more surprises to come.

On a stage that somehow lit up not too far from our car, in an apparent vision, we spotted nine hens dancing and kicking up their heels. Ten roosters were leaping up around them, and eleven turkeys were piping out tunes on piccolos. The climax was when a dozen ducks came quacking down the street pounding on snare drums. {<u>Yeah, more 'D' characters for me to deal with</u>}

Overcome with all the strangeness, we herded the kids into the car and left those twelve days of Christmas ghosts to simmer in their strange maelstrom of ectoplasm. My throbbing head felt like I'd been hit by a frying pan, as I nervously drove to where Daisy had parked her car to meet me. I followed her and the kids home, where we had no difficulty convincing them to go upstairs to bed. The two young ones seemed unfazed by the oddities of the evening and knew that Santa wouldn't come unless they were asleep.

Daisy and I kissed them and I told them, "Okay you rug rats, off the bed now. I think I saw Santa and his reindeer skipping over some rooftops on the drive home tonight."

Dooby just smiled, winked, and patted me on the back.

"This has been a humdinger of a night, so I won't piddle and let you and mom go simmer down and get some rest. I love you, so whatever loony things have been going on and traipsing around here had better quit it," he told us.

We kissed our oldest son on the cheek and swatted his behind in a gesture of affection. He grinned and went up to bed. Daisy and I retreated to our bedroom, where I heard the puppy scratching at the bathroom door. I took care of the little mutt and cleaned up after him. That would be the kid's job after tonight. Cah Cah was so tired she didn't even see the fish in the aquarium, so her surprise would be set up for tomorrow morning.

Daisy and I went to our rooms and locked the door behind us. We each were zonked and truly flustered by what we saw and experienced in the park.

"That strange manger scene made me want to scream," she said.

"Me too," I replied. "Before we dine tomorrow, I think I'll go visit that Catholic Church we passed coming home. I think some prayers are in order, don't you?"

"Yes, I do. Please light a candle and say some for all of us." she declared.

Suddenly, out on the lawn there arose such a clatter that I sprang from my bed to see what was the matter ... yeah, I know ... you've guessed what comes next.

Daisy inquired, "What was it, dear?"

I snarled and said, "No, it's no deer. It's a little, old driver so lively and quick ... that I'd like to go down and beat with a stick."

∗ ∗ ∗

Christmas morning was as joyous and chaotic as you might imagine. Brighton Early began to crow at daybreak, but Daisy and I set our alarm and beat him up by fifteen minutes. When he did hop up on our bed and started his morning reveille call, Daisy and I greeted him with blaring canned air horns at full blast. That nutty rooster was so stunned he fell back onto the floor and fainted. I grinned at Daisy and bent down over the bewildered pullet.

"How do you like getting a dose of your own medicine?" I shouted.

That silly rooster roused and disappeared before I could further berate him. The kids too were startled, but it took them only a few moments to wipe away the cobwebs before they raced downstairs to the den.

There, their bounty of gifts overwhelmed and delighted them. When Daisy came in with the puppy, their glee went over the top. They surrounded him, as the dog smothered them in sloppy tongue kisses. Its tail wagged so fast I thought it might fall off.

"What's her name?" asked an excited Dippy.

"Well, he's a boy," I stated. "Santa told us it's up to you kids to name him and care for him."

As they played with the puppy, Daisy leaned and whispered to Cah Cah.

"Check out the aquarium. I think I saw a new addition in there."

Cah Cah ceased petting the puppy and ran to the fish tank. Little Nemo didn't disappoint her, for it swam past like a soldier passing in review of a general. She laughed and her mouth flew open in surprise.

"Nemo!" she yelled. "Yippee! Santa brought me, Nemo."

When it got around to Daisy and I opening the gifts we got for each other, I bought her a two-hundred-dollar gift certificate to the local Central Market where she could browse and purchase any one of the thousand different items they sell there. She squealed with delight and gave me a big kiss. Then I watched carefully, as she opened the present containing the music box. She tore through the wrapping and smiled with joy when she saw the two elegant ceramic white doves on top. I suppose I should have anticipated what occurred next, for when she reached to open the music box and play the programmed song, the two white doves suddenly animated, flapped their wings, and flew up into the air. Their short flight took them towards the den wall. Upon banging into it, they simply crashed and their fine porcelain bodies crumpled into a dozen pieces.

Patti parrot, who'd been given a full bag of peanuts by Daisy, tossed a spent nutshell from its beak.

She then squawked, "Pappy purchased possessed poultry."

And so, our holiday began.

\* \* \*

Later in our den, after the twins arrived and we all opened presents, Wayne nervously wiped his hand across his brow

He said, "Yes, as I was pulling up, I could've sworn that I saw a herd of chickens leap out in front of my car. I swerved to miss them, but—"

I interrupted Wayne, "Yeah, I bet you knocked over the brick mailbox."

"I did, but how'd you know? Of course, I'll have it repaired again."

"Don't worry about it," I told him. "I now keep your brick mason's number on speed dial."

"Maybe Clancy wasn't as crazy as we thought he was and did see hens when he hit the mailbox that day," said Dwayne.

"Yeah, maybe you're right, Bro. At any rate, I'm going to ask the doctor to lower the strength of my allergy meds," replied Wayne.

I clapped my hands tightly and led the twins into the dining room where Daisy had the table decorated in a holiday style. The dishes, glasses, and cutlery were all set up for our family Christmas meal. When the twins were seated, I called outside to the kids who were busily playing with their toys. Dippy was zipping all up and down the driveway on his new bike, while Dooby was busily flying his new drone. Cah Cah played chase with the new puppy.

I told the kids, "Okay, ya'll, it's time for our meal, so put down your toys and come inside to the table."

Daisy opened the oven door to check on the hasenpfeffer. Looking inside, she saw a fat hen wearing goggles and a hazmat suit spooning gravy on top of the stew. It squawked at her and winked. Daisy just shrugged her shoulders, closed the door, and then turned off the oven.

"I think the stew is done. Have a seat everyone and we'll start serving," she stated.

Then she re-opened the oven door and the hen was of curse ... I mean of course ... gone.

Wayne helped Dwayne with the napkins, silverware, and where his plate, water glass, and tea glass were placed.

Daisy placed the stew on the table and Wayne perused it and the other food that Daisy and I prepared. Dwayne sniffed the air and licked his lips.

"Hasenpfeffer, you say? Exactly what is that?" he asked. "It smells delicious."

"It's a stewed rabbit, with carrots, onions, tomatoes, garlic, and a hint of basil," declared Daisy.

When Cah Cah heard that she remarked, "Oh no, we're not eating Peter Rabbit are we?"

I laughed and assured her it wasn't Peter. I don't think she believed me though.

"We also have baked potatoes, corn on the cob, baked beans, rolls, and a Waldorf salad," pronounced Daisy.

When everyone was seated, including our rambunctious kids, I stood at the head of the table, much as Paul Plump had done on Thanksgiving, and did as he'd done by tapping a knife to an empty glass to get everyone's attention.

I then gave my speech, which this time did not include words beginning with 'P'. No, we were a new breed in this home and since our name begins with a 'D' … that was the basis for the speech I presented without any knowledge or control overusing that alphabet letter.

I said, "Doodledoo daddy does declare to a devoted, dashing, desirable, dedicated, darling damsel of domicile dwelling our desire to duly dole, devour, and digest delicious doses of divine dinner delicacies and drink that my diligent dame didst dispatch to directly divvy out." I said, without any hesitation or means to prevent the 'D' diction anomaly.

"Deactivate, decompress, dismantle, disengage, and decrease with the distributed 'D' dogma," declared a dazed Daisy.

I thumped my head and shook it, attempting to douse, deter, and disregard my sudden propensity to speak in 'D' words. Wayne and Dwayne looked dumbfounded and yet devoid of any opinion about my diminutive, devised, digressed diction.

"My apologies," I stated. "I'm not sure where that came from, but if you'll bow your heads, I'll try saying the blessing over this feast before us."

Somehow, I managed to say grace without repeating any daunting 'D' words. After that, we passed the helpings of food around the table and everyone partook of a nice, Christmas meal, mixed with good conversation and sharing in friendship and with family. When were we finished, the kids helped clear the table and assisted their mother to clean up and put away the dishes, pots, and pans.

We men retreated down to the basement and watched a football game on television. At least, Wayne and I did, while Dwayne had us explain almost every play and touchdown made. All in all, except for a few oddball instances it was a wonderful Christmas day with no more poultry-geists stirring up any nonsense. Wayne and Dwayne were very pleased with the gifts we got them and we were more than happy to have them share this holiday time with us.

# CHAPTER 17: Fore Score & One Duck

The next day, I came out of the house, got in my car, and started down the driveway. As I pulled away, I waved at the bricklayer as he was arriving in his truck. I stopped and rolled down my car window. He smiled at me and shook his head, for he saw the wrecked mailbox he'd already repaired three times. Again, it was disheveled, broken down, and lying about in the street and yard.

He said, "I'd have come yesterday, but my wife made me stay home with the kids while she went shopping."

"I understand. Wives are like that. Just do your thing, Juan, and leave your bill inside the box when you're done."

Then, I pulled away and drove to the collision shop I'd contacted. They were to repair the front bumper on the Jeep, plus replace and repaint the front right-side panel. Fortunately, they provided me with a loaner vehicle until my Jeep could be repaired.

Before leaving, I took my golf clubs out of the trunk and placed them in the loaner car. Despite it being December, it was another chamber of commerce day with temps in the low 70s. I was to meet Wayne and Dwayne on a nearby golf course to play a round ... although I had no idea how Dwayne was going to play since he was still mostly blind.

I drove up to the plush country club where we were to play. It surprised me that I only saw five cars in the parking lot. I pulled up, parked, and got out. Before I could get my clubs out, a valet in a golf cart pulled up and stopped behind my car.

"Good morning, Sir. Welcome to Shady Oaks Country Club. If you'll just open the trunk and have a seat in the cart, I'll get your clubs and drive you up to the clubhouse."

I opened the trunk and sat down in the cart. He removed my golf bag and attached it to the rear of the cart. He then smiled, hopped in behind the wheel, and drove me to up the posh clubhouse.

"The Kockle twins are waiting for you inside at the bar. I'll drive your cart around to the first tee," he told me.

I reached into my wallet to get a few dollars to tip him, but he raised his hand to stop me.

"No, Sir. We aren't allowed to accept any gratuity for services rendered. It's a rule of the club owners, but thank you for the gesture."

I thanked him and strolled up to the lavish clubhouse. I took note that the balmy weather for this time of year was still amazing. There was barely a cloud in the sky.

Inside, I was met by Wayne, Dwayne, and Sweetroll. Wayne walked over and playfully slapped me on the back.

"We're glad you decided to join us. Maybe a nice game of golf will help you unwind and relax," he remarked.

"I certainly hope so," I said. "Thanks for inviting me."

"Would you like something to drink or eat before we tee off?" Wayne asked.

"No thanks, I brought some coffee in a thermos. It's so warm today that I should have brought cold sodas instead."

Dwayne remarked, "Yes, for the day after Christmas this is remarkably warm weather we're having."

Wayne commented, "Maybe it's due to the global warming patterns."

A few minutes later, we were standing on the tee box of the first hole. Sweetroll ran chasing after some birds that were on the fairway. I watched his antics and looked around to see if any other golfers were being disturbed by his barking presence.

Not seeing anyone else on the course, I commented, "I hope Sweetroll's barking doesn't disturb other golfers today. The management might not like it if he does."

Wayne chuckled and stated, "No worries, there's no other golfers out here today ... except for us ... the course is closed. Since we own the club, I don't think management is going to mind his barking or being here."

I laughed and wasn't surprised that these two owned the club. I'd come to expect the unexpected with them.

"I see," I said. "Then no, I doubt management will object. I've never played on a course before where my group was the only one on it."

"Then we defer to our guest, letting you tee off first," declared Dwayne.

Knowing that my golfing skills were severely lacking, I teed up and swung my driver at the small white ball. As it occasionally does, I topped it and it dribbled only about fifty yards off the tee box down the right side of the fairway.

"It's always nice to get that first swing out of the way," commented Wayne. "Would you like to take a mulligan?"

"No," I said. "I'll play it where it lies and try to do better on my next swing."

Wayne stepped up with his big club. He swung smoothly and effortlessly. His ball flew about two-hundred-eight yards straight down the middle. Now, it was Dwayne's turn, and I was curious to learn how a blind man could play golf.

Sweetroll returned to Dwayne's side and Wayne handed Dwayne an odd-looking driver. He then guided Dwayne to a spot on the tee box, leaned over, teed up Dwayne's ball, and then stood back to give Dwayne room.

I was puzzled by this action, but Dwayne approached the ball with his club and even faced in the proper direction of the fairway.

I whispered to Wayne, "He's still mostly blind. How can he possibly know where the ball is to hit it?"

Before Wayne could answer, Dwayne stopped, turned, and pulled out a small inner rubberized piece stuck in his ear canal.

"Another of my inventions, Dabney," he said. "You see, my ball emits a high pitch sound inaudible to humans, but is easily picked up by my earpiece and the sensors inside my clubs."

He placed the earpiece back in, stepped up to the ball, and positioned his club behind it. He swung as hard as he was able, and to my astonishment, the ball flew almost as straight and even farther down the fairway than Wayne's. Then Wayne led him back to their golf cart.

Dwayne continued explaining, "There are three tones for which I listen. One tells me when the club is positioned right to hit the ball."

Wayne replaced the driver in Dwayne's bag and got in to drive the cart. I got into my cart and prepared to drive to my ball.

"And the other two tones? What are they for?" I asked.

Wayne and I drove next to each other in the carts while going fifty yards to my ball.

"When I hear the other tones, I squeeze the club's handle twice and I get a voice telling me how far the hole is, and what club I should use. The third sensor tells me the wind direction, plus what degree and direction to turn for aiming purposes," explained Dwayne.

I stood over my ball with a hybrid fairway club, swung as hard as I could, and this time my ball traveled down the fairway to within a nine iron of the green.

"Amazing!" I screamed out.

"Did you hit a good shot?" asked Dwayne.

"Oh, it was alright. Better than my first effort for sure. No, I meant it's amazing that you could come up with something like that, Dwayne. Your genius always impresses me."

He smiled and the three of us and Sweetroll drove our carts down the fairway. Wayne and I hit our next shots, and each of us was in the fringe near the green.

Dwayne's second shot was perfect and landed on the green, rolling to within six feet of the hole. He smiled and grabbed onto Sweetroll's harness, as the two of them walked toward the green. Nearing it, I parked my cart and saw a squirrel leap from a nearby oak tree. It raced onto the green and for some reason attacked Dwayne's ball. The squirrel slashed at it with his front feet, tossing it about in the air.

Seeing this, Wayne uttered, "Uh, oh!"

I watched the squirrel, silently wondering if it were rabid.

"What's wrong with that crazy squirrel?" I questioned.

"Squirrels hate the high pitch sound emitted by Dwayne's ball," stated Wayne.

A second later, Sweetroll caught sight of the squirrel. He tore off towards it, with Dwayne still gripping onto the dog's harness.

"Sweetroll hates squirrels," declared Wayne.

Wayne and I watched as Dwayne stumbled forward. He let go of the harness, but his momentum tossed him face-first into a deep sand trap near the green. From our vantage point, all we could see was Dwayne taking a nosedive, and then disappearing from view. As Sweetroll chased the squirrel up another tree, Wayne and I quickly raced towards the sand hazard.

As we cleared the rise of the green, we saw Dwayne stuck head first in the sand ... covered up to his waist. Just his feet were visible, and they were crazily wiggling.

"Great!" exclaimed Wayne. "This is the second time this week I'll have had to pull him out of a sand trap."

I suppressed a giggle and joined Wayne, as we latched onto Dwayne and lifted him from the sand. He spits grains of sand, wiped his tongue across his lips, and spewed out spittle. His hat was missing and his hair was a mess.

Wayne helped brush the sand off his brother and stood him up on his feet. I pulled out his shirttail and released the grit trapped inside there. Wayne dug his hands into the sand and retrieved Dwayne's golf cap. Dwayne wiggled his legs and the sand poured out of his pants onto his shoes.

Dwayne grumbled, "Another squirrel, I presume", as his lips blew away grits of sand.

"Yes, and I imagine your golf ball has a few rodent teeth marks on it," said Wayne.

He winked at me, as he placed Dwayne's cap back on his brother's head.

"Yeah, I'll bet it does," stated Dwayne. "I certainly know why they call these sand traps."

An innocent acting Sweetroll returned to his master, who leaned down, patted, and hugged his squirrel-chasing dog.

"It's okay, boy. I guess I'm going to have to change the tone frequencies of my ball."

"Either that or next time I'll bring you a pail and shovel and let you play in there till we finish," teased Wayne.

One thing I learned for sure about the twins; they were both talented athletes and certainly were not cabbage pounders when it came to golf. Neither one hit a ball out of bounds nor even off the fairway. Wayne was three-under-par at the turn onto the back nine. Dwayne was two under ... and he was blind. I felt like I was the one with a handicap ... mine being that I was a lousy golfer.

Later, on the back nine of the course, near a large pond, I needed to sink a five-foot putt for a par on the hole. I lined up my ball and bent to putt. I was just about to strike the ball when something distracted me and demanded my attention.

# POULTRY-GEIST

I heard the quack of a duck nearby. {Yeah, guess who} I raised my head and looked out onto the pond next to the green. What I saw there made my blood boil. I knew it seemed impossible, but it looked like the same pesky drake mallard with three white neck rings that I'd tried to rescue that day from my frozen pond in Ohio. My face reddened and my right eye twitched nervously.

I quickly straightened up and then waved the putter wildly above my head. In a complete rant of rage, I raced off the green and dove headlong into the water. I struck out with the club at the duck and splashed the water about, but when I stopped ... I no longer saw the fowl critter. As was always the case, this putrid poultry-geist {no, I refuse to capitalize their name any longer} it just disappeared.

I was left standing knee-deep in muddy water with a Lilly pad that hung from one of my ears. My clothing was soaking wet and I felt like the village idiot of a lost jungle tribe.

Then, before I could react, the duck came zooming by on the wing. It knocked off my golf cap and pecked me on the head. With another knot raised on my noggin, I threw a temper tantrum and wheeled about flailing my putter in the air.

Wayne rushed to the edge of the water and offered me a hand. I took it and sloshed out of the water onto the bank.

Concerned, he asked, "What's going on, Dabney?".

"It was that stupid duck again," I stated.

He looked at me like I was crazy and asked, "What duck? I didn't see anything, except you swinging at the air with your putter.."

"No, of course not ... you wouldn't," I replied.

Dripping wet, I stood in silence. My eyes boiled with anger and my head hurt. The knot the duck's bill gave me was joined by the pecks on the head Brighton Early had given me two days before. Frustrated, I broke my putter over my knee, stalked off towards the golf cart, got in, and started driving toward the clubhouse.

Wayne held out his arms and seemed confused. "Where are you going? We still have a few holes left to play."

I screamed back at him as I drove off, "Forget it. I'm done for the day. Thanks for inviting me."

On the green, Dwayne shrugged his shoulders and practiced his putting stroke.

Wayne remarked, 'Poor guy. I think he has a flock of pigeons nesting in his attic.'

He slowly walked up to join Dwayne on the green,

Dwayne said candidly. "It's just speculation, but I'm guessing he missed his putt."

\* \* \*

The next morning at 5:30 A.M. we heard the rooster crow in our bedroom, Daisy and I slid out of bed and began our morning routine. When I opened the door to my closet, before me there stood a flamingo on one leg and holding a tie in its beak.

I nodded silently, shook my head at the bird, and then remarked, "No thanks, I'm going casual today."

I cringed and shut the door slowly. When I jerked it back open, naturally the flamingo was gone.

After I showered and shaved, I got into my robe and went downstairs to where Daisy and the kids were eating cereal for breakfast. I suddenly remembered that today was Monday and I had two things to do. My appointment to see Dr. Andropoff was at 11:00 A.M., and I wanted to go see the facility where all the hens were raised and fed. The Kockle's egg business was almost as lucrative as the processed chicken.

Before I sat down to eat, I remembered that this was to be the first day of my subscription to have the Lancaster paper delivered. I tucked my robe around me, walked into the hall, and opened the front door. The newspaper was lying out front near the recently repaired brick mailbox.

"Good," I thought. Now I could sit down before each day and enjoy reading the news, cruise through the entertainment and sports pages, and then peruse all the ads for bargains in local stores and shops.

When I walked outside to get the paper, I noticed the distinct chill in the air, as if winter were like an overflowing lake whose dam was about to crack and fail ... allowing all that pent-up force to be released at any moment.

# POULTRY-GEIST

I picked up my newspaper and paused on the sidewalk in front of the house. I gazed in wonderment with a sense of accomplished satisfaction that Daisy and I had somehow managed to provide this type of home and lifestyle for our kids and ourselves. I gazed at the house with its steep gables, dormers, windows, chimney, pitched roof, and sturdy brick and stone walls. My mind searched for answers as to why I experienced the uneasiness I did about this place that was now our home.

I knew the fly in the ointment was all the madness that had occurred here since we arrived. The discomfort I had wasn't caused by the house but centered on the unwelcome visitors, visions, and disruptions caused by the fowl spirits that haunted this town and this place.

I looked about the neighborhood and saw the same red-tailed hawk still nesting high in that tree down the street. The other four houses spread apart on our cul-de-sac street were equally as lavish and regal as the one the twins had given us. I wondered if any of these neighbors had any problems such as ours. If they did, I wasn't sure how to go about asking them without seeming like a crazed kook. No, whatever problems we were encountering, I'd deal with them and was determined to somehow overcome these interruptions to our happiness and fulfilling our dreams.

* * *

On my second visit to Dr. Andropoff, I was led back into the quiet room by the female assistant where I immediately knew the routine and laid down on the leather couch. I searched the room for any sign of Rooster Galldern, but he did not appear. I could smell the doctor's pipe tobacco, as smoke wafted under the door to his office. I closed my eyes and tried to relax. Soft orchestral music played through speakers hidden in the headrest of the couch. I found that to be a soothing touch to help dim the tension in my body.

A few minutes later, the doctor made his grand entrance. Similarly dressed as before and smoking his pipe, he waltzed in and sat down in the armchair beside the small table where he kept his intercom and notebook. He picked up the notebook and turned his head towards me.

"After our previous session, I wasn't sure you'd return for another," he stated as he crossed his long legs. "I trust this time you won't seek to read the notes I scribble on my pad."

"No," I remarked. "I'll avoid that at all cost ... which I understand is now five hundred bucks an hour, so let's have at it."

"Very well, how are things now that you've had a few days to relax and enjoy the holiday?"

"Well, holding a tie in its beak, a flamingo was in my closet this morning; we saw an interesting manger scene with poultry in the park; a unique performance of the 'Twelve Days of Christmas' by a bevy of feathered fowl; I have three knots on my head from being pecked by a cartoonish rooster and a demonic duck; I chased the dead duck's ghost out of a golf course pond, and my car was egged by a cartoon rooster weather forecaster while I was at an Amish farm. So, how are Bob and Neil? Did you have good seats at the concert?" I asked in an annoying tone.

The doctor puffed on his pipe and remained silent. Annoyed, he sneered and wrote on his pad. I could tell by his shift in posture and by the tenseness in his jawline that he was agitated. I sensed in him a revulsion of my explanations, my candidness, and the fact that I did not fawn over him like he was some guru with the answers to all of life's ... and my problems.

"To begin with, yes, the concert was super and Bob is still a paranoid schizophrenic. I did not get Neil's autograph for he did not come back after he left the stage, but the concert and the tickets were marvelous," he told me in an equally bothersome tone.

He then paused, smiled, and switched legs he crossed.

His irritated voice proclaimed, "That sentence and this one will take approximately fifteen seconds for me to utter, which if broken down into dollars per second, that diatribe of yours and this nonsense reply has cost you about five dollars so far. Is there anything else you'd like to know before we begin to derive some way to help relieve your sense of being haunted by Poultry-Geists ... as your wife described them when my assistant spoke to her on the phone the other day."

He inhaled and exhaled smoke, then added, "I've got till 1:00 P.M. before my next patient, so waste all the time you'd like. And that's another five bucks added to the tab."

He was beginning to remind me of the Dr. Malcomb character played by Jeff Goldblum in the movie, "Jurassic Park."

Like the owner of the dinosaur theme park, Mr. Hammond, said about, Dr. Malcomb, "I really, really hate that man."

I wiggled on the couch and sat upon the edge of it with my feet on the floor and faced the good doctor.

"Let's cut to the chase, then," I declared. "I'm still going loony tunes and hearing and seeing things that others cannot. If I'm losing my mind, what can you do or tell me to prevent that from happening?"

He told me, "If I thought it would do any good, I'd recommend aversion therapy whereby you are isolated from any possibility of becoming exposed to any of these visions and voices you hear and see. That would require you being confined to an institution, so I don't think you or your family want that, do you?"

"No, of course not," I stated. "Besides I'm not sure where I could go to escape the pranks of the fowl contagion haunting my family and me."

"In any therapy, if at first, you don't succeed, then you're about average. In your confusion, are you telling me that all these things you're encountering are an honest response, or is there in you a deception to every rule?" he asked in words drenched with further sarcasm.

"I swear to you that all I've told you is true. Whatever these things are that haunt me, I assure you that to me ... they are real," I declared.

He calmly stated, "I don't disagree that you believe they are, but in my analysis, I cannot accept that such things are possible. No, in your batteries are not included scenarios, and what you think is real, I proclaim they are merely illusions of the mind. From what I can gather, you've not been exposed to any mystical moon rays, witchcraft, possession by demons, an imbalance of bodily fluids, or a brain tumor—"

"Hold on," I interrupted him. "When I had blood drawn lately, the lab came back and told me my blood revealed an anomaly and that I tested as having the DNA of a rooster."

He scoffed at me and said, "Nonsense! Now I know you're joking. That's not humanly possible."

"I'm just telling you what they told me," I said bluntly.

The doctor remained silent and wrote this on his pad:

"I feel like I'm speaking to a bedpost. He's a squirrel's idea of nirvana ... he's nuts. He's got a noggin as empty as last year's bird nest."

Then he said, "Dobney, you're confusing me with facts that make no sense."

I angrily responded, "I told you before my name is, Dabney, not Dobney ... Dr. Androopinoff."

"My apologies, Mr. Doodlebore, there is one more thing we might try."

"Yeah? What's that, Dr. Androidoff?" I mocked.

He stood and walked over to a wall cabinet where he pulled out a drawer and removed an article that had wires attached to a small lithium battery pack. There was also what appeared to be a metalized object about the size of a large dog collar.

He brought the whole contraption over and sat back down in his chair. He placed the metalized collar around his throat and attached one wire into a plugin to the collar. He then took the other wireline and attached that to the battery on one end. On the opposite end was a push-button device that he held in his hand.

"What's all that?" I asked curiously.

"This is a device I created that I use for mild shock therapy. Whenever you encounter one of your visions or hear voices, then you stop what you're doing, put this on, and then press this button ... as I'm about to do. You'll receive a gentle electrical stimulus that will pulse through the wire onto the collar around your neck."

"I'm not a dog that's attempting to leave the boundaries of its front yard. Where'd you pick that up ... at Petco?" I teased.

With that said, he pushed the button and his face grimaced a bit, as he received a mild electric shock to his neck.

"See, for the most part, it's quite harmless, but effective," he stated as he rubbed his neck.

I ridiculed him more and said, "Great! So, with all the crazy things I've been seeing, I'll be electrocuted and my brain fried like a boiled egg."

He explained, "It only sends a low voltage current into your neck to shock you back into reality. However, it is a cumulative instrument and the amount of shock you receive depends on how long you hold down the button. A caution though, for the intensity of the shock will increase with every occurrence. That is done to teach your brain to avoid shock by refusing to accept that you're seeing the apparitions. This behavior therapy should help resolve the distorted actions, attitudes, and emotions you have because of your hallucinatory fowl ghosts. You see, Mr. Doodleburn, you have within you the desire and capacity to self-solve this problem and fulfill your full potential."

He paused and I listened to more of his cornball, conceited educated explanation.

"This is basic Pavlovian or respondent conditioning. The conditioned stimulus is neural (the shock collar); the unconditioned stimulus is biologically potent (the visions you encounter) and the unconditioned response to the unconditioned stimulus is an unlearned reflex (your brain resisting the use of shock curing you of seeing the visions)."

"Sure, that psycho-babble makes perfect sense to me ... not," I replied sarcastically.

As he was speaking, suddenly Rooster Galldern appeared tapping his boot on the ground. His spurs twirled and he had a sneer on his face. He removed the slingshot from his holster, winked at me, and strolled up behind the doctor. He twirled the slingshot and quickly re-holstered it like a professional gunfighter. He tapped the doctor on the shoulder.

"You know, Pilgrim, listening to this sidewinder is about as effective as feeding oats to a dead horse. That dog won't hunt."

When the doctor heard Rooster's John Wayne drawl, he reeled and turned in his chair. Seeing the feathered pullet dressed in cowboy boots, hat, and vest ... and wearing an egg belt, slingshot, and an eye patch, the doctor went into a full-out hissy fit. His finger reacted involuntarily and pressed down hard on the shock button ... sending wave after wave of electric shocks to the collar. His eyes began to bulge, tear up, and turn red. His legs gave way and he collapsed back into his armchair.

Rooster shook his head and told me, "This ain't a proper place to park your carcass, Pilgrim. Besides, I wouldn't trust a man for five minutes that looks like he's been dead for twenty years."

I stood up, walked over, and pulled the button sending the shocks to the doctor's neck out of his tense hands. He slumped over and gasped for air. His neck was fiery red and his bloodshot eyes stared at Rooster and me like we were aliens from another planet. Perhaps he was right about Rooster.

With a smirk on my face, I shrugged and pointed my arms at Rooster.

I told the unhinged doctor, "Well, here he is, doc. Believe me now?"

Rooster told him, "No odor of commonality hangs about you, mister. So, stow your wares under somebody else's wagon and leave my Pilgrim here alone."

I grinned and told Rooster, "Well said, my eggs-pert, egg-o-tis-tic nimrod."

Dr. Andropoff could only nod his head and watch as Rooster tipped his hat and dissolved into thin air before him. I recognized the look of astonishment on the doctor's face and backed away out the door to the reception area. The doctor sat frozen and clinging to the arms of his chair. He shook his head as if to beg for mercy.

As I passed his assistant's desk, I heard his nervous voice over her intercom.

"Ms. Décolletage, please see that no more appointments are booked for Mr. Doodlemier ... and cancel all my other appointments for today. I'm going to see my psychiatrist, Dr. Feelgood."

"Alright, doctor. Are you okay in there?" she asked, but there was no response.

"Doctor Andropoff, I said, are you okay?" she asked again over the intercom.

Again there was no response. She stood and walked to open the door to his quiet session room. When she did, she saw three fat hens standing over him pushing the shock button, as he was getting zapped by the hens time and time again. She gasped and shrieked when she witnessed the impossibility of cartoon hens being real.

When he saw her, all his weak voice could manage to utter was, "Just shoot me, I'll never feel it.

# CHAPTER 18: Going Cah Cah

At supper time that evening, I went to the bottom of the staircase and called out for Cah Cah to come down from playing in her room to eat supper. Moments after my second call, she appeared lazily on the upstairs landing. She gazed down at me with her bright eyes. In her arms, she carried the faceless Amish doll that Daisy had given her.

I met her at the base of the stairs where she leaped into my arms.

"Dah Dah, I love you," she said sweetly. "I love my dolly too. See, I gave her a mouth and she now talks to me."

I smiled, but then did a double-take when I saw what she'd done to the doll. Instead of a mouth, it now had the beak of a chicken.

"It's a beautiful doll, Cah Cah, but that's not a mouth you put on it, but rather the beak of a bird," I said. "Where did you get it?"

"Dolly got it, Dah Dah ... that's what it told me it wanted."

In most cases, I would've dismissed such words from a child her age, but under the circumstances, with all that's happened I had to believe what she was telling me was real and the doll did speak to her. For a brief moment, I thought I saw the doll's beak move up and down as if trying to say something. I scowled deeply and my chin began to tremble. I sat Cah Cah down and spanked her behind playfully. She giggled and waved the doll at me. I was worried, yet hid my emotions from her.

"Alright, little one, go into the kitchen, and let's eat supper."

Patti parrot was perched on the kitchen faucet.

She squawked out these 'D' words, "Dainty daughter's doll does dispense deceptive dialogue."

From the irritation that caused me, I tossed a roll at the parrot and it flew off into the den to its perch.

"What was all that the parrot was saying?" asked a concerned Daisy.

"Don't pay any attention to that crazy bird, Mom," said Dooby. "He told me there was a deplorable dead duck designated to descend to dunk and doom Cah Cah's dumb fish."

Dippy chuckled and stated, "That's silly. How can a dead duck do anything?"

"Exactly," replied Dooby. "Just ignore that stupid parrot."

I rubbed one of the lessening knots on my head and wasn't so quick to dismiss what the parrot said.

After nibbling at her supper, Cah Cah took up her doll and began to sing, "Old McDoodledoos had a farm, E-I-E-I-O. And on this farm, they had some chicks, E-I-E-I-O. With a chick, chick here and a chick, chick there ... anywhere you look there's a chick everywhere. Yes, old McDoodledoos had a farm, Quack, Cluck, Quack, Cluck ... Quack."

As the boys laughed, Daisy and I just sat there with our mouths open and sighed.

"My dolly taught me that song. Quack, cluck, quack, cluck," she repeated.

\* \* \*

That night, Daisy had a dream; rather I should say ... a nightmare. She told me about it. In it, she said she found herself outside in the swimming pool in the middle of a snowstorm. The water was freezing cold and she saw the bubbles from her exhaled breath floating downward instead of up.

Her constricted throat tried to scream, but there was only silence and the sound of her heart pounding in her chest. Her lungs felt like they were about to burst when she realized she was upside down in the water. She flailed, got herself acclimated, and then pulled with her arms to try and reach the surface.

When she came up to the surface and her head reached above the waterline, she gasped for air and treaded water. She had to brush away the snowpack floating atop the pool, wiped her face, and then cleared the wetness from her eyes. She squinted as her vision cleared, and she began peering around.

Wearing only the nightgown she'd worn to bed; she groaned and inhaled a deep breath. Disoriented, very cold, and confused, she glanced to the north end of the pool, where she saw the rooster, Brighton Early. He was springing up and down on the diving board. He wore inflated floaters on his wings. With each bounce, packed snow on the board scattered and fell into the icy pool. He pointed his wingtip hands, crowed, and then dove in headfirst, causing a wave in the pool that swamped Daisy. She said she choked from swallowing some cold water, and then paddled herself around as she heard something from the other end of the pool.

Our two boys were casually dressed only in their swim trunks and were trying to teach three bikini-clad, fat hens how to swim. Dooby dove into the cold water on the shallow end and stood up in the waist-deep liquid where he swept away the floating snow. Icicles hung from his nose and chin, but he didn't appear to be phased at all by the cold. Meanwhile, Dippy rotated his arms, mimicking what the hens needed to do when they were in the water. However, once they leaped off into the pool, the hens sank like rocks to the bottom. Dooby pulled them out by their neck and lifted each one back onto the pool deck. Daisy claimed that as she watched all this, Brighton Early swam by her on his back and spitting water and snowflakes into the air.

Just why she didn't try to swim to the pool's edge and climb out on the ladder was a mystery to her, for she seemed unable to stop treading water right where she was. Her eyes then caught sight of me. I was up on top of the garage roof perched on my haunches like a pullet and began to flap my arms and crow ... over and over according to her. She then saw Rooster Galldern crawling on his knees and leading an apparent sightless Sweetroll around the pool. The dog had on Rooster's eye patch and walked on its back legs while holding onto the harness attached to Rooster.

She told me the climax to her nightmare and the last scene before she woke up screaming was that of Cah Cah floating in the pool inside a giant, transparent eggshell.

As Cah Cah came close to Daisy, she heard our daughter utter, "Momma, they are almost here."

That's how a distraught Daisy described to me what she saw. Sitting up on our bed, she was shivering and tears flowed from her eyes as I held her to me. She remained motionless for several minutes, as she hugged me and tried to catch her breath. I glanced at the alarm clock next to our bed. It was 3:00 A.M. The room was dimly lit by the lamp on the end table beside our bed. I leaned over and switched it off, as darkness filled the room. I embraced her and kissed her cheek.

"It's okay, hon. You're here with me now and safe. You just had a bad nightmare. Try to relax and get some more sleep. I'll be right here to wake you if you start dreaming or become agitated again,"

"I'm better now, thanks," she told me. "I don't know if I can get back to sleep, but I do need to go rinse off in the bathroom."

I let go of her and switched back on the lamp. She got up from bed, pulled on her robe that was in a nearby chair, and then slid her feet into a pair of warm, fuzzy slippers that I gave her for Christmas. She made her way into the bathroom, flipped on the light, and then I heard the water running as she sponged her face and body with a wet washcloth.

As she brushed her teeth, I heard her start to sing the same song that Cah Cah had sung at supper.

"Old McDoodledoo had a farm, E-I-E-I-O."

\* \* \*

By the end of the week, the weather had turned rather iffy and they (being Rooster Galldern on the Fox channel) were predicting snow after New Year's Day. Thankfully, we had no further incidents with <u>Poultry-Geists</u> from that Monday through to New Year's Eve. Instead, Daisy and I busily made plans to celebrate Cah Cah's birthday that day. When Daisy was pregnant with her, we'd hoped Cah Cah would be a Christmas baby. Instead, she blessed us with that December 31$^{st}$ date, and became a tax deduction we could claim for the entire year. She was by far the cutest of our three kids, and to us like a precious jewel and angel sent from God.

That day I spent helping Daisy and the boys decorate the house for Cah Cah's birthday. We hung up Happy Birthday signs on the walls and readied for the party soon to come that afternoon.

"How many kids are you expecting?" I asked Daisy.

"The three girls she's met on our block, plus Wayne and Dwayne's two little nieces," replied Daisy.

"I didn't realize they had another brother," I stated.

"They don't. They have a sister that's from New York. They're her kids."

I asked "Nice, is she coming too?"

"No, she couldn't come, so Wayne and Dwayne sent a private jet to get the girls and bring them here this week."

"I see. I guess we just haven't learned how to act rich yet, for that seems expensive."

Daisy laughed and placed bright ribbons around the lamps and scattered bits of confetti on the end tables of the den.

"You finish up down here," she said. "I'll go set out the cake and make sure the boys and Cah Cah are ready."

She left and went into our bedroom to get ready for the party in half an hour. Cah Cah snooped around in the kitchen rattling some of the presents we got her and trying to guess what was inside them. She clung to her faceless doll with the hen's beak and would place it up close to her ear as if she heard it speaking to her.

When Daisy came out a few minutes later, the boys and I took our turns and went to get dressed for the party. As I showered quickly, dressed casually, and brushed my hair I heard the doorbell ring. A few minutes later from the dining room, I heard several loud and laughing kids. They wore party hats and were blowing whistles. They sat around the table and the birthday cake with Cah Cah's name and five candles on top.

She saw me, giggled, and yelled, "Happy birthday ... to me, Dah Dah!"

I smiled and kissed her on the head. "Yes, my angel, happy birthday to you."

Wayne and Dwayne shook hands with me and introduced me to their two little nieces.

Daisy introduced the other three moms and their girls. One mother seemed very nervous and distracted by all the frivolity.

Sitting next to the cake, Daisy lit the candles with a fueled lighter. She, me, the boys, the moms and twins plus the five little girls began to sing Happy Birthday to Cah Cah. My angel's cherub face lit up with joy as she made her wish and blew out the candles.

As Daisy began to cut the cake into slices and set them on plastic plates, two other moms dished out vanilla ice cream to all of us. As I checked the aquarium for one of Cah Cah's birthday surprises, the nervous acting mother approached me. She seemed rather sheepish.

"Dabney, I should have walked us down here, but I'm afraid I drove my car and had a little accident while I was trying to park in front," she stated in an embarrassed manner.

"Oh, don't worry about it. We have a good bricklayer that can repair the mailbox."

"Yes, that's it, but how did you know I—"

"Ran into it when a bunch of hens raced out in front of you," I declared confidently.

"Yes, and I tried to miss them but swerved into your brick mailbox. I'll pay for having it repaired. For the life of me, I can't figure out where all those hens went, for they just seemed to vanish. Maybe I need a vacation."

"Nonsense, you and your daughter just enjoy the party. I hope your car is alright. Mine's still in the shop for having done the same thing for the same reason."

She shot me a puzzled look and said, "It's got a bent bumper and fender, but it shouldn't be too expensive to repair. I just hope my husband doesn't blow his top when he sees it."

After the kids gulped down the cake and ice cream, Daisy brought in Cah Cah's presents. She lit into the wrapped prizes like a man dying of thirst who found a pond of fresh water in the desert. Cah Cah giggled and excitedly opened each present and thanked those that brought them to her.

I walked to the wall between the kitchen and den that displayed the aquarium. I pressed a button on the wall and sliding doors raised on each side of it, giving me access to the fish tank.

Cah Cah had expressed concerns that little Nemo didn't have anyone of her kind to play with within the tank, so I'd gone back to that same pet shop and purchased another orange and black Clownfish. This one was inside a plastic bag filled with air and tied with a rubber band. I called Cah Cah over and showed her what was inside the bag.

She and the other girls cheered and clapped their hands. Then I untied the bag and released the Clownfish into the tank.

"Oh, doody, now Nemo has a Nemette girlfriend to play with," she excitedly told the girls.

"Yes, that's right, sweetie. The new fish is a girl. Or so I was told by the pet shop owner."

No sooner did that happen, than Daisy and I heard the far away quacking ... of a duck. {Yes, it still grates on my nerves to write that word}

Daisy turned towards the open kitchen window in time to see a mallard duck swoop in through the window, fly through the kitchen, and land with a splash in the aquarium. She and I looked at the duck and then grimaced at each other. I noticed right away that it had those same three rings of white-feathered markings around its scrawny neck.

"Does that duck look familiar to you?" I asked Daisy.

Yes, but it can't be. It was shot dead," she remarked.

Before I could react, the duck winked at me, and then dove with its head into the aquarium water, grabbed the first one, and then the other of the Clownfish ... and gobbled them down whole. Cah Cah and the girls were horrified and began to cry.

Angry, I went bonkers and raced to the fish tank. I grabbed that duck by the neck, lifted it out of the tank, turned it over, and began slapping it on the rump.

I screamed, "Oh no you don't, you devil drake! Spit 'em out, you crazy web-footed mongrel!"

The choking duck coughed and soon spit up the two fish. They plopped back into the saltwater, shuddered, and then wobbled away to safety behind a rock at the tank's bottom.

Everyone's face broke into a smile and I was pleased that by my actions this time I'd got the better of that fowl vermin.

Happy little Cah Cah raced to the tank and yelled, "Whoopee! Dah Dah saved Nemo and Nemette."

She shook an angry finger at the duck that I held by the neck.

She cried out, "Bad duck!".

The duck suddenly began to squirm and I lost my grip on its neck. It twisted and freed itself from my hand, flapped its wings, and before I or anyone could react, the duck flew back through the open kitchen window and disappeared as quickly as it had come.

We finished the party, thanked everyone for the gifts and for coming, and then wished everyone a Happy New Year. The twins had a flight to catch, as they were going to return the girls and spend the evening in New York with their sister in Times Square watching the ball drop on 2019 and turn into the New Year. At least Wayne would see it and describe it to Dwayne.

We planned to go into Lancaster where they were having fireworks that night, along with live music on a downtown stage. We planned to eat dinner at one of our new favorite restaurants in town and return home, as we knew the kids would be exhausted long before midnight. I had champagne on ice at home and Daisy and I would ring in 2020 by sharing in the bubbly and making our resolutions for the upcoming New Year.

After dinner, we joined the throng of others in town to watch the display of fireworks accompanied by patriotic music. It was about forty degrees outside, so we bundled up, found a spot in the park to view the show, spread a wool blanket on the ground, and then an hour after dark the fireworks began. Despite the chill, with my family beside me, I put away my worries and angst for a half-hour as we observed the uplifting, colorful array of bursting light filling the clear, star-filled night skies. As quickly as they appeared one after the other, each round of fireworks shot into the sky and then vanished into thin air ... leaving but a smoking trail behind from the brilliance displayed moments before. A gentle breeze stirred from the north and floated away the clouded powdery aftermath to clear the way for the next rising contrail of light and explosive luminosity.

Next to a couple of weeping willow trees devoid of their leaves, we watched eagerly as the dramatic climax to the show began to fill the skies with bang after bang and flash after flash of amazing color and light. I hugged Daisy and the kids to me as we all were awed by the spectacular conclusion of this marvelous celebration. That is, until the final volley and burst of fireworks displayed to us a rather unexpected sight. The very last combination of rockets formed in the dark skies the image of that rascal, Rooster Galldern, who tipped his hat to the crowd and grinned. All of it was done through the magic of some pre-planned program by whoever set off the fireballs.

"Oh, my Lord," I grumbled. "Is there no escaping that two-bit egghead?"

Daisy remarked, "The T.V. station must be responsible for that, Dabney,".

"Yahoo!" shouted Cah Cah as the show ended.

A strange cold sense of disappointed aloofness numbed my mind. I looked at my watch. It was 8:15 P.M., so we gathered up our things and drove home. I thought maybe I'd watch a football bowl game on T.V. and that it might help relieve some of my anxiety. At home, the kids departed upstairs to their rooms and I strolled down into the basement. Daisy removed her clothes, got into a comfortable gown and robe, and curled up in a den recliner with a romance novel she'd been reading.

In the media/game room below I reclined in a theater seat and turned on the television to the game I wanted to watch between Penn State and Notre Dame. I'd checked the small fridge and was certain the champagne was ready for Daisy and me to celebrate at midnight. The game went as I'd hoped, and Penn State got out to a two-touchdown lead by the half. I stood up, stretched, and retrieved a bag of salted peanuts from the bar cabinet. After relieving my bladder in the basement bathroom, I opened the door to the game room and what I saw astounded me. A horde of uniformed roosters dressed as soldiers were shooting at each other with muskets. Some clashed hand to hand with sabers and bayonets. One group of roosters wore confederate gray uniforms and the other wore union blue.

A rooster general sitting on a white sawhorse peered through a spyglass at his gray-clad troops, but fifteen feet away.

I saw one rooster race up to him and yell, "General <u>Leroy</u>, we're taking heavy casualties and can't afford to risk another charge."

I heard the general reply, "Yes, Captain <u>Barnyard</u>, I guess you're right. General <u>Thicket's</u> troops have got the high ground upon that pool table and are picking our roosters off like chickens being led to the packing house."

The blue general atop the pool table raised his saber high and screamed, "Troopers, we've got them feather-headed rebels on the run, so pour it to 'em."

A group of blue-clad rooster soldiers rolled up their slingshot egg canons and began to lob the shelled artillery at their enemies. On the other side of the room, gray-suited chicken soldiers were being creamed with egg yolks, egg whites, and sticky shells.

I heard an officer for the blue army tell his superior, "General <u>Banty</u>, our barrage is weakening their lines. I see that their general has even hoisted a white flag of surrender."

I looked and saw the gray-clad general waving what looked to be a stick with a handkerchief attached to it. In looking closer, I recognized the hankie, for it was one of mine and bore my monogram.

The blue general issued a command to his officer. "Colonel <u>Rhode</u>, take sergeant <u>Island</u> and corporal <u>Red</u> and go out to meet with that officer to accept his surrender."

I'm certain the entire battle scene was staged to disturb me and make me angry. As before in the park, I'd concluded that there was no getting away from these poultry pests. So, I decided to be coy and pretend they didn't exist. I grabbed my bag of peanuts and began walking through the crowded mob of chicken soldiers. I passed through them like they were vapor and I noticed I got some disbelieving stares from the two rooster generals that I sauntered past. I whistled, hummed, and started to sit down in my chair to watch the second half. I motioned at several of the roosters fighting in front of my T.V. to move to the left and right so that I could see the start of the third quarter. As I did, two eggs slammed into the side of my head. The gooey mess and eggshells stuck to my hair and some of the yolks entered my ear canal. My hand flew to my head and I felt the goo run down my neck and onto my shoulders.

However, rather than lose my cool and frolic in anger, I turned, stared at the eggs-e-cuted artillery, the blue-clad general, and then forced a wide grin.

"Congratulations on your victory, Generals Thicket, and Banty. Now if you don't mind, remove yourself and your troops behind the Mason Dixon line outside, for I want to watch the rest of my game in peace."

When Patti parrot came swooping into the basement and lit upon my shoulder, the battle group dispersed and vanished, as I knew they would. Patti somehow smelled or knew I had peanuts.

She squawked, "Demoralized, demobilized, denizens defeated. Dear Daddy does dole out delectable, delicious peanut doses to Patti parrot."

I fed the stupid bird, but dang it, Notre Dame came back to win by a field goal on the last play of the game. When it was over, I grabbed the bottle of champagne from the small fridge and went up to check on Daisy. She was entwined in the chair with the opened book she'd been reading. She was snoring and still exhausted because of the nightmare and having lost so much sleep.

# POULTRY-GEIST

I checked my watch and it was still about a half-hour away from midnight. I let her sleep and carried the chilled bottle of champagne into the kitchen where I stowed it away in our large fridge. I supposed it would wait until another celebration was in order. Then I washed my face and neck and wiped away the remnants of my uncivil chicken war egging. I then heard the sound of soft feet padding down the stairs. I peeked out into the hall and saw my little Cah Cah slowly descending the stairs onto the floor below. She dragged her faceless doll and looked drowsy and confused. I walked up to her and bent down on my knees to look into her sleepy eyes. I held my arms on her shoulders, which seemed to prevent her from falling over.

"Hey, pumpkin," I said. "Why are you up so late? Is something wrong?"

She rubbed her eyes and yawned. "My dolly told me that it couldn't sleep ... because I was roly-poly and had the wiggles."

I looked at the doll and I swear its beak formed a grin.

I picked Cah Cah up, kissed her cheek, and then carried her upstairs. I placed her in bed and tucked the covers around her. Her sleepy eyes could barely stay open and although she wanted to keep it beside her, I removed the doll and placed it in a chair across the room. I then turned off the lamp and checked on her. She was asleep before I could get to the doorway. As I closed the door halfway, I glanced back inside ... and saw the faceless doll again lying in bed beside her.

I stepped back inside, grabbed the doll, and carried it with me downstairs. Annoyed and upset, I walked into the den, opened a drawer in a wall cabinet, and slammed the doll inside it. Slamming the drawer shut created a noise that woke Daisy. Drool ran from her mouth and when I tried standing her up, she slumped back into my arms. I wound up lifting and carrying her into our bedroom, where I placed her in bed and covered her much in the same way as I'd done with Cah Cah.

She immediately fell back to sleep. I sat on the edge of our bed across from her and glanced at my watch. It was twelve minutes till midnight. I went into the bathroom, brushed my teeth, and combed through my hair. The effort removed even more of the egg yolks I'd missed when in the kitchen.

As the master of the house, I wondered if perhaps I wasn't indeed becoming nutty as a fruitcake. The home was supposed to be a place where one resided and retreated in private; a refuge where one felt comfortable and relaxed, could unwind from the stresses in life, and enjoyed the peace that dwells within there. As I stated before, our residence had become a conning tower, a superstructure for the <u>poultry-geists</u> to use as a docking station. In their spatial dimension, I felt as if we were merely pawns, they used to grease us down the road to insanity.

From the bathroom, I walked back into the den and checked to make sure the front door was locked and secure, as I always did before going to bed. After seeing that the deadbolt was thrown and the door locked, I chuckled to myself, thinking a fat lot of good that does, for the fowl threats for us come through walls whenever they want.

As I sauntered back to our bedroom, I heard the clock on the wall in the den strike. It chimed twelve times, so I realized it was midnight.

"Happy New Year," I whispered to no one. At least I thought it was to no one.

In the semi-darkness of the room, I heard, "It will be, Pilgrim, if you quit lollygagging and hither which do something about this boondoggle."

Yes, the first words I heard in 2021 proved to be the familiar voice of Rooster Galldern.

I asked, "What boondoggle? What are you crowing about, you bobble-headed moron?"

"We've been on ice for a coon's age, Pilgrim, so saddle up and take care of business if you expect to be fetchin' tranquility in this here forthcomin' era," he stated firmly.

Great! I was directed into the New Year with not a clue as to what that stupid fowl meant.

# CHAPTER 19: Hair Today - Gone Tomorrow

Daybreak the next morning came early as Brighton Early lived up to his name and woke me at 5:00 A.M. I yawned, crept out of bed, and stumbled into the bathroom. I reached into the shower and turned on the faucets. I sprawled out on the toilet and after I saw the steam forming, I slipped off my undershorts, stepped into the shower, and closed the glass door behind me. I stood in the warm spray, then soaped down my face, head, and hairy chest.

Through sleepy eyes, I glanced into the fogless mirror on the tiled walls. My thoughts harkened back to midnight and what Galldern had told me. I wondered what he'd meant by a 'boondoggle' or that remark he made about being on the ice. I could make no sense of it. Even in the warmth of the hot water, the melancholy I felt swept through me like the sudden chill from an icy blast to my psyche. The promises of today and tomorrow seemed only to present me with more problems and I knew there was to be more trouble ahead if I could not somehow rid myself and my family of the persistent poultry pests that haunted us.

Meanwhile, as I showered, the rooster, Brighton Early, materialized in the bathroom and opened a drawer where Daisy and I kept our grooming items. He chuckled, as he removed the bottle of cream oil that I used on my hair when I combed it. As he listened to me mumble to myself in the shower, he emptied the bottle and replaced the contents with one of Daisy's products that she uses to remove hair from her legs. After filling it three-quarters of the way, he poured back some of the cream oil and screwed the top to the bottle.

Brighton placed the bottle back in the drawer, flashed a prankish grin, and then disappeared into the wall. After I finished and exited the shower stall, I wrapped my robe around me and put on clean underpants. Then I walked over to my space at the long vanity. From my drawer, I took out a can of shaving cream and lathered up my face. Careful not to cut myself, I used my double-edge razor and shaved away the stubble. I returned the shaving cream to the drawer, picked up a bottle of after-shave lotion, opened the top, and then splashed some of the lotion onto my hands. I patted the lotion on my face. As always, I winced at the slight discomfort but enjoyed the manly smell and its cooling menthol that soothed my shaved skin.

Next, I took out a comb, and then removed the bottle of cream oil that Brighton Early had tampered with and filled with mostly hair remover. I poured my usual generous amount of the white lotion into the palm of my hand. I noticed it seemed a bit thicker than normal and smelled different, but I just shrugged off that fact and began to apply the contents onto my scalp and hair. I vigorously rubbed it in; for I liked the way the cream always gave me a glossy head of controllable hair that seemed healthy and free of any split ends or dandruff. I picked up the bottle, sniffed my hands, scowled, and thought that since I'd had this bottle for almost six months, perhaps it was losing some of its consistency and it was time I bought a new bottle.

I combed through my hair dozens of times, spreading the cream thoroughly into my thick mane and scalp. As I always did, it was a two-step procedure and I reapplied more of the cream oil, repeating the procedure and massaging more of the lotion into my hair.

When I was satisfied with the way my hair looked, I placed the top on the bottle and tossed it into the trash can nearby. By now, it was almost 6:00 a.m. I walked into the bedroom, where I saw that Daisy had gotten up as well. I supposed she was in the kitchen getting the kids' breakfast ready. I dressed and put on my shoes, and went waltzing downstairs into the kitchen. What I saw there made me stop in my tracks.

My sons, Dippy and Dooby were crawling across the floor on their knees. Cah Cah poured grape nuts onto the tile floor, as the two boys pecked at the specks of grain, and licked up the small nuggets ... all the while cackling like two banty roosters.

I yelled at them, "Dippy! Dooby! What are you doing?"

Holding up the cereal box and clinging to her faceless doll with the beak, Cah Cah shot me a blank look.

She snarled her lip and asked "Why'd you put my dolly in a dark drawer, Dah Dah? She no like that."

I scratched at my itching head and wondered how the heck she found that doll.

I pretended that I was sorry, "Forgive me, sweetie. I thought you were done playing with it."

"I'm feeding the boys breakfast, Dah Dah. Here, chick, chick, chick," she cooed.

Annoyed, I grabbed the boys by the arms and lifted them off the floor.

"Stop that!" I commanded. "Get up to the table and eat with a spoon from a bowl."

I then asked Cah Cah, "Where's your mother?"

Little Cah Cah meekly pointed upward with her tiny finger.

"Is she upstairs? What's she doing? She should be down here fixing your breakfast." I declared.

Dippy and Dooby kept on cackling as they got their cereal bowls. However, when I left to go find Daisy, they poured the cereal onto the table and began pecking at it again. Cah Cah laughed and smiled at her faceless doll. I couldn't locate Daisy in any of the upstairs rooms. As I was about to give up and return downstairs, I heard a shuffling noise coming from the attic. I opened the door that led up there and when I topped the stairs onto the landing of that storage area, I saw Daisy curled up in a dark corner. She too was cackling as I approached her.

I heard her begin to sing, "Old McDoodledoos had a farm, E-I-E-I-O."

I leaned down over her and when she looked up into my eyes her expression was like some brooding snail had crawled across her face. Her lips were pursed, drawn thin, and twisted into a contorted frown. Her eyes were wild and her cheeks rosy as if she had a fever. I felt her head and it was sweating. I guessed she was physically okay, but she didn't look altogether.

"Daisy, what's wrong, dear? Why are you up here alone in the attic?" I asked.

Babbling like a child she said, "They're cooped up. Gotta be freed."

"Who's cooped up and needs to be freed?" I asked.

"Them. They're coming." She said as she became more agitated and eager.

She grabbed me by the arms and glared into my eyes, "Quit lollygagging, Pilgrim, and do what must be done."

I bounded backward onto my backside, for those were the identical words I'd heard Rooster Galldern utter at midnight. What blithe spirits had taken hold of her to cause her to say that? I shook her and my eyes filled with tears, but she just calmly stood, tilted her head, seemed to come out of her daze, and then looked down at me.

She glanced about and then at me.

I said firmly, "Daisy, what on earth are you doing up here in the attic? I've looked all over for you. Dust yourself off, get out of this dark attic, and come down to breakfast."

* * *

I led her downstairs and into the kitchen where the boys were scratching with their feet and scattering grape nuts all across the room. They cackled like hens and flapped their arms up and down. Cah Cah was sitting on the floor with a contented look on her face. Daisy thought they were playing a game and she too began to flap her arms and cackle. When Cah Cah carefully rose onto her haunches, underneath her was a hen's egg.

"Look, Dah Dah. Me laid an egg." she giggled.

The blood drained from my face and I felt as if I was swimming upstream and pushing on doors marked, 'pull.' My head itched, so I began to scratch it. When I did, my hand brought back several strands of hair. Great! Now all this worry was making my hair fall out.

"Cah Cah, I hope you got that egg from the fridge," I said. "And you boys stop acting like a couple of old hens. And stop encouraging them, Daisy."

I pointed at the table where the kids and Daisy joined me, as I glared at them like they were sheep and I was a pouting, impatient shepherd.

"Now, get it together people. Let's face the facts that we're all being influenced and obsessed by these pesky hens, roosters, duh {I almost said ducks ... dang it, I did say it}, and other fowl that are making us act and perform as if we're going goofy." I stated firmly.

The boys grinned at me and Cah Cah grinned at her stupid faceless doll. Daisy just looked at me, said nothing, and gathered the kids into her arms like she was a mother hen swaddling her chicks.

"Now, I want you all to resist any urges you don't understand. Right now, I think we're like a wheelbarrow that's being pushed around and can be too easily upset." I proclaimed, knowing that Cah Cah likely had no idea of what I meant.

"Just stay together and have faith. Whatever's causing us this grief, I'm going to find a way to stop it ... no matter what," I said confidently.

As Daisy was about to speak, the phone rang in the den. I sighed, got up, and walked in to answer it.

"Oh, hi Wayne. Happy New Year to you and Dwayne too." I paused and listened. "Oh, my! What does an alarm like that mean?" I asked.

From his end of the line, Wayne stated into the phone, "It's likely a false alarm, but if it's not then there could be a fire inside the hatchery or in the processing plant. The fire department is on the way, so I'll keep you posted."

"Alright, I'll go over to meet them and to see what's happening"

"No, not yet. They'll call me if there's a fire and tell me if it's safe to go near the plant. Some of the fertilizers we use on the fields around there might give off toxic fumes or even explode if they catch fire, so hang tight and I'll let you know what they find."

"Okay, I'll wait here for your call."

Worry was etched on my face, both for my family and for the plant. Silently, I wondered if perhaps the pesky poultry-geists had anything to do with the alarm and possible fire. I couldn't imagine though that they'd burn down a facility where live hens were being raised.

* * *

A nervous forty-five minutes went by before Wayne called me again.

"Good news, Dabney, there was no fire, but someone broke into the plant's tower room. Dwayne and I are going down now to meet with the police to see what they know about the break-in."

"I'm glad there was no fire. I'll get ready and meet you there in a few minutes," I said.

"You don't have to do that, it's New Year's Day. Stay home, relax, and watch some football. We'll take care of this."

I sighed and reluctantly told him, "Alright, but I'll be in tomorrow morning for certain."

"Okay, enjoy time with your family and we'll see you then," he told me.

I hung up and turned to Daisy, who had a queer look on her face. She walked up to me, placed a hand in my hair, and then when she removed it her hand was filled with familiar-looking dark brown hair ... mine to be exact.

"My Lord, Dabney, what's going on with your hair? It's coming out in clumps," she whined.

I ran my hand over my scalp and was horrified to see another clump of oily hair that dislodged from my head.

"I don't know what's going on," I squalled as I ran into our bedroom and stood before the mirror over the vanity. Sure enough, more than half of my scalp was vacant of any hair. I panicked, tossed off my clothes, and turned on the shower. I didn't wait for the water to warm up, for I quickly grabbed the shampoo and began to squirt it on my noggin.

I scrubbed hard, thinking that whatever had caused the hair loss must be due to something I was either allergic to, or else what I'd put on my hair to cause this. Eliminating radiation as a source, I soon concluded that it must have been the cream oil I used. I remembered it smelled funny, but I'd been using that brand of hair tonic for almost twenty years and there was never this type of reaction. As my mind pondered the possibilities, Daisy entered the bathroom. To my further anguish, I saw that the shampoo only served to loosen the remainder of my hair. The floor of the shower was soon packed with cranial hair. So much that it stopped up the drain. I ran a hand across my scalp and it felt as barren as a baby's behind.

"Oh, no!" I bellowed like a bull. My knees trembled and I slid down the tile walls onto the floor. The hot water poured upon my limp body and hairless head. From my mouth then came a faint cry of unassisted woe. I felt like a man driving with the brakes on that got stopped just short of insanity. Still, I felt I was skidding into it and out of control.

"Darling, are you alright in there?" questioned Daisy, her voice tinged with concern. "I think I know what's happened to cause you to lose your hair," I heard her say.

I sniffed away a forming tear and vowed silently not to cry. This was a hard tumble, but I then got annoyed more than scared and vowed not to fall over my cliff. I rose to my feet, opened the shower door and Daisy handed me a towel. I wrapped the towel around my waist and stepped out onto a bathroom rug. Immediately, I saw Daisy's startled expression as she stared at my bald head. Her mouth formed a peculiar twist and I knew by her chewing on a fingernail that she was trying not to laugh.

I growled, "So help me, if you say one word about being married to, Yul Brynner, I'll scream."

"Of course, I won't, dear. I guess it depends on how you look at it, but I think you more resemble a handsome, Bruce Willis."

I snarled at her and again looked at myself in the mirror. Still wringing wet, I saw my face form a sultry sneer and squint like Bruce might do in a movie. Daisy could hold it back no longer and burst out laughing.

"I'm sorry, dear. Please don't be angry, but I think someone put my creamy hair remover into your bottle of cream oil."

She held up a bottle of her hair remover that was almost empty.

"I bought this just last week and haven't used any yet. Now, it's almost empty."

She held up my bottle of cream oil and sniffed it.

"Yep, this has the distinctive smell of my cream, so I'd say you are the victim of a cruel prank."

I sighed, slipped on my robe, and sat down on the edge of Daisy's marble tub.

"Yeah, and I have two choices as to which detestable rooster did it," I stated. "So, how long do you think it'll take for my hair to grow back?" I asked her.

"Well, that depends on how your scalp reacts to the potent remover. It could take a couple of weeks or only four or five days."

"Jumpin' Jehoshaphat! What if it's permanent and I stay this way?"

"Then we'll drill three holes in your head and use you like a bowling ball," Daisy said teasingly.

I curled my lip in defiance and said, "Very funny. Stop with the chin music, tap the brakes, and show a little mercy for a frustrated, globe-headed man."

"Yes, darling, I'm sorry for your loss, but you have an awe-inspiring shaped sphere atop your neck and shoulders; one that any man would be proud to display. How's that?" she asked, with a broad smile on her face.

With that, I stormed out into the bedroom and dressed in my jeans, slippers, and a T-shirt. Daisy went upstairs to help Cah Cah bathe the new puppy. I avoided the boys and secluded myself in the basement den to watch a football bowl game. As I leaned back in my recliner, I noticed how chilled my head was, so I got up and put on a wool toboggan cap that I found in the basement closet. I returned to my recliner, sat down, and with the remote turned on the television.

Instead of the game, the image that came on the set was that of Rooster Galldern. I angrily used the remote and began switching from channel to channel, but on each one, his ugly mug appeared on the set.

"Hey, Pilgrim, you seem lower than a gopher hole and look like something the cat dragged in. With a noggin that's as slick as a boiled onion, I'm guessing everything ain't hunky-dory," he alleged.

"Leave me alone, you dirty, rotten, fratter-hazophat. {Whatever that means ... I was just frazzled and mad} Haven't you done enough damage for one day? Get out of my life and T.V. Just let me watch my game."

Rooster drawled, "Hold on, Pilgrim. I know you're all bum-fuzzled with your nose out of joint, but before you get all whomper-jawed and het up about it, I'm not the one that slapped you bald-headed.".

"Maybe so, but I bet you had a hand ... a wing ... or influenced someone else who did."

He drew a deep breath and puffed out his fluffy rooster chest.

With rancor in his voice, he said, "Go ahead and cry till the cows come home. You're just whistling in the wind like always. Farmers ought to hire you to keep their windmills running. Talk till you're blue in the face, but that's how the cow ate the cabbage, Pilgrim. I know you've had your slats rattled, but quit blaming me for your problems,"

I retorted, "I've tried picking up the crumbs of sensibility, but you're like Indian underwear; you keep on creeping up on me. You're more agitating than a washing machine and despite what you say; you are the cause of all my troubles."

He responded, "Kiss my true grits, Pilgrim. I know I'm about as welcome around here as water on a leaking ship, but you're gonna have to learn to butt with your head ... and in case you don't know, it's that hairless, brainless knob atop your shoulders."

I pointed the remote at the television and growled, "Well, right now I need what only you can provide ... your absence. And anytime in the future that you pass by our house we'd sure appreciate it."

Rooster snarled, grabbed his slingshot, and pointed it at me. "Later, Pilgrim, I have to get back to my rat killing."

With that, I fumed in anger, shut off the television, and then stormed upstairs. My boys were in the den already watching a football game on T.V. Lying on the carpet on their stomachs watching the game, they saw me and bid me come watch it with them.

"Hey, Pop, it's raining so hard at this game in Miami that some guy just intercepted a pass, got confused, and ran the wrong way into the other team's end zone," declared Dooby.

"I know how he must feel. I've been running in the wrong direction ever since we got here," I said dejectedly.

I plopped down in another recliner, threw my feet over the chair arms, laid back, and placed a hand under my head while I gazed at the frog strangling rain in the game being shown. In two minutes, we watched two fumbles, four dropped passes, and the ball being centered twelve yards over the head of a punter.

"It's hard by the yard today. I hope those players don't rust," said Dooby, laughing at the absurdity and tribulations of the teams playing that game.

"Hey, Pop, what's with the toboggan in the house? Is your head cold?" asked Dippy.

I pointed to the television. "No, I'm wearing this to practice keeping warm for when I race at the Olympics on the downhill bobsled."

The boys laughed and together we watched the remainder of that sloppy game, won by the team that got the touchdown by the wrong-way player.

* * *

That night, I sat for hours patting my head with a washcloth-soaked poultice Daisy made me from a combination of hydrogen peroxide, menthol aftershave, and Epsom salt dissolved in warm water. It made my scalp tingle a bit and I hoped it helped to nourish and stimulate the hair follicles below my skin line ... to grow back sooner rather than later.

She prepared me a frozen dinner and I ate supper in our bedroom. The kids asked her if I was getting sick, but she assured them I was okay, just tired. After they went to bed, I raided the fridge and made myself a large sandwich, and drank a glass of iced tea.

I knew I'd have to face my children the next morning, but by then perhaps Daisy would have time to tell them not to laugh or give me a hard time.

"I'll tell the kids, but what are you going to tell the twins when they see you've lost all your hair?"

I told her, "I've been thinking about that. I'll tell them I accidentally used your hair remover instead of my cream oil. That's a half-truth, and should sound plausible."

✳ ✳ ✳

Daisy and I woke the next morning to Brighton Early's crowing reveille. I tried to catch him before he dissolved, but had no luck. So, I got dressed to go to the plant. When I looked outside, there'd been a two-inch snowfall overnight and it was only 29 degrees. That afforded me the perfect excuse to wear the wool toboggan cap. I drew it over my barren scalp and picked up my heavy coat to put on when I'd venture out in the cold.

I first made my way downstairs and ate some cereal with the kids.

"Dah Dah, you look funny in that cap," giggled Cah Cah.

"Yeah, Pop, you should take it off while you're eating," Dippy stated.

I glanced at Daisy, who raised her brows and turned her face away so that I wouldn't see her chuckle.

"It's going to be cold this winter, so I'm wearing it to get used to the feel of having to put one on every time I go out," I told him.

"Good idea, Pop. I'm going up to get mine too," said Dippy, and then he ran upstairs to get his cap.

Daisy shook her head and buttered the toast for me that popped up out of the toaster. After eating, I kissed her and the kids, while Dippy gave me a thumbs up. He smiled and sat there smug while wearing his toboggan cap.

Since the holidays were over, Dippy and Dooby were heading back to school today and after breakfast walked down the street where they were picked up by a school bus. Cah Cah remained at home with Daisy, but we discussed sending her to a local preschool nearby.

I walked out, got into my loaner car, and backed out of the driveway. As I did, I saw a Fed Ex truck pull up near our mailbox. In my rearview mirror, I saw the truck swerve and hit the mailbox, sending it into pieces. As expected, I witnessed the stunned driver hop out to see ... no hens ... only a destroyed mailbox and his truck's bent bumper. I adjusted my rearview mirror and grumbled. I took out my cell phone and hit the dial button.

Soon the man on the other end answered.

"Good morning, Juan, "I said. "Are you available again today?" I asked.

After he replied, yes, I told him, "Good, then come on over, but this time leave the concrete base and we'll put a potted plant there instead. Please, then pour a new concrete pad and build the mailbox on the other side of the yard."

"Si, señor. You know, at the rate this is going, I'll make enough money to retire in a year. When I do, I'll give you the number for my cousin, Jose." he said jokingly.

"And I'll give you the number of my psychologist," I said sarcastically.

\* \* \*

Meanwhile, back at their home, Daisy stood looking at her reflection in the large mirror over her vanity. Her belly seemed somewhat extended, and she checked her plump profile in the glass. She patted her stomach and winced. Patti parrot flew into the bathroom, turned its head sideways, and looked at Daisy.

"It then squawked, "Damsel Daisy does discover dropping a delivery."

She swatted at the intruding parrot with a rolled-up newspaper, but it flew away back into the den.

"Dropping a delivery?" she pondered. "What did that crazy parrot mean by that

# CHAPTER 20: Egg Head Nest

After I arrived at the plant, I got several stares and snickers from some employees because of my hairless head. Wayne and Dwayne took it in stride and told me it actually didn't look bad at all. They said my bald head combined with my full mustache made me appear very masculine. Of course, Dwayne had to get closer to me. He ran his fingers slowly over my head as if he was doing a cat scan of my skull.

Later, I got curious about such practice and discovered on the Internet that back in 1786, a physician named, Franz Gall, {not Marshall Galldern's relative I hope} created a pseudoscience he named, 'Phrenology.' It was a practice of determining how the structure and measurements of the human skull directly affected one's personality, aptitude, and general health. To me that all seemed like a lot of hooey, but I silently wondered if perhaps that wasn't why Dwayne was so thorough when he was feeling my slick head. At any rate, I survived the ribbings that morning that I took from folks there. I was hopeful my cranial hair would grow back in a week ... or two ...or sooner I hoped.

In the afternoon, the twins and I rode out into Lancaster County to an Amish farm where Wayne told me the farmer there was interested in selling off part of his lucrative farmland.

"Why would he sell off part of his acreage?" I asked Wayne.

"I'm not sure. These Amish folks are very confidential about why they do anything."

Dwayne commented, "We've purchased several portions of land from the Mennonites and Amish around here. Because they plow under the manure from their farm animals, all their land and the soil are fertile and rich in nutrients. In addition to the large hen barns, Wayne showed you near our plant, we free-range hens on these types of properties and get a premium in the markets for the eggs and fryers we raise there. As a result, we've made a lot of new friends among the locals, which is always good business. It also affords us insights into their culture that other competitors don't have."

I knew the twins were shrewd businessmen and understood how important t was to remain friendly and deal with the local farmers around the area.

When we pulled up the long snow-covered path leading to a beautiful farm with a huge barn, silo, corral, and large two-story farmhouse, four warmly dressed kids raced to meet our car. As we pulled up to the house, a bearded farmer rode up in a black, covered, one-horse buggy like so many other of his kind drives in Lancaster County. He too wore a warm coat and had on a fur-trimmed hat with flaps that pulled down over his ears. Wayne parked and got out to meet him, as I helped Dwayne out of the car's passenger-side door. Sweetroll immediately began to chase after a grouping of chickens that strolled casually around the yard.

"Hey, you egg-sucking dog, get back here and leave those chickens alone," asserted Wayne.

Sweetroll reluctantly ceased his chase and returned to Dwayne's side.

The farmer gathered his kids and shook Wayne's hand. The wife remained at the door to the house smiling out at us, but she did not come outside in the cold. He then walked over to meet Dwayne and me.

He smiled and said, "Hello, I am Herman Pick. These are my children, Dora, Flora, Clara, and Auto. Welcome to my family farm," he stated. "That's my wife, Alfrieda, in the doorway. She's ill, so please excuse her for not coming out."

The twins and I waved to her and she waved a weak hand back at us. The farmer then hopped up into his buggy and led us out to the land he wanted to sell. We followed him in the car down a pathway, up over a rise, and then he stopped atop a hill. From the buggy, he pointed out at the pristine farmland below. Even with snow-covered fields, we saw two separate streams flowing through the land, plus dozens of oak trees, and land bordered by hand-strewn wood rail fences on three sides. To me, it all looked like a Currier and Ives postcard.

We parked and met the farmer at the crest of the hill overlooking the lush valley.

"Here it is gentlemen. These fifty acres have been in my family for over a hundred-twenty years. I regret to say that with only four children and having two hundred other acres to plow, I cannot work this parcel any longer.

I could sell it off to others of my Amish neighbors, but I desire to get a premium price for this premium land so that I can afford to better care for my family. If you buy it, I may even buy one of them smelly tractors.

"Herman, after seeing this magnificent acreage, the price you quoted us is more than fair. We'll take it. I assume you want the cash," stated Wayne.

"Yes, thank you. So, if you'll come back to the house, I'll draw up the papers. Once you bring me the money, you can get the deed recorded in your name at the tax office."

As the twins started to get into their car, I strode over to Herman as he crawled up onto his buggy.

"Herman, is it alright if I ride back to the house with you in your buggy?"

"Of course, brother Dabney. You're very welcome."

As Herman drove the buggy, the warm air I exhaled from my lungs formed fog in the chilled air. Wearing my gloves, the toboggan, and warm linen pants with a heavy coat, I wasn't uncomfortable on the ride back. The crisp air made me feel alive and invigorated. For a brief few moments, I forgot all my problems. That is ... until I heard a voice coming forth from the back seat of the buggy.

"If you don't climb the mountain, you can't see the view, Pilgrim," declared Rooster Galldern.

Startled, I almost asked the farmer if he'd heard that remark, but from his expression and focus upon the path the horse traveled and where the buggy followed, I could see he had taken no notice of words spoken by our added passenger.

"Pilgrim, I've been told your human ancestors hung by their tails from trees. Of course, somewhere in the past one of your forefathers must have been a cuckoo. Mine hang by their feet on metal racks and their heads chopped off in your twins' processing plant," he stated angrily.

I gritted my teeth and swatted my hand behind me in an attempt to shut him up. It did no good.

"Yeah, now take your new Amish friend here. Nice guy, but around him, I'd feel about as safe as a rooster in a barnyard with the preacher coming for dinner," he stated.

"Stop it!" I yelled out as the buggy pulled up to the house. Rooster waved and then disappeared behind the buggy.

The farmer looked at me with an odd expression and was not sure why I was yelling.

"Here we are, brother Dabney. Come in the house and warm up while I draw up the papers. I have some warm cider that I think you'll enjoy."

As I exited the buggy, I looked back toward the rear seat, but Rooster was gone. A moment later, he came loping around the buggy on his sawhorse and setting up straight in his saddle.

He glared at me and said, "I don't mean to drop a rusty bucket down your well, Pilgrim, but your missus is home moping around like an old hen with an egg broken inside her. And baby sister is cuter than a speckled pup and a bowl of sunshine, so quit acting like a thundercloud and go feather your nest."

"My nest?" I exclaimed as the farmer guided us toward the house.

"Yes, you're right. In the old country we do refer to a home as being our nest," said Herman.

I looked over my shoulder and as usual, Rooster was gone. I spent the next half-hour in discomfort and worry about what that ornery yard bird had said. What had he meant and was Daisy okay? In the house, we drank some of the delicious cider the farmer offered us. We also met his sweet wife that was sick with a stomach virus. I excused myself and went into another room to call Daisy on my cell phone to check on her and the kids.

The phone rang several times before she answered. "Hello! Yes, dear, I'm fine. The boys are home from school and down in the basement playing pool and chasing Bingo. Cah Cah's playing with her doll, and I'm in our bedroom lying down."

"Chasing Bingo?" I asked.

"Yes, that's the name Cah Cah came up with for the new puppy," she told me.

"Okay, well I think we're about done here, so I hope to be home in about an hour or so. Can I bring you anything?" I asked.

"You might stop at the feed store and pick me up a bushel of corn and some bird feed," she bluntly declared.

Startled, I knew then that not all was well at home. I recalled the way she'd acted in the attic and now was asking me for what was essentially chicken feed. It made me cringe.

"Daisy, are you sure you're okay?"

Of course, I am hon. I'm warm and as cozy as a hen in an incubator."

Once again, I cringed. "Hon, please, just get some rest. I'll cook supper when I get home."

I heard a loud happy cackle on the line and she hung up.

* * *

In our bedroom at home, Daisy opened some built-in drawers in her closet and began to take out soft cotton and nylon undergarments. She patted her stomach once more, and then began to arrange a nest-like circle of undergarments, plus the straw she'd gathered from outside onto the carpeted closet floor. She slumped against the wall for a moment. Wearing her nightgown, she then straddled the straw and garments, squatted on top of her nest, folded her arms, and then began to rock slowly and methodically back and forth on her haunches.

A quiet, quirky purring came forth from her throat and she seemed in a state of bliss. Her hand moved slowly to her abdomen in an unconscious gesture like that she'd had when she was pregnant. She sank into the softness of the grassy bed and fabrics, nested comfortably, and hummed softly.

Later as I drove home, the snow increased in its intensity. Large flakes began to fall and soon the roads were covered in the freshly packed snow. The loaner car I drove had snow tires, but no four-wheel-drive like my Jeep. I wanted to get home as soon as possible but do so in one piece. Despite the near white-out, I was able to make my way safely onto the Pleasant Place cul-de-sac where we lived.

As I approached the driveway, to my surprise the bricklayer, Juan, was bundled up in a thick overcoat and hood working on the mailbox he'd moved to the other side of our property line. He'd made a concrete pad and was slapping mortar onto the frozen brick. Though his hands and nose turned cherry red, the brick mason laid one brick after another onto the stack, tapped them down, and picked up another. He stopped long enough to wave at me, as ice cycles hung from his chin.

My only thought was, "Now there's a man who loves his work."

Inside the house, I called out for Daisy, but she did not answer. I walked into the kitchen, but she was not there. I heard the boys laughing below in the basement and the pup, Bingo, growling and happily racing around after them. I walked through the den into our bedroom. Daisy was just coming out of the closet and seemed disoriented. Her hair was a mess and her gown was soaked in sweat. I helped her as she sat on the corner of our bed.

"Are you alright?" I asked. "You seem delirious and confused."

She looked at me with eyes that didn't quite seem to focus.

"Huh? Yes, I'm okay, just a bit dizzy," she said.

I helped her lay back and went into the bathroom where I ran some cold water over a washcloth. I brought it back and set it on her forehead. I wiped her brow and held her hand. It was clammy and I patted it as she sighed and closed her eyes.

In a quiet voice, she told me, "I'll be alright, hon. Just let me rest for a while."

I drew her feet onto the bed and she laid back. I fluffed her new 'foam' filled pillow under her head, kissed her cheek, shut off the overhead light, and walked to the doorway.

"I love you, Daisy. Get some rest while I fix supper for us."

"Don't worry about me," she whispered. "Just make something for the kids and you. I'm not hungry."

\* \* \*

That night after supper, I went into the den where I saw Cah Cah laughing and watching a Disney channel cartoon on the television. She gripped her doll and I saw her whisper to it as she giggled. A silent scream rushed through me and I felt tempted to snatch it out of her hands and tear it to shreds. Still, I saw that she took comfort from it, so I ignored my urges and sat down in my recliner to read the newspaper. When I opened it to the front-page headlines, there I saw a photo of Rooster Galldern, sans his hat and displaying his rooster's comb. Out of his uniformed cowboy outfit, he was dressed up in a spiffy suit and tie.

The headline read: "President Galldern to visit China." I snarled and turned to the second page, which had several advertisements with more photos of Rooster. In one, he was posing in a bathing suit with his eye patch upside down and on a different eye.

The ad read: "Enjoy the warm waters of this Caribbean paradise. Fly Southern Airlines."

I growled as every page had some photo posted of that crazy rooster. He was a football hero catching a pass in the end zone; a race car driver holding up a trophy; a doctor touting a newly-discovered wonder drug; a suspect wanted in a robbery; a photo of him doing his televised, weather forecast; and of course, my favorite ... the photo and obituary of a local politician.

"Would that it was so," I whispered.

I angrily crumpled the newspaper and took it to the fireplace. I tossed it onto the gas logs and then flipped on the switch that ignited the logs. To my relief, the newspaper soon turned to ash. However, I knew the effort would not stop the regeneration of this pest, for he seemed indestructible and kept probing his spurs into my psyche.

The lights in the den suddenly dimmed and all that remained was a soft glow from the firelight of the gas logs. Cah Cah turned off the T.V. and ran upstairs to her room. Standing there alone, I then heard only Rooster's voice in my head.

"You're like that duck you hate, Pilgrim. Although you appear calm on the surface, underneath you're paddlin' as hard as you can to stay afloat. Come on, quit worrying, smile, and don't be such an old sourpuss."

I shrieked, "Shut up, you will-o'-the-wisp prowler."

"You might as well laugh at yourself once in a while, Pilgrim; everybody else does."

I shouted back, "My New Year resolves to get you out of my life, so scram and go make an omelet out of what's left of that bird brain of yours."

He boldly stated, "You know, Pilgrim, you're like an Easter egg. You're ornamental on the outside but hard-boiled on the inside. I'm holding up here in your world and an itch that you've got to keep scratching ... like it or not,"

I smirked and replied, "And you're an infectious plague-carrying phantom that speaks to me in riddles and vague blurbs that drive me crazy trying to figure out what the heck you mean."

"When the time comes, you'll know the ropes, Pilgrim."

There was a swoosh of wind that stirred the fire, and then silence. I knew that he was gone again. I went upstairs to tuck Cah Cah into bed, and then set out the boy's clothes for the next school day.

I then went downstairs and shouted down to the basement, "If you boys have any homework do it before bedtime. So, quit playing, take the dog with you, and go upstairs."

They complied and soon went up while I joined Daisy in our bedroom. She was fast asleep. I didn't get much of my own that night for worrying about what might come next.

# CHAPTER 21: Into the Breach

The next morning, after getting ready for work, I called out to Daisy, but she did not answer me. I strolled into the kitchen, where the boys were buttering toast and drinking milk.

"Something's wrong with mom," stated Dooby.

"What do you mean?" I asked. "Where is she?"

Dippy swallowed a drink of his milk he motioned towards our bedroom.

Dooby grimaced and said, "She came in here, smiled, opened a can of corn, poured it on the table, and wobbled out. She looked like she's been sleepwalking, Pop,"

I strolled back into our bedroom and peered into the bathroom, but she wasn't there either. I listened and then heard a weak sound coming from Daisy's closet. I walked closer, and there was the distinct sound of a hen cackling. I slowly opened the door and looked inside.

My eyebrows rose, and then I stopped and inhaled a big breath. My wife was sitting in the corner of the closet. In her hands, she had knitting needles and yarn. Around her were soft undergarments and even a few strands of straw.

When she saw me, she stopped cackling and smiled innocently.

"What are you doing?" I asked meekly. "The boys are up and said something was wrong with you. What's all this?"

She slowly shook her head to disagree.

"I'm fine and needed more here," she stated candidly.

I knelt beside her and brushed the matted hair from her face. She put down her knitting.

"Daisy, are you sick? Please, tell me what's going on."

She smirked and slowly raised. Underneath her in the soft nest of clothes was a speckled egg as large as one laid by an ostrich. She leaned and patted it gently with her hands.

"It's a miracle. I laid it just after sunrise. I think it's a girl," she stated emphatically.

I backed away against the closet wall. An electrifying shudder raced through me. A convulsing shaking seized my body and I visibly trembled with anxiety. I looked at Daisy as if she'd lost her mind.

"Isn't it beautiful?" she said.

"Beautiful?" I screamed. "Daisy, it's an egg. You're not a platypus, humans don't lay eggs."

"I know, but somehow I did. Aren't you happy?" she asked me.

"Happy? No. I mean ... I—"

My cell phone rang and I instinctively answered it.

"Yeah, hi, Wayne. What? Another break-in? Sure, I'll be there. I'm on my way."

I scowled, but bent and kissed Daisy as I rose to my feet. She rocked back gracefully on her heels. I pulled reluctantly away from her and held her at arm's length. I glanced at the huge egg and smirked. She looked up to see me pause just inside the closet door. I stood there for a moment trying to decide what to do or say next. She seemed almost catatonic.

"An Egg! My wife laid an egg! I'm haunted by an eye-patched rooster, by another that crows at dawn and walks on ceilings, and a stupid duck that should be dead. My world has unraveled and become insane," I cried out in desperation, "Please, Daisy, just get up and ... and—"

I had a brain freeze, and then could only blurt out, "I can't deal with this right now. I'll call you from work," I told her.

When I disappeared from the closet, Daisy carefully covered up and tucked her egg into the downy clothing. She then came out of the closet and crept upstairs, where she paused at the hall landing. She gazed down the hall at Cah Cah's room and slowly toddled toward it. The door to the room was slightly ajar and Daisy glanced inside to see our daughter soundly sleeping next to the faceless doll. She smiled and turned to walk back down the stairs, where she heard the boys open the front door and race out into the cold to catch their school bus down the street.

In our bathroom, Daisy sat down and looked at her reflection in the vanity mirror. She stretched dreamily and seemed to savor the feeling of well-being that she'd experienced from laying her egg. She began brushing her hair in a soothing rhythm, all the while humming the tune, "E-I-E-I-O.

A chick, chick here ... a chick, chick there ... here a chick ...there a chick ... everywhere a chick, chick."

\* \* \*

The snowfall from the night before had ceased, but the forecast, according to the Fox channel's crackerjack meteorologist, Marshall Rooster Galldern, declared we were in for more winter weather on the way.

After leaving the house, the skies again began to darken and the cold winds began to howl. The chill in the air didn't bother me nearly as much as my chilled spirit. I wondered if anything was ever going to be right again. I thought about the egg in the closet I saw under Daisy. My brows drew together in an agonized expression. I considered that 'thing' to be a miscarriage conceived by conspiring poultry-geists intent on committing their surly, grotesque deeds upon us. I concluded that they'd somehow convinced Daisy that she'd laid that egg, when in fact it was a deposit left by one of those fowl foes.

At the plant, I struggled to open the front door, for the wind blew against it as I stepped inside. I immediately removed my gloves and toboggan cap. The receptionist, a middle-aged woman with dark hair greeted me.

"Good morning, Bruce ... I mean, Mr. Doodledoo," she said teasingly. "The twins are in the tower room where the beak-in occurred. They're expecting you."

"Thank you, Sara," I said. "Wait, did you say beak-in?"

A soft gasp escaped her and she corrected herself, "Oh, I meant break-in."

I wondered if her tongue-tied words were an accident, or if she'd just experienced some of the fowl madness with which I'd been dealing.

I changed the subject. "Is there any coffee ready in the beak room ... I mean break room?"

"Yes, I made a fresh pot of it just before you came."

"God bless you. I'm so cold I may drink the whole pot."

"Yes, it looks like winter arrived and will stick around till late spring," she said. "The man on the radio said an Alberta Clipper is headed our way and we're going to get buried in snow by the end of the week."

"Perfect," I stated sarcastically. "With my luck, we'll probably have a nuclear winter. I may just go find a snowdrift, sit in it, and break both my legs with a hammer."

Sara laughed, but then she noticed that I wasn't joining in the mirth and was indeed distressed. I winced and walked toward the break room. She peered out at the ominous forming storm clouds rolling across the skies.

In the tower room, Dwayne and Wayne were settled in behind a computerized workstation near the conveyor where Wayne was scrutinizing numerous video monitors. He saw views from several angles of what was security footage of last night's breach into the area where the grilled poultry was gravity tenderized. They introduced me to two local detectives who also watched closely as the HD video playbacks were shown.

"Was anything stolen or damaged?' I asked.

"The conveyor line was thrown out of synch and the locks on the rear door were disabled," said Wayne. "However, we can't find that anything was taken or broken."

"It might have been some teenagers just trying to get in and swipe some chicken," stated a detective.

As I looked at the videos, I quickly recognized one of the culprits. I pointed at three of the monitors and exclaimed, "There they are. I recognize one of them, but the other three are none I've seen before."

One of the detectives glared closely at the monitor, and then at me with an inquisitive look on his face.

He asked "There who is? We've looked at these security tapes for almost an hour and there's nothing on them except the equipment and some dead chickens. Some of the carcasses do seem to be moved and jostled around by something, but we reason that's a glitch in the video monitor."

"Wait, Dabney. Are you saying you see someone you know in the videos?" Dwayne asked.

I bristled, but then wondered if it wasn't another trick of the pesky poultry-geists.

"You're telling me you can't see that big one-eyed, egg-toting cowboy rooster, that scruffy-looking wolf, and the fat old hen?" I asked of the trio.

"No, as a matter of fact, we don't see that. If you are, I have to wonder what you've been snorting or smoking," stated the other detective.

I struggled to keep my composure, but it had already been a bad start to the day and I didn't need this guy's condescending attitude thrown in my face. I knew what I was seeing. The fact that they didn't or couldn't see the three perpetrators annoyed and angered me.

Wayne stepped in between the detective and me. "Dabney's recently moved here from Miami. He's tired and stressed, so give him a break and slack off the attitude."

The first detective flailed his arms in disgust and said, "Alright, Wayne, but we've got better things to do than wasting our time looking at videos of invisible phantoms."

The other detective pointed at me and said, "Joking about a crime is no laughing matter, Mr. Doodledaft."

The second detective then stated mindlessly, "I decree, disavow, and declare to a degree your defenseless decorum's a doleful, delicate delusion directly derived, dispensed, and dispatched by disparaging double talk."

The first detective with ice water in his veins replied to his partner, "Enough already, Mack. I might also ask, what have you been smoking? Get your coat and let's split."

He handed his card to Wayne. "Call us if you find any evidence of something missing, or something strange on these tapes."

\* \* \*

A few minutes after the detectives left, the twins and I shut down the videos and walked back into the office area.

Wayne seriously questioned, "Dabney, you're serious about what you saw on those videos?"

"I know what I think I saw. It was as I described," I told him.

"Dwayne and I would ordinarily make you an appointment to speak to a therapist, but after what that cop spouted with all the "D's" and what we were compelled to say in that café when we all went "P' nuts ... I tend to believe you."

"I've already been to a therapist and he was as loony as I seem to be of late. I wouldn't blame you if you didn't believe me, for it does seem crazy.

Sadly, the fact is that stupid rooster and other cartoonish fowl have been pestering me and my family ever since we got here."

Dwayne grunted and pounded his fist on the desk in front of him.

"I knew it. Dad wasn't going insane. He did see all those things he told us about."

"What things?" I asked.

"Well, for one, he said he was being hounded by some crazy acting rooster that of all things spoke in a John Wayne accent and was dressed like a cowboy. We dismissed it, for the doctors told us it was just his dementia causing him to hallucinate."

"Whoa!" I stated anxiously. "Then he too was a victim of this insanity? My condolences to him and you, for its indeed a lot to deal with and a heavy load to carry."

All of a sudden, the alarm went off in the tower again. That was followed by two other alarms sounding from the processing plant and hatchery. It was chaos. We looked at each other in total astonishment.

"What's happening now?" I shouted.

"Alarms are going off all over the facilities," Wayne said excitedly.

"We'll go check the ones in the plant and hatchery. The other's the shutdown alarm in the tower room," said Dwayne as he held onto Sweetroll's harness.

"You two go check out those others and I'll join you after I see what's happening in the tower room," I told them.

I threw up my arms, tossed my coat on the desk, and dashed out of the office toward the tower room. As I quickly made my way there, I withdrew my cell phone from my pants pocket. I tried to call home, but for some reason, there was no signal strength, so the call did not go through.

Inside the silo tower room, I found that the conveyor line of grilled chickens had come to a full stop. I located the reset switch and flipped the lever to the ON position. However, the line still did not restart.

I grumbled under my breath, and then I heard voices. I walked toward the tower where the grilled chickens tumbled over and fell upon the stainless-steel platform pan. From fifteen feet away, I stepped behind the conveyor and crouched down out of sight.

# POULTRY-GEIST

There, to no surprise of mine, I saw Rooster Galldern standing near the bottom of the tower. He stared up at the top from where the chickens fall. My eyes trailed upward too and I saw the same fat, old cartoon hen I had on the video monitor. She inched her way towards the edge of the tower where the grilled chickens tumble off.

I heard Rooster's Foghorn Leghorn-like yell, "Now what in the high and gosh almighty is that old hen up to now?"

I watched as the hen closed her beady little red eyes, pointed her wings outward, and then dove headlong off the tower.

"I'll be horsewhipped. She jumped!" Rooster hollered.

He reacted and raced to where she'd fall. My mouth took on an unpleasant twist as I observed the hen tumbling and falling through the air towards Rooster. A moment later, she dropped safely into the strong wings of Galldern, who snatched her out of the air and brought her to a complete stop. He groaned and seemed to have momentarily lost his breath.

He sighed and snarled, "Hello, ma'am! What's the big idea, lady? You almost scared me outta ten years of my life, which I can't spare."

The frizzled feathered blue hen had a dumb, surprised look on her face. As Rooster set her down and stood her up, I saw her flash him a look of pure delight.

He grinned and asked, "Hello there, wide sister. What might your name be?"

She smiled and dropped her gaze in an embarrassed manner.

"I'm Fanny Frizzle. Why'd you catch me?"

"Had to ma'am. I'm Marshall Rooster Galldern, and it's what I do," he stated and winked at her.

Her beak formed a tight, demure smile and she asked, "That so? Are you single and uncommitted, Marshall?"

He burst out laughing and said, "Committed? Me? That'll be the day."

She smirked and glared at him. "What's that you say?"

"Uh, I said it's a nice day, ma'am," he stated humbly.

Rooster placed a wing around her, and they walked around and off the steel platform. Curious, I continued to listen to their conversation.

"Rooster, I'm just a useless, fat old hen that can no longer lay eggs."

He comforted her and began to flirt and whisper into her ear ... or at least where a chicken's ear should be. She exuded a loud, blissful cackling.

"Pa-cawk!" she squawked. "You say you're a movie star?"

"Sure thing, missy. You ever see the movie 'True Grits? ... The Search Chairs? ... A Quiet Rooster?' I lost my voice in that one and couldn't crow."

"Well, I don't get out much these days, but how exciting to meet a famous actor."

"Well, yes I suppose I am. You should have seen me in the other flick. I engaged with Lucky Nude Pepper and his gang. He lost all his feathers when I shot him and he fell back into a pot of boiling water down on Goose creek. Once again facing him, I loaded and drew my slingshot, grabbed my goat Bo and put the reins in my mouth, charged them ruthless brigands ... and ... well, feathers flew that day, I want to tell you. All except for Lucky Nude Pepper that is."

She asked meekly, "Well, I imagine a fine-looking one-eyed rooster such as yourself has many hens in your coop. Why would you save an old cluck like me?"

"Some things a rooster just don't get over so easy. Like the sight of a plump hen tumbling through the air, the light reflecting off her feathers. Like her lying still in my arms, with a face and beak fresh as a dry well ... I mean a young pullet," he stated with his tongue in his cheek. {If a rooster has a tongue ... I guess he does, for he sure flaps it a lot}

Rooster then pulled the old hen close to him, looked down at her, and then peeled up his eye patch revealing both his virile and beckoning eyes. He blinked at her and she swooned.

Then he boldly said, "I mean to kiss you in one minute, Miss Fanny ... or see us hitched in Fort Smith at Judge Quacker's convenience. Which'll it be?"

Fanny went limp in his arms, acted faint, and then placed the back of her hand over her feathered forehead.

"Oh, Rooster, you had me at hello."

I snarled at the absurdity of this whole unlikely romantic interlude and backed away towards the front door. It was about then that I heard the rear door creep open. I stopped and hid behind another area near the conveyor.

As I looked over the edge of the conveyor line, I saw a stealthy cartoon wolf sneaking towards the grilled chickens lying just off the stainless-steel pad of the conveyor that carried them into the flash freeze and loading zone to be shipped out.

He carried a duffle-type bag labeled: "Rooster Costume." He slobbered, opened the bag, stepped into the loose suit with white feathers, and then pulled a zipper that tightened the suit about him. Once settled into the costume, the wolf appeared to be identical to a rooster.

My sharp eyes couldn't believe the ridiculousness of this whole scenario. The alarm was off, so I decided to leave and have Wayne and Dwayne come in to see what was holding up the conveyor line. I hoped by then the witnessing of the wolf, plus Rooster and his romantic urgings with the fat, old hen would be gone. However, as I attempted to stand and walk away, my shirt got caught on one of the conveyor sprockets.

I grumbled and leaned over onto the conveyor. As I did, the line suddenly restarted and began to roll again. The wolf in his rooster guise took a position beneath where the chickens began to fall. He rubbed his hands together, as drool dripped off his fake beak.

I yanked at my shirt, but it did not loosen. Instead, I soon found myself being dragged along and approaching the tower. I placed my foot upon the conveyor line and tried to break my shirt free, but this only complicated the issue, for then my pants leg got snagged onto one of the paddle-like pans. I scrambled and kicked as hard as I was able, scattering several grilled chickens off their paddles and onto the floor, yet I was still pinned to the one that carried me ever closer to the position where the paddles elevated and began to rise up the tower. Like a roller coaster, the chain pulled me up like it would anxious, anticipating thrill park riders.

I screamed out but found myself being lifted upside down into the air. The conveyor lurched but did not stop. I was lifted higher and higher up the tower towards the top. Meanwhile, the wolf withdrew and opened another large bag, in which he began to stuff grilled chickens. Rooster just watched and cocked his head, evidently curious as to what this other rooster was doing.

As I reached the top of the tower, I saw a small, yellow-feathered cartoon chicken wearing thick eyeglasses and a Mexican sombrero. It scarcely took notice of me as I squirmed and panicked trying to get loose. As my body was pulled along and across the top of the tower, I noticed the title of the book the chicken was reading: "Chicken Little."

"Chicken Little? I screamed. Help me, I'm falling!"

"No, señor. I'm Pepe Polo, a leedle cheek-en. Yes, you are right, theez guy eez falling."

I about fainted as I reached the edge of the tower, despite my efforts and straining to pull loose, like the chickens ... I tumbled down the incline and over the edge of the tower. I plummeted towards the ground and the steel platform. My life flashed before my eyes and I saw Daisy and the kids, the twins ... and finally before I figured I was about to cash in my chips ... I saw Galldern and that stupid mallard duck with the two-neck rings.

Below, the unsuspecting wolf in rooster clothing glanced up. Though he heard me cry out, it was too late for him to move out of the way. My tense body slammed into the wolf, sending white feathers flying in every direction. The conveyor suddenly hung up again and no other chickens fell.

Oblivious to what had happened to me or the chicken-suited wolf, near the edge of the silo, Rooster opened a door to go outside with the old hen. When he did, the cold wind slammed him in the face. He grabbed Fanny by her wing and spun her to him. He kicked the door shut and a faint light twinkled in the depths of his one eye. He held Fanny close to him.

He remarked, "Brrrr! That there wind's colder than a frozen river."

Hearing my crash to the floor, he turned and witnessed the tangled mess that squirmed about beneath the tower. I was numb both physically and mentally and wondered why I was still alive. If I were, I had no idea how that could be from having fallen from so high.

Rooster and Fanny sashayed over to the tower, where they heard me groaning. I supposed I was still alive but probably squashed like a potato. I moaned, sat up, and saw six red birds flying around my head. As Rooster approached, one stopped and lit upon my bald noggin.

He saw that I appeared like someone completely out of his gourd. It was no wonder considering the force of the impact and my fall. I attempted to focus my eyes, but the room spun as if I was on a merry-go-round.

"Whoa, Pilgrim! Your eyes look like two minnows swimming in a fish bowl," said Rooster.

From beneath me, the wolf finally popped his head out. His fake beak was twisted and stars swam above and about his head. When Rooster stood next to us, the wolf tried to stand but wavered back and forth.

"I smell a rat in rooster's clothing," Galldern snarled at the wolf.

I must have had a brainless expression on my face, for I sat merrily watching the little red birds swirling about my head.

Fanny looked at me, and then at the costumed wolf in a rooster suit. His hairy tail was hanging out.

She commented to him, "Hmmm, you're kinda frazzled, but not bad looking. Are you single?"

Rooster steadied the wolf and brushed him off.

"Fella, you look like five miles of bad road," he stated.

When the wolf saw the large rooster, he tried to run away, but Rooster would have none of it. He grabbed the wolf by the throat.

"Now hold on there. If you're lookin' for trouble, young fella, I'll oblige ya."

The wolf's legs wobbled and he attempted to sit down. Fanny tried to calm Rooster.

Instead, he became quite agitated and angry.

"I know, I know. I haven't lost my temper, but fella, you could've gotten somebody badly hurt today. Somebody ought to belt you in the mouth," he declared.

He paused and then said, "But I won't! I won't!"

Fanny swooned and made goo-goo eyes at Rooster. His eye blazoned with anger and he reared back and made a winged fist.

"The heck I won't," he declared in a gruff voice.

He slammed the wolf's face, knocking the loco Lobo silly and away from me. The wolf, with a large knot rising on his forehead wobbled and tried to crawl off.

Rooster stuck out a large boot, stepped on him, and stopped him from doing so.

He cried out, "Pretending to be a rooster. I should spread-eagle you over a wagon wheel."

I somehow garnished enough strength to try and stand up, but immediately I fell onto my face. Rooster snatched me up and stood me on my feet once more.

"You gotta get back in the saddle, Pilgrim. I won't always be here to pick you up."

My face formed a silly grin. I wavered and stumbled, but remained standing.

He cautioned me, "Take it easy there, Pilgrim. One foot in the stirrup at a time."

I wobbled on weak legs and swayed back and forth.

Mostly incoherent, I mumbled, "I should have bought a squirrel."

From out of nowhere, another rooster swooped in and appeared before me. He stopped near the wolf and stuck out his chest. He was dressed in a Marine's uniform, with high-top black boots and a sergeant's stripes on his sleeve.

He yelled at me, "I'm Gunny Sergeant, Earl Lee Riser. You need to shape up, Maggot. Toe the line and come to attention."

Still cockeyed, I flashed him a stupid expression, took a step forward, and fell again onto my face. My eyes were crossed and I dizzily sat up. I managed to get my legs under me and I tugged on the sergeant's arm. My mouth formed words that came forth from a scrambled brain.

"Hey occifer, I swear to drunk I'm not as good as you think I am."

He sneered, his eyes narrowed and his back became ramrod stiff and straight.

I continued to utter nonsense, "I'd like to help you out, sarge. Which way did you come in?" I then mumbled, "I know how Wile-E-Coyote feels and you're just jealous because the voices only talk to me."

There was a sudden jerk of the conveyor, and several more cooked chickens began to roll off and fall from the tower. Several of them smacked me right in my already jumbled-up noggin.

I heard my voice stammer, "Under the spreading chestnut tree, the village smithy stands." I held out my hands, palms up. "Look, it's raining chickens."

Rooster stepped forward and pointed at me. I now had a bluebird perched on the index finger of each hand.

He told the sergeant, "This wrangler's stirred up like a bowl of oatmeal and ain't up to followin' no marchin' orders, you olive drab blunderbuss."

Earl Lee shoved Rooster aside and got up again in my face.

He snarled at Rooster, "Out of my way, Tubby. I'll make a Marine outta this peckerwood, or else."

Somehow thinking he was speaking to me, I stammered, "Peckerwood? I'm a bald-headed eagle, not a woodpecker."

Dazed and groggy, I snatched hold of a flitting bluebird. I patted it on the head and ruffled its feathers.

"I uttered, "Pretty bird. I will love him and squeeze him ... and I will call him, George."

Rooster bristled at Earl Lee and reached for his holster. He fondled his slingshot.

"Tubby? Listen, fella, I ain't never shot no one I didn't have to, but in your case, I may make an exception."

Earl Lee laughed and replied, "Is that a fact? Well, what're you going to do, Tubby, egg me to death?"

He pointed at Rooster, and then fondled and patted the colt .45 pistol in his holster.

"Now this here's a real bludgeon master, Sheriff, so wipe that stupid look off your ugly face."

Rooster hitched up his britches and declared, "I can't help this stupid look, and I'm a Marshall, you cock-a-mammy, stiff-legged moron. Brandishing such a hog leg, you must think I'm a real dangerous rooster."

It was then that the first instrument of my binomial state occurred ... whereby I became part human and part rooster.

Noticing my bald head, in a quick move, Rooster reached up and snatched the rooster comb off his head, and slammed it down onto mine.

He then commanded me, "Here, Pilgrim. Hold onto this for me. I don't want to get it damaged."

I felt the floppy appendage with my hand. It seemed firmly planted atop my head and had suddenly attached itself to my skin as if grown there.

Earl Lee went eyeball to eyeball with Rooster's one un-patched eye.

blowing backward where he came to rest at Rooster's feet. The two of them went into a stare down like two bulls about to butt heads. Miss Fanny backed away and opened the rear door. The wind knocked the wolf down. He fell onto the floor and rolled like tumbleweeds

Without flinching, or taking his eyes off Earl Lee, Rooster bent his knees, took the wolf's neck in one big wing hand, and then flung that scruffy critter ten feet away. He momentarily broke eye contact with Earl Lee and glanced with a puzzled look at the wolf, now unzipped and free of his rooster suit. The wolf still held onto his bag of cooked hens.

"Who the heck are you, anyway?" Rooster inquired of the dopey wolf.

The scrambled wolf muttered, "I'm Justin Casey Howells ... the third."

"The third?" laughed Rooster. "Yeah, you do look sort like a recycled old pair of underpants at that,"

Earl Lee snarled and said, "Never mind that egghead. Are you gonna draw or not, you one-eyed fat fowl?"

Rooster's eyes narrowed and he ruffled his feathers. His hand swiftly went to his holster and the two roosters crowed.

"Fill your hands, you son of a painted hen!" yelled Rooster.

The two roosters had their hands perched over their holsters, but neither drew their weapon.

Rooster gritted his teeth and whispered, "Now, you understand, sarge. Any move you make, accidental or not. Your fault, my fault, nobody's fault ... it don't matter. I'm gonna scramble that thick egghead of yours ... and these unfertilized spawns of mine were rotten a month ago."

Earl Lee countered with, "And you understand, Tubby, that if you draw down on me, I'll split you in two like a ripe melon."

The two slowly backed off from each other. The tension built, and as my head cleared somewhat, I crawled away to a safe distance from them. About this time, an Italian rooster stepped out from behind the tower. {I know he was from Italy, for he had on a shirt that had written on it, "I'm from Italy."}

To my complete surprise, he yelled, "Cut! That was-a-great. It's a wrap for today. We'll return tomorrow to shoot the climax."

Rooster looked at Earl Lee. The two laughed and shook hands. Rooster put a wing around Earl Lee, and the two of them marched off towards the rear exit.

"How'd you like the ad-lib about me calling you an olive drab blunderbuss, Earl Lee?" asked Rooster.

"About as much as you did by me calling you, Tubby," laughed Earl Lee. Fanny walked off arm and arm with the battered wolf.

"So, Justin, you say you are single," she commented. "You remind me a lot of my grandmother, and you have such large teeth."

The Italian rooster approached and assisted me, as I sat down onto a canvas-backed chair of his that had written on it: <u>Sir Gio Leon – Director</u>.

"That was-a some fine acting there, Mr. Doodleblurb. I'll-a-see about getting you the standard day scale for your performance," he stated.

Rooster slapped Earl Lee on the back and said, "Come on, Semper Fi, I'm kinda dry, so let's mosey over to our favorite watering hole."

He commented, "Sure thing. I'm also kind of hungry. What say we then grab some corn from the crib ... my treat."

My head ached but began to clear. I glanced up at the distance from where I fell and wondered how I'd survived with no broken bones. I became peeved when I felt the floppy rooster's comb drape across my head. I glanced toward Rooster and wanted to complain about it, but he, Earl Lee, and the rest of that cast of clowns began to fade into the walls.

About this time, Wayne made his way into the tower room. All the players were gone, but he saw me and came over to me to help. When he saw the rooster's comb atop my head, he stopped in his tracks. He had a puzzled squint in his eyes. He winced and spoke with as reasonable a voice as he could muster while he helped me up.

"My dad once told us that you never truly understand anything until you can explain it to your grandmother. So, pretend I'm your granny and try explaining this," he said touching the floppy red object atop my head.

"Sure, no problem," I stated on wobbly legs. "But first, I need to go see my <u>psychiatricalist</u>. I mean my <u>psychologicalust</u> ... that crazy dude with the paneled walls. He's a very sick man and needs my help."

He held onto me to steady my balance. "Are you sure you don't mean padded walls?" he asked candidly.

I stammered, "Padded what?"

He shrugged and said, "Never mind. Your wife called. She said you must come home at once, but I don't think you can drive."

Dwayne ambled in too with Sweetroll guiding him. "That you, Pard? Good news is they were only false alarms and the system's been rebooted. Also, we sold twelve more new franchises yesterday."

I was led back into the office by Wayne who sat me down and told me to call home. He gathered my hat and gloves and brought me my coat.

# CHAPTER 22: A Fowl Wind Blows

Dwayne somehow knew what Wayne was doing and asked me, "Leaving so soon?"

Wayne picked up the phone and dialed Daisy at home. She answered and he put me on the line.

He told Dwayne, "Something's happened and he's got to go home."

I tried to remain calm and listened to my egg-laying wife as she explained the crisis. I wondered how it could be any worst, but I soon discovered it could be.

I heard Daisy's panicked voice, "Dabney, you've got to come home. Something terrible has happened."

I leaned forward in the chair and scratched at the floppy skin atop my head. Wayne sighed and his astonishment was still evident. He glared at the strange growth that dominated my skull.

I told Daisy, "Calm down, sweetheart. What's happened now? Your egg didn't hatch, did it?"

Wayne's eyes rolled and he slipped down into another chair beside my desk. Dwayne's hand nervously grabbed Sweetroll's harness and jerked it upward in an unexpected reaction.

"No, not yet," she said, "It's Cah Cah. After the boys caught the bus to school, she ran into the den to watch cartoons on the T.V."

"Doesn't she always," I stated.

Her voice cracked as she explained over the phone, "Yes, but when I went in later to check on her, she wasn't there."

"She didn't run off, did she? There's a snowstorm coming this way. She doesn't need to be—"

She interrupted me, "No, it's worse than that."

"Worse How?" I questioned her.

Daisy began to whimper and cry. "I ran around the house calling for her, but she didn't answer. I looked outside and checked with the neighbors."

"Well, did you find her?" I asked, noting the tension in my voice.

"I think so ... sort of I believe," as her voice trailed off.

I became annoyed and replied, "You think so? Did you find her or not?"

There was silence on the line, and I then heard Daisy sobbing.

"Daisy? Speak to me."

In a shrieking voice she proclaimed, "Dabney, I heard her call my name. I followed the sound and"—

She paused and I bit into my bottom lip.

"And what?" I asked desperately.

"She was on T.V.; rather she was in it. Somehow, she was caught up inside the set and in one of the cartoons she likes to watch."

I leaned back in my chair and placed my hand over the receiver. I thought to myself, "Daisy's lost her mind."

Wayne and I looked at each other in total wonderment. Dwayne just sighed and patted Sweetroll. Emotions whirled and skidded through my head.

She continued with her explanation, "I think she's okay though, for she was laughing and bopping knots on Wile E. Coyote's head."

"Ouch! I know how that feels," I stated as I rubbed my head.

"What?" she asked.

"Never mind, Daisy. Just try and relax and I'll be home as soon as I can."

"Yes, please. I'll keep watching her and leave the T.V. on the Cartoons."

The twins watched as I hung up the phone and buried my head in my hands. Wayne grabbed his car keys and tapped me on the shoulder.

"Come on, Dabney, we'll drive you home."

The jagged, painful thoughts that coursed through my mind caused me to gather my lost strength and leap up from the chair.

"No, I'm better now. I'll drive home as quickly as possible to try and make sense of what's happening there."

"Do you think it's possible that Cah Cah could be trapped inside a T.V. set?" asked Dwayne.

After all, that's gone on this morning, I have no idea of what's possible, real, or imagined anymore?" I replied.

"I can't imagine the weight of the burdens you've been carrying. Now this happens," said a concerned Wayne. "We'll follow you in case there's something we can do to help."

I turned my head and my raw feelings injected an unexpected sarcastic reply, "Well, standby, we may need to borrow the plant's incubator. That and maybe you know of a good network exorcist."

Bewildered Wayne asked, "Did Daisy lay an egg? How is that possible?"

"She told me she did and there was one lying in the nest she built in her closet," I told him.

Dwayne stated, "Actually, I do know a holy, old Indian medicine man that's into spirituality issues,"

"Are you serious?" I asked him.

"Yes, my friend has a reputation around town for clearing homes of bad spirits and poltergeists."

"Yeah, but how is he with Poultry-Geists?" I asked {Yeah, I am re-capitalizing those two horrid words}

I continued, "I made up those words to describe the roosters, hens, and duck foes driving us crazy. So, does your Indian medicine man have any experience with casting out fowl spirits?"

"I'm not sure, but we can swing by and pick him up. We'll then meet at your place and try to solve what's been happening to you," Dwayne stated. "Please drive safely for you still look a bit woozy."

I told him, "I will, and there's no need to solve it, for I know what's been happening to us. I just want to get rid of those feathered fiends that haunt us."

* * *

After forcing down two cups of coffee, Wayne helped me to my car. I drove carefully and slowly through the icy wind and blowing snow that began an hour before. My hands gripped the steering wheel and I wiped the fog off the inside of the windshield so I could see the road ahead.

You've now seen how I got this way, and also know the dilemma I'm facing at home. Besides myself, my wife is going nuts and my daughter has disappeared; supposedly into an electronic cartoon world. I glanced in the rearview mirror at my bald head and the rooster's comb I now possessed.

I yanked the toboggan onto my head and muttering to myself, I said, "I look like a deranged reject from the funny farm, and it's freezing outside."

It wasn't until I realized I was driving on the freeway instead of the road to our home that I understood I shouldn't be behind the wheel of a motorized vehicle. I swooned and began to lose my train of thought. I pulled at my neck and shirt, with the slightest recognition that I may be about to pass out. The car swerved and almost ran off the road.

It was then that I heard a familiar voice again, "Hey, Pilgrim, scoot over and let me in that saddle. I'm not too familiar with these new-fangled, smoke-burning contraptions, but I expect even I can do better at the reins than you can right now."

As I felt myself slip into the darkness of unconsciousness, I saw Rooster grab the wheel and begin to steer. The car did a few side-to-side swipes across various lanes, but somehow that crazy Marshall managed to get me and the car back home in one piece. When there, he shook me, and the next thing I knew I had returned to reality and awareness. I sat up in the passenger seat.

"Alright, Pilgrim. Your steed here is back in the corral. Though you seem limber as a dishrag, it's time you gathered your sittin' hen, shooed off that pesky parrot, rescued baby sister, and let that frisky pup of yours lead you to the truth."

Once again, I was puzzled by what he was squawking about, but I did appreciate that he somehow got me home. Before I could thank him, he vanished like he always did. Wayne's car was in the driveway, so I hoped he and Dwayne had found the old Indian medicine man.

Wearing my coat and the wool toboggan over my head, I forced open the car door. In the stiff, cold breeze, I made my way up the drive and the three steps to the front door. Inside, I struggled to close it against the blinding snowstorm that was happening with a fury.

I heard Daisy call out to me, "That you, dear? We're in the den."

I toddled into the den, where a warm, gas-flamed fire glowed in the fireplace. There, I saw Daisy, Wayne, Dwayne, Sweetroll, Dippy, Dooby, and an elderly man with dark skin and black hair. They were all sitting cross-legged on the carpet. There were several small pots with burning incense; its aromatic smoke encircled the room like a cloud of perfume.

In the middle of their circle was Daisy's egg lying on a satin pillow. It had now grown to the size of a large oval watermelon. I approached them and removed my coat. Dippy conversed with the dark-haired man.

He asked him, "So, Punjab, you don't eat meat of any type?"

"No, my son. I am a vegan," said the dark-haired man whose name was, Punjab.

I thought, "Wait, Punjab doesn't sound like any Indian name I'd ever heard."

Dippy smiled and commented to Punjab, "That's cool, we're Presbyterian."

"What's all this?" I asked candidly.

It was then I noticed Cah Cah on the television screen. She was dressed like Elmer Fudd, had a shotgun in one arm and that stupid faceless doll of hers in the other. She curled her mouth and whispered, "Be vewy, vewy quiet, Dah Dah ... I'm hunting wabbits."

When she laughed that goofy laugh, I felt the hairs stand up on the back of my neck.

The elderly dark-haired man stood, put his hands together, and bowed to me.

I looked at Daisy, the speckled egg, and shrugged dismissively at the old man named Punjab.

"Is that really Cah Cah inside the T.V.?" I asked the others. "And who's this old guy?"

Punjab addressed me again, "Greetings, Sir. I am Punjab. Dwayne asked me to come here to check out bad spirits in your home."

I looked down at Dwayne and my face formed a scowl.

"You said he was a holy, old Indian man," I declared to Dwayne.

Punjab remarked, "I assure you, Mr. Doddledoo, I am wholly a man. There are no girly parts on me."

I slapped Dwayne on the shoulder. "You said he was a medicine man."

Dwayne turned his head toward me and stated, "He is. He's a seventy-year-old retired pharmaceutical salesman from Mumbai, India."

Punjab added, "Which was formerly known as Bombay."

Frustrated and angry, I plopped down on the floor next to Daisy.

"Great!" I said to Dwayne. "I expected a native shaman, and you bring me a retired slumdog, pill pusher."

"Please, Mr. Doddledap—"

I gnarled my teeth and grumbled, "It's Doodledoo, not Doddledap, you old medical misfit."

"You must have patience. I've spoken to spirits in your house. They are very strong and determined," he remarked.

Yeah, determined to drive us crazy," I replied.

Suddenly, from outside the piercing winds began to howl. The house began to shake and the walls rattled. Lamps turned over, pictures fell from the walls, and chairs tipped over on their sides. Wayne leaped up and rushed to the front window. As the house shook, he glanced outside. I could tell by the startled expression on his face that he was alarmed.

Sweetroll and Bingo the pup began to whine. They tucked their tails and Sweetroll hid under Dwayne's arm, while the pup inched under Dooby's legs.

Patti the pesky peanut-eating parrot squawked, "Danger Doodledoos! Dismount, dismiss and detour downstairs as downwind air disaster directly disburses and dispatches demolishing doom."

Heading directly towards our home and forming not from a raging thunderstorm, but rather from the intense snow clouds, was the roaring, spiraling vortex of a white tornado.

Wayne yelled out, "What the ... such things don't happen here in winter."

The odd funnel steadily approached and Wayne turned to issue us a desperate warning.

"Quick, grab what you can and everybody get down to the basement."

The house continued to shake. Light fixtures ripped from the ceiling and smashed loudly to the floor. Daisy screamed, as the power to the television suddenly went off and the images of Cah Cah racing through the background of the cartoon woods vanished.

Daisy and Wayne grabbed her large egg and every one of us raced down the steps into the basement. The lights soon blinked and went out. In the darkness, I heard Sweetroll and Bingo whimper, as did the two boys. They, Daisy and I, with the big egg between us, bundled together on the floor. I then recalled a flashlight I'd seen in a nearby drawer. I fumbled in the darkness, found and withdrew the flashlight, and then turned on the beam of light.

Seeing our dire situation and with the house falling apart around us, I led us into the small equipment room where the water heater, sump pump, and water softener were kept. Daisy rolled her egg inside and it seemed even bigger than before.

Sweetroll, Dwayne, Wayne, and Punjab curled up in a protective ball in one corner of the room and we were in another corner. Moments later, in the dim light of the single beamed flashlight, as I huddled next to Daisy and the boys, I saw the egg suddenly expand to the size of a beach ball. Patti parrot followed us into the basement, but then flew back upstairs and out a window where the glass had blown out. The winds zipped her away and we never saw that ornery, feathered oracle again.

Punjab raised his arms to the ceiling. He began to chant in a language foreign to us. As the vortex of the funnel passed directly over the house, the entire above-ground structure strained to remain intact, but the high winds were like a hunter eager to devour its prey. The entire house frame above ground level was swept away in one big swoosh.

The bitter cold swept through us and into the now open-topped room. Hundreds of white feathers mixed with snow then drifted to the ground covering us all like a downy blanket. Only a few things were left untouched in the basement, including the group of us gathered in that small equipment room.

Dwayne released his grip on Sweetroll. Wayne sat up, spit out feathers, and then turned his face to the now open, dark, white sky above us. As he did so, a large bolt of lightning flashed from the white clouds. Amazingly, it struck Dwayne right on the top of his head. He toppled over like a bowling pin. His hair singed, but for some reason, it did not burn. Nor did he appear to be injured by the curious, powerful blast.

Wayne screamed, "Oh, my God!" He leaped to help his brother but was relieved when Dwayne inhaled and somehow managed to sit up.

He cried out to Dwayne, "Holy cow, where'd a lightning bolt come from? Are you okay?"

Dwayne scratched his head and felt a small nodule rise there, but otherwise, he seemed alright.

"Yeah, I think so, Bro. But you still can't have her phone number."

Wayne laughed and hugged Dwayne to him.

As quickly as it came, the cloud dispersed and there was a sudden calm. The wind no longer howled, and in the dim flashlight beam, I watched feathers fall silently about us. I was relieved when I saw the boys were alright. Daisy sneezed and opened her eyes. Sweetroll had his butt in the air, as he'd done that day in the boat on the duck hunt. Bingo was licking Dooby and Dippy's faces. Then he stopped and ran over to the egg, which by now to my amazement was as large around as a car tire. It appeared ready to explode.

It rolled away from Daisy and into the concrete block wall. My toboggan was loose and came off my head, exposing my rooster's comb to everyone. Daisy sneered at it, but her focus was on the egg, at which Bingo had begun to lick and bark.

Wayne shook his brother's shoulders and had a concerned look on his face.

Dwayne still smoldered a bit from the lightning strike, but overall seemed no worse for the wear. He brushed himself off and then turned his head towards me.

"Dabney? Is that you? You look good bald, but what's with the red skin flap atop your noggin?"

Wayne and all of us looked at Dwayne, who continued to brush feathers and debris off himself.

Wayne exclaimed, "Wait a second! Dwayne, can you see?"

Dwayne snickered and said, "Well, of course, I—"

He stopped brushing, raised his head and his eyes flew wide open.

Giddy as a sailor on furlough, he screamed, "Hold it. Yes, I see! I can see!"

He and Wayne stood, hugged happily, and the two brothers began to dance around in circles. Sweetroll wagged his tail and happily barked.

Meanwhile, Dippy noticed that something inside the egg was beginning to stir and seemed to be trying to break out of the shell.

He pointed at the enormous egg, "Mom, Pop ... the egg."

Daisy sighed and the blood drained from her face. The two boys and I watched, as the egg's shell slowly cracked open. To our delight and surprise, inside it, a curled-up little Cah Cah began to emerge. She was wet with a thick goo but seemed to be alright.

Seeing her parents, she smiled, rolled to her knees, and stretched out her arms.

"Her first words were, "They were here."

As tears filled Daisy's eyes, she and I clutched Cah Cah into our arms. The egg white substance she was covered in rubbed off on us too, but we didn't mind in the least. The boys picked away pieces of the shell and they too did a happy dance. Cah Cah's rag doll no longer had a beak, and its face now even had eyes and a smiling mouth.

Punjab stood among us, stepped out of the room, and looked about him at the ruins that a few moments before had been our house. Light snow now trickled down, as Punjab lifted his arms to the sky. His face formed a look of satisfied contentment.

He uttered, "This house ... is ... clean. It's gone ... but it's clean."

The boys playfully ran their hands across my skinhead. Dooby pulled on the rooster comb and I yelped.

"Ouch! Don't do that, Son."

"Sorry, Pop. I was just curious if it was real or not."

"I'm afraid it is, but hopefully it'll be gone and my hair will grow back soon."

I shrugged my shoulders, congratulated Dwayne on regaining his eyesight, and hugged my sons, daughter, and loving wife. Bingo joined us in our gleeful reunion. Despite now being homeless, we all laughed and joined Wayne and Dwayne in their mirth. My underarms tickled, and when I raised my arms to scratch, I discovered another enhancement, as Daisy called them. Yep, that's when I discovered that besides the discomforting rooster's comb, I also had downy feathers under my armpits.

Bingo began to sniff around next to the north wall on what was left of our basement. He barked and began to scratch the floor next to the wall. As Bingo and Punjab stood close by in the wasted ruins, a part of the north wall of the basement collapsed, opening up what appeared to be a passageway. As Punjab stepped forward, he saw that the passage led about ten feet into a dark hidden room. He snapped his fingers, and then as if remembering something, retrieved a small penlight attached to a set of car keys from his pocket. He turned on the penlight and shined it into the room.

In the meantime, Daisy and the others followed me out of the equipment room into the open-air space of the basement. It was still snowing lightly and we had to endure the cold. I wrapped Daisy and Cah Cah in a blanket I'd had next to my recliner. I'd grabbed my coat before coming down, so I was alright, but the boys, Punjab, and the twins were shivering.

I saw the soft illumination from Punjab's penlight coming from the passageway and left Daisy's side to see what it was behind the collapsed wall. Daisy again looked at my head devoid of hair but sporting the rooster's comb.

She inquired, "How'd that ... thing ... get there?"

Deflecting her question I said, "I'm not sure, but I'll go check it out. You and the boys stay here and keep as warm as possible."

"No," she said. "I don't mean that passageway, I mean how'd you get that rooster's comb on your head?" she again asked.

"Yeah, I know what you meant, but look ... I can't explain it any more than you can about how you laid an egg, nor how Cah Cah got caught up in Loony Tune World. It's there, so I'll find a way to deal with it."

As I backed away towards the passage, she nervously touched it with her hands. Seeing that the basement stairs were intact, I pointed to them and motioned at her,

I told the two boys, "Be careful, and take your mom and Cah Cah upstairs and try to make it out to my car. Here are the keys and my flashlight. All of you get inside and turn on the car heater to warm up. I'll be along soon, but first I want to check out what's behind this wall."

"I hope the car's still there and didn't blow away in the storm," said Daisy.

"Good point," I replied. "If it isn't then look for a neighbor's house that you might go to get warm. Call 911 on your cell ... if it's working, and let them know what happened here. They'll send help for sure."

As they started up the still existing stairs, I entered the passage and the semi-dark room beyond. To my complete surprise, Punjab was in the corner holding what appeared to be metal movie canisters. I could barely see but did recognize that there were hundreds, if not thousands of canisters stacked on shelves around the large room.

About then, from upstairs I heard Cah Cah yell out, "Oh, doody! Nemo, Nemette, and my other fishes are okay."

Somehow, although the rest of the house had been destroyed, that aquarium wall with the fish had been untouched and was still intact. With the cold, I knew we'd have to remove them soon and get them into a warmer, safer environment ... us too, for that matter.

Punjab held up one of the large cans and seemed enthralled by its contents.

In the dull light, I asked him, "What's all this?"

Punjab shook his head and had no definitive answer. From behind him, Wayne and Dwayne stuck their heads inside the room. Dwayne lit a candle that he'd found in an end table drawer in the basement. He looked around, picked up a canister, and smiled. I examined some of the stacks of metal canisters.

"They seem to all be containers ... of animated cartoons ... Warner Brothers, Disney, Woody Woodpecker, Popeye, Betty Boop, Tom and Jerry, Popeye, plus others," said Dwayne.

"Cartoons?" I asked. "Where'd they all come from?"

Dwayne stared at my head, and a small giggle exuded from his lips.

"I'm sorry. I don't mean to stare, but you look like a fugitive from a bad horror movie," he said.

"Yeah, thanks for reminding me," I snarled.

Wayne then commented, "I remember as a kid ... these houses weren't here then. We'd drive out by here and our dad would tell us about an old drive-in movie that was once on this land."

Dwayne added, "Yeah, and now that you mention it, I'm pretty sure this is the exact spot where it used to be located. A nice old couple—"

"A Mr. and Mrs. Goldstein.," interjected Wayne.

Dwayne lovingly picked up another canister.

"Dad said they had twelve grandchildren and opened the drive-in so those kids could come out on weekends and watch cartoons. There was no Disney channel or Cartoon Network on T.V. back then."

"Yes, they ran cartoons all summer. Dad loved it. He said it was great fun. I'm sorry we missed all that," replied Wayne.

A nostalgic Dwayne stated, "I remember, he claimed they made the best chili dogs and hamburgers he ever ate. It was dark and moist here in this underground room, so this must've been an old enclosed storeroom where they kept the animated films and cartoons."

I held one of the canisters and ran my hand across the top of my head tweaking my rooster's comb. I was frustrated by all that's happened.

"What happened to the drive-in?" I inquired.

"Progress and new technology, I suppose," replied Wayne. "That, plus I heard the couple just got too old and feeble to keep it open."

"Word was that in the sixties, they closed the drive-in, plowed it all under, and dad bought the land to raise corn for our poultry," added Dwayne. "I guess he never knew this room was here."

Wayne stated, "Anyway, he sold the land later to a developer, and you know the rest."

I pondered for a moment and alleged, "The loony things that have been happening to us must somehow be connected to that drive-in and the cartoons. I think I know now what these comical <u>Poultry-Geists</u> have been trying to tell me."

From in the corner of the room, I once again saw Rooster Galldern. He removed his hat and had no rooster's comb now ... for I had it. He tipped his hat to me and a silly grin crossed his beak.

Speaking words only I could hear, he told me, "Pilgrim, before this, you indeed were an unfinished attic and didn't know beans from buttons. By golly, now you finally figured out how the cow ate the cabbage. So, what're you going to do now?"

I smirked and told him, "Get this disgusting flap of yours off my head, plus armpit feathers I inherited from you ... and I'll consider helping you."

The twins and Punjab looked around to see to whom I was speaking. Rooster just winked at me with his one uncovered eye.

"I'd remove it if I could, Dabney, but I think you'd be better off getting a surgeon to remove it." replied Wayne, thinking that I was speaking to him.

"Huh?" I spoke. "No, I wasn't speaking to you. I mean, yeah, I'll look into seeing a doctor ... I suppose."

I shook my finger at Galldern, formed a fist, and shot daggers from my eyes at him.

"No, I won't take it back just yet, Pilgrim. You look quite dapper with it, although on me it does seem much more defining and dandy."

# POULTRY-GEIST

He laughed and vanished, leaving me in the state you found me in at the beginning of this story.

# CHAPTER 23: And They All Lived

As you might recall, that quack, Dr. Muzzkauff, and the therapist, Dr. Andropoff, proved to be total washouts. With our house gone, Wayne and Dwayne put us up in the posh hotel in Lancaster. The morning after my infertile visit to that quack doctor in town, by force of habit and out of sheer orneriness, I purposely woke the entire family by crowing at dawn.

After my frustrating day at the quack doctor's office the prior day, this morning I discovered the rooster's comb and underarm feathers were gone and my scalp and pits were back to normal ... whatever that is. I even had the short stubble shadow of hair re-growth on my head.

We settled in at the posh Lancaster Hotel while an insurance claim for the destruction of our home was being filed. Inside the heated area, I leaped off the diving board into the stylish indoor pool, came up from the warm water, and hen ... I mean then ... swam over to Cah Cah and the boys.

Daisy was laid out on a chaise reading a book. It was glorious having my family all there. We were laughing, playing, and not having a care in the world ... or being bothered by snow, cold, and you know what. Still, I wondered if I'd seen Rooster Galldern and company for the last time.

Meanwhile, in the rear of the Lancaster Preservation Society, an enclosed panel truck backed up to a stop at their rear docking area. A driver hopped out and walked to the rear of the truck. He opened its roll-up door and inside were hundreds of the movie canisters from the hidden storeroom we found next to our basement. The man and a helper began unloading them onto carts and taking them into the building's storage area.

We donated the old canisters of cartoons to the local Preservation Society, which refurbishes old films. In turn, we agreed to pay a fee for having the cartoons and animated films transferred over onto digital formats for modern technology to project onto movie screens.

That morning, Daisy and I went to a business that houses all sorts of weather equipment, radar tracking monitors, and other weather-gathering data.

A man there that we spoke to on the phone looked at his charts and data, shook his head, and finally threw up both hands in frustration.

# POULTRY-GEIST

The man told us, "The strange lightning strike, plus the powerful and peculiar winter winds that swept through and destroyed your house can not be explained by the local weather bureau or any national ones. The odd thing is yours was the only property damaged in the area."

"Oh well," I said, "at least they helped by cleaning up all the feathers. We donated them to a pillow factory in Philadelphia," proclaimed Daisy.

He did not seem amused and when we left, the poor man was still trying to calculate a reason as to what happened with our house and why it occurred.

\* \* \*

Two months later in February, on the site where our home used to be, carpenters were nailing on sheets of plywood decking, as a new home was being constructed on the same lot. No, it was not our home, for we chose not to rebuild there.

Down below, inside one of the open-framed rooms was Juan, the bricklayer, examining a set of blueprints. After rebuilding our mailbox so many times and liking the location, we gave the property where our house was to him. Thus, he contracted to build his family's new home there. He has been a bit confused though and can't quite figure out why he's rammed into that same mailbox three times already. He claimed to see what he thought was a gathering of hens that raced out in front of his car when he was pulling up to where they were building the new home. Poor man ... I'm not talking anymore about that Twilight Zone ... and don't you say anything either, or else you just might experience a stopover by a certain cartoon rooster and grouping of fowl visitors.

\* \* \*

In a national television studio in New York City, Punjab was seated on a couch across from a famous female talk show hostess. He'd been traveling the talk show circuit for the past week. As the cameras rolled, the lady held up a book entitled, "Feathers in the Wind." She showed its cover to a national audience that viewed her daily talk show program.

She asked him, "Punjab, what made you write this best-selling book? It's sold millions of copies in just a few weeks."

The old Indian medicine man grinned and said, "To help people calm their karmas and tell them how to ward off and tame angry spirits."

\* \* \*

Meanwhile, around the first tee at the Pebble Beach Golf Course in California, a large crowd gathered and cheered on Dwayne, as he slammed his opening drive on the first hole almost three hundred yards straight down the fairway.

A sign over the tee box read: "Welcome to the Purina Pro-Am Tourney."

With his eyesight miraculously restored, Dwayne went on to become a professional golfer. He won millions of dollars on the tour that summer and was now playing in a celebrity-pro-am tourney. He stopped inventing after a failed experiment with an even more powerful electromagnetic device, unfortunately, pulled three NASA communication satellites back to Earth, plus a Russian weather satellite spun out of orbit ... making for an extremely upset group of Russian scientists and an angry bunch of U.S. government agencies.

Sweetroll had saddlebags slung over his back, and inside each bag were Dwayne's golf clubs.

Yep, you guessed it. Sweetroll became the first canine caddie on the tour. As Dwayne lined up his second shot at the green, Sweetroll barked. He rushed up to Dwayne and clamped down with his teeth on the golf club before Dwayne could swing.

Dwayne stopped, looked at his dog, and asked, "The wrong club? Which do you suggest?"

Sweetroll bent his head back and bit down on a club from the saddlebags. He pulled it out with his teeth, secured it in his mouth, and then walked it over to Dwayne.

Dwayne glanced at the green and said, "A nine iron, huh? I think maybe you're right."

He addressed the ball, swung, and the ball rolled to a stop three feet from the pin. The crowd roared. Dwayne reached into his fanny pack and withdrew a cinnamon bun, which he tossed to Sweetroll. The canine caddy scarped it down in one big gulp.

All went well, until the PGA tourney in August when Sweetroll was banned because of a squirrel incident. He went bonkers and chased after a squirrel, as golf clubs flew out of his saddlebags, scattering them all across the fairway. He pursued that squirrel under a television tower, knocked out a leg on the tower, and it collapsed onto the ground with two surprised cameramen and four bewildered spectators. Everyone was okay, but the network lost its video feed on that hole. Dwayne got fined and canine caddies were banned from then on at all pro golfing events.

That day at the pro-am championship, Dwayne's amateur golf partner was putting on the $18^{th}$ green. He needed to sink the putt for him and Dwayne to become the champions. It was a simple-looking three-foot putt with no visible break. The man stood over the putt, looked at the hole, and stroked the ball solidly. It rolled in line and directly towards the cup. However, but inches away it encircled the cup by an inch or more and wound up on the exact opposite side of the hole. The golf announcers calling the action on T.V. saw what happened and were astonished.

"Wow! What the heck caused that ball to react that way?" asked one announcer.

Dwayne's golf partner went bonkers, started swinging his putter at something unseen, and chased after whatever it was he saw, all the while cursing and angrily kicking at the air.

A second announcer asked, "Who was that man, anyway?"

The first announcer stated, "He's a wealthy investor that owns numerous poultry processing and hatchery plants across the nation. He recently bought out the plants that his playing partner used to own."

"What is he shouting"

Then they each heard his scorn, "Come back here you no good, one-eyed rooster?"

The announcer remarked, "What rooster? I think he's been out in the sun too long. At any rate, we apologize for those unnecessary expletives he uttered."

\* \* \*

Yep, Wayne, Dwayne, Daisy, and I all sold our interests and left the poultry business behind. We used our lucrative shares of wealth to invest in new ventures that involved buying stocks in cereal companies, candy manufacturers, and the tech industry. It proved to be very profitable and allowed us all more free time to be with family and friends. Daisy and I used a good portion of our new prosperity in giving to our church, hospitals, charitable missions, helping the hungry, and homeless folk, and to PETA and the SPCA.

As for Wayne, he now wore a thick beard. This day, he was in his kitchen helping to prepare a meal. Next to him was Karen, the girl he met that day at the airport. No, Dwayne never gave in and provided him with her phone number ... because he was just teasing Wayne and never really had it. Wayne smiled at her and leaned over to kiss her, but she playfully tossed flour in his face.

If you're wondering how they did meet again, let me explain: While driving his car, Wayne turned to whistle at a cute young lady and drove smack into a tree. The nurse that cared for him at the county hospital was ... you guessed it ... Karen. After getting well, he finally talked her into giving him her phone number. Later, they got together on a date, and that eventually led to a romance, marriage, and the soon-to-come new arrival to their family. Yes, he lost his heart to her and found true love. She also makes wonderful oatmeal and raisin cookies.

As for me and my family, here's my update: I was this summer afternoon in our den sipping on a glass of iced tea. As I lounged in my recliner, I looked out the rear window of our new farmhouse, where outside down a slope was a large pond. Swimming in the pond was the duck {*yeah him*} with three white rings around its neck.

# POULTRY-GEIST

Learning that we preferred a farm to the city, Daisy and I bought a hundred acres and a five-bedroom house outside of Paradise near the main highway, but not on the Interstate. There on the pond, I kept seeing our phantom duck swimming each day; come rain, shine, or icy cold with snow covering the pond. I know it's just his ghost, but his being there made me smile and shiver at the same time.

Later, I was joined by Daisy outside, as Cah Cah and the two boys happily chased their dog, Bingo, around our huge backyard surrounded by acres of corn and soybeans. The kids were happy when we brought them back to live on a farm where we had dairy cows, and hens that we didn't eat, but did their eggs. We had a tractor and combine for me, horses for the two boys, plus a tame pony for Cah Cah. We were even able to save the dumb fish and arranged with a professional designer to build and furnish a new aquarium in the house for them.

Let's face it, we got filthy rich franchising our grilled chicken restaurants, and were even more so now. It made us feel good to be able to do good for others with a fair share of what our investments made for us. Now retired from work before I turned forty, we had let our friend, Juan, the brick mason, run the hatchery and processing plant. He's now the CEO under the new regime of ownership. However, I did hear that he's been rather jittery these days and has been seen exiting Dr. Muzzkauff's and Dr. Andropoff's offices a couple of times.

\* \* \*

Now, if you'll excuse me, it's dusk and almost time. I placed an Amish hat over my re-grown cranial hair and scratched my Amish-style beard. No longer wearing a mustache, I stepped around the corner of our house into the cleared field near the roadway. There by the side of the road on a ten-acre plot was the newly opened drive-in-movie theater we built.

In front of the large movie screen, was a playground with swing sets, slides, merry-go-rounds, and a place to play catch with Frisbees or balls.

The marquis sign in front of the theater stated: <u>CARTOONS – EVERY SPRING, SUMMER, AND FALL WEEKEND.</u>

It was almost time to open. I'd best get over to the concession stand and projection room to make sure things get started okay. Daisy kissed me, and I turned to walk away. After all that happened, we figured we owed it to the kids of Lancaster County to continue an old tradition long ago lost. So, we built this new drive-in movie theater with digital projectors and digitized all those cartoons. Having more than enough money ourselves, all our profits went to charities.

Wayne drove up in his sports car with Karen. He tipped his hand to me, placed dollars in the charity jar, and pulled into the theater. Beside him, Karen patted her swelled abdomen and grinned at her handsome husband. She opened the doors and let Wayne's two nieces out to run and play upfront until it was dark enough for the cartoons to start.

Nearing dark, the drive-in lot began to fill. As was the case, even some Amish families showed up driving their simple one-horse buggies. They enjoyed letting their kids watch the old cartoons and play on the swings and other playground items we added. Up near the movie screen, parents laughed and played with their kids. They too would swing, slide, and spin on the merry-go-rounds. Little Cah Cah was usually there, along with her two brothers and Daisy.

Here at this drive-in, kids left their Wii, Playstations, X-Boxes, and video games awhile; to come out, play, watch cartoons, and just be kids having fun with one another and their parents.

When Darkness approached, all over the lot car horns began to blow, and all around was heard the sounds of kids cheering and laughing. Kids and parents brought back goodies from the concession stand to their vehicles and tuned in their car radios to the AM station where we broadcast the sound in synch with the cartoons.

Soon, the large screen lit up with familiar sounds from "Merry Melodies" and numerous other cartoons, some of which hadn't been seen in many years. Usually, we'd arranged with other major distributors to show popular animated features as well. In the concession stand, we served hot dogs, hamburgers, candy, popcorn, drinks, and fresh fruit, but no grilled chickens or other poultry products. We didn't want to tempt fate again.

Almost two hours later, with the weekend's cartoons over, the patrons and workers left for home, and the lot cleared of cars and people. As always, I was the last to leave. I closed everything down and locked up the concession stand. When I was done, I turned on a flashlight, twirled a key ring on my finger, and waltzed towards home in the dark.

As I strolled happily along, beside me and joining with me as usual while I sang, was my new old pal, Rooster Galldern.

We walked arm in wing as he and I blurted out: "Camp town ladies, sing this song ... Doo Dah ... Doo Dah ... all the Doodledoo day."

## C.S. RAMAHON

"I'll be seeing yawl, Pilgrims."

www.ingramcontent.com/pod-product-compliance
Lightning Source LLC
Chambersburg PA
CBHW051339020726
47501CB00007B/2160